MY
HEART
IS
A
CHAINSAW

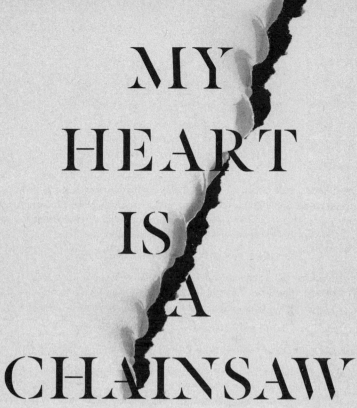

MY
HEART
IS
A
CHAINSAW

STEPHEN GRAHAM JONES

SAGA PRESS

LONDON SYDNEY **NEW YORK** TORONTO NEW DELHI

AN IMPRINT OF SIMON & SCHUSTER, INC.

1230 AVENUE OF THE AMERICAS, NEW YORK, NEW YORK 10020

Saga Press
An Imprint of Simon & Schuster, Inc.
1230 Avenue of the Americas
New York, NY 10020

First Saga Press hardcover edition August 2021

SAGA PRESS and colophon are trademarks of Simon & Schuster, Inc.

For information about special discounts for bulk purchases, please contact Simon & Schuster Special Sales at 1-866-506-1949 or business@simonandschuster.com.

The Simon & Schuster Speakers Bureau can bring authors to your live event. For more information or to book an event, contact the Simon & Schuster Speakers Bureau at 1-866-248-3049 or visit our website at www.simonspeakers.com.

Interior design by Jaime Putorti

Manufactured in the United States of America

1 3 5 7 9 10 8 6 4 2

Library of Congress Cataloging-in-Publication Data

Names: Jones, Stephen Graham, 1972– author.
Title: My heart is a chainsaw / Stephen Graham Jones.
Description: First Saga Press hardcover edition. | New York : Saga Press, 2021.
Identifiers: LCCN 2021014273 (print) | LCCN 2021014274 (ebook) |
ISBN 9781982137632 (hardcover) | ISBN 9781982137656 (ebook)
Classification: LCC PS3560.O5395 M92 2021 (print) |
LCC PS3560.O5395 (ebook) | DDC 813/.54—dc23
LC record available at https://lccn.loc.gov/2021014273
LC ebook record available at https://lccn.loc.gov/2021014274

ISBN 978-1-9821-3763-2
ISBN 978-1-9821-3765-6 (ebook)

to Debra Hill: thank you, from all of us

The slasher film lies by and large beyond the purview of the respectable

—Carol J. Clover

NIGHT SCHOOL

On the battered paper map that's carried the two of them across they're not sure how many of the American states now, this is Proofrock, Idaho, and the dark body of water before them is Indian Lake, and it kind of goes forever out into the night.

"Does that mean there's Indians *in* the lake, or does it mean that Indians made it?" Lotte asks, a gleam of excitement to her eyes.

"Everything here's named after Indians," Sven says back, whispering because there's something solemn about being awake when everyone's asleep.

Their rental car is ticking down behind them from the six-hour push from Casper, the doors open because they just wanted to look, to see, to soak all this in before going back to the Netherlands at the end of the week.

Lotte shines her phone's light down onto the fluttering map and looks up from it and across the water, like trying to connect what she's seeing in lines and grids to what she's actually standing in.

"Wat?" Sven says.

"In *American*," Lotte tells him for the two-hundredth time. If they want partial course credit for immersion, they have to actually immerse.

"What?" Sven repeats, the word belligerent in English, like trying to make elbow room for itself.

"That should be the national forest on the other side," Lotte says, chinning across the water because her hands are struggling to get the map shut.

"Everything's a national forest," Sven grumbles, angling his head as if to peer deeper into the darkness at all these black trees.

"But you can't do *that* in the king's forest, can you?" Lotte asks, finally getting the map folded in one of the six different ways it's possible to fold it.

Sven follows her eyes across Indian Lake. There's little floating pinpoints of light over there that only really come into focus when you look into the darkness right beside them.

"Hunh," he says, Lotte coming up behind him to rest her chin on his shoulder, hold his waist in her hands.

Sven breathes in deep with wonder when the lights rearrange themselves, suggesting great yellow necks in the inky blackness: strange and massive animals, piecing the world together one lakeshore at a time. Then, a ways down the shore, a ball of flickering light arcs up into the velvety sky and hangs, hangs.

"Mooi," Lotte says right next to his ear, and Sven repeats it in American: "Beautiful."

"We shouldn't," Lotte says, which of course means the exact opposite.

Sven looks back to the car, shrugs sure, what the hell. It's not like they're going to be here again, right? It's not like they're going to get another chance to be twenty years old in America, a whole lake at their feet like it bubbled up just for them to dip their toes into—and maybe more.

They leave their clothes on the hood, the antenna, draped over the open doors.

The mountain air is crisp and thin, their skin pale and bare.

"The water will be—" Sven starts to say, but Lotte finishes for him, "*Perfect*," and with that they're running the way naked bare-foot people do across gravel, which is delicately, hugging them-selves against the chill but laughing too, just to be doing this.

Behind them Proofrock, Idaho, is dark. Before them a long wooden pier is reaching out over the water, pointing them across the lake.

To get their nerve up for how cold this is going to be, once their feet find those wooden planks, Lotte and Sven stretch out and really run, not worried about the chance of nails or splinters or falling. Sven howls up into the vast open space all around them and Lotte snaps a blurry picture of him with her phone.

"You brought that?" he says, turning around to jog backwards.

"Document, document," she says, her arms drawn in like a boxer's now that Sven's looking back.

He raises an imaginary camera, takes his own picture of her.

Lotte is looking past him now, though, her eyes not as sure as they just were, her strides shortening, slowing, her hands and elbows going into strategic-coverage mode.

There's a much *closer* light flickering at what's got to be the end of the pier, and it looks for all the world like a fisherman in dark rain gear, holding an old-style lantern up at face level. No, not a fisherman: a lighthouse keeper who hasn't seen another soul for three years. A lighthouse keeper who thinks that holding his lan-tern close to his own eyes will improve his vision.

And then the light's gone.

Sven's hand finds Lotte's and they slow to a shuffle, the sky yawning empty and deep above them. All around them.

"Wat?" Lotte says.

"In *American*," Sven chides, forcing his smile.

"I don't anymore think we should—" Lotte starts, but doesn't finish because Sven, walking now instead of running, is jumping on his left foot, his right splintered or nailed or stubbed, something sudden and unpleasant.

The light at the end of the pier comes on, curious.

"Look," Lotte says to Sven.

When he stops hopping and grabbing at the sole of his foot, the light goes back off.

He nods, getting it, then stomps his hurt right foot down with authority.

The light glows on.

"Try it," he says to Lotte.

Hesitant, she does, stomping, getting no response. But then she jumps with both feet, comes down hard enough to jangle whatever bad connection is happening down there.

"Gloeilamp isn't screwed enough," Sven diagnoses, pulling her ahead.

"Screwed *in* enough," Lotte fixes, traipsing behind.

When they get there, step into that puddle of wavering light, Sven licks the pads of his fingers and reaches up under the rusty cowl to tighten the bulb, the light losing its thready flicker immediately, shining an unwavering cone of warmth down onto their pale thighs now, their shadows stark behind them, bleeding off into the darkness.

"We're gonna fix this place up *right*," Sven says, meaning all of America.

Lotte darts in to kiss him on the cheek, then, her eyes locked on Sven's the whole while, and still holding his fingertips until she can't, she steps over the end of the pier as easy as anything.

Sven turns his head against the splash, smiling and cringing both, but the splash doesn't come.

"Lotte?" he says, stepping forward, shielding his face from the water he knows has to be coming.

She's in a dark green canoe that's rocking back and forth—she must have spotted it while he was fiddling with the lightbulb. Sven raises his hands, snaps another make-believe picture of her, says, "Cover up, this one's for the grandchildrens. I want them to see how amazing their grootmoeder was when I first was knowing her."

Lotte purses her lips, unable to hide her smile, and Sven steps down with her, arms wide so as not to roll them.

"This isn't stealing," he says, reaching up to unhook the canoe's rope. "It was just floating here—out there, I mean. We had to swim out even to get it, to save it."

"We're gonna fix this place up!" Lotte says as loud as she can around Sven, leaning on the shaky little left-behind cooler to push them away from the pier. She trails her hands in the water and, drifting out from the pier now, can just see their rental car. It looks like a laundry bomb exploded over it. No: it looks like two kids from the Netherlands fizzed away from pure joy, disappeared into nothing, leaving only their clothes behind.

"What?" Sven asks in perfect American.

"We don't have a paddle," Lotte says. It's the funniest thing in the world to her. It's making this little expedition even more perfect.

"Or pants, or shirts . . ." Sven adds, taking both sides of the canoe and rocking it back and forth.

"*Koude*," Lotte agrees, hugging herself. Then, like a dare, "Warmer in the water."

"Out where it's *diepere*," Sven says, correcting himself before she can: "*Deeper*."

They reach over to paddle with their hands, the water bitter cold, and after about twenty yards of this Sven liberates the white lid off the little cooler. It's a much better paddle than their hands, and—importantly—it doesn't care about freezing.

"My hero," Lotte says in precise English, pressing herself into his back.

"It can be warmer up here too," Sven says, but doesn't stop drawing them farther out onto the lake.

Lotte presses the side of her face into his back, her new vantage point giving her an angle into the now-open tiny cooler.

"Hey!" she says, and extracts a clear baggie with a sandwich inside, its peanut butter smearing.

"Ew, pindakaas," Sven says, and pulls deep with the cooler lid, surging them ahead.

Lotte unceremoniously shakes the sandwich out into the water without touching it, crosses her finger over her lips so Sven will know not to tell on her about this, then drops her phone into the baggie and neatly seals the top, blowing into it at the very end so the phone is in a make-do balloon.

"Your ziplock tas can also be a flotatie device," she says in her best KLM flight attendant voice.

Sven chuckles, says, "*Flotation.*"

The phone in the bag is still recording. Lotte angles it away from her, holds it up so it can see ahead of them.

"What do you think they are?" Sven asks, nodding to the lights they don't seem to be any closer to yet.

"Giant fireflies," Lotte says with a secret thrill. "American fireflies."

"Mastodons met—*with* bioluminescente tusks," Sven says.

"Air jellyfish," Lotte says, quieter, like a prayer.

"Isn't there a tree fungus that's fosforescerend?" Sven asks. "Being serious, nu."

"*Now,*" Lotte corrects, still using her wispy-dreamy voice. "It's the Indians. They're painting their faces and their bodies for revolt."

"Until John Wayne Gacy hears about it," Sven says with enough confidence that Lotte has to giggle.

"It's just John Wa—" she starts, doesn't finish because Sven is jerking back from leaning over the side of the canoe, jerking back and pulling his hands up fast, something long stringing from them. He stands shaking it off, trying to, and the canoe overbalances, starts to roll. Instead of letting it, he dives off the other side, his Netherbits mostly hidden from the phone's hungry eye.

He slips in almost without a sound, just one gulp and gone.

Alone on the canoe now, Lotte stands unsteadily, the back of her hand coming instantly up to her nose, her mouth—the *smell* from whatever stringy grossness Sven dragged in over the side.

She dry heaves, falls to her knees from it.

They've drifted into . . . what? A mat of algae? Lake scum? At *this* altitude, snow still in the ditches?

"Sven!" she calls to the blackness encroaching from all sides now.

She covers herself with her arms, sits on her heels as best she can. No Sven.

And now she knows what that smell has to be: fish guts. Some men from the town gutted a big haul of them over the side of their boat, the intestines and non-meaty parts adhering together with the congealing blood to make a gooey floating scab.

She coughs again, has to close her eyes to keep from throwing up.

Or maybe it wasn't a whole net of fish—they can't do that here in inland America, can they?—but one or two of the really *big* fish, pulled up from the very bottom of the lake. Sturgeon, pike, catfish?

Sven will know. His uncle is a fisherman.

"Sven!" she calls again, not liking this game.

Not necessarily in response to her call, probably more to do with his lung capacity, Sven surfaces maybe twenty feet to Lotte's left.

"Gevonden—got it!" he's yelling.

What he's waving over his head is the bright white lid of the little cooler.

"Come back!" Lotte calls to him. "I don't want to see the giant fireflies anymore!"

"Mastodons!" Sven yells back, clapping the lid on the water, the sound almost unbearably loud to Lotte, like drawing attention they don't want. She looks to the lights on the far shore to see if they're all turning this way.

She gathers her phone-balloon, shakes the camera so it's facing her, and says into it in perfect English, "I hate you, Sven. I'm cold and scared and when you're asking yourself what you did wrong, why you didn't get any in the big state of Idaho, you can play this and you can know."

Then she wedges the phone backwards half under the canoe's bow deck, up against the stem—the pointy hidden corner at the front where you can stuff a ziplock baggie you've blown up and hidden a phone inside.

"Come to me!" Sven says. "I don't want to touch that . . . that hair again!"

"It's not hair!" Lotte calls back. "It's fish gut—"

What stops her from finishing is the distinct sense that someone was just standing behind her. Which would be impossible, of course, since behind her there's only the lake. Still, she whips around to the other end of the boat, certain there was a shadow there, just in her peripheral vision, already gone.

"It is kelp?" Sven's asking now. "Is that how you say it in Engels?"

"*English*," Lotte corrects, losing patience with this.

"Fuck English!" Sven says back. "*Het is haar!*"

It's not hair, though.

If it were hair, that would mean that . . . Lotte doesn't know: would it mean that a moose or a bear or a cowboy horse had died out here, or floated out here while dead and bloated, then burst in the heat of the day, geysering blood and gore up in a chunky fountain?

The canoe *thunking* into something where there should be nothing tells her that's just what it has to be.

She shrieks, can feel sudden tears on her face, her breath the kind of deep she's about to lose control of.

"*Sven!*" she screams, holding hard to the side of the canoe, and now, instead of another thunk, what she hears, fast like little footsteps, is a series of . . . not quite splashes, but some disturbance on the surface of the water. Fish in a line, jumping? A formation of bats snatching insects from the top of the lake? A rock someone skipped in the daytime, still making it across to the other shore?

She pushes away from whatever it is.

"Sven, Sven, Sven!" she's saying, less loud each time, because it feels like her voice is putting a bullseye on her back.

They never should have come to America. This isn't some big adventure.

Lotte looks back to the pier, to the light she knows is real, and right when she looks is when it blinks off then on again—no, no, it didn't go off, something passed *between* her and it.

Seconds later, a profanely intimate sound squelches across the water to the canoe, like a wet ripping. From where Sven was? Is she even still in the same place in relation to him?

Lotte stands, feels more exposed than she ever has, even though she can't see her own arms.

She falls back, almost over the side, when Sven starts screaming. In Dutch, in English, in *human*, except more primal—the way you only ever scream once, Lotte knows.

All Lotte can make out is "*Wat is er mis met haar mond?*" before his voice gargles down, stops abruptly.

Lotte reaches in to paddle back, away, she's sorry, Sven, she's sorry, she's sorry to America too, they shouldn't have violated her at night, they should have driven all the way around Idaho, she'll tell everybody, she'll warn them all away if she can just—

Her arm is up to the elbow in the mat of hair and rot and guts, it's stringing off her, draping into the canoe, wrapping around her but she doesn't care, she's lying on her stomach now to pull harder for the shore, her fingertips pushing down to where the water's even colder.

Once, twice, twenty times, and then—her hand connects with something solid? Her head is instantly filled with the slow-motion image of a dead horse floating underwater, the pads of her fingers brushing the white diamond between its eyes, her lightest touch pushing the huge dead body drifting down even deeper.

She pulls back, sits up holding her hand to herself like it's injured, and then what she touched with that hand bobs past.

The white cooler lid, streaked red.

Lotte shakes her head no, no, no, and then, because what else can she do, she rolls over the other side of the canoe, fights through the tendrils of decay, some even going in her mouth, trying to reach down her throat, and then she's to open water, swimming hard for the dim lights of Proofrock like only an elementary school swim-meet veteran can.

The phone she left behind in its foggy balloon is just recording the empty aluminum canoe now, and one blurry corner of the little cooler. But it's listening in its muted way.

What it hears is the front part of Lotte's scream.

She doesn't get to finish it.

JUST BEFORE DAWN

Jade Daniels slouches—that's the only word for it—into the staging area for Terra Nova on a twelve-degree night on the thirteenth of March, the Friday before spring break officially gets going for Proofrock.

In the left pocket of her thin custodian coveralls is a box-cutter, what her dad would probably call a "shitrock" knife, and in her right is her fist. Under her overalls there's just a girl-cut Misfits t-shirt, probably technically too small if that matters, and her threadbare jeans, most of the holes in the thighs not from washing dishes at the pancake house or moving boxes in a shipping warehouse—Proofrock isn't big enough for either of those places—but from scraping at the fabric with her fingernails during seventh period, her state history class, which she calls Brainwashing 101. Her finger-nails are black, of course, and her hair is supposed to be green, that was the plan one hundred percent, it was going to look killer, but Indian hair doesn't take the dye like the box says "all hair" should, so she's got a bobbed orange mop to deal with, which was what started the fight at her house thirty minutes ago, spitting her up here.

If her dad had just been able to watch her cross from the front door to the hall without saying anything, she'd probably be in her bedroom right now, headphones clamped on, a bootleg slasher crackling on the screen of her thirteen-inch television set with the built-in VCR.

Her dad can never keep his mouth shut, though, especially six beers into a night that's probably going to take a whole case to get through.

"You *got* to stop eating so many carrots, girl," he said with a halfway chuckle, punctuating it with a drink from his bottle.

Jade stopped like she had to, like she guesses he must have wanted her to.

His name, Tab Daniels, is the one he earned in high school, because he threaded fishing line back and forth across the headliner glued to the roof of his Grand Prix, festooned it with fishing hooks, and then proceeded to hang enough pull tabs onto those barbed hooks that the headliner finally collapsed onto him one seventy-mile-per-hour night.

The wreck should have killed him, Jade knows. Or wishes. She was already on the way by then, so it's not like it would have blipped her out of existence. All it would have blipped her to would be a less crappy version of her life, one where she lives with her mother, not her so-called father.

But of course, because she's doomed to grow up in the same house with her own personal boogeyman, the wreck just broke his bones, Freddy'd his face up, because, as he always tells anybody who doesn't know to have already left the room, God smiles on drunks and Indians.

Jade would humbly disagree with that statement, being half as Indian as her dad and getting zero smiles from Above, pretty much. Case in point: her dad's drinking buddy Rexall chuckling about her dad's orange-hair joke, and tipping his chin up to Jade: "Hey, *I* got a carrot she can—"

Hating herself for it the whole while, Jade had actually bared her teeth at this, expecting her dad to backhand Rexall, living reject that he is. Or if not backhand him, at least give him an elbow in warning. At the very very least Tab Daniels could have whispered *not so loud* to his high school bud. *Wait till she's gone, man.* Anything would have been enough.

He'd just chuckled in drunk appreciation, though.

Maybe if Jade's mom were still in the picture, then *she* could have thrown that maternal elbow, glared that glare, but whatever. Kimmy Daniels's place is only three-quarters of a mile away from Jade's living room, but that might as well be another galaxy. One not in Tab Daniels's orbit anymore—which is exactly the idea, Jade knows.

She also knows that stopping in the living room like she did was a mistake. She should have just kept booking, pushed on, shouldered through the smoke and the jokes, landed in her bedroom. Once you're stopped, though, then starting again without a comeback, that's admitting defeat.

She fixed Rexall in her glare.

"My dad was saying that about eating carrots because girls who want to be skinny try to eat *only* carrots, and the whites of their eyes will sometimes go orange, from overdoing it," she said, touching her hair to make the connection for Rexall. "I'm guessing you being such a shit-eater explains the color of your eyes?"

Rexall surged up at this, clattering empties off the coffee table, but Jade's dad, his eyes never leaving Jade, did hold Rexall back this time.

Rexall's name is because he used to deal, back in whatever his day was, and Jade's pretty sure it was exactly that: one single day.

Jade's dad chewed the inside of his cheek in that gross way he always does, that makes Jade see the knot of spongy scar tissue between his molars.

"Got her mother's mouth," he said to Rexall.

"If only," Rexall said back, and Jade had to blur her eyes to try to erase this from her head.

"That's right, just—" she started, not even sure where she was going with this, but didn't get to finish anyway because Tab was standing, stepping calmly across the coffee table, his eyes locked on Jade's the whole way.

"Try me," Jade said to him, her heart a quivering bowstring, her feet not giving an inch, even from the oily harshness of his breath, the ick of his body heat.

"This were two hundred years ago . . ." he said, not having to finish it because it was the same stupid thing he was always going on about: how he was born too late, how this age, this era, he wasn't built for it, he was a throwback, he would have been perfect back in the day, would have single-handedly scalped every settler who tried to push a plow through the dirt, or build a barn, tie a bonnet, whatever.

Yeah.

More like he'd have been Fort Indian #1, always hanging around the gate for the next drink.

"Might have to take you over my knee anyway," he added, and this time, instead of continuing with this verbal sparring match, Jade's right fist was already coming up all on its own, her feet set like she needed them to be, her torso rotating, shoulder locked, all of it, her unathletic, untrained body swinging for the fences.

It should have worked, too. Tab's head was turned for the last drink in his bottle, and she'd never tried anything like this before, so he wasn't special on-guard. He *had* been getting sucker-punched his whole stupid life, though, and had some radar as a result. Either that or God really was smiling on him.

Him, not his daughter.

He caught her fist in his open left hand easy as anything, pulled her face right to his, said, "You do not want to do this with me, girl."

"Not with," Jade said right into his lips, "*to*," bringing her knee up into his balls like there was a rocket in her boot heel, and then, in the time it took him to keel over into the coffee table, clattering empty bottles away, Jade was running through the screen door, exploding out into the night, never mind that she wasn't dressed for it.

The only reason she got her work coveralls at all was that they were hanging on the laundry line, skinned with frost—nobody expected weather to have rolled in over the pass like it had. She didn't put the coveralls on until the end of the block, though, and when she did she was watching the street the whole time, her eyes the only heat she had anymore.

"*Alice*," she says to herself now, shuffling through the open gate of the staging area for the Terra Nova construction going on twenty-four/seven across the lake.

Alice, the final girl from *Friday the 13th*, has sort-of orange hair, doesn't she?

She does, Jade decides with a cruel smile, and that makes this dye-job not a disaster, but providence, fate. Homage. This is Friday the 13th, after all, the holiest of the holies. But she's pissed, she reminds herself. There's no smiling when you're the kind of pissed she is. All that's left to do now is turn up somewhere with hypothermia. What she'll tell Sheriff Hardy is that her dad was partying like always and kicked her out just like last time.

All Jade has to do is tough it out. Go past shivering to something more blue-lipped and dry-eyed. Her loose plan had *been* to walk down the town pier to get that done—it's public, it's dramatic, somebody'll find her before she's all the way dead—but then she'd seen the flickering glow from the staging area, had no choice but to moth over.

The flickering glow is a fire, it turns out. Not a bonfire, but . . . she has to smile when she gets what she's seeing: the grunts on the night shift have used the front-end loader to scoop up all the wood and trash from around the site, probably their last task before clocking out, and then they left all that trash in the big steel bucket, kept it lifted a foot or so off the ground, and dropped a flame in, probably on a shop towel they held on to until the last finger-burning instant.

Burning's one way to get rid of a load of trash, Jade supposes. With Proofrock trying to dip down into single digits, maybe it's the best way.

What gives Jade license to come right up to the fire with the rest of the grunts, by her reasoning at least, are her work coveralls, grimy from afternoons and weekends mopping floors and emptying trash and scrubbing toilets. Her name—"JD" for "Jennifer Daniels"—sewn onto her chest in cursive thread proves she's like them: not important enough to bother remembering, but the front office has to have something to call you when there's a spill needs taken care of.

"Howdy," she says all around, trying for no lingering eye-contact, no extra attention drawn to her. She immediately regrets *howdy*, is certain they're going to take that as insult, but it's too late to reel it back in now, isn't it?

The one with the yellow aviators—shooting glasses, right?— nods once, leans over to spit into the fire.

The guy beside him with the mismatched gloves backhands Shooting Glasses in rebuke, nodding to Jade like can't Shooting Glasses see there's a lady among them?

To show it's no big deal, Jade leans over into the heat, her frozen face crackling, and spits all she can muster down into the swirling flames, her eyelashes curling back from the heat, it feels like.

The grunt with his faded green Carhartts tucked into his cowboy boots chuckles once in appreciation.

Jade wipes her lips with the back of her bare hand, can feel neither her lips nor the skin of her hand, is just using the brief action to case the place.

It looks the same from inside as it does through the ten-foot chain link: pallets and pallets of building material, ditch witches and scissor lifts, tired forklifts and crusty cement chutes, trucks parked wherever they were when dusk sifted in, brought the real chill with it. The heavy equipment like the front-end loaders and the bulldozers are all herded onto this side of the fenced-in area, the silhouette of the backhoe rising behind like a long-necked sauropod, the crane the undeniable king of them all, its feet planted halfway between this fire and the barge that ferries all this equipment back and forth across Indian Lake.

The day that barge was delivered by a convoy of semis and then assembled on-site, just before Thanksgiving break, it had been enough of an event that a lot of the elementary school classes took a field trip to watch. And ever since that day, Proofrock hasn't been able to look away. It never seems like that long, flat non-boat can carry one of these ten-ton tractors, but each time it just squats down in the water like it thinks it can, it thinks it can, and then, somehow, it does. Watching through the window during seventh period, Jade hates the way her heart swells, seeing the monstrous backhoe balanced on the nearly-submerged back of the barge again.

Does she want the backhoe to slide off, plummet down to Drown Town under the lake, or does she want the water to just rise and rise around its tall tires, nobody noticing until it's too late?

Either will do.

At the other end of that ferry trip is Terra Nova, which Jade despises just on principle. Terra Nova is the rich development going up across the lake, in what used to be national forest before some fancy legal maneuvers carved a lip of it out for what the newspapers are calling the most gated community in all of Idaho—"So exclusive there aren't even roads around to it!" If you want to get there, you either go by boat, balloon, or you swim, and balloons fare poorly with mountain winds, and the water's just shy of freezing most of the year, so.

What "Terra Nova" means, all the articles are proud to reveal, is "New World." What one of the incoming residents said, kind of famously, was that when there are no more frontiers, you have to make them yourself, don't you?

Right now there's ten mansions going up over there at a pace so breakneck it looks almost like the houses are rising in time lapse.

What those entrepreneurs and moguls and magnates probably don't know, though, is that if you walk the shore around to the east from Proofrock to Terra Nova, having to tippy-toe along the dam's spine at a certain point, the one clearing you'll stumble into will be the old summer camp, long gone to seed: nine falling-down cabins against a chalky white bluff, one chapel with open sides so it's pretty much just a low roof on pillars, like a church that's sinking, and a central meeting house nobody's met at since forever. Unless you count the ghosts of all the kids murdered on those grounds fifty years ago.

To everyone in Proofrock it's "Camp Blood." Give Terra Nova a summer or two, Jade figures, and Camp Blood will be the Camp Blood Golf Course, each fairway named after one of the cabins.

It's sacrilege, she tells anyone who'll listen, which is mostly just Mr. Holmes, her state history teacher. You don't remake *The Exorcist*, you don't sequel *Rosemary's Baby*, and you don't be disrespectful about soil an actual slasher has walked across. Some things you just don't touch. Not that anybody in town cares. Or: everybody likes the fifteen dollars an hour Terra Nova's smooth-talking liaisons are paying anybody who wants to hire on for the day. Anybody like, say, Tab Daniels. Thus the surge of beer he's been riding the last couple of months.

The transaction's not what they think, though, that's the thing. They're not selling their time, their labor, their sweat, they're selling *Proofrock*. Once Camelot starts sparkling right across Indian Lake, nothing's ever going to be the same—this rant courtesy of Mr. Holmes. Before, all the swayed-in fences and cars with mismatched fenders on this side of the lake were just the way it was, the way it had always been. Now, with Terra Nova's Porsches and Aston Martins and Maseratis and Range Rovers rolling through to park at the pier, Proofrock's cars are going to start seeming like a rolling salvage yard. When people in Proofrock can direct their binoculars across the water to see how the rich and famous live, that's only going to make them suddenly aware of how they're *not* living, with their swayed-in fences, their roofs that should have been re-shingled two winters ago, their packed-dirt driveways, their last decade's hemlines and shoulder pads, because fashion takes a while to make the climb to eight thousand feet.

As Mr. Holmes put it on one of his sad digressions—it's his last semester before retirement—Terra Nova wants to make the *other* side of the lake pretty and serene, nice and pristine. It's not quite so concerned about Proofrock, which before long is going to be just what gets left behind on the way to something better: cigarettes ground out under boot heels, quick pisses behind tires as tall as a house, little jigs and jags of angle iron pushed into the dirt along with layer after sedimentary layer of lonely washers and snapped-off bolts, which is why no way will Jade be staying here even one more minute than she has to after graduation. That's a promise. There's Idaho City, there's Boise, there's the whole rest of the world waiting for her. Anywhere but here.

But that, like the hypothermia, is all later.

Right now it's just rubbing her hands together over the fire, never mind the sparks swirling up. If she flinches from them, she's a girl, she won't deserve to be here at this hour.

"You all right there?" Shooting Glasses asks.

"Excellent," Jade says back, giving him a sliver of a grin. "You?"

Instead of answering, Shooting Glasses tries to make subtle eye contact with the other grunts, except quarters are too close for "subtle."

"I interrupting something?" Jade says all around.

Mismatched Gloves shrugs, which means yes.

"Feel like I just barged into a wake, I mean," Jade says, going from face to face.

"Good call," Cowboy Boots says while wiping at his nose.

"I'm not Catholic," Jade says, pulling back with all of them from a long swirling exhalation of sparks, "but isn't there usually more drinking at a wake?"

"You're thinking Irish," Mismatched Gloves says with a sort-of grin.

"Let me guess," Jade says. "Your name . . . McAllen? Mc-Whorter? Mc-something?"

"That's Scottish," Shooting Glasses says, staring into the fire. "Irish is O'Shaunessy, O'Brien—think luck *O'* the Irish, that's how I remember it."

"Which of them has leprechauns?" Cowboy Boots asks.

"Shh, shh, you're Indian, man," Shooting Glasses tells him. "We're talking Europe stuff here, yeah?"

"Me too," Jade says.

"You're a leprechaun?" Mismatched Gloves asks, smiling now as well.

"Indian," Jade says, and, by way of formal introduction to Cowboy Boots, "Blackfoot, my dad tells me."

"Isn't that Black*feet*?" Shooting Glasses asks.

"Montana or Canada?" Mismatched Gloves adds in.

Jade doesn't tell them that, in elementary, until she caught the Montana return address on what turned out to be a Christmas check, she'd always thought she was Shoshone, because those were the Indians her social studies class said were in Idaho. So, being in Idaho, that's what she must be. But then that return address, and that tribal seal by the address—she'd saved it, kept it hidden alongside her *Candyman* tape. Too, back in those days she'd had the idea that, since she was starting *out* half Indian, that as she got bigger and taller—got more and more physical actual blood—someday she'd be full-blood like her dad.

"Black*feet*," she says back with faked authority. "What the fuck do you think I said?"

"Yeah," Mismatched Gloves says, holding his different-colored hands high and away, not touching this anymore, "she sounds Blackfeet all right."

"Adopted," Cowboy Boots says about himself, by way of introduction. "Could be anything."

"What he's saying is he's a mutt," Mismatched Gloves says.

"Mutt *your* ass," Cowboy Boots says back, and Jade files that away: on this job-site, "*your* ass" is the add-on way of turning anything around. Her kind of place.

"So who died?" she says to whoever's answering.

"He didn't die," Cowboy Boots says, blinking something away.

"Depends on what you consider dead," Mismatched Gloves adds.

"Greyson Brust," Shooting Glasses says, being respectful with the name.

"Hired on with us," Mismatched Gloves tells Jade, then shrugs an exaggerated shrug, like trying not to think of something.

"Zero days since the last accident?" Jade asks, aware of the eggshells she's walked onto here.

Shooting Glasses chuckles kind of humorlessly.

"Place is cursed," Jade says, which gets *all* of their attention, a few more unsubtle glances among them. "Probably, I mean," she adds.

"So where you headed?" Cowboy Boots asks, trying to get Jade's eventual exit started.

Jade, not a poker player, accidentally sneaks a glance in the direction of the great void in the night Indian Lake is, shrugs.

"She's not going *to*," Mismatched Gloves says, watching Jade hard. "She's going *from*, right?"

"Killer name," she says back to him, the answer to a question he hadn't even been asking a little.

"Say what?" Cowboy Boots says.

"Greyson Brust," Jade says, obviously. "That's—he sounds like horror royalty, I mean. You can hear it, can't you? 'Greyson Brust' is right up there with Harry Warden, with Billy Loomis, with John Wakefield, with Victor Crowley and Sammi Curr. With . . . I'm gonna say it . . . Jason *Voorhees*. Some names just have that killer ring, don't they?"

"You good, there?" Mismatched Gloves asks, and Jade looks down to where he means: the red blooming slow in the left pocket of her coveralls, from when she was flicking the utility knife's razor blade open and shut against her leg on the walk here.

"Got some red on me, yeah," she kind-of-quotes, shrugging his inspection off, all the tiny scars up and down her thighs and hips crawling over themselves to be seen. And then, because now nobody's saying anything and everything's awkward and starting to suck, Jade backs up a smidge from the fire, says, "But you're right, yeah. I have to be careful here. Shouldn't be standing so close to open flames like these, I mean."

"You were—" Cowboy Boots starts, then tries again: "I thought you were talking about—"

"*Slashers*," Jade says with her best evil grin. "I was talking about slashers. They're why I can't catch fire here. I'm a janitor, I mean, a custodian, and what's that but a caretaker, right? I'm practically Proofrock's caretaker when I'm wearing this. And if I stand too close, catch a sleeve on fire, and the rest of me goes up, then . . ."

Jade has to gulp her smile down.

"I'm talking about Cropsy," she says, looking from face to face for even a hint of recognition. "Slashers from 1981, Alex."

"Um," Shooting Glasses says.

"Okay, okay," she says, backing up in her head to figure out where to start for them. "Say you're the main and only caretaker for Camp Blackfoot. The one from *The Burning*, I mean. Not the one from *Camp Blood*, which is a movie to them, a place to us around here, but forget that for now. It's just—it's the same way Higgins Haven is in both *Friday the 13th Part III* and *Twisted Nightmare*, right?"

"You're the janitor for this camp," Cowboy Boots fills in, playing along.

"If I'm Cropsy I am, yeah," Jade says, ignoring everything else. "And I've got my own cabin and everything. But these kids, these punks, they don't really appreciate the way I've been 'taking care' of things, so much. Remember, this is sleepaway camp. It's its own little closed system of punishment and reward."

"Think I know that camp," Shooting Glasses says.

"*You* went to camp?" Mismatched Gloves says.

"I know the punishment part, I mean," Shooting Glasses says back to him.

"So I'm Cropsy, I'm the janitor, the caretaker," Jade goes on, before they forget they're listening to her. "It's my job to clean up all the blood in the showers. It's my job to tump the cut-off fingers out of the bottom of the canoe. Any deaths by wasp-nest or arrow or axe, I clean them up just the same. But then all these kids get it in their head that I need to be taught a lesson, so they elect to play a harmless little prank. Kind of a time-honored tradition of camp, right?"

"Got a jacket in the truck, you want one," Cowboy Boots says to Jade. Probably because of the way her jaw's chattering and the muscles around her eyes are jerking. But that's not cold, that's excitement. Usually Mr. Holmes will have cut her off by now, his big hand up between them, telling her he's not letting her write any more papers on horror movies, sorry.

But she can do them out loud, too.

"The prank these kids dream up," she explains, her voice gearing down, really getting into this, "it's that they sneak a probably-fake human skull into Cropsy's—into *my* bedroom while I'm sleeping, leave it there with two little candles burning in the eye sockets, and then bang on the window to wake me up. You can guess what happens next. The prank works—I'm scared, terrified, I've woken up to a nightmare—my cabin's on fire! Lesson learned, right? Wrong. In my half-asleep panic, I knock this skull over, the sheets catch fire, and then for some reason I've got a full can of gas in there with me. Probably to keep it away from the kids. To keep them from hurting themselves with it in some stupid way."

"Shit," Shooting Glasses says.

"Now fast-forward five years after that explosion," Jade says, like it's a campfire they're gathered round. "I, Cropsy, I lived *through* that burning . . . somehow. Kind of. Because I'm all melty and cratered, I wear trench coats, and my hat's always pulled down low because any sunlight practically hisses against my tender skin, my pizza knots of scar tissue—this is three years *before* Freddy, cool?"

"Got some gloves too," Cowboy Boots offers, starting to pull his off.

"I don't need a glove," Jade says, set up so perfect. "First person I kill, it's with scissors."

"Should we—?" Shooting Glasses says to everybody but Jade.

"Shh, shh," Mismatched Gloves tells him, getting into this.

Jade grins a not very secret grin. "By the time I make it back to the lake Camp Blackfoot's on, though—that's Black*foot*—those scissors have gone magnum. They're full-on hedge clippers now. And . . . why scissors, you think? Why hedge clippers? That's what I'm wanting to get at here. Maybe you can guess it. My history teacher couldn't."

"There somebody we can call?" Shooting Glasses asks.

"Think back to that initial prank, right?" Jade says, stopping at each face like an interrogation. "*Two* candles burning like eyes in that skull? Now, say I just woke up, saw that in the very last part of what I'm going to come to consider the good part of my life, wouldn't my first impulse be to cover those eyes, to ruin those eyes, to stop this scary shit from happening? But, if I just had a letter opener, say, I'm screwed. I have to either stick it in the left eye or the right eye, which doesn't make the scare go away, it just turns it into a pirate. But, if I've got scissors like *Schizoid* from the year before, well. Then I can pop both eyes at once. They're the perfect weapon for this terror I've woken up to. But now it's five years later and I'm back at good old Camp Blackfoot, and there's just a metric *shit*-ton of killing that needs to get done. So I ditch the scissors. Hedge clippers, though, with them I can stay back at a safe distance, just chop-chop-chop." Jade mimes it for them, coming at each of their throats. They just watch her. "And anyway, hedge clippers, they've, one, never been used in a slasher before 1981, and, two, when held up so they kind of flash in the light, they kind of make you feel like you're already dead."

"Can I give you, you know, a ride somewhere?" Shooting Glasses asks.

"But also," Jade barrels on, having to remind herself to breathe, "scissors *and* hedge clippers, they kind of fit the name, don't they?

Think about it. 'Cropsy.' If the name is at all descriptive, then it has to mean *cropping* things. Cutting them shorter than they were. Look it up in the dictionary when you get home. To 'crop' is to cut off the outer or upper parts. This is what I do as revenge to these campers, this summer. I *crop* the living shit out of them. In the woods. On a raft. In a mineshaft . . . all things we have right here in Proofrock."

"What are you saying?" Cowboy Boots says, looking around like to check if he's the only one of them wondering this.

"I'm saying that this is why I say I should be *careful* here," Jade tells him, opening her hands to the fire. "If I get too close to this and go up in flames, then I'm going to come back in five years and carve through this town like, like—but I forgot to tell you all the other stuff. Shit. Did you know that on the set of *The Burning*, Tom Savini still had Betsy Palmer's decapitated head from *Friday the 13th*, and the actors actually got to play with it like a volleyball? And, talking *Friday*, did you know it and *Mother's Day* were filming across the lake from each other in 1979? Yeah, yeah, the crews would get together at night and drink beer, and they, no way could they have known that the f-f-floodgates were about to open, like—like those elevator doors in *The Shining*, right? It must have—it was, it had to be—can you even imagine—"

Jade hates it, but she's crying a little bit now.

Maybe kind of a lot, really.

And now Shooting Glasses has her by the arm, his jacket off, around her shoulders.

He guides her away from the precious heat of the trashfire, delivers her into the passenger seat of a late-model dust-caked car that's out of place for a construction site.

"I—I'm f-fine," Jade finally manages to get out, trying to prove that it's okay, she can stay, she can talk all night, she did all her slasher homework, she knows every answer, please, just ask, ask.

"I'm taking you to—" Shooting Glasses says from the driver's seat, grubbing the keys up from the passenger seatback pocket, which makes it feel like his fingertips are touching her back. "Are you really, like, running from something?"

Jade considers this question for long enough that it becomes an answer.

"Where can I take you, then?" Shooting Glasses asks, cranking the engine.

"This your car?" Jade asks him back, wiping her face, finally breathing, and breathing too much now, too deep, like she's about to just collapse into a girl-shaped column of tears and wishes.

"It's like Cody out there," Shooting Glasses says, nodding back to either Mismatched Gloves or Cowboy Boots. "We *adopted* it."

Cowboy Boots, then.

"Adopted it your ass," Jade says, pausing for a slice of a moment to clock if he hears that she's talking like them. "Adopting a car means—it means you s-s-stole it."

She hates shivering like this, showing weakness like this, having to have a body like this. But it'll pass, she knows. You only shiver for a bit, when your body still has hope it can get back to warm.

"It was in the way of loading the barge last weekend," Shooting Glasses says with an easy shrug. "We moved it in here to keep it from getting dinged up."

"That d-doesn't mean it's y-y-yours."

"We'll give it back whenever whoever's it is comes for it."

"Maybe it's m-mine," Jade says, her shoulders jerking in spite of the jacket she's wrapped in.

In answer to that, Shooting Glasses plucks a glittery pink Deadwood shirt off the dash, holds it up.

Jade has to smile, caught. No way can a horror fan claim a shirt like that.

"Now where we going, final girl?" Shooting Glasses says.

Jade's heart stops, being called that. It stops and then inflates like a balloon in her chest. But, "That's not me," she has to say, looking out the side of the car, through her own reflection. "F-final girls are virg—they're p-p-pure . . . they're not like me."

"Question stands."

"I'll show you," Jade says, and nods to the right, into downtown Proofrock, then says to Shooting Glasses, "N-now you."

"Me what?" Shooting Glasses says, easing the car one tire at a time over the fence panel laid on its side that Jade guesses is a gate. Close enough. When he turns the headlights on, though, she reaches across, touches his arm, shakes her head no. He sucks the light back into the front of the car. It makes it feel like they're driving through church.

"I'd never even been here before," Shooting Glasses says about Proofrock, sleeping all around them.

"Lucky," Jade says, a wave of shivers rolling up her back again, her lips set against this physical betrayal. "Here."

Shooting Glasses hand-over-hands the wheel to the left again, easing them past the drugstore, past the bank, and it's not like church anymore. Now it's like they're coasting through a painting: "Quaint Mountain Towns." "Lakeside Pastoral." "What If 1965 Never Stopped Happening?"

"Your turn," Jade tells Shooting Glasses. "I told you—I told you some stuff. Now you tell me some stuff. That's how it works. Quid pro quo, Clarice."

Shooting Glasses shakes his head side to side slow, apparently impressed that, in spite of these early stages of hypothermia, the girl's still got it.

Jade nods that, yes, this is her, this is what she does.

"Where were you the last four years?" she says to him, kind of accidentally out loud.

"I was—" he starts, then hears it like she means it, just purses his lips, peers ahead into the unheadlit darkness.

"This is where you tell me about your buddy," Jade explains to him. "The one that *wasn't* a wake for back there. The one who didn't die all the way or whatever."

"Greyson."

"Did he go live with a distant aunt to recover? Was her barn full of pitchforks, her hands full of s-sewing needles, her head full of bad ideas?"

Shooting Glasses looks over to her about this.

"That's how it usually goes, I mean," Jade explains, trying to show she means no insult. "The wronged party, victim of the prank, has to go somewhere long enough that everyone else can forget all about him, so it can be a s-s-surprise when he's back."

"You said this place was haunted," Shooting Glasses tells her.

"By all the ghosts of who everybody used to want to be, before they died inside," Jade says.

"What were you doing out here?" Shooting Glasses asks.

"Did you know *Friday the 13th*, it was trying to cash in on *Halloween*, yeah, sure, but then right at the very end it forgot what it was doing, started thinking it was *Carrie*?"

"Why do you talk about horror so much?"

"Slashers," Jade corrects, is always correcting.

"I mean, and don't take this the wrong way, but, have you considered that maybe you're just hiding be—"

"Can't I just like horror because it's great? Does there have to be some big explanation?"

"I'm just, your leg, I think maybe that's blood. I think maybe I should—"

Jade doesn't hear the end because she's popped the door, is rolling out into the cold, can't take any more of this—her dad, this town, high school. Questions, glances, judgments. The sad way stupid Sheriff Hardy looks at her. The way Mr. Holmes is always asking her these exact same questions, every time she turns in a paper. Now even construction grunts she doesn't know are treating her like she's in need of special-delicate handling.

Fuck that. Fuck all of them.

She falls on the heels of her hands and her knees, doesn't let that stop her, is already running like a ragdoll down the town pier, that kind of running that's all untied boots, that you have to lift your chin for, because you know you're going so fast. Halfway to the end of the pier, the stolen car's brights blast on, throwing her shadow out ahead of her, where it plunges past the wooden planks, into the water.

Jade tries to stop but it's slick, so, yeah, the perfect capper to the perfect night: she goes flailing over the end, just like every kid all summer long, except it's not summer yet, and she's seventeen, and it's cold-thirty in the dead-dead morning.

The last thing she thinks as she's slipping over the end is how stupid it is that that shaky light is steady for once, isn't flickering out, and then she's holding her breath for the icy plunge, is trying to insulate herself with slashers that happen in the snow but can only come up with *Cold Prey* and *Cold Prey 2*, and that's not going to be enough to keep her blood from freezing.

Instead of splashing into the lake or cracking through the thin sheet of ice that has to be there, she *thunks* into the bottom of the green canoe always tied there, BYOP-style: Bring Your Own Paddle.

The canoe rocks and founders, doesn't quite roll.

Jade sits up holding the back of her head, the world blurry and getting blurrier, then, hearing footsteps coming for her, she lets the scratchy nylon rope loose, reaches out with one boot to push off into the darkness, the scrim of ice on the surface crackling around her in large, slow sheets. So she won't have to see Shooting Glasses standing there looking for her, she fetals down on her side in the bottom of the canoe, the gunwales to either side hiding her and her orange hair, her blue lips, her red left leg, her pitch-black heart.

And she hates it more than anything, but she's sobbing now.

No, she can never be a final girl.

Final girls are good, they're uncomplicated, they have these reserves of courage coiled up inside them, not layer after layer of shame, or guilt, or whatever this festering poison is.

Real final girls only want the horror to be over. They don't stay up late praying to Craven and Carpenter to send one of their savage angels down, just for a weekend maybe. Just for one night. Just for one dance, please? One last dance?

That's all Jade needs in the world, she knows.

Instead she's got Tab Daniels for a father, Proofrock for a prison, and high school for a torture chamber.

Kill em all, she says in her heart of hearts. *Let God sort them out.*

Or just leave them unsorted, floating facedown in the shallows. That works too.

Jade chuckles to herself through the tears, pats her chest pocket for the cigarette she doesn't have, because these coveralls were just hanging on the line.

Once she's drifted far enough out that the light from the pier can't reach her, she sits up, takes stock, and keeps monologuing even though the trashfire is just a flickering speck of light on shore: "Did you know that kid the shark eats in *Jaws*, his name's 'Voorhees' too?" she asks the construction grunts, all three of them so ready to smile with wonder at this. "Yeah, yeah, Voorhees kids should maybe stay out of the water, think? But that's not even what I meant to say, okay, sorry. I was just—when Jason comes up out of the water in mossy slow motion for Alice, floating there in her safe canoe, roll-the-credits music already cueing up, that's *Friday*'s *Carrie* moment right there, that's the stinger that would set the mold for the Golden Age of the slasher, the eighties, and, and . . . the way he comes up and hugs her from behind, it's not because he means her any violence, any harm, it's just that he's—he's a little *kid*, goddamnit, he's a helpless messed-up little kid and he's fucking drowning, he's terrified, he's holding on to whatever he can, right? He's scared, and she's . . . she's supposed to protect him, save him, keep him *safe*."

Jade lowers her face, because the air at her chest has to be warmer. Her lungs feel like they're iced over, filling with something solid and permanent.

This isn't just going to be hypothermia, Sheriff Hardy, Mr. Holmes.

She's Alice at the end of *Friday the 13th* now, she knows, when Friday's starting to be Saturday, she's Alice and she's floating out on the lake in her canoe, waiting for the magic to happen, trying to stay out there long enough that Jason notices her up at the surface, starts rising, rising—

"Here I am," Jade says, loopy with cold now, smiling because it doesn't hurt anymore, and just to give Jason some color to find her, some of what he likes, she holds her left wrist out, uses her right hand to flick the razor from the utility knife like a sharp little tongue, and she cuts longways and deep like opening a fountain, doesn't scratch some side-to-side plea-for-help gash.

Her blood pours steaming from the fishbelly part of her left forearm and she studies it, says, "Here I am, I'm—I'm . . ."

What stops her is how fascinating her blood is, pooled on the surface of the gelid lake. She's seventy percent certain a misshapen face is looking up at her from the murk, its mouthful of gravestone teeth trying to grin. She smiles back, looks all around in farewell, to Proofrock where she grew up, to Terra Nova where she's never been, to Camp Blood, where her heart is.

"*Momma I'm coming home*," she says with that Ozzy lilt, and she knows no arms are coming up from behind her for her big finale, for the slasher version of a death roll, which is really just a hug, but she closes her eyes all the same, pretends.

SLASHER 101

And then there was one. Of me, I mean, Mr. Holmes,
one Jade Daniels to take you by the hand and
walk you up and down the video rental aisles of
slasherland to make up for what I missed from the
Freddy Glove Incident at freshman detention, which
wasn't even really my fault, and that Freddy glove
has PLASTIC blades anyway. It's almost October
though, and horror is my religion. Can I not
celebrate orthodoxly and honor my church's holy
days?

But I need to explain SLASHERS to you now, in
under 2 pages.

It's easy to think that the slasher started
with <u>Halloween</u>, previously called <u>The Babysitter
Murders</u>, or that it got a face when <u>Friday the 13th
III</u> put a certain <u>Black Christmas</u> hockey mask on,
but still, a lot fans and true believers will go
back to <u>Psycho</u> and <u>Peeping Tom</u>. However though if
you ask yourself "Who was the first masked killer?"
then you can go all the long way back to <u>Phantom
of the Opera</u>, which you might remember seeing on a
high school outing probably.

What's first and almost first isn't as important
as what's INSIDE the slasher though, sir. And that
is REVENGE plain and simple.

To explain, years ago there was some prank or
crime that hurt someone and then the slasher comes
back to dispense his violent brand of justice, and
he's not listening to excuses or apologies because
there's not one single one that could ever be even
halfway enough, his mission is carving and he's not
stopping until he's stopped.

So in the case of Jason Voorhees and Freddy
Krueger, what made them into a slasher is that

Jason DROWNS through massive and obviously wrong neglect, and Freddy is EXECUTED by a mob illegally, and the counselors who allowed this drowning and the parents who became this mob never get punished, just get to keep on keeping on, and it's that unfairness that powers the slasher. As for Michael Myers, his Ahab Dr. Loomis says he's evil, but he's been MADE evil, Mr. Holmes. The crime done to him is that his sister his BABYSITTER should have been watching him closer not stripping down and sexing it up. Michael could have been run over in the street. He could have choked on candy. He could have found a knife and got all stabby.

Only one of those three ended up happening, Mr. Holmes. It would have been a pretty short movie otherwise.

As for Ghostface from <u>Scream</u>, sure Billy aka Ghostface says it's scarier when there isn't a motive, but that doesn't mean he doesn't have one, sir. Final Girl Sidney's mom had an affair with his dad, breaking his family up, so a year later all the revenge starts up.

So what I'm saying is that in the slasher, wrongs are always punished. The crew that did the Bad Prank years ago gets the just dessert they deserve, with a bloody cherry on top, and when they least expect it, making it all better, which should convert you to my side of the movie aisle and the water's fine over here, Mr. Holmes, really. A little bloody maybe, but all the dead people are people who were asking for it. Which is my argument in a gory nutshell.

SLAUGHTER HIGH

Eight weeks is the vacation Henderson High gives you for at-tempted suicide, apparently—*seven*, really, Jade thinks, since spring break was one of those weeks.

Still, seven works, even if she had to spend them in a psych ward down in Idaho Falls. She should have thought of this par-ticular scam years ago. Better yet? She's kind of an escaped mental patient now, she thinks. Close enough.

And that story only ends one way.

"What's so funny?" Sheriff Hardy asks her across the console of his OJ-white county Bronco—the chariot delivering Jade back for the last week of class, so she can go through the motions of finishing out her senior year.

"This," Jade says, hooking her chin out to the hug-n-go lane they're mired in.

"But you understand about the community service?" he asks, switching hands on the wheel with a groan, a wet cartilaginous *pop* coming from the depths of his lower back.

"Twelve hours," Jade recites for the third time this trip. Twelve hours picking trash for—

Get this, she would say to her best friend, if she had one: the community service is for "Unauthorized Use of the Town Canoe."

"Is that really what it's called?" her imaginary best friend would hiss back with just the right amount of thrilled outrage.

"Exactly," Jade would say, this interchange nearly making those twelve hours of picking trash worth it.

Instead, they just sort of pre-suck.

Still, she guesses she's going to be a star at school today, right? This will be her official fifteen minutes. The returning antihero. The teen every parent fears the worst. The one who almost got away, before Hardy got Shooting Glasses's frantic call and fired his airboat up, skipped out to Jade's frozen spot on the lake, kept her wrist compressed just long enough for the LifeFlight to touch down on shore, all of Proofrock gathered behind it in their slippers and robes and, for all Jade knows, half-dead as she was, wearing those sleep caps with the long cartoon tails trailing behind, that, in real life, would have been dipped into toilet water five hundred times already.

It's a fun enough image to dwell on, and Jade's had weeks and weeks at the Teton Peaks Residential Treatment Center to do it, but what she always finds herself watching instead of the crowd that night is Sheriff Hardy, coming up out of the shallows with her in his arms, giving her all the body heat he has to give, his sixty-one-year-old jowls quivering with each bellow he lets out about how this girl is goddamn well *not* going to die, not on his watch.

In slashers, the local cops are always useless. It's a hard and fast rule of the genre. Sheriff Hardy not sticking to that is just one more nail in the coffin of Jade's dreams.

By now that coffin's pretty much all nails.

"And you don't have any blades hidden here, right?" Sheriff Hardy confirms, nodding to the front doors of the school they're finally stopped at.

"Axes and machetes count?" Jade asks back with her best evil grin, her hand already to the door handle, but . . . there's a manilla-brown PROPERTY envelope suddenly and unaccountably in Hardy's right hand?

Hardy breathes in like Jade's paining him here, says, "You want, I can just take you back to—"

"*No*, Sheriff, no weapons on school grounds. Everybody knows I keep my axes and machetes over at Camp Blood, right? Buried under the floorboards of cabin six?"

Hardy licks his lips and Jade can tell he doesn't know what to do with her.

Just as she wants it.

"That's for me?" she says about the mystery envelope, and Hardy hands it across uncertainly.

"I just want you to—to be safe, you know?" he says.

Jade's trying for all the world to hold his eyes while also weighing this strangely-heavy envelope in her hand. *Property?*

"Consider me saved," she says, her door open now, right foot reaching for the ground, and she's no more than shut the door and spun around before a dad in a gold Honda kisses her shins with his plastic bumper, his tires chirping.

Jade has to hop back to keep the contact from getting real, hop back and slam both hands onto the hood. She looks down through her electric blue bangs to her knees, to this insult of a near-disaster, and then she brings her eyes up slow across the hood, bores them through the windshield, and Hodders her head over to look into this father's soul. It, like his chest, is pretty much just covered in coffee. She removes her hands one at a time, only looking away at the last moment. Holding her mummy-wrist high, envelope low and trailing, she stalks away, wades through the crush of bodies, under the wilting flags, and steps into the hallowed halls of learning one more time, breathes that morning napalm in.

It smells like hairspray and floor cleaner and secret cigarette smoke.

"Woodsboro High, here I am," she says.

Nobody notices.

The gauze on her arm itches, wants to just come off already, but the gauze is her armor for the day, so it can't come off. And Hardy was too gentlemanly to even question it, though Jade did catch him looking: Why would Suicide Girl still need dressing over stitches that had long been pulled, over a skin-weld of scar tissue she's already considering getting a tattoo around, a tattoo of dead fingers clawing their way up and out? The answer of course is that she doesn't need it. But she also really-really does.

The mummy-wrap is stolen, of course. All the best things in life are stolen, Jade knows. Like this envelope.

Since nobody's got eyes on her, she steps into the Quiet Room by the main office, which any student can retreat to if anxiety has their thoughts circling the drain, from their parents getting divorced, from their boyfriend or girlfriend not texting them back, from finals or "life," whatever.

Jade unwraps the red string keeping the envelope closed and reaches in for this so-called property.

First is the name-patch from her custodial coveralls, probably all that was left after the medics attacked her with their blunt-nosed scissors. Jade tucks it into her front pocket, to carry ahead to her next pair of coveralls. Next is a plastic baggie with the earrings she was wearing the night-of. One's a pearly-white smiling face maybe a half-inch across, and the other's the same face, just sobbing blood, a pentagram Manson'd between its eyes. Because: the Crüe. She chocks the envelope under her arm and reinserts *Theatre of Pain* into her ears, apologizing to Vince and Nikki and Tommy and Mick that she never even missed them.

But the patch and the earrings aren't the real weight in this envelope. The real weight is a sandwich baggie with a rhinestone-and-pink phone inside.

"What are you?" Jade says, shaking the phone out, trying to wake it but it's been dead since the night-of, she guesses. Or earlier.

Why would Hardy think this is hers, though? Was it in the canoe? Is it one of the medics'? Why does it smell like peanut butter?

Jade peels the pink case off for the ID or emergency credit card tucked in back. Instead there's just an if-found sticker, with a +31 phone number and a name that probably goes with that country code: "Sven."

Jade dials the number into her own phone, listens to it ring and ring, finally landing at a voicemail in a language she doesn't understand. She looks "+31" up, lands on "Netherlands."

"*Any*way," she says, and, now that the phone number's in her call list, peels the if-found sticker, crumbles it into the trash so that, as far as teachers or principals or sheriffs might know, this is her phone. To prove it, she shoves it into her right rear pocket, moving her own phone to her bra, which she knows is some sort of breast cancer danger, but screw it. Maybe her imaginary best friend will text and Jade will feel that buzz immediately in her heart, right?

Right.

All the same, she guesses it was pure luck she wasn't checking her phone on the ride in with Hardy. He might have clocked the phone in her lap, had questions about the one in the bag, with the pink case Jade would never have for herself, now that she's thinking about it.

That pink, though, it reminds her of . . . what?

Jade squints, trying to dredge the memory up, connect it to

something, and zombies back out into the bustle of two minutes before first bell. She's not going to chemistry, though. Not yet. First it's the ladies' room by the men's gym, because it's always the least crowded. The whole way there she's expecting conversation to stop around her, for feet to shuffle to a stop when she scowls past, but instead it's just the usual treatment: eyes flicking away when they realize it's Jennifer Daniels again, or Jade, or JD, or whatever she's going by this year. Even her beacon of an arm hardly draws a second glance.

What, did somebody else suicide after her, and better? Is she old news already?

She ducks into the ladies' room and pulls down the community eyeliner from the top of the far mirror, the one with SKANK STATION scratched into the tile above it, either by one of the rah-rahs who would never stoop to risk an eye infection, or by that rah-rah's mother, fifteen years ago.

No way can Jade face the day without her black binoculars to look through, though.

She opens wide, traces it on raccoon-thick, has her face right to the mirror when the voice comes from behind her: "Oh. So there *will* be thirty-two Hawks this year, I guess."

Jade refocuses, sees the reflections of Rica Lawless and Greta Dimmons swishing for the exit, their word balloon practically hanging in the air behind them for Jade to study.

Thirty-*two* Henderson Hawks?

Counting Jade back into the graduating class . . . she's no mathlete, but shouldn't it be thirty seniors *without* her? Does she count twice now that she's back from the dead, or did some salmon of an overachieving junior jump a grade?

More important: does she care? Is she going to let Rica and Greta occupy even one one-hundredth of her precious headspace? The only reason they're even counting graduates is because they're both yearbook staff, meaning the class photo is their responsibility—that stupid series of wide snapshots by the trophy case that every group of seniors gets Shining'd into. It's one of those cardboard cutout things like for coin collections, except the coins are the graduates' faces, and each of their faces is set into an actual Henderson Hawk, brown feathers and all, the scroll at the bottom promising they're all going to *soar into the future* or *take the snake by the tail* or *have a bird's-eye view of history*, Jade forgets all the stupid embarrassing hawk stuff.

But yeah, "I'm back, bitches," she says out loud to the door closing behind Rica and Greta.

It's punctuated by a toilet flushing.

Jade holds the eyeliner a smidge from her lower lid, waiting for a pair of combat boots to step down from a toilet, followed by a dark robe slowly descending over the ankles, but instead—

Oh, shit, Jade nearly sputters out.

This is why no one cares that Suicide Girl is stalking the halls again. This is why the count of graduating seniors is off by one.

Jade's eyeliner pencil goes clattering down into the sink, leaving slashes and dots of black in that porcelain whiteness.

It's from who's pulling the stall door in, stepping around it, gliding effortlessly to the sink right by Jade's. She's nobody from Jade's past, nobody Jade recognizes at all except by stature, by type, by bearing. If this girl had an aura, it would be "princess," but the cut of her eyes is closer to "warrior," the kind of face that's just made to come alive when a spatter of blood mists across those perky, flawless, no-acne cheeks.

Jade isn't sure whether this girl actually reaches forward to turn the water on or if the water, knowing it needs to be on to better kiss these hands, just comes on all on its own. For half an accidental moment, Jade catches herself checking the air around them for cartoon bluebirds carrying a gossamer wrap.

"Oh, hey," the girl says as easy as anything, of course not offering to shake hands—this is a bathroom—"I'm Letha. Letha Mondragon?"

The question mark hanging between them now translates out as *You've heard of me, yes?* but not in an off-putting way, not in a way that's assuming anything.

Jade feels her face flushing warm in response. It's maybe the first time in her life that's ever actually happened to her. She wonders if it shows on her Indian skin or not, and then she's wondering if this "Letha Mondragon," being Black, is even accustomed to reading people's emotional states from the blood rushing to the surface of their skin.

In the same instant she decides this is racist as hell, gulps it down as best she can. All the same, she still hasn't managed to look away from this Letha Mondragon's reflection in her own mirror, has she?

It's not because she's Black, either. Black isn't *completely* unheard of in Idaho, though it is less and less heard of the higher the elevation gets. No, the reason she's caught in this vortex of staring, it's . . . is it Letha Mondragon's hair?

It's not just glamorous and perfect, flowing down her back but kind of spiral-curled too, it's, it's—oh, Jade knows what it is, yeah, of course: online at four in some bleary morning, lost in the wishing well of her phone, she'd chanced onto a smuggled-out snapshot from the set of a shampoo commercial. One of those ones where the model's long luxuriant locks are cascading in slow-motion waves all around her, a silky bronze extension of her dopey smile.

What Jade had always assumed had to be strategically-placed fans blowing and lifting all these models' too-beautiful hair turned out to be a faceless green humanoid—someone in a skinhugging bright green turtleneck and thin green gloves, with green nylon pulled tight over their head so they can disappear in the camera's eye. So they can guide the model's hair up like this, and like that.

Letha Mondragon must have a whole crew of those green humanoids following her around, always underfoot, lifting her hair up, around, everywhere.

And, the thing is? Jade can tell by the polite way Letha's just waiting for Jade's response, lips pursed, eyes big, hands sudsing up, that she doesn't see the little green people. She isn't even aware of them.

"And you are?" she says to Jade, her face hopeful for some interaction but not being pushy about it. "I don't think I've seen you here before, have I?"

Jade makes herself lean back into the mirror with her face, her numb fingers grubbing the eyeliner pencil up, fully aware now of the SKANK STATION carved above her. And, as if her own grudging awareness of that heading has made it blink, Letha Mondragon's eyes flick up to it and then down just as fast, almost demurely, and now it's not just Jade's face glowing with heat, with awareness, with knowledge, with possibility, it's—and she could never say this out loud, not in a thousand-million years—it's her *heart*.

Letha Mondragon is embarrassed, not *of* the profanity, but that it even has to exist. Because that's the kind of pure she is. That's the only answer here. She probably, Jade knows—no, she *surely* already has a job volunteering somewhere in town. Not a church, but that's just because churches, in spite of their own good intentions, have their own bad history. And that's not for one such as Letha Mondragon. She would never sully herself that way, even by association. No, she's probably volunteering . . . not at the high school library, Mrs. Jennings is a famous drunk and smokes menthols besides, and no candy-striping at Doc Wilson's either, as handsy as he gets late in the afternoon, and there's no thrift store where Letha could fold third-hand clothes after school, no animal shelter she can bottle-feed kittens at. Wherever it is she's doing her good and necessary work, she walks there with purpose, Jade can tell, her books pressed tight to her chest, but Jade can see under that as well: Letha Mondragon is volunteering to help, yes, that's most important, of course of course, but she's also volunteering because, if she weren't busy, then she wouldn't have any acceptable excuse for not showing up when Randi Randall's parents are gone for the weekend. If she wasn't already busy, she'd have zero reason not to step down into Bethany Manx's famously-smoky basement whenever Principal Manx is at a conference.

And, stacked like she most definitely is, she probably can't press *too* many books to her chest, Jade guesses. Nobody's arms could be that long. But even covering up like that, there's still her legs, which, even in jeans, are obviously the human version of "gazelle," probably from volleyball or water polo or the four-hundred, and the rest of her is perfectly proportioned just the same, almost sculpted, all . . . five feet *eleven* of her?

Shit, man. Is she even real? Jade tries to focus on the business end of the eyeliner, halfway wondering if somebody dosed it. Because—can there actually *be* specimens like Letha Mondragon in the actual world, not just in the airbrushed jack-off fantasies of every wishful-thinking penis-haver out there?

But, as if designed by those dreams, she's not *too* tall either, is she? That would be intimidating to the insecure male set. And, though pigtails and poodle skirts aren't the order of the day even in high-valley Idaho, "pigtails and poodle skirt" is still the impression Jade's getting from Letha Mondragon. Maybe that's just because there's no visible piercings, Jade tells herself. Maybe it's just because there are no tattoos peeking up from a collar or flicking a sharp forked tongue down from a shirtsleeve.

No, Letha Mondragon would never even consider such self-mutilation, such external expression of "inner turmoil," such obvious pleas for help. She doesn't even wear her jeans too tight, or have big rhinestone crosses on the rear pockets like every second ass out in the hall, because placing shiny crosshairs on yourself, well, that's for other girls.

Jade wants to hate her for that, for all of it at once, she wants to lash out from instant jealousy or the basic unfairness of random biology, but she can't seem to muster it, is anesthetized just from being this close, is still saying that name over and over in her head: Mondragon, Mondragon, Mondragon.

If "Greyson Brust" is as killer as Harry Warden, then "Letha Mondragon" is easily as inviolable as Laurie Strode, as Sidney Prescott, both of whom dress conservatively, neither of whom would ever bleach her hair with stolen peroxide in a hospital sink, then dye it electric blue.

No, Jade will never be any kind of final girl, she knows, and has known for years.

Final girls don't wear combat boots to school, untied in honor of John Bender. Final girls' wrists aren't open to the world. Final girls are all, of course—this goes without saying—virgins. Final girls don't wear "Metal Up Your Ass" shirts to school, with the indelible image of a knife thrusting up from the toilet. Final girls never select the SKANK STATION mirror, or wear this much eyeliner—they don't need to. Their eyes are already piercing and perfect.

Instead of getting lost in Letha's, Jade sneaks a quick look down to the shoes this impossible girl-woman has to have all the way down there, and, yep: no pumps, nothing stiletto or even near-stiletto. Because she's too young for that, is still Cheerleader Sandy, not Leather Sandy.

Jade could puke, except she also wants to cry, and isn't sure which is maybe going to happen, is just watching Letha's hands under that solid sluice of water now, the suds sliding away, the

hands tending each other, the nails unpainted, of course, and neither long nor French.

"Jade," Jade manages to cough out, her throat clenching shut
again immediately after.

Letha turns the water off, reaches the other way for a paper
towel.

"Jade," she says, her eyes practically glittering. "That's my birth-
stone, wow."

"You're—you're—"

"From Terra Nova," Letha says, shrugging as if embarrassed by
all this unasked-for notoriety. "Or, once our house gets finished, I
will be. So I guess we're neighbors then, aren't we? Just across the
lake? Maybe we can hang out some afternoon?"

"Terra Nova," Jade says, stabbing the soft dull point of the eyeliner into the white of her eye and not letting herself flinch from
the burn. Relishing it, actually. Using it to ground herself in this
moment, not float away.

"I better—" Letha says, leaning sideways towards the door, and
like that she's gone, the bell probably holding its breath for her to
find her classroom, then ringing in celebration.

Letha Mondragon, the new girl, the final girl.

"Unauthorized Use of the Town Canoe," Jade whispers to her
moments after she's gone, and it takes her a halting breath or two
to understand what the black drips are in the sink she's holding on
to by both sides.

Tears.

She's crying and smiling, everything all at once.

SLASHER 101

Don't feel bad, Mr. Holmes. Not everybody knows
about the Final Girl in the slasher. But let me
give you this blood pass. It's like a hall pass,
just all the lights are off.

First and this goes without saying, final girls
have the coolest names. Ripley, Sidney. Strode,
Stretch. Connor, Crane, Cotton. Even Julie James
from I Know What You Did Last Summer has that
double initials thing going on, that kind of gets
your mouth addicted to saying her name. They're
more than cool names though. As you can tell by
what they're called, they're also the last girl
alive. But that only means she's last, maybe by
luck, and not "best," when the actual REASON she's
last is that she IS the best of us all.

The REASON she's final is her resolve, sir. Her
will and her insistence not to die. She runs and
falls of course, and probably screams and cries too,
but this is because she's started her horror journey
out bookish and timid, with good values, the home by
nine-thirty good big sister type. But of everybody
in the movie she's the one with "more" inside her, by
which I mean at a certain point in all the running
away, during all the stalking and slashing, when
the bloodletting's reached a sort of crazed frenzy
where the bodies are just falling left and right and
between, this Final Girl stands up through the heart
of it all, through the fragile shell of her old self,
and she goes toe to toe with this bad evil.

The Final Girl is a hero for our times, sir,
kind of like a certain student Principal Manx can't
really prove was me leaving that bucket of pig's
blood in the rafters of the Sadie Hawkins dance,
that wasn't even really pig's blood.

But the best ever example of a real and actual
final girl is from Just Before Dawn where Constance
finally turns to face her mountainous hillbilly
slasher, who's already carved through the rest of
her friends. She's had enough. Being attacked over
and over, it hasn't weakened her, it's cut away her
restraints. The slasher thought he was tormenting
her. He thought he was the one in charge. Wrong. He
was fashioning his own death. He was building the
perfect killing machine.

What this Final Girl does is turn around, scream
into his face that she's so sick of this, that
this is ENOUGH, that this is over. And then, in a
move not matched in all the years since, not even
by Sidney Prescott, not even by slow motion Alice
when Pamela Voorhees won't stop coming at her, not
even by Jamie Lee Curtis in that long dark night
of Haddonfield, Constance climbs up her slasher's
frontside and because she has no weapon, because
she IS the weapon, she forces her hand into her
slasher's mouth, down his throat, and then she
reaches in deeper, and comes out with his life
pulsing in her fist.

To put it in conclusion, sir, final girls are
the vessel we keep all our hope in. Bad guys don't
just die by themselves, I mean. Sometimes they need
help in the form of a furie running at them, her
mouth open in scream, her eyes white hot, her heart
forever pure.

THE INITIATION

The rest of the day blurs past for Jade. It's like she's moving at normal speed, but everyone else in the halls and classrooms and cafeteria are superfast ants. Either that or it's her that's going slow, her that's trying to wade through syrup.

In seventh period, probably because he's tired of teaching the same old history unit—the Shoshone and the Oregon Trail, mining and Drown Town—Mr. Holmes shows them a video he's taken from the ultralight little airplane he's been buzzing around in all year, and sometimes parks in the parking lot even though his house is only three blocks away.

Because there are no airspace laws over Indian Lake yet—"But wait, wait," he says all sad-like—he can drift over to Terra Nova if the wind's not too bad, report back on the progress of construction. That's maybe why he built the ultralight in the first place, Terra Nova being his pre-retirement paranoia. But the ultralight's pretty cool, Jade thinks—it's pretty much just a sky go-cart. She's surprised he hasn't already killed himself with it.

Now that he's mounted one of the school's videocameras to the frame, it won't be long, she imagines. Tilting his fabric wings this way or that for a better angle, a longer shot, that's a good way to take a header into a flagpole, a tree, the tall brick side of the drugstore, or even just the hard surface of the lake.

Like he's always saying, though, we all become history at some point or another, right? And, if Jade's right about there being a final girl in town at long last—if that's in fact what Letha Mondragon, sitting two rows up and one over, is—then what that means is that a slasher cycle is trying to get started, meaning life's about to get real cheap around these parts. A lot of people's insides are about to start being on the *out*side.

Jade can hardly help smiling. Best graduation present *ever*.

But it's not a for-sure thing yet, she reminds herself. It can still be wishful thinking on her part. When you're wearing slasher goggles, everything can look like a slasher.

What she needs is proof the cycle's starting, and in the slasher that proof only ever takes one form: a couple of randos getting eviscerated, usually while half-dressed. It's the blood sacrifice the ritual needs to get going right.

Who will it be, though?

Jade cases history class, looking for any of the telltale signs of impending death: a water bottle sloshing with something a lot harsher than water (check); a text thread exploding with a party's address (check); a pair of pupils dilated well past mellow (check, check, check); the purple corner of a condom wrapper sticking up from a wallet or purse (it's already torn, but still: check).

And—will this slasher be punishing the graduating class due to some long-ago forgotten prank their parents were part of, or will this have more to do with trespassing, with waking something that should have been left sleeping? If it's the trespassing build, then Camp Blood will probably play a part, since that kind of horror always has tendrils connecting it to the black-and-white past. If the slasher's here for something the parents have done and *know* they've done, though, then the slasher and the final girl will probably face off at the scene of the original prank, which will most likely be the lake.

Either way works.

Jade can't help but smile.

"Ms. Daniels?" Mr. Holmes says, reeling her back to class.

"I'm watching, I'm watching," Jade says, and she sort of even is. On the rolled-in television screen Mr. Holmes has tied the videocamera into, he's just crossed the opposite shore of Indian Lake, is skimming the top of the pine trees about a quarter mile to the north of Terra Nova.

"Wait for it, wait for it," he says from the front of the classroom, and then dives forward for the pause button when he clears the last tree. "Trigger warning," he turns around to announce, a mischievous glint to his eye. "All vegetarians, prepare to upchuck the celery and beets you had for lunch."

Mr. Holmes is always arguing that he wouldn't eat cows if they weren't made of meat, which is enough of a groaner to sort of wrap around to endearing, in a sad way.

"More like cucumber, right, Ambs?" Lee Scanlon announces to the room single entendre–style, Amber Wayne kicking his chair from behind.

"Now now," Mr. Holmes says, and the way he does slow-motion with the playback is by tapping the pause button over and over, inching his flight forward. It's like a slideshow now, Jade guesses, and settles in to see what he saw on his last big trip across the lake.

From the front of the room, Tiffany Koenig, closest to the screen, gasps and covers her face, turns away. Mr. Holmes just smiles, tapping the pause button with delicious slowness.

In the high sloping meadow just past the tall line of trees right on the shore, spread out so you can kind of still see the formation they were in, are ten or twenty dead elk, their legs and heads all twisted and contracted into grotesque configurations.

Jade leans forward in her desk, because there was definitely some real and unique pain in this lonely meadow. Some roving Cenobite got its pound of flesh, and then the rest of the pounds of flesh as well.

Banner Tompkins stands, crowds the screen, a couple of the other football players suddenly interested in history class as well. It's kind of a first.

"What—what did it?" Letha asks, and all heads turn to her.

She's not looking away, but the pain in her voice, on her face, is about to spill over into tears, it sounds like. For the sad innocent animals.

"Such a *tragedy*," Banner says, trying to match her emotion.

"Please," Jade hears herself scoffing, and Banner looks back to her, flashes his grin that she's pretty sure means *Shhh, shh, I'm almost into her pants, here.*

If only he knew who he was dealing with.

"What did it, yes," Mr. Holmes is saying, doing that thing where he thinks on his feet while the image is paused and trembling. "As you can see, there are no bullet or arrow holes, no holes at all."

"Beaver fever," Lee says, and gets a high five from Banner, a sneer from most of the girls.

"Giardiasis," Mr. Holmes corrects, as if considering this possibility. "But . . . wouldn't an elk's four-chambered stomach take care of most parasites? Or, would nineteen elks' stomachs *fail* to do so, and all at the same time?"

"Griz," Banner finally says, and, as if his judgment here is final, he takes his seat.

Mr. Holmes comes around slow on the heel of his right loafer, his left skating just over the floor, stopping him perfect, a move Jade's always appreciated—not that she'd ever tell him.

"Mr. Tompkins may be on to something," he says. "Do you see how the bull's neck there has been broken? What other animal out there would have that kind of raw power?"

"A bear?" Letha says, as if just making the connection between it and "griz."

"*Oh my,*" Amber adds with fake drama, covering the O of her mouth with her so-delicate fingers.

"There is wildlife on that side of the lake, Ms. Mondragon, yes," Mr. Holmes informs Letha. "One of the many perils of living in what was formerly a national preserve."

"Can we—you know?" Tiffany K pleads, rolling her hand forward for the play button please.

Mr. Holmes grins, lets his flight glide on past this meadow of dead elk and then bank high over the forest, swoop back in the direction of Proofrock—

"Wait, wait," Letha says, coming up from her seat a bit.

Mr. Holmes catches the pause key and Jade realizes she has been gone a long time: not only have the houses of Terra Nova been getting real and actual skins over their wood frames the last two months, but there's driveways being carved out, unlikely pools and ponds being scraped into the rock, and an actual *dock* latched onto the shore now.

Tied onto the dock somehow, but probably anchored too, because the lake is deep on the steep side of Pleasant Valley, is the kind of yacht Jade's only seen in movies. Ones about drug dealers.

Did it get lifted in on a fleet of cargo helicopters, or was it trucked in on one of those wide-load rigs?

"Oh, that's just Tiara," Letha says, not so much with pride as with . . . defeat?

Tiara must be the bombshell blond *white* woman tanning in a nothing-bikini on one of the many decks of the yacht. She's straight out of *Cheerleader Camp*—easy to hate.

"Sister?" Banner says hopefully.

"Stepmother," Letha says curtly, no malice at all, but maybe a trace of what sounds to Jade a lot like forced pleasantness. It's the first chink she's seen in Letha's final girl armor, but really it's just more support for her *being* a final girl: before getting sucked into the slasher cycle, the final girl will have to have some sort of pre-existing issue. For example, Mr. Holmes: in *Scream*, Sidney's pre-existing issue was her mother's death. In *Urban Legend*, Natalie's trying to live down the death she accidentally caused years ago.

Letha's issue must be this trophy wife who's supposed to be her mom. Either that or—or it's whatever happened to her actual mom, all wrapped up with how fast her dad found a replacement, one who could be Letha's older sister.

Had this "Tiara" already been cued up, possibly? Were the circumstances of Letha's mom's death perhaps . . . mysterious?

Jade has to look down into her lap to keep her eyes hidden.

"Go on, go on," Amber says to Mr. Holmes, just to get Tiara's bikini away from the front of the classroom, and Mr. Holmes, having old man fingers, of course cues ahead and then stabs the pause in again, this time holding on the shaky-guilty image of his left hand, a cigarette cocked between the fingers—cigarettes it's common knowledge he's promised his wife he's done with forever. Cigarettes that Jade has to guess fall down out of the sky all over Proofrock. Cigarettes that could be anybody's, but aren't.

The dirty dog.

It kind of gives Jade a new respect for him. Never mind his complete inability to cue the recording past that image. At least it gets him to usher them all gone before last bell. Jade walks out into the parking lot alone, already unwinding the gauze from her wrist. She lets it trail behind her all the way over to Golding Elementary. It's not usually her beat, but that's where Main Supplies is: her next pair of coveralls.

"Bye, now," she says to the gauze, watching it dance higher and higher in the breeze, a long skinny ghost.

Jade goes into the elementary the back way, finds Main Supplies first try—this *was* her school for six years—and has her pick of the leftover coveralls. Yay. She steps into the least stained of them, stands into the shoulders, and shoots her arms down through the sleeves. They're too big again, smell like whoever wore them last, but whatever. At least the zipper works.

She uses her Crüe earrings to pin her name-patch to the chest, over the thread-holes from the last unlucky soul.

"So it begins," she says, tying her hair back as best she can, as short as it is, and ducked ahead like that, she sees the old timecard rack behind the open door, a relic of more analog times. Rexall, the janitor for these parts—he's a natural with throwup—has his phone tucked in there, charging.

It reminds Jade of the mystery phone still in her back pocket.

Moving quietly now, as if that makes a difference, she unplugs Rexall's, starts this pink one charging on its cable.

Three forever minutes later, Jade tapping energy into the floor the phone can have if it wants, it powers on. *Five* minutes later, Jade can't even dream what the passcode might be. "SVEN"—7836—is a fail, as is 1234, 4321, and all the corners and diamonds both ways. She's about to shrug and say screw it, go outside and do some drop tests because why not, but then . . . she palms her own phone, goes to the last call, the one to the non-U.S. number, and redials, ready to hang up to duck any overseas charges.

The phone she's holding doesn't ring. Of course. If your if-found number rings the phone that's just been found, then you don't deserve to get your phone back. And if you were thinking that was going to happen, well, Jade isn't sure what she deserves.

She sits on the stool that's right there, starts punching a flurry of random codes with both thumbs, is probably ninety seconds into it before she realizes she's not alone, that there's a shape looming beside her, and sort of behind. A shape with a distinctly acrid scent, undercut with . . . is that Jergens?

"Trying to give me a fucking heart attack, man?" she says to Rexall.

He steps forward, his coveralls matching hers. Before this exact moment, and counting all the nights he spends passed out on the couch fifteen feet from her bed, she's always managed to avoid being in tight places alone with him.

"You'll never get it that way, Blue," Rexall says about the phone, his breath some sort of minty, which doesn't fit with the rest of how he presents.

"Just forgot the code," Jade mumbles. "Trying all my usual ones."

"That's why you're two-fisting it?" Rexall says about the fact that she's holding more than one phone. He licks his lips long and slow, presumably so they won't crack when he grins the lecherous grin Jade knows is coming.

"You know," she says to him, resetting, "here in a little bit, Hardy's going to be looking for suspects for . . . for something that's about to start happening. You're maybe going to be at the top of that list, might want to have your alibis in order."

"I didn't even know her, Your Honor," Rexall says, holding his Boy Scout fingers up but then leaning over to take a profane sniff of the back of his middle finger.

"Just remembered," Jade says, "I don't talk to you anymore."

Rexall holds his left hand out for the pink phone, snaps twice when Jade doesn't give it.

"What for?" she asks.

"She said without talking to him," Rexall halfway-quotes back to her, and—what the hell—it's either surrender it or continue this conversation. "Wouldn't believe how many of these get perma-nently lost over here," he goes on, stepping over to a PC buried under about fifteen half-done computer repair jobs. "I crack them, wipe them, jailbreak them, they go for hundred and fifty each, easy like Sunday morning."

"I'm not looking to sell it, I'm just—"

"Yeah, yeah, it's your backup phone," Rexall says, plugging it into the PC, tabbing over to a terminal window. "Fifty dollars."

"I don't have fifty dollars, Rexall. I don't even have fifty cents."

"Show me a little something then?" he says. "*Couple* of . . . not-so-little somethings?"

"Um," Jade says, no eye contact, resisting the urge to check the zipper of her coveralls. "I'm seventeen? Not that that's even an appropriate request if I was legal."

"Had to try," Rexall says with a no-harm no-foul shrug, then out-louds the magic key-combo he's typing that runs his program: 36-26-36.

"You sure you should be working around kids?" Jade asks. "Or even around, you know, living people?"

"Tried the morgue in Boise," he says. "There was . . . an incident. Ask your dad about it sometime, he was there."

Jade waits for him to guffaw or chuckle, because this has to be a joke, doesn't it? Please? Finally she just says, "How about you do this for free, I don't narc you out to Hardy. Not for cracking this phone, I mean. For . . . inappropriate requests?"

Rexall stiffens but doesn't turn around.

"I was just goofing," he says as if hurt, hitting return grandly, the pink phone flashing twice then going black.

"Great, your fancy program bricked it," Jade says, taking it when he hands it to her. "Thanks."

"Power her up," he says. "No passcode anymore, all the data remains. You're welcome, jailbait."

"You give scuzz a bad name, Rexall," Jade says, holding the pink phone's power button in.

"Thank me now or thank me later . . ." he says. Then, about his own phone in the timecard slot: "Plug mine back in, won't you? It's . . . it's *doing* something."

Jade nods her best noncommittal nod, is waiting for the pink phone's startup to finally get over with.

"And—and don't, like, look at it?" Rexall adds on his way out, eyebrows raised like he's just asking for common courtesy here.

Jade doesn't dignify this, just stares him down until he's gone. A half step later she has his phone, is powering it down without having to log in, mostly because she doesn't want the distant thrill it would probably give him for her to type that "36-26-36" in. When the phone's cycled down, she steps up onto the stool, hides his phone in the ceiling, pulls the tile back into place, says in monotone, "Sheriff Hardy, the evidence you need is right above Main Supplies, I saw him tucking it up there one day."

The pink phone buzzes awake in her hand. Jade taps through this and that, most of it in a language she doesn't know. But then she lands in the photo album, because selfies are the universal language.

The most recent is a video.

"What have we here . . ." she says, ducking out of Main Supplies, watching and walking, trying to beat the rush of elementary kids to the exit doors.

At first it's just foggy nothing playing back at her, but then the phone's camera figures out how to focus through whatever that is—that same sandwich bag?—and it's a naked blond girl, flashes of a naked blond guy.

"Unauthorized Use of the Town Canoe," Jade tells them, unwinding her earbuds and clocking the date: six days before her "attempt," as the therapist in Idaho Falls calls it.

She guesses she's lucky the town canoe had even found its way back by the time she needed it, right?

As for who these kids are, first, their English is all intoned

funny, and second, around here they'd be Towhead 1 and Towhead 2—blond mops she'd have shared crayons with, freckled
faces she would know. And she doesn't.

"Sven," Jade says then, turning backwards to push through
the double doors, out into the sunlight. Inside Golding Elementary the bell rings, meaning Jade's just ahead of the tidal wave of
coughing and sniffing and yelling and crying.

It could wash right over her and she wouldn't even notice.

The guy—Sven—has just gone over the side of the canoe.

Jade stops walking, stops breathing.

"What the bleeping bleep . . ." she says, looking around for if
any of the parents in the hug-n-go lane have cued into the momentous thing happening on this phone's screen. They're just
staring, waiting for her to move already, please.

Jade nods sorry, sorry, and steps along, scrubbing the video back
to when Sven goes over, the pale soles of his feet there and gone.

The girl is all alone now, and, going by what Sven called her at
the pier, her name is . . . 'Throat Murder?' 'Thromudder?' 'Crone
Mother?' Jade settles on the easier "Blondie." As in, Just *what* is
Blondie flinching away from?

Jade looks up, out to Indian Lake, as if she can see what was
terrorizing this blond girl that night.

She rewinds again to Sven going over the side, memorizing
every splash, every breath, every moment of this magical thing
that happened after Proofrock was asleep, and this time through
she flinches *with* Blondie, even turns around with her, trying to
see over all sides of the canoe as well.

"This could have been you, horror girl," she says to herself.

Same lake, same pier, same boat, almost the same night.

Now the girl is paddling away from something alongside the
canoe, and now—no, no—she's slipping over the side because
swimming has to be faster. Meaning Jade can only hear now.

The girl's scream splits the night in two and then cuts off just as fast, the silence after it quieter and deeper than any Jade's ever experienced.

In *Friday the 13th*, it's two blond counselors who get the blade to start the ritual, Barry and Claudette. In Proofrock, in whatever this is going to be called, it's two blond out-of-towners. Two Netherlanders, Sven and Blondie.

"Thank you," Jade says to them, kissing the screen then flinching back from the pink phone *ringing* against her lips. She rubs the sensation away, and then, on the fifth ring, because the kids flowing past are watching her, wondering if she's going to, she answers—holds it up to her ear, anyway.

It's that same language from the video. The one word that's the same, evidently, is "detective."

That's all Jade needs to hear.

Calmly, not in any kind of panic, just another wrong number, she hangs up, bends to attend to her right boot, and when she stands, she's sliding the pink phone under her chunky sole. When she moves ahead with the surge of kids, she's sliding the phone out into the road, into a puddle. It slurps the phone right in, but then the phone bobs up to the surface—the case must float, shit. It's just hanging there like a flat cork, so pink, so obvious, ringing *again* now, two fourth-graders stopped by Jade to watch this unfolding tragedy.

"Oops," the taller of the two girls tells Jade.

Jade's just staring.

"Here—" the shorter one says, stepping forward to retrieve the phone for Jade, who's evidently too heartbroken, too scared, but Jade, her palm stabbing out to the girl's chest, stops her, a bus swishing by in that same instant, honking loud and long, close enough that the tips of the girl's hair rub along the dingy yellow paint.

Behind Jade, a woman screams, the kind of scream that makes Jade feel like she just got punched in the gut, it's from so deep.

She looks back in wonder, half-expecting it to be the blond girl from the video.

It's Misty Christy the rhyming realtor, rushing to the shorter of the two girls, pulling her into a hard hug.

"You saved her," the tall girl says up to Jade, and Jade looks to the retreating bus, to Misty Christy clutching her saved daughter, and then to the puddle. Pieces of the shattered phone are bobbing in the water.

Jade swallows, and then Misty Christy is hugging her too, hugging her and crying, and Jade, unable to speak, doesn't tell her that it was an accident, that she was only keeping this elementary schooler from getting the phone, she wasn't trying to save any lives, be any kind of hero—that's not what she does. Kind of the opposite, really.

When Jade's finally released from this hug, there's a half-moon of parents arrayed on the grass, all watching her, waiting to see what the horror girl's going to do now. Jade presses her lips into a sort of smile, is kind of wondering what she's going to do as well. Finally she just thrusts her hands in her pockets, shoulders around to hide from them all, and the first step she takes is deep into the puddle that ate the phone.

Her foot goes cold and wet and she keeps moving, and half a block later she finally sputters a breath out, draws another in deep-deep, her hands steepled over her mouth.

Those Dutch kids in the lake. They—what them dying like that means . . . it means this is—

It's started, Jade knows. It's finally happening.

SLASHER 101

Actually the slasher ISN'T impossible or just in
the movies, sir. But it does need certain minimum
requirements after the initial prank.

The 1st thing is the Blood Sacrifice. Think
Judith Myers the big sister in <u>Halloween</u> or Casey
Becker from <u>Scream</u>, or her 1960 version Marion
Crane in, you guessed it, <u>Psycho</u>.

The 2nd thing a slasher needs is Adults,
surprise. And by adults I mean those parents and
teachers and cops who dismiss all this tomfoolery
of the kids being just kids. Think <u>A Nightmare on
Elm Street</u> where Nancy's dad the police detective
should listen to his daughter. Or Officer Dorf
from <u>Friday the 13th</u> who can't even drive his own
motorcycle but with a name like Dorf what do you
expect. If the adults and police were competent
then all this could be stopped.

Or go to <u>Final Destination</u>'s Bludworth, who is
really and forever Candyman Tony Todd, an adult
who actually BELIEVES these kids, but because of
that he can't talk to any other adults. Or even
when the adult knows for sure and believes beyond
any shadowy doubts, which is rare like Dr. Loomis
in <u>Halloween</u> or Crazy Ralph in <u>Friday the 13th</u>,
then nobody believes THEM, which is the main sucky
part about being a kid. Well it's 1 of the sucky
parts but don't get me started because then I'll be
talking about how it's not really suspension worthy
if someone replaces the sex ed videotape with that
arrow coming up from Kevin Bacon's throat, but this
paper is of such educational value that it should
make up for that.

3rd of what the slasher needs is for all this
to happen pretty much Overnight. The reason you

need that is because a slasher that happens over a
single bad night in Haddonfield, it's believable
that the adults who could put a stop to it are
distracted or it's their night off. The 3rd and
a half necessary ingredient which is kind of part
of "Overnight" is a Party. Slashers love to crash
parties. Think what if Proofrock were getting a
slasher. What night might we all be in one place
for for this bloody business?

Next and 4th is the Signature Weapon. Jason
has his machete, Michael has his kitchen knife,
Ghostface has a hunting knife, Freddy has his
glove, Cropsy has those hedge clippers, the
Fisherman who still knows what you did last summer
has that hook, and, 5th, the pentagram number, you
need someone to WIELD that weapon, sir.

Enter the Slasher and his opposite the Final
Girl, our #6, who you know from me telling you when
I was a freshman.

So in conclusion once a slasher comes back from
the "dead" and does the Blood Sacrifice with a
Signature Weapon, then the Adults go incompetent,
there's an Overnight Party, and a Final Girl
stumbles out of the library and into this meat
grinder, but don't forget about #7.

That's the Sequel, Mr. Holmes, which this paper
will ALSO have, where you'll be thrilled to learn
all about 2 other necessary things, Masks and
SlasherCam, but that's next semester, since right
now I have to either do this interview project for
half my history grade or die trying.

GRADUATION DAY

Jade's dad doesn't sit for the ceremony, but he's there with Clate Rodgers, onetime Henderson Hawk, now working out of a garage over in Ammon. The two of them are stationed against the fence right by the grooved aluminum steps leading up to the stands, are Chuck from *Footloose* and Wooderson from *Dazed and Confused*—walking, talking, drinking cautionary tales, seemingly there specifically to scare this next graduating class straight, make sure they get those college applications in, lest they end up stationed at this fence as well. At least that's what the two of them are until Sheriff Hardy saunters past then slows as if he's just smelled something but doesn't exactly want to turn around, see what it might be—see if Clate Rodgers is actually daring to show his face in Proofrock after all these years.

Tab lifts his coozied can to Hardy, daring him to check if it's beer or not, Clate snickers and rubs his nose with the whole side of his index finger, and with that they slope away to some less public place. Jade, pretending not to have clocked this sad but typical interaction, lets her eyes keep roving across the crowd, up into the bleachers.

The way graduation usually works is that the thirty-odd seniors' parents get to the football field early enough to stake out the middle seats with blankets and thermoses of coffee, but this morning was different. Some of the construction grunts were already there, and had been there since before dawn, or so Jade gathers from all the grumbling. But there's some awe there too, isn't there? So far the incoming residents of Terra Nova have just been a golf cap moving down an aisle at the drugstore, a tanned and Rolex'd forearm at the diner, an Aston Martin nosed into a slot down by the banks—all sightings have been one at a time, but never all of them together. Even the newspaper articles just had them in their own frames, not grouped together like some superhero team.

Word now, though, is that the construction grunts still staking out the center seats up in the bleachers aren't there for themselves, don't have any graduates in this particular race yet, are just holding these seats, are just yellow-vested harbingers of the fable about to unfold at this graduation.

Because of that, the buzz and whisper is different. Both more hushed and more thrilled, like a formation of Oprah Winfreys are about to parachute down through the clouds, giving cars out to you, and you, and also you.

Jade tells herself that, should that happen, she won't be one of those simpletons grubbing for outflung pennies, but, at the same time, she one hundred percent knows that it's easy to be aloof when those pennies aren't in play yet.

Where she's seated is front row behind the low stage, and what she's wearing underneath her gown are her custodian coveralls, because she's on-duty right after this. It's stupid that real life is having to start the moment all this so-called magic is over, but, at the same time, it's like she's in a music video too, isn't it? The kind where you walk fast away from graduation into a montage of what's waiting for you next, the bassline charting your steps:

unmopped hallways, horrorshow restrooms, chalkboards needing a good Etch A Sketch shaking, to be blank for the next round of students.

Jade bobs her head two or three times, starring in that video, but then stops when she clocks the line of Bentleys rolling into the parking lot.

"Oh, shit," she says.

"What?" Greta Dimmons asks, touching her hair, her hat, and her shoulders all in fast succession.

Jade doesn't answer, has already turned away from the Bentleys, to who they'll matter the most to: Mr. Holmes, up on stage.

"Well, fuck," he says loud enough for even the row behind Jade to pick it up, judging by the snickers. Judging by how Principal Manx's back straightens, it was loud enough for him, too.

Fuck is the only response, though. The Terra Novans are finally showing their faces in town. Jade hates it, but her back is sort of straightening too, to see better, to not miss a thing.

The Bentleys ease up to the gate and the tycoons and magnates step out in their languorous way. The women aren't wearing gowns, but hip-hugging skirts and trim little blazers, effortless heels. The men aren't wearing tuxes, but suits tailored and then tailored again, sunglasses that ride just low enough to look casual, accidental. The packed dirt path wending from the gate to the bleachers is a red carpet for them to pick down, hand in hand.

First is Mars Baker, the founding partner of some storied law firm in Boston, whose legal maneuvering is, according to the papers, what carved Terra Nova out from the national forest. He's mid-fifties like all of them, mostly bald, and beaming, his severe wife, Macy Todd, holding his arm—*the* Macy Todd, who skated on a tabloid murder back in the nineties, then married the brilliant lawyer who'd gotten her off. Their twin girls Cinn and Ginny, twelve or thirteen if Jade remembers right from the profile in the newspaper, are tagging along, wearing matching flower-girl-looking dresses, though there are no flowers.

After them is tall gangly Ross Pangborne, with all his Bill Gates awkwardness and matching boyish charm. *Also* bald, Jade notes, and wonders if hair-burning testosterone and financial domination are somehow related. In the profile she read of him at the drugstore, instead of carrying a phone that can keep him up to date on the social media juggernaut he started for kicks and grins, he carries a simple flip phone, and sometimes not even that. His wife Donna is the female version of him. They look like brother and sister more than husband and wife, but Jade suspects maybe it's just the same way a dog will come to look like its owner after enough years. Not that she can tell which of them is that dog. Their ten-year-old daughter, Galatea, whose name means something fancy, Jade can't remember, is slouching behind in blue jeans and a sweater, probably the most formal they could convince her to get. *Good for you, girl,* Jade sends across the bouncy red track. *Don't ever change.*

Next is Deacon Samuels, *full* head of hair and a hundred-watt smile. It's what he's used to become a real estate magnate, apparently—well, obviously—and it's also what he flashes on the cover of all the golf magazines whose covers he graces. Jade scoffs in her head. Holding hands with Deacon Samuels is his famous ex-model of a wife, Ladybird, the "first lady of style" or something vapid like that, though Jade does have to appreciate how smoothly she navigates the bleacher steps in those impossible heels. When Deacon gets to the seats Terra Nova's workers have been saving, he makes a show of passing discreet but not too discreet bills to each of them, which is their dismissal.

Hundreds, probably. Good work if you can get it.

When the construction grunts start to try to squeeze past the Terra Novans flowing in—the papers have been calling them the

"Founders," since they're founding a new community—Macy Todd, somehow with just her eyes, informs them that they'll be going the *other* way, the long and awkward way down and out, thank you.

While they're retreating, cowed, their yellow vests practically glowing with humiliation, two or three of their slouching manners familiar to Jade, Llewellyn Singleton makes his timid entrance up the bleacher stairs, smiling with embarrassment from all the eyes on him and his wife, Lana. He's not used to public scrutiny, probably, would rather be in the office at his chain of banks, or franchise of banks—they're like eggs the *Aliens* mother laid all across America, careful to leave one in each town. No, actually in, as the ad used to famously say, "every *single town*," ha, ha, ha. Ha. But either Llewellyn or Lana must have a cool bone somewhere in their body, or at least their sordid past: their son, six years old, is "Lemmy," which has to be after Motörhead's frontman, as there can be no other Lemmys.

After them is Theo Mondragon and his shiny-new wife, the aptly-named Tiara. Theo holds Tiara's elbow as she balances on her even *more* impossible heels up the aluminum steps, and with his other hand he sneaks a single wave into the wall of graduates— to Letha. As near as Jade can tell, and not counting her own dad, who's just Indian-dark and already skulked back into deeper and danker shadows anyway, Theo's the only Black person in the bleachers at all. But he'd stand out anywhere, she's pretty sure. His college-football shoulders tapering down to a thirty-year-old's waist, the short work he's making of the stairs, and just the fact that he's the headliner, here. Not that it's a bank-account pissing contest, but it kind of is, Jade suspects. And in today's world, a media empire trumps banks and law firms and real estate brokerages, maybe even social media.

The five couples take their seats, and, because this is what kings do at these kind of functions, Theo Mondragon, the alpha of this group of alphas, stands and rolls his right hand in a sort of restrained amusement, kindly telling everyone they can proceed. Carry on, carry on.

Jade does, or tries to, but . . . it's like gravity was explained to her, sophomore year: each planet is a bowling ball on the trampoline that spacetime is, and all smaller bodies roll downhill to it, just naturally, helplessly, the same way all eyes at this graduation, including hers, keep finding these Founders and their wives. It's why Brad Pitt doesn't eat at Burger King, she knows—all the eyes, all the attention—but bowling balls are going to do what bowling balls are going to do, aren't they? People in Proofrock have never even seen anyone like these Founders, and now they're literally, physically rubbing shoulders with them.

Which is to say, all of Mr. Holmes's prophecies about Terra Nova's disastrous impact are coming true.

Jade manages to look away from Theo Mondragon, find her history teacher now in the speaker area kind of off to the side—because this is Mr. Holmes's last go-round, Principal Manx is giving him the mic to say his farewells, lay down his final pronouncements and prognostications, deliver one last lecture, who knows. His left hand is patting his jacket pocket over and over, like being sure his cigarettes are going to be there the moment this ceremony is done. To get over what's happening right now up in the bleachers, though, Jade bets he's going to have to chainsmoke the whole pack, crushing the butts underfoot until he's standing in a pile of dead soldiers. And maybe that won't even be enough.

To add to his woes—and delay his retirement—Jade's got a petition in with him to let her please please please complete her coursework for his class. All the other teachers were happy enough to let her slide on the last couple months' work, but Mr. Holmes is Mr. Holmes, and so far he's not letting his last act as a teacher involve sacrificing the "no excuses, no forgiveness" policy he's always been known for. What that means for Jade is that this ceremony is a sham, as she still doesn't have her last history credit done, and now, with Mr. Holmes's replacement not here until August, when can she finish it? And will the replacement let her fudge the assignments, write about history through the lens of slashers, and never exactly get around to state history, so much?

She knows the answer to that.

Without meaning to, she rubs the inside of her *un*scarred wrist, wonders if a matching set is what she, and the world, really needs.

Sitting beside Mr. Holmes, wildly enough, is Rexall, in something approximating a suit. He's being honored as well. It's sick: Misty Christy, whose daughter almost got slapped by that bus, wrote a letter to the superintendent of the district, thanking and praising that "elementary school janitor" for saving her daughter's life, and somehow never quite using a pronoun in the process.

When Rexall's radar pings on Jade's glare, he looks back, gives her a nasty smile and a slimy nod, and then waggles something suggestively at her from his lap. Before Jade can help it, she's already looked: his phone. He found it. Meaning it can't be used against him anymore, shit. Also meaning that, since he couldn't have found it by calling it or pinging it, there must have been a pinhole camera in Main Supplies, watching her. Which would be the only reason he left her there "all by herself" so easy, just on the chance she might change bras in slow motion.

Jade's skin wants to crawl off her, slither away. She shivers, shakes her shoulders, and tips her head back to see the top row of the bleachers, which she's telling herself is where she'd rather be. And she sort of is—a pale version of her, anyway: her mom is up there in the high corner, sitting off by herself even in the crowd.

It's the first time Jade's seen her . . . since just after Christmas maybe? Since her last slide and skulk through Family Dollar, anyway. Kimmy Daniels. Technically she and Jade's dad are still married, but she's been living in a trailer with some other Tab for nearly five years now. As far as Jade knows—and she guesses she does know—her mom is the most senior check-out girl at Family Dollar, or in its history altogether, probably. More important, if the store's not crowded, and if the manager's putting out some fire in a far aisle, Kimmy will let Jade walk past without paying for the hair dye she's always needing. Jade's never been sure if she's stealing it or if her mom pays for the hair supplies herself, but that's mostly because they never speak. Jade just walks and glares, and Kimmy just drinks Jade's every step in, her own leg muscles maybe tensing and relaxing, because she remembers being that old, that young.

The reason she's up in the bleachers now, Jade imagines, is because Jade's doing what she never did, as she was pregnant with Jade by what would have been her own graduation. Pregnant and staking out the hospital over in Idaho Falls, to see if the love of her life was going to wake up after his big wreck or not.

If only you knew, Mom, Jade sends across to her. *I'm not really graduating. This is all fake for me.*

Which is to say: it's a fitting end for her high school career.

Maybe Jade should have used her roll of masking tape to say all that to her mom on the top of her mortarboard cap instead of doing her standard happy face with X's for eyes, but screw it, right? Being here one day out of a whole childhood doesn't exactly make up for anything. Next cruise through Family Dollar, Jade's taking the whole *shelf* of hair bullshit.

Take that, Mom.

As for the color she got special for today, for the big day— bright pink—it's not dye, but spray-on Halloween paint. Because Indian hair won't go light enough for full-on electric pink. But screw it. It's not like anybody's going to be touching her hair, or studying the hatband of her mortarboard.

Her earrings are full-size dangling dice, because life's a gamble and then you die, and her lipstick's black like her heart—sticky, too—her fingernails blood-red.

Soon enough Letha Mondragon, the new girl with no real history as a Hawk, is up at the mic, delivering the commencement speech to louder and louder rounds of applause. The loudest is when she cedes her valedictorian medal to Alison Chambers, since "Grade-point averages transferred *in* don't reflect feet-on-the-ground grades, do they?"

She really is perfect, isn't she?

If Jade had any doubts about her final girl status, they're melting away more and more with each word of the speech, each round of applause.

When it finally dies down, Principal Manx saunters up to the podium, holds two fingers up for eventual silence—his V'd fingers are wolf ears, which means "stop howling, *listen*"—and then shuffles his papers, tells the crowd this next speaker needs no introduction. At the institution of Henderson High, he *is* an institution, teaching wave after wave of students Idaho state history, because, "as everybody knows, if we don't know what's happened before, we're doomed to repeat it."

A smattering of compulsory applause follows Mr. Holmes up to the mic. The first thing he does is page through the sheets of paper Principal Manx left behind, holding them up just enough that the graduates behind him can see that they're all blank—props. Because Manx has done this same ceremony so many times, he could sleepwalk through it.

Mr. Holmes straightens the papers, sets them back down, and then he turns, looks from left to right at all of the graduates before coming back around to stare down all the faces in the bleachers.

When it's finally pin-drop silent, he leads off with, "The saying is actually 'Progress, far from consisting in change, depends on retentiveness. Those who cannot remember the past are condemned to repeat it.'" To punctuate this never-asked-for correction, he clears his smoker's throat, even has to sneak a hand up, tug at the loose skin over his Adam's apple like trying to make room for the air he's going to need here. "It's from George Santayana, a Spanish-American philosopher from the first part of the twentieth century. He also famously said that history is a pack of lies about events that never happened, told by people who weren't there."

He takes the podium in his hands and leans onto it, glares out into the bleachers, adds, "We, however, are all here in this moment. Yes, in the months and years to come, our stories of this momentous day will become just that—stories—but for this, for right now, for the moment we're in, perhaps we can, as a group, understand just what it is that's happening here. Just a little."

Now it's Principal Manx's turn to offer a corrective, in the form of a cough probably meant to remind Mr. Holmes of some conversation they had about the content of his retirement speech, here.

Mr. Holmes doesn't seem to hear it.

"We have guests among us today," he says, holding his hand out to the Terra Novans, giving everyone license to look to the center of the bleachers again. He holds his hands up to the side to clap, but there's something distinctly mocking about it, so the few who fall in clapping with him trail away almost immediately.

"And I say 'guests,' but please, Mr. Mondragon, Mr. Baker, the rest of you—I don't mean to suggest your stay here will be temporary, of course. We should hope it won't be. You're the saviors of this mountain town, this lake, this valley, this *county*—of all of us." Mr. Holmes stops again to clear his throat, and when he comes back to the mic, he's nodding with resolve. "There is of course another filter we can understand 'guest' through, as many of these graduates will know, from having processed through my classroom. In Ancient Greece, the gods would come down from Mount Olympus to walk among the mortals, but they would come in the form of travelers, of beggars, and so what developed in that society, due to that belief, was an etiquette built around abject fear. Completely sensible fear. If they didn't comport themselves properly, offer a bowl of soup, say, even their last bowl of soup, then . . . then Zeus could stand up from those beggar's robes and strike them down, erase them as if they never were."

Mr. Holmes lets that settle, then repeats it for emphasis: "As if they never were."

"Mr. Holmes—" Principal Manx starts, coming up from his chair, but Mr. Holmes holds his hand back, not asking for another minute at the mic, but informing Manx that he's taking that minute.

Go, sir, Jade says inside, grinning with wonder.

"But this is America, of course, not the Mediterranean," Mr. Holmes says. "I should be more even-handed, use iconography more associated with this soil. Apologies. Let me . . . here, I know. Pre-contact South America, how's that? We can find an apt example there, I believe. Look to the Inca, say. Not the Inca as they were when the Spanish blundered into the Andes, but as that empire had been rising and falling for millennia, all on their own. And, before you ask, I don't mean to say that this mountain we live on is the Andes, or that gods and rulers walk among us. But, these ancient Inca, whose technological sophistication rivaled and surpassed any of their contemporaries across the globe, they eventually achieved a level of social stratification that essentially deified the ruling class, the wealthiest of the wealthy, and how this played out for them is something we should perhaps pay attention to ourselves, still keeping to our Santayana, as that ruling class, the wealthy elite, they didn't only lock all the resources up for themselves, casting the working classes into not just penury but destitution, but they so revered themselves that they would build elaborate houses for their mummified dead, and continue to serve them food, and assign servants to them, and a society this top-heavy is of course doomed to topple over and over again, until it finds a more stable, and even-handed, way to persist and thrive. Or if you resist Santayana, then perhaps you'll listen to Mark Twain, who said that history doesn't repeat, but it does rhyme. I only hope that Proofrock won't be part of that couplet. But, please, I don't want any of you associating these Incan houses of the dead with the very nice homes going up across the lake, of course. We're not the Inca, are we? Neither should we be the Ancient Greeks. When the gods knock on our doors, instead of offering them our last ladle of hard-won soup, we should perhaps, instead, offer them the point of our spe—"

"Thank you, *thank you* for that riveting tour through history, Mr. Holmes," Principal Manx says, finally stepping between Mr. Holmes and the podium and then turning to the side to lead another round of applause—*farewell* applause.

In the bleachers, Theo Mondragon is the first to stand, clapping loudly, but then Mars Baker is standing alongside him, and Ladybird Samuels, Macy Todd—all of them, beating their hands together, not a smile among them.

Mr. Holmes turns back to the graduates, says, just loud enough, "It's not just soup they want," and Jade's the first to shoot up from her seat, clapping, sneaking a look over to Letha in the second row—the only other row. Her lips are moving uncertainly, but she can't stand with her classmates, *against* her dad, and Jade hates herself for it, but she regrets having led this round of applause. No, what she regrets is this whole stupid ceremony. This whole stupid town.

As if confirming how stupid it is, Principal Manx, trying to salvage graduation, motions for Rexall to rise, accept his certificate for going, as Manx says into the mic, "Above and beyond the duties of a custodian." The applause continues, and Jade knows that out in the parking lot, her dad's lifting a can for Rexall, which has to be why he was there. Not for his only daughter, the *second* Indian non-graduate in twenty years. The only words the two of them have had about graduation at all is when Tab asked her where she was moving out this summer.

What Jade told him was that it was none of his concern, thanks.

What she didn't tell him was that it would pretty much either be Camp Blood or the couch of whoever her mom was living with.

Rexall shuffles up to the podium, his phone still tight in his hand like a life preserver, but when Manx steps to the side to formally present him, Misty Christy stands up from the crowd, waving her hand back and forth like can Principal Manx please call on her?

It stops the ceremony, everyone looking to Misty Christy.

Misty Christy is shaking her head no, pointing *past* the podium.

To Jade.

Jade shrinks, slouches, licks her lip, probably frying her lipstick, blackening her tongue. For the first time in maybe ever, she wishes her hair wasn't so easy to find in a crowd.

"It was *her*, not him!" Misty Christy is saying, her voice unamplified but loud enough.

Principal Manx looks back to Jade and Jade has to look past him, past the bleachers, past all of it.

"I saw too!" Lucky says, from another part of the bleachers. He drives the school bus. He was the one who almost hit Misty Christy's daughter.

"Me too!" Judd Tambor, Proofrock's other realtor, calls out, his voice booming.

Jade's ninety-nine to a hundred-and-fifty-percent certain he wasn't there that day, but this is his chance to stand up for the unstood-up-for, and no way in hell does he let his main rival get all the good will for that.

And now, after Judd Tambor, Jade can't clock all the other Proofrockers chiming in that they were there, they saw, they know. Part of it's that herd-thing Mr. Holmes is always telling them about, Jade knows, which is like the underbelly of mob mentality, but part of it too is that, if they don't stand in support of her, then Rexall gets that certificate, and they probably know him and his high school days and further exploits better than Jade ever will.

She closes her eyes, counts to three for all of this to be over, but then she looks again at the count of two. Not to Misty Christy, not to Judd Tambor, holding his toddler daughter up and waving her back and forth like some sort of proof of the hero Jade is, not to *everyone* clapping now, but to the very top corner of the bleachers. At her mom.

She's smiling that close-lipped smile she has.

Jade closes her eyes tighter, is *not* going to fucking cry right here, in front of everybody. And then, right on cue, her dad steps out from under the bleachers, not in from the parking lot. He's banging two trashcan lids together like cymbals, his beer clenched between his teeth, splashing onto his face and down his shirt.

It shuts the rest of the clapping down, but he keeps clanging those lids until Hardy thins his lips, walks down along the fence that direction.

Jade closes her eyes again, harder. Reminds herself that with every good, there's two bads. That's just the way it is. Maybe it's a thing with Indians, or maybe it's just her, it doesn't really matter. True's true.

When she finally looks again, peering up from under her bangs, Rexall's seated and Principal Manx is leaning down to the mic to "Get these degrees handed *out!*"

Because the alphabet is what it is, Jade's second to walk the stage, second to have to shake Manx's hand, and the first and only to receive no hoots or applause or confetti cannons going off, since her dad's been removed from the premises, and her mom couldn't handle everyone looking up to her, has slunk away under cover of all that clapping.

When Letha walks, though, in heels for once—she's got to be six-plus feet in them—the yacht nobody realized was drifting in behind them does a long airhorn blast that sends a choreographed whole *flock* of white doves up from some hidden place on shore.

Of course.

Sidestepping down the second row to take her seat, Letha squeezes Jade's right shoulder in a sisterly way, a supportive way, and Jade hates more than anything the way her eyes heat up from this contact.

Where were you *all my life?* Jade says to Letha in her head, which is when she remembers having said that once before, or close to it.

Shooting Glasses.

Jade scans right to left for a yellow safety vest that hasn't made a complete exit, and sure enough, there he is leaning against a stanchion of the bleachers on the right side, as if he hasn't earned a seat up in the bleachers. Not after having stolen them from their rightful owners.

Jade nods once to him and he nods back, tips the shallow brim of his hardhat in congratulations, then steps away, and she realizes that's all he was waiting for: her.

Because she's the one he saved, and he wants to see her all the way through?

Because he . . .

Jade shakes her head no, not that, not her. No way can he be into her. She shakes the possibility off, finds her eyes locked on

Theo Mondragon again. He looks for all the world like Bruce Wayne, with Batman just under his tasteful suit. He's entrancing, has to own every boardroom he sweeps into, every shareholders' meeting he graces, every dinner table he settles down at.

Every town he builds a house in.

Jade can't be sure, but, from the angle of his head, she's pretty sure Mr. Holmes is either watching him too, or memorizing all the Terra Novans' faces, to burn them in effigy later. Some people count sheep, and some light matches under their enemies, Jade imagines. She knows which of those types Mr. Holmes is. Except he doesn't use matches, just flicks his lit cigarette to the gas-soaked tinder under their feet.

Go, sir, Jade says again.

This is what she'll remember, she knows. That she wasn't the only one at this laughable, embarrassing event who would rather have burned it all down. It's good being the horror chick, sure, always standing away from the rest of the crowd, smoking bitter cigarette after bitter cigarette, she'd have it no other way, but it's nice to make eye contact with someone else with a black heart, too, and then breathe smoke out slow, like judgment.

When it's time to throw the hats, Jade holds on to hers, smuggles it off the football field, and leaves it smiling up from the last trashcan on the way back to the high school for her mop and bucket, and whispers to the camera surely watching to hold on those X'd-out eyes for a few seconds more.

They're a good preview of what's coming.

SLASHER 101

For my Interview Project on Proofrock History,
since I couldn't interview an ACTUAL slasher as they
don't take appointments and are kind of known for
leaving anyone within slashing range dead, usually
along with their pets and classmates and family, I
had to interview someone who had once been slasher
ADJACENT, which you said I could do if I could find
such a personage. Well I did, Mr. Holmes. I think
you were joking when you said it, but if you were
then allow me to introduce you to the punchline.
It's Mrs. Christine Gillette at Pleasant Valley
Assisted Living, who will be 100 2 years from now.
    Perhaps this will be a break from all the other
interviews in this stack of papers having to do
with mining history or with Henderson-Golding or
with Glen Dam or with Indian Lake or with Caribou-
Targhee National Forest, which I'm guessing
must taste like backwash to you since it's all
stuff you told us already this semester, which a
student would only know if she had been studiously
listening the whole time and hardly that absent
if you think about how much she's HERE when she's
here, and yes this is supposed to be 5 pages, but
since I haven't started the actual interview,
I'm not even counting yet, this is all just bonus
introducing material I'm doing now.
    As for the slasher in question it's Stacey
Graves the Lake Witch, surprise. Common knowledge
known locally is that she's an urban legend like
Bloody Mary, that she's the Idaho version of
Slender Man for the generation that lived and died
by <u>Leave It to Beaver</u>. But this is just due to the
rust of time covering up the truth, sir, and this
interview is the rust remover, bam.

My original and initial plan was to find a
survivor of the rampage at Camp Blood, but this is
better in that it's previous to that. And it's even
got old timey details that I could never in a hundred
tries make up. Let me give you a perfect example.

Evidently when mining collapsed from all the
producing mines in the new town of Proofrock getting
swamped by Indian Lake having risen and risen,
people started having to boat across the new lake to
hunt elk if they didn't want to starve. No seasons,
no limits other than how many bullets you had and
how smart the elk were. But the problem that came
up really fast was getting those big heavy elk back
across the lake to town. You can search online that
they weigh anywhere from 500 to 730 pounds.

The solution to all that heaviness was to use
rawhide string or a belt to tie the elk's mouth
shut, and also plug up their aft end, as Mr. Krabs
might say and I don't want to think about, and then
using your mouth to blow as much air as you could
into the elk's nose holes and plug them up with mud
before the air can whistle back out.

What you've done now is turn this big dead
animal into a flotation device, sir. So one day
Christine Gillette's friend's dad Mr. Bill got an
elk, and only shot it in the head instead of the
side so there wouldn't be another hole to plug with
mud. And there he is floating that kill back to
town like a champion hunter when that elk thrashes
awake in the water and blows its two nose plugs
of mud up onto Mr. Bill's boat like dog droppings
fresh from the dog, and you can tell we're in
the interview now, since this is Paraphrase and
Distillation instead of Transcription, just like
the example you gave us.

What had happened, Christine Gillette says
because she wants me to get an A for this project
and therefore save my semester grade in one fell

swoop, was Mr. Bill had evidently shot that elk
only in the BASE of its horn, not the skull, so
the elk was only knocked out. And Mr. Bill hadn't
dressed it out by cutting its stomach open because
then all its air would leak out too.

So now this awake and severely unhappy elk was
tied to his actual boat, which has to be a panic
situation. What Mr. Bill had to do in order not to
sink down to Drown Town, which was still Henderson-
Golding to him, was shoot that elk between the eyes
and then cut the rope, at which point that elk sunk
and sunk.

End of story? Not even close, sir.

That was too much good meat to just kiss goodbye
in starvation times, see. So Mr. Bill came back
with an iron hook from the hardware store and
paddled back and forth all night until he hooked
onto what he was sure was that elk. Either that or
a submarined log. But he didn't think it was going
to be a log. Because it was too heavy to lift with
arms and shoulders, he brought in this local dude
Cross Bull Joe, who drove the model A version of a
tow truck. This means he had a cable and winch on
his truck. And what he did was back that truck all
the way down the old pier, as Christine Gillette
called it, the outsides of his rear tires hanging
over the actual edges on both sides.

What I asked her here as I'm sure you can guess
was "OLD pier?" As in, there was another before the
one that's there NOW? How do we not all know this?
What ELSE do we not know, sir? This is why history
class is a requirement. If I wasn't for sure
graduating, I could take it again and again, until
I knew about ALL the old piers.

But, Christine Gillette. Or, Cross Bull Joe,
really. His winch strained and pulled and I imagine
that, like Quint in _Jaws_, he had to pour water on
that winding-up cable. What he finally pulled up

made all the women scream, all the children fall to
their knees, and all the men take a long step back
like whoah.

It was an Indian girl, sir.

Which, I know what you're thinking, Mr. Holmes.
You're thinking that it's sad but people drown in
lakes every day, probably more back then before
life jackets and safety signs, and that Indian Lake
is cold enough that they don't even decompose,
just bob around in Ezekiel's Cold Box, waiting
for the day somebody with a tow truck hooks them,
pulls them up into the light. I know this is what
you're thinking because it's also what I was
thinking.

But we're both wrong, sir.

The way Christine Gillette told it to me, the
way they knew this wasn't some random Shoshone or
Bannock in a stolen and rotting water logged dress
was what happened 10 seconds later. But let's
time these explosions if we can. The first for
me sitting there in room 522 of Pleasant Valley
Assisted Living was what you're probably asking
now, which is "Stacey Graves was INDIAN?"

If you're rocked and shocked, it's because this
is not exactly common knowledge and it's also not
part of the accepted lore about our Lake Witch.
But evidently Stacey Graves had been half Indian,
meaning that since her dad was all white, her mom
must have been full blooded. Which everybody used
to know and I guess we still would if we talked to
the right old people. Christine Gillette told me
that the boogeyman of Indian Lake used to not even
be Stacey Graves in the first place, OR Ezekiel with
his big hands. It used to be Stacey Graves's MOM,
always walking around the shore line looking for her
lost daughter, and taking any kids after dark back
to her cave where she would hold them to her, in
Christine Gillette's picture painty words, "leathery

dugs" and make them drink her milk, which pretty much did the opposite of real mother's milk, so the lesson there was to not go out after dark, kids, get it?

Anyway, with THAT explosion of Stacey Graves having been Indian hanging in the air above me and Christine Gillette, she activated her inner demolition man and detonated the next charge, even sort of acted it out so I'd be sure to get it. What she did in her wheelchair was reach her right arm up for the big iron hook coming in under Stacey Graves' chin, gouging up into her head like she was a fish wriggling on a trotline. And then her left hand joined her right, and using the strength of both she pulled herself up off that black hook, which Christine Gillette said was a good 2 dollar one, which is probably a fact we could check to verify the truthfulness of her story.

Because of the barb at the point of that hook that caught in this little girl's chin right at the very end, when she was already trying to fall away and do what Stacey Graves DOES, which you of course already know from having lived here for so long and heard the stories, the final releasing of her hands made her hang sideways by only her jaw and everybody thought it was going to crack off and tear away. But then only SOME skin tore instead and runny black blood spurted out and then she was off the hook and to the races, and everybody was shrieking and pulling their hair and going to church first thing and promising not to go across the lake for elk anymore, which is kind of the secret real birth of the national forest if you ask me.

And Christine Gillette saw all of this 1st hand, Mr. Holmes. She was 14 that year. And the way I know she's not making it up is that the story went on after that, and not because she was just trying to keep me there since nobody ever visits her according to the sheet I had to sign.

After what happened HAPPENED, nobody would go out
onto the old pier anymore. Not even Cross Bull Joe
to get his truck. So then one morning they heard a
cracking and crashing sound, and by the time anybody
looked out there, the old pier had mostly collapsed
under the weight of that tow truck, probably when
one bird too many landed on that black hook and that
tall V of pipe holding the cable. If a pier can be
a camel's back, then a bird can be a straw, right?

Christine Gillette's dad told her he would give
her 1 whole dime if she would swim out there and
untie that 2 dollar hook for him, but Christine
Gillette says that her life was worth more than ten
cents, which back then was a lot more than today of
course.

So that hook's still out there, I guess. And
maybe that truck too, all rotted and flaked away,
the window glass all turned to crumbles.

And also Stacey Graves, Mr. Holmes.

You had to know that's where I was going.

So in conclusion and wrap up for the WHOLE
SEMESTER including my course grade which maybe
shouldn't be history, what we thought was just
fiction has in fact a basis in eyewitness testimony.
And the way you can know I didn't make this up is
that if I were the one coming up with that then at
the end of the story Christine Gillette would huff
air out through her nose and two plugs of mud would
splat onto the ground between us, and then I'd look
up the moment after a shape just left from looking
in the window, and there would probably be scary
piano and violin playing too.

But none of that, sir.

Christine Gillette just reached a shaky hand for
her coffee cup of only water, and I helped her by
guiding the cup closer to her hand, and then held
my breath when she drank because it was always
about to spill but never did.

Then when I was leaving after many nods and grins and thank you's, me the whole time imagining being 14 and seeing a live dead girl hauled up from the cold depths, Christine Gillette hummed a little bit, sir. It stopped me. I looked back to see what was up and if maybe she was having an episode or what.

"We used to jump rope to it," she explained, and then added that they would jump rope to it when they could steal a rope from their dads' shops or the beds of their trucks or from the "tack" shed.

"Jump rope to what?" I asked, because the good interviewer prompts with pertinent facts and phrases, as you told us.

What Christine Gillette came back with, sir, was straight out of a Freddy dream pretty much, and you know I don't write poetry, so this is all her 100%:

Stacey Stacey Stacey Graves
Born to put you in your grave
You see her in the dark of night
And once you do you're lost from sight
Look for water, look for blood
Look for footprints in the mud
You never see her walk on grass
Don't slow down, she'll get your--

Christine Gillette didn't do the obvious rhyming word, but she didn't need to. I felt the shiver all the same, and am still hearing her and her friends' feet slapping the packed dirt as they chant this, being sure to get indoors before dark, because Stacey Graves isn't just a campfire story, Mr. Holmes.

The Lake Witch is real, and she's still out there, coming soon to a nightmare near you, near all of us, we can only hope. Or, if "we" can't hope, then don't worry.

I've got enough for all of us.

CURTAINS

*S*tab, *Stab, Stab*.

Jade jams the sharp end of her litter stick into a Styrofoam cup and imagines the cup writhing, moaning, begging for mercy. She hikes the stick up, uses her gloved left hand to push the dying cup off the stainless steel tip and into the canvas bag slung over her left hip like the most cavernous purse.

Today the bright yellow litter stick is a spear, but in the afternoons since graduation it's been a pike for bulls, except that made her feel evil; a long push-dart for wolverines and badgers—rabid, of course; a laser beam that cooks whatever trash it comes into contact with (lots of hissing sound effects); a blood-sampler for crocodiles, also probably rabid; and, like so many of her fantasies, the weapon found sticking up from her father's right eye socket.

But the left can work too. She's not picky.

Stab.

In the *Scream* franchise, that's what the movie dramatization of Gale Weathers's tell-all book is called. That and a nickel'll get you five cents, Jade knows, and can't help smiling about.

Because nobody's around to catch her, she can smile all she

wants. Smile and sing, thrash with Cyco Miko in her earbuds, even do a cartwheel if the urge strikes and her inner cheerleader just has to express herself. This is what summer-janitoring for the county is about: there are no kids to clean up after in the halls of the schools, so you become custodian for the whole town.

And, to be sure, if Jade has an inner cheerleader, it's one of those ratted-out punk ones from that Nirvana video—the pep rally from hell. That's nineties not eighties, but so was *Popcorn*, so was *New Nightmare*, so was *Scream*.

"Without memory, there can be no retribution," she mumbles, eviscerating a Copenhagen tin's shiny thin lid with a nice *pop*. "Without memory, there can be no retribution" is a line from *Popcorn*, maybe *the* line. That's another thing she can do since no one's out here: quote horror all the day long to test herself, to keep her slasher Q up. It's just her and the blowing trash, after all, and, somewhere out there, surely, an *actual* slasher rising from the depths.

As near as she can suspect, it's either going to look like or *be* Stacey Graves, which will be pretty wicked, or it'll look like or be Ezekiel from Drown Town, the scary-ass preacherman with the big hands and too-wide mouth, the better to sing with— think *Poltergeist 2*, "God is *in*, his holy *temp*-le," which Jade delivers at high and sudden volume to the birds that keep gathering around in case she uncovers something tasty.

One of the early extra credit papers she did for Mr. Holmes had been on him—Ezekiel, not the *Poltergeist 2* preacher. It was a two-pager, which she had mostly copied from online: when Henderson-Golding was being flooded with what would become Indian Lake, he'd locked his congregation into his one-room church with him, and they sang until the waters swamped the town, and are maybe, Jade said in her conclusion, still singing, awaiting the day they can rise from the depths to punish the town that replaced Henderson-Golding. And then they turn their attentions to Glen Dam, let the waters of judgment flow forth, down-valley, freeing their beloved, soggy little town.

The problem with Ezekiel, though, it's that he's not really slasher material. What's there for him to revenge? The people of Henderson-Golding had found him in the woods, nursed him back to health, taught him language even though he already had white hair. They'd probably even given him the Bible he would use like a hammer to smite down what-all he saw as sin—everything, pretty much. If Ezekiel was hanging around, it should be to thank all those people who found him, not choke their descendants out with his big hands.

No, Ezekiel's more like a dark and scary force. The only thing he's got against teens, or anybody, is that they're all sinning. But, according to him, the whole world is sin, right? Therefore, the whole world needs to burn. He's more like Nix from *Lord of Illusions*: came for the mayhem, stayed for the massacre.

Stacey Graves, then. Either her or someone dressed up like her. Someone killing like she probably *would*. Case in point: those two Dutch kids out on the water.

Jade spears a tissue she doesn't want to touch even with her thick glove, then stabs through the side of a Diet Coke bottle, then goes for a triple-stacker—a long, faded receipt in *addition* to the Diet Coke and tissue.

Lifting gently, slowly, she guides them all into her bag of infinite holding. Infinite smelly holding.

Stacey Graves does make sense out on the water, she supposes. But it's not like Ezekiel doesn't. The lake is both of their territory, and probably the shore too.

Jade looks out across the lake and mimes poling ahead with her litter stick, both hands, has to jog to catch a candy wrapper trying to make it to the tall grass. Candy wrappers are always the fastest. Something about their no-friction paper and their basic weightlessness, and how each upflung tatter is another sail.

Stab. Stab.

When the candy wrapper flits up into the air instead of riding her spear into the bag, Jade tries to move slow enough to impale it at eight feet high and spiraling. When she misses three times in a row, just scaring it higher away, she takes a couple of running steps and hurls her stick like a spear at it.

One one-hundredth of a second after the handle's gone from her hand, she thinks to look ahead to where her litter stick might be landing.

Time slows for her, hardly even moving at all.

At the other end of this not-a-javelin's arc is—is . . . there's the sheriff's big plate glass window, there's two county vehicles, there's the light pole with the frosted glass bulb by the sidewalk leading *to* the sheriff's building, there's a blue post office box which it's probably a federal crime to puncture.

Jade turns her head away to not have to witness this, and, when it has to be over, her future decided, she takes a timid peek.

The litter stick landed point-first in the hump of grass. A small brown bird flutters down, perches on it, and gives Jade the eye, like this new and unexpected vantage point is his, now, thank you very much. Jade looks past the bird to Sheriff Hardy's window, which has to be like his big television screen, the one always tuned to "Proofrock." Just, now it's got this one girl traipsing across it.

This one girl who owes him some community service. Which she can't dodge anymore, can she?

"Might as well," she says. She has to go over there anyway to collect her litter stick, doesn't she? Maybe signing up for some hours can be her payment for the luck of not having broken out any windows, perforated any car roofs.

Jade waves the bird away, its sharp claws not letting go of the stick's handle until the last possible instant.

That would for sure be scary, Jade thinks, tracking the bird zigging and zagging away: a human body with a sparrow head, like the owl-head dude in *Stage Fright*.

Slashers these days tend to be more off-the-shelf, though, don't they?

As if to prove this, Jade pulls the so-called lapel of her coveralls over on the left side, to check if the dull white Michael Myers mask she's got stashed there is riding well. It's just a hard plastic shell with a wimpy elastic band, your basic face eraser, but no way can she risk carrying a sixty-dollar pull-on full-head bleached-out Captain Kirk around in her pocket just for kicks and grins. No, in circumstances like hers, keep a little two-dollar clearance job that you can leave behind if need be. It's not like she paid the two dollars for it anyway.

Now that she's actually here at Hardy's building, though, this close to the threat of community service, she's kind of having second and third thoughts.

What if he wants her to wash his Bronco? What if he tells her to use her litter stick out in the shallows of Indian Lake, where every third piece of flotsam is going to be not just a rubber, but the rubber of someone she *knows*?

No thank you.

Maybe she can just cross the summer with those twelve hours untouched. What's he going to do, arrest her? Keep her from graduating any more than she's already not graduating?

Moving sneaky, she dislodges the gross tissue from the top of her canvas bag o'smells, lets it go in a gust of wind, then jogs backwards-like, being as conscientious a litter-stabber as she is, she has no choice but to run catch it. Except it keeps being one stab ahead of her stick. And again, again, until she has to be out of sight of Hardy's office window.

The life of the summer janitor, yeah. Gloriouser and gloriouser, until she can't contain the gloriousness anymore, has to burst with sunshine from the pure joy welling up inside her.

Which is only halfway a lie: the longer this slasher takes to rise, the more her anticipation has been ratcheting up. Time and again, watching Letha Mondragon walk from her stepmother's slick little Audi to the pier for their cigarette boat the *Umiak*, Jade's reached out for her, to warn her, to explain it all to her, but she's never reaching with her hands, quite. Just with her eyes. She's going to have to actually tell her at some point, though. It's not stacking the deck, it's just common courtesy.

But, Jade has to admit, she guesses the reason she hasn't approached Letha Mondragon yet is that she's not a hundred and ten percent absolute certain that this isn't all just in her head, that she isn't a victim of wishful thinking. Maybe all her videotapes have rotted her mind. Maybe all the hatred balled up inside her has started sending tendrils out into her thinking, to blacken her thoughts, dim her perception of the actual world.

If she starts seeing tracking lines in the sky, that's when she'll know, she tells herself.

Until then, she'll just keep watching, and waiting.

Except—except it has to be true this time, doesn't it? Letha Mondragon wouldn't be here if there weren't a slasher in the vicinity, would she? That's not the way it works. Jade guesses she doesn't know which came first, the slasher or the final girl, the chicken or the bloody egg, but she does know that where there's one, there's gonna be the other, so it doesn't really matter.

And, okay, she does know which came first: the slasher, of course. It rises to right the wrongs, then when it gets all carried away, nature spits up its governor, its throttle, its one-woman police force, its fiercest angel: the final girl. She's the only cap the slasher cycle recognizes.

But Jade's not writing her cute little papers for Mr. Holmes anymore. Those days are over, gone forever.

Now she's *in* a slasher.

Stab.

This time it's a dead bird. The meaty feel and muted crunch comes up through the fiberglass pole into Jade's palm, and she makes it last as long as she can, imagines a paternal hand spread on the ground, fatherly fingers clutching at the gravel, a left work boot jerking involuntarily, blood leaking down into the whorls of an ear. Right or left, it doesn't matter.

Instead of burying the bird in the trash bag at her hip, she uses her heel and the point of the stick to scrape a deep-enough hole under a bush by the post office. It's Saturday, so nobody's there to ask her what she's doing.

She pushes the dead bird in, covers it up, then studies the dark blood on her stainless steel prod.

It makes a lump swell in her throat. This is what stories mean by "gorge," she knows.

She turns away, spits long and stringy but doesn't quite throw up. Technically.

Just from a one-ounce bird, yeah.

Real brave, Jennifer, she tells herself. *Very metal.*

To deal with the trauma, she works her way around to the side of the post office then sits there for an hour she measures in cigarettes smoked, the shadows lengthening all around her, the temperature clicking down with the sun.

If she doesn't get back to Golding Elementary in time to turn her stick back in, big loss. It'll just mean not being in Rexall's hidden camera, and that can't be the worst thing in the world. And Hardy's not even in his office to catch her not working. From here she can see him out on the water, skipping around in the airboat he bought with the insurance money for his daughter's death back when.

"Get him, sir," Jade says.

She's talking about Clate Rodgers, Hardy's daughter's junior high boyfriend at the time of her drowning.

What was her name? Jade's mom used to say it sometimes, as if, had this dead girl lived, the whole town would be different, better, as if, with that one girl walking down its streets, Proofrock could be what it was meant to have been. Not the current thing it is.

Melanie, that's it.

It's lettered right there on the sides of Hardy's airboat, were Jade close enough to see. The first time she sounded the name out, just trying to make it be a word, not a jumble of blue letters stuck to his hull, she was . . . second grade? But it could have been first, she supposes. In the summer, it's tradition for all the kids who don't think they're too old to line up on the pier in their swimsuits, line up and hold hands, Sheriff Hardy coasting his airboat back and forth before them like a drill sergeant, informing them about water safety, about how all of them, if they follow his instructions to a T, can have the best, and safest, summer ever.

The whole time the kids are flinching and trying not to run away, especially when he hauls the rudder over fast and guns his big fan, performing a neat little kick turn on the water.

They're waiting, they're holding their breath over and over, but they have to breathe too. Jade remembers it so well, so clearly. She was holding Bethany Manx's hand on one side, Tim Lawson's on the other, and she wasn't that weird horror chick yet, was just another kid, nine years old, the whole summer spread out before her, waiting.

Sheriff Hardy just kept lecturing about water safety, though, and he kept not doing it, and *not doing it*, and she was about to ex- plode with anticipation, they all were, they couldn't wait any longer, and Jade remembers seeing Hardy's lips trying not to smile, and then he ran his left index finger up the bridge of his nose, pushing his chrome sunglasses all the way on, and then he finally did it, finally gunned his airboat's throttle all the way up, hauling the rudder over hard, pelting the whole line of kids with a spattery wall of ice-cold water.

After which he just kept going, standing up in his airboat, skipping out deeper and deeper into Indian Lake.

This was maybe ten years after his daughter washed up, Jade guesses.

He probably needed his sunglasses on better to hide his eyes.

No, when he carried Jade up from the shallows, no, he *wasn't* going to let any more girls drown in his lake.

Jade wipes her eyes, tries to keep her chin from being a stupid prune, and tells him she's sorry, okay? She's sorry, she couldn't help it. And she hopes he fucking kills the goddamn shit out of Clate Rodgers.

Maybe some of his friends too.

She sniffles in, stands up against the post office wall, and wonders if that's it, then: will the slasher this time be dressed like a local cop, like the melty terminator from *Judgment Day*? Maybe that's what this slasher cycle will be called when it breaks on the national news: "Judgment Day." Except it'll probably be "Wilderness Massacre," something insulting like that.

No, of course: "Camp Blood, Chapter 2." Because, like Randy says in *Scream 2*, the sequels always have to be bloodier. Unless whoever it is *is* actually wearing some giant Stacey Graves getup, in which case: *The Lake Witch Slayings*.

Jade likes the ring of that one.

That's all later, though. Right now she needs to clock out, always keeping her eyes on the floor so she doesn't accidentally look into any of Rexall's—

She flattens herself against the post office wall, holding the litter stick across her chest in both hands, her lips set.

A Jeep is blasting past, top down, packed with former Hawks cheerleaders.

It's on a collision course with the *Umiak*, surging across the lake, Tiara Mondragon at the flashing chrome steering wheel, her hips wrapped in a gossamer sarong from a fashion catalog, her top a black string bikini, her eyes in, of all things, ski goggles.

When the *Umiak* slides in for a sideways stop, washing water over the top of the pier, Letha Mondragon rises from below.

Jade steps away from the wall to see better.

The cheerleaders in the Jeep are standing, calling Letha over. Jade catches "finally" and "it's going to be great!" For them, two weeks after graduation is still a celebration. But that's probably because their tassels are in frames on the wall already, not burned string by string with a series of cigarettes, just to watch that soft nylon curl up in pain, try to get away, climb back into the safety of high school.

Letha looks back to Tiara, and Tiara shrugs, washing her hands of this, so Letha hops down from the tall side of the boat as graceful as any cat burglar, touches down on the slick wet boards like sticking this landing is no big thing, just everyday for her.

Jade cannot *wait* to see her go up against the tall shape on her dance card. It won't matter if he's got a chainsaw or a harpoon gun or is two-fisting machetes like nunchucks, faster and faster. Letha Mondragon, final girl extraordinaire, will walk open-eyed into those whirling blades, come out with a dark heart in her hands.

She's everything Jade always wished she could have been, had she not grown up where she did, how she did, with *who* she did.

It's going to be epic, this final-girl-against-slasher high noon.

Unless Jade's just making it all up, she reminds herself.

To prove she's not, when Letha Mondragon chocks her sneaker up onto the rear tire of the Jeep and vaults in, sitting under the roll bar not on it, Jade steps out from the wall she's been hiding against, tracks the Jeep's exit to get a read on where the party is tonight. Right before the shadows take Letha, she looks longingly back across the lake, as if beaming apology over to the yacht, to her family, for doing something for herself for once.

Jade knows that look.

She outgrew it in fifth grade, but still, she remembers not wanting to leave the house, broach into the big scary world.

"But everything's scary," she reminds herself, gathering her coveralls at her throat because too much exposure to Proofrock might finally just do her in. When the Jeep's headlights finally kiss each other goodbye, fold themselves into the dusk, Jade beats the darkness back by lighting a cigarette. It flares harsh orange, and, her lungs swirling with death, her litter stick hidden far up under the bushes, she falls in behind the Jeep and just goes ahead and says it out loud: "The party was great on . . . *Girls Nite Out.*" It's the slasher where the killer wears the bear suit with whackadoo-dle eyes. But, extra points for the blades hidden in the paw, right? 1982 too, a couple of years before the Springwood Slasher would have knife fingers. But Jade can't get lost in her head, needs to keep up with the Jeep long enough to get a read on where this party's going to be. But these girls—the driver's Bethany Manx, Jade's pretty sure—are making it easy. The way they're hugging the shore, the only place they can be going is Banner Tompkins's house, right on the lake. His parents aren't jet-setters or anything, but it is bowling night up the road in Ammon, and bowling usually takes until two in the morning to weave back from. Leaving time to invite a few friends over. Say, twenty of them, and all the booze they can carry?

Jade knows it'll be swim trunks and bikinis until about midnight. After which it'll be nothing but smiles.

On the twenty-minute walk to get there, skirting the Bay and Devil's Creek, Jade keeps finding herself looking to the left, across the lake. She tries to come back, watch for tripping hazards, keep from busting her face on a tree root, but her chin keeps cranking over, her eyes tunneling across all that water, to Terra Nova.

She hates it on principle, sure, but it's also what's delivering a final girl to town, so maybe she should give it a sort of grudging pass. At least until this slasher cycle is over. After that it can burn, be a haunted husk in the cold open of the sequel, where that installment's blood sacrifice happens, well away from prying eyes that might try to shut things down before they even get going proper.

Why is she watching it now, though?

She actually stumbles when the obviousness of it hits her: she's not watching Terra Nova at all. She's glaring back at Letha's father, Theo Mondragon, the one who rolled his arm forward for the graduation crowd, telling Proofrock it could get on with its little ceremony.

The chip on her shoulder for him isn't only about that, though. It's . . . it's that he's a father of a sort-of young girl, isn't it? An *innocent* girl, at least.

Shit.

Jade collects herself, walks faster, with more purpose.

Her job here, it's not only to educate Letha on what's coming. It's also to keep her safe so it all *can* happen.

That includes keeping her safe from her father, who, by marrying a woman half his age, is already whispering to the world that he's not averse to stepping well outside his age group. Maybe even has a taste for it.

Is *this* the chink in Letha Mondragon's otherwise impervious armor? Final girls these days do have those pesky pre-existing issues, Jade knows. She thought it was whatever happened to Letha's real mom, which would be enough, but—no no no—she has something more intense, doesn't she? Something in her past, in her *childhood*, that's left her skittish, that fundamentally broke her confidence in the world.

Her father.

It all tracks, doesn't it? Letha isn't timid and conservative and right-moral'd from nature, but because she's trying to make up for something, trying to cover it with good deeds. Something that wasn't even her fault. She was just a little girl left alone with her dad for the afternoon.

Jade is crashing through the bushes now.

Chancing another look across the water, she can nearly see Theo Mondragon up in his office in their yacht, getting off scot-free one more time, skating like he always has with his wealth, his privilege, his good looks and charm. His funny excuses, his believable lies.

He's smug because no one is ever going to know. Letha sure isn't going to tell, and, from what Jade hears, it's just them over there—the Mondragons. The other Founders swing through on and off to check on the progress of Terra Nova, but they've got empires to run, and their yachts are probably cutting through other waters anyway, the world being their playground and all.

"You're being paranoid," Jade tries to tell herself. But she doesn't slow down any. What she's seeing now that she's deeper in the trees, cutting across to the flickering bonfire at Banner Tompkins's, what she can't help but picture, is Theo Mondragon in what he would probably call a skiff or a dinghy, with a silent little trolling motor. Not the *Umiak*, as everybody knows that one, and of course not the pontoon boat with all the seats that they use when the other Founders are in town. It's got festive lights strung all over it now anyway. And the catamaran with the big sail would be like advertising his progress across the lake, and the gondola boat tied to their dock has to be purely for show, and wouldn't last out in Indian Lake's chop anyway, and the canoe and rowboat are too slow, too labor intensive for a CEO, and the stupid white pedal boat with the high arching swan neck and tiny aristocratic swan head has to be just for any kids who show up, doesn't it?

No, a little flat-bottomed jonboat with a trolling motor. It's like putting a silencer on a small-caliber pistol. Theo Mondragon's probably sitting in the bow right now, his hand on that steering handle, the wind in his tight hair, his five o'clock shadow raspy, his eyes brimming with the most expensive wine.

Does he have a spotting scope up on that tallest part of the yacht? Has he been tracking the party?

Jade can't say there's not a sliver of a chance.

And, right now, Letha, she's in a between-place, she's unaccounted-for, it's her first big night out on her own. Anything can happen.

Jade slows a few feet back in the trees, eases the Michael mask out, fits it over her face just in case, fluffing her purple-tinged hair out over the elastic band. Watching like this, a mask just feels better. It's not the first time she's done it, of course—she treats parties like anthropology field work, taking mental notes the whole time—but it's the first time she's doing it for a reason that might make sense later.

The bonfire blazing in the yard is the jumbo-size version of her dad's yearslong fire pit in the backyard, that he makes her scrape out some Sundays.

The Jeep is already there.

Jade creeps over, holds her hand close to the tailpipe, feeling for heat, then finally thins her lips, just clamps right on.

It's only warm.

Letha's in the house, then. With all the music, all the loud talking, all the squeals.

Good for her. She deserves this. Be a kid before it's too late, this is the last summer for it.

Jade feels around for the right tree to stand behind, for the right dip to crouch in, for the right pile of junk to mask her pale coveralls, and it doesn't match the mask, but she can't help doing the sound effects a bit: *ki-ki-ki, ma-ma-ma.*

She's not here to carve through the party, though. Let them have their fun, she doesn't care. She's here because—because what *if* Theo Mondragon is about to drag his Saturday night special jonboat up onto the shore?

Jade would never kill anyone just because. With reason, though, yeah. Twice-over, with interest, and more than a little attitude, maybe even something a little extra, for style points.

Her plan is to wait until Theo Mondragon throws Letha down in the tall grass. Then Jade'll step into frame, having filched a piece of rebar up from the scrap pile, limbered an axe up from a stump. There's always an axe around when you need it. If there's one thing horror movies have taught her, it's that.

For now, though, she just lips her new cigarette, knows better than to spark up.

Already couples are traipsing out to the cars, steaming up the windows. Meaning all the beds inside must be occupied.

Normally, in a town the size of Proofrock, there'd be even money that she'd have gone to seventh-grade homecoming with one of those naked backs in the front seat, that she'd have a secret matching tattoo with the prom queen who's just bare feet-on-glass, that she'd have written love notes to whoever's in that car with the squeaky springs. Guy or girl.

There's nothing normal about Jennifer Daniels, though.

By seventh grade she was already the death metal girl, the D&D

girl, the devilchild, practically *was* the walking, talking cover for *Sleepaway Camp II*. She knew all the songs the other kids' *parents* knew, had memorized all the movies those parents had screamed to in their own junior high, and she could reel them out on command, from the slightest provocation, like weaving a cloak of protection around her, and pulling tight.

Anyway, she doesn't need the stupid rituals of parties like these, does she? All the laughter is nervous and forced, all the come-ons and invitations so inelegant.

It's better to just watch, she tells herself. It's better to hide in the trees, part the leaves, take notes in her head, not missing a single thing, because you never know what's going to matter. And then when it's time, she'll step out with that sharp piece of rebar, step out and drive it through a thick fatherly chest, and the blood is going to mist across her graduating class's faces, and they're going to thank her, because this night could have gone the complete other way.

Jade can see it all in her head, from every angle.

Hours later the bonfire is down to embers, though, and nothing's happened yet, *except* in her head. There's less cars, but there's no dragon silhouette taking shape in the shadows. She taps her knuckle on her hard plastic cheek like a metronome, to anchor herself in the moment, to stay awake, and, finally, thirty minutes before midnight, ten minutes after telling herself screw it, the side door off the garage opens, spills thready blue light.

Ah.

They're watching movies in there, then. Horror movies, probably. What else would you watch in a garage, with a group, at this time of night?

It's something she's seen, Jade knows—she's seen everything twice—but still, she wants worse than anything to just catch a glimpse, to make the movie out from a single frame. One of the

*Child's Play*s, maybe? *Ringu*? Dialing all the way back to *The Texas Chain Saw Massacre*? She wants worse than anything to speak up from the back of the garage, let them in on the true story of this cursed production, on the trivia about the movie's limited engagement in Italy, about how the soundtrack in the theatrical release isn't the same as the one that was released on VHS. For reasons she can explain and trace and unfold for however long they'll sit there listening.

Wasn't meant to be, though. Either she's one of the flock, or she knows horror movies. Not both. And they're probably jeering at the effects anyway. Overplaying their reactions to the jump-scares. Not even paying the right kind of attention.

Jade's *glad* not to be in there. She lifts her mask to spit, and when the eyeholes settle down again like binoculars, the doorway opens. A girl steps into it, two girls, *three* girls now, the second helping the first.

The second is Letha Mondragon in a pair of bright white shorts she must have borrowed at the party, since she didn't have them on at the pier. And of course the second one is her. She would never be stumbling drunk like the first one obviously is. But she would keep the drunk one safe.

The third one is Bethany Manx, the Jeep driver, the principal's daughter, always trying to shake that mantle off. Jade can tell it's her from her rail-thin profile, her mod cut, longer in front than back, and the flash of silver from her mouth: the tongue stud Daddy Dearest doesn't know about, that she only, famously, puts in for get-togethers like this.

Bethany peels off, has some errand back at the cars, leaving Letha and the drunk one—it's Tiffany Koenig. She's throwing up into the tall grass by one of the cars, which, if scuttlebutt heard over bathroom stalls is right, is kind of her party trick. Letha is patiently threading Tiffany K's hair back from the puke.

The good thing about people throwing up outside is that the janitor doesn't have to clean it up. In the great outdoors, raccoons are the janitors. And they love their job.

After it's over and Tiffany K's crying—you do that when it comes out your nose as well as your mouth, you do that when you panic that you're never going to be able to breathe again—Letha stands her up, steadies her a bit, and starts to lead her into the dark house, to clean up.

Tiffany K pulls away. It's embarrassing, looking like this. Vomit stringing between your fingers. Cheeks wet with hot tears.

This party *is* happening right by a giant sink, though . . .

Letha looks around for help, for guidance, for Bethany who's nowhere, and finally just leads Tiffany K carefully around the coals of the bonfire. Because unsteady people shouldn't lean out over the water alone, she takes her shoes off and squelches into the mud of the shore with Tiffany K, helps her splash her face.

Jade creeps closer, trying to see if this—"friendship"—looks like it does in the movies. Of the two of them, she imagines she's Tiffany K here, the self-destructive one. Not the responsible one. Not the good friend.

It's best she leaves now, she knows. It's best she was never here. There's no corporate tycoon trolling across the lake to rape anybody. There's no dragon, using its mighty tail to cut through the water.

Jade turns, her breath heavy and close in her mask, knows that as soon as she's twenty steps away she's going to be lighting up, breathing deep, holding the smoke in for as long as janitorially possible—but then she stops, cocks her head back to the lake.

Someone's walking through the water?

It's Letha.

"*What?*" Jade says out loud, on accident, but nobody looks her way. The problem here is that this isn't on-script, this isn't in the genre, isn't a trope. The final girl in the first act isn't *curious*. Curiosity is what's going to get all those *other* girls killed, not her.

Jade steps closer, into the dull glow from the dead bonfire, the skin of her neck contracting in the heat, the plastic of her face impervious.

Letha's wading out farther now, is getting her borrowed white shorts wet.

Jade shakes her head no, no, but then she sees what Letha's after.

There's . . . it's someone *floating* out there.

Her heart thumps once, deep.

"Don't," she says to Letha, not even close to loud enough for Letha to hear, but Letha senses Jade all the same—final girl radar—and looks back for long enough that Jade is aware of each red coal flickering off her mask.

These are just work coveralls, she wants to whisper across these thirty feet. They're not Michael Myers coveralls, they're just work clothes.

Her white face isn't so easy to explain.

Letha, either having seen Jade or not, turns back to her task. Her duty. She steps out again, again, up to her stomach now, then, all at once, her armpits.

She's a short pull away from this floating person now.

"Hello?" she says, splashing water up onto him, or her. It.

No response.

This could be a practical joke, Jade wants to warn. Banner Tompkins is kind of famous for them, and this is home ground for him. Maybe it's a sex doll they keep in the shed for a floatie. Maybe it's a punching dummy from when he was in martial arts with Mason Rodgers, sophomore year. Maybe it's a deer some old-fashioned hunter was trying to float across the lake.

Letha gives herself to the water, pulls with her arms to this body and grabs on, turns around immediately, paddles for the shore.

Tiffany K is just sitting there hugging her knees now, crying like you do when you're drunk and you know it's not over yet. She's not seeing what Jade's most definitely seeing: the final girl being a final girl, hauling a corpse in. Finding the first body.

Inside her mask, Jade smiles wide, with unadulterated wonder.

This is—this is . . . this means it's real, doesn't it? That it's not all in her head, but outside it too, for once.

She almost goes to help Letha drag this dead body in, beach it, announce it, but no, this has to be all the final girl. This is all Letha Mondragon. And she's athletic and capable and determined enough that she should be able to do it.

She gets it into the shallows, anyway.

It bobs in the give-and-take of the lake's surface, the water cleaning the pondweed from its head at last.

At which point Tiffany K starts screaming. And screaming.

Letha, probably having gone through lifeguard training one country club summer, turns the wide-shouldered body over in a way that says she knows how to administer CPR, and is honor-bound to try.

Except some of the pale skin from the corpse's back sloughs off onto her right hand, an oozy black welling up where the skin's torn away.

The only reason Jade sees the next part is that Letha's white shorts are wet, but they're still bright. And they're right behind this boy's Dutch-blond head. The head that's in her lap. The face.

There's no lower jaw.

Jade's laughter wells up from deep-deep inside, lives inside her mask, fills her head.

"Well then," she says, striding fast away before the party can convene over this tragedy, and by twenty yards out she's running just for the thrill of it, the branches tearing at what would be her face, her coveralls keeping anything sharp from touching her.

Once she's far enough away she skids to her knees in a clearing, in the moonlight, and rips the mask off, leans back pushing the heels of her hands into her eyes, because she can't stop crying.

First the final girl. Now the blood sacrifice—proof that the recording on that pink phone was real.

This is Laurie Strode seeing Michael Myers outside her school. This is Sidney Prescott, seeing that black robe descend in that last bathroom stall.

And now there are steps that must be taken—a letter that has to be typed in and printed out. But first, first all Jade can do is hug herself tight and shake with gratitude.

It leaves her panting on her knees, panting and smiling, looking at the darkness all around her.

He could be anywhere, couldn't he?

He already is.

SLASHER 101

Hello, Letha Mondragon. You may remember me from
the bathroom by the gym. I had blue hair. Enclosed
please find A Bay of Blood from 1971 by famed
Giallo director Mario Bava, which let me tell you
changed my life in 6th grade when I found it.
I was in Idaho Falls for a doctor's appointment
I couldn't do in Proofrock and I was in the gas
station for the bathroom while my mom was having a
conversation with herself in the car about will she
won't she and then this movie was in the bargain
bin like trash. But let me tell you it wasn't.

The reason I'm selecting to pass that same sacred
copy of A Bay of Blood to you in this clandestine
fashion is that many including me consider it to
be the main grandfather of the slasher genre. When
you're watching A Bay of Blood you'll notice the
eerie similarity in the opening credits to Indian
Lake. The first time I was watching it in secret
my heart dropped let me tell you. I thought it WAS
Indian Lake.

But as to A Bay of Blood's ancestoriness, there
are many who say that Sean Cunningham the director
of Friday the 13th 9 years later modeled his
slasher ON A Bay of Blood. The reason for that is
partially the set up and mostly the kills. However
Sean Cunningham objects that it's really just great
minds thinking alike. But one of the main premises
of A Bay of Blood is some teenagers going to party
at a lake and having sex and then they get killed
in the most violent and satisfying ways, which is
also the set up for Friday the 13th.

But what you need to pay attention to with A Bay
of Blood isn't that the way to avoid a blade to the
face is to leave the lake. What to pay attention

to is the 13 ways there are to be killed AT a lake, and also that you can't trust anyone not to be the killer.

What I'm telling you is that pretty soon, probably at our annual July Fourth party on the water, Proofrock is going to be turning INTO A Bay of Blood, I promise. Instead of explaining pranks and revenge and red herrings and final girls and reveals all right here I'm just going to instead fold in a lot of the papers and interviews I wrote for Mr. Holmes in History Class, including a bonus on Jaws since that matters. Those papers can be your bible and your map and guide and gospel. What I'm telling you is that the Dutch boy you found in the lake is the beginning, not the end.

As for the end, nobody not even an expert in the slasher genre like me can guess it this early, but the rules say that whoever is already chopping necks is going to use for disguise the thing we're already afraid of. Here in Indian Lake that's Stacey Graves. 2 years ago I 100 percent believed in Stacey Graves. But I realize now that the age of the supernatural slasher was the Golden Age, with Michael and Jason and Freddy and Chucky. This is the age of Ghostface and Valentine, which is mostly people wearing masks for revenge.

But you should know about Stacey Graves the Lake Witch all the same. That's why I'm including the interview paper about her.

My number is inside Bay of Blood if you want to talk more.

SILENT RAGE

On the way out of the darkened library—custodians have keys and keys and keys—when Jade's using every last bit of her effort and attention to get the glass front door lifted enough on its saggy hinges for the deadbolt to slide home, a man's voice knifes out of the darkness, straightening her back, flooding her veins with adrenaline, her head with static, and priming her throat with a scream she barely manages to swallow.

"Thought Connie and her husband were having a dust-up again," the creaky voice says from the book return alcove right by the door. "That she was maybe sleeping up here for the night, y'know?"

Jade shuts her eyes in instant regret. She should have gone out the *back* way. She should have just slept in the breakroom. She should have shrouded the computer monitor she was writing on with one of the big cardboard boxes. She should have *remembered* that Hardy always finishes his day out with one last cigarette on the bench by the lake, the one dedicated to his daughter. The one just a hop, skip, and gulp from the library—emphasis on the *gulp*.

"Sheriff," Jade says.

"But then I swung by Connie's place," Hardy goes on in his good-old-boy way, "and both cars are there, you know? Living room window's blue like from a television show."

"She watches *CSI*," Jade says, finally getting the deadbolt to click over, hold the tired door up for the few hours the night has left.

"Yeah?" Hardy says, just super conversationally. "Hope you didn't leave any trace evidence in there, then . . ."

Jade doesn't have to be directed to follow him when he shoulders off the wall, spins his toothpick into the mulch under the bushes, and starts ambling over to his Bronco, so bright white in the darkness.

"What you got there?" he asks about the sheaf of papers still warm enough from the copier that they're trying to curl up against the night air.

When Jade doesn't answer, Hardy looks back to evaluate, then holds his hand out for them, not even having to snap. Jade surrenders them, sure her life is over now, that this is the end. It was fun, y'all, but I've got to go to hell now, see ya. My secret diary's getting logged as evidence, is probably going to indict me six ways from Sunday on multiple charges, not the least of which will be wishful thinking.

Hardy stops on the bulging sidewalk, pulls his bifocals up to his face to read the first line of the top page: "*And then there was one. Of me, I mean, Mr. . . .* Holmes?"

The question mark and the exaggerated drama are all Hardy.

He considers Jade over his specs, flips to the next paper—Jade stapled them all one by one, so Letha wouldn't get lost: "*Don't feel bad, Mr.* Holmes. *Not everybody knows about the Final Girl?* What's that, the 'final girl'?"

"It's just a thing for history class," Jade says, shoulders seriously sagging.

"*Actually the slasher isn't impossible or just in the movies, sir,*" Hardy reads next, hitting "sir" especially hard and dropping his glasses back, his neck strap taking their slight weight, the glasses hardly bouncing. Jade knows because that's where she's looking. Not up into his face.

That doesn't mean she can't feel him watching her.

"*Slasher?*" he finally says.

Mentally backpedaling, Jade stumbles into the hole she'd always meant to bury her high school diploma in, and, because that's all she's got to save her life here, she uses it. "Summer work for Sherlock," she mumbles, looking out across the black-black waters of Indian Lake.

It's a Hail Mary pie-in-the-sky flying fuck at a rolling donut, but it's all Jade has in the world right now. Her first last and only prayer.

"Last I heard, Bea—Mr. *Holmes* doesn't let students call him that," Hardy says, holding her door open because cops are always directing traffic. "*Former* students either."

"I'm not exactly former," Jade says, her voice dwindling down into the sincere, embarrassed octaves. "Still need a history credit to graduate."

"But you were there for the ceremony," Hardy explains—objects.

Jade steps up into the truck.

Hardy, still not sold, still *standing* there, flips deeper into Jade's stack of print-outs, spiraling Jade deep into pre-wince mode, since shuffled in there somewhere, she's not sure where—stapling got complicated—is "*Hello, Letha Mondragon,*" and that letter's so damning that Hardy'll probably just read the whole thing out loud like entering it into evidence.

"*How—how about we just consider this the very end of my . . .*" he reads, having to breathe in for the next part: "*Extra* credit *career, if that works for you, Mr. Holmes."* He looks up to recite the last part: "The *end*?" he says incredulously, flopping the pages closed and then riffling their edges as if counting, or weighing. "How long has this career *been*?"

"He keeps a basket on his desk," Jade says. "He calls it the extra credit kitty."

Hardy's shoulders shake with some internal amusement and he closes her door, rounds the Bronco, climbs up himself.

"So you figured to play to your strengths," he says, firing the truck up. "Blood and guts, werewolves and zombies."

"Just slashers," Jade says, probably not even loud enough to make it across to him.

Hardy backs the Bronco out, swings them around, only turning the headlights on when they're on blacktop, and Jade doesn't know if she's being hand-delivered back to the hospital in Idaho Falls or down to the holding cell behind his office or what, at least not until he turns onto her street. He pulls up in front of her house, doesn't take his truck out of gear, so everything in Jade's mirror is washed red.

"I won't tell Connie about the janitorial staff using her ink and copy paper up, I don't guess," he says, handing Jade her stolen paper and ink. "But I probably will mention it to Bear next time I see him down at Dot's, make sure this is schoolwork, not personal."

Grady "Bear" Holmes, aka "Sherlock," the flying history teacher and secret cigarette fiend.

Fucking Idaho.

The radio under Hardy's dash squawks, straightening Jade's back *again*, and she of all people is supposed to know jumpscares more or less. But maybe that just makes her more vulnerable to them, not less.

Meg Koenig's voice comes through fuzzy and urgent. Hardy dials it down and leans over the wheel with both arms, hugging it to him so he can study the front of Jade's house without having to stare at the side of her face as well.

"He working across the lake these days?" he asks, about Tab.

Jade nods once.

"All righty then, I guess I'll see you . . ." Hardy leads off, pausing to narrow his eyes, do some mental calculations, "*Friday* to start your community service. How's that sound?"

"Can't wait," Jade says. "Guessing I should wear clothes I don't care about?"

Hardy chuckles like he'd been expecting that, pulls the mic down from its hook by the rearview mirror, says before he thumbs the line open, "Filing for Meg, cleaning the coffee pot, I don't know. She'll find something for you to do. Let's say . . . hour a day, next couple weeks, get it over with?"

Meg Koenig, Tiffany Koenig's mom.

"Yippee," Jade monotones.

"Hardy here," Hardy says into the mic, either just like a movie cop or . . . or maybe the movies aren't that made-up.

Jade steps down, shuts the door, and Hardy waits until she's on the porch and really for sure going home to roll away. Jade's still standing there staring down into her dad's muddy boots—*fresh* muddy?—when the door she's facing flashes red and blue: a few houses down, Hardy's turned his lights on, is accelerating hard, screeching around the corner to some emergency.

In Proofrock, at two in the morning?

Jade steps back down to track him, can't, so keeps walking to the end of the street, where she can look across the lake, see Terra Nova.

It's just the same glittering lights as it's been for the last few weeks: giant yacht, night construction.

"Hunh," she says, and studies her dark neighborhood, the darker town.

It has to be Blondie, she finally decides. The Dutch girl. She finally floated in.

Jade looks down to the pages fluttering in her hand. She flips to her own random line somewhere in the middle of the sheaf, sees an eight-year-old girl named Stacey Graves living like a cat in some pioneer version of Proofrock, always looking across the rising lake for the mother who abandoned her.

Who's to say, though, right?

Life isn't like the nature shows. In the documentaries the coaches play in biology, the mother rabbit will stand up to the snake or the coyote or the hawk when it's after her baby rabbit, will stand up to them when she doesn't have even one chance in all of hell at fighting off this perfect predator, but she throws her little body into those claws and fangs all the same and kicks for all she's worth, for all her baby's worth to her, which is . . . everything?

"Not likely," Jade mumbles, and is glad she doesn't have a stupid diploma, because that would mean she took some test where she answered *yes* to "this is how a mother rabbit protects her young," which would have been a lie.

But fuck it.

Not every mom is a Pamela Voorhees, going after *all* camp counselors because one or two of them let her baby drown.

And Jade is far from a baby anymore, either.

She steps forward again, again, drilling her eyes across the lake, trying to picture what Holmes painted for them one seventh period: the fire of 1965, coming right up to the shore over there, Proofrock holding its breath, all of Idaho ready to burn.

But it didn't.

It never does.

Jade shrugs like *just wait*, spins on a combat heel, and slouches back up her street almost grinning. All in all, this night's been almost a win, hasn't it? Hardy could have confiscated her papers, meaning she'd have had to have broken into one of the schools to reprint them from her email, and, who knows, she might have walked in on Rexall cleaning the lenses of all his hidden cameras.

No thank you.

Jade kicks dramatically across her lawn—no, she *Holden Caulfields* it across her lawn. As far as Jade knows, nobody at Henderson High ever turned that into a way of walking, an *attitude* of walking, so it can be all hers.

She Holden Caulfields it up onto her ramshackle porch again, endures the gauntlet of the living room, her dad making a show of pausing *The Night of the Hunter* to let her pass, and then she clamps her headphones on, pulls her little television close, and pushes the *The Hitcher* tape in, tells herself it's *Prom Night II* after that, hating the whole time that she kind of wants to sneak back into the living room, see if she can catch any of *The Night of the Hunter*—see if that old-time preacher in it is maybe some figuration of Ezekiel. Maybe him being on-screen in her own house is a sign, even, that she shouldn't dismiss Drown Town so fast for this slasher cycle. Jade pauses Rutger Hauer on her thirteen-inch, tries to eavesdrop on Robert Mitchum in there on the twenty-seven inch, and it takes enough effort that part of her sort of drifts off, is partially awake on the couch in the living room, her dad quietly spreading a blanket over her.

Jade jerks awake blinking hard, trying to shake that image, flush it, and scans her videotapes for that orange pumpkin sticker she put on the spine of *Halloween* years ago, so it can be the last thing she sees before conking, so she can take *it* with her into sleep, and the next time she opens her eyes it's nearly noon, meaning she's sleeping through today's litter-stabbing expedition. But fuck it. Let the trash stab itself for one day. Like Rexall's watching her time card that close? No, his cameras are more zoomed in on her chestal area.

Jade shudders, trying to shake the grime of his eyes off.

Carrying a box of Honeycombs and not exactly moving at top speed—the house is empty like the tomb—she folds some of her old pants around her prize *A Bay of Blood* tape, and then she ties a white ribbon around it both ways, to be sure the boxy VHS won't clatter out at Tiara Mondragon's feet, get kicked away like a roach.

Next she folds all the papers shut, and instead of hiding them at the center with *A Bay of Blood*, she slips the thick little bundle under the ribbon's bow like some long, heartfelt, meandering girl-to-girl note about boys and make-up and . . . and whatever normal girls talk about. Then it's just suiting up and trucking through the muck around the lake, tightwriting it across the spine of the dam, and clomping up the dock at Terra Nova forty-five minutes later, knocking on whatever passes for a door.

Except the yacht . . . isn't there?

Jade cases the lake slow. Where can something that size *be*?

Camp Blood, it turns out, which she'd saluted down to on the way over, from the top of the bluff.

"*Excuse me?*" Jade says out loud, truly affronted about this transgression—about *them* being at Camp Blood. She comes right up to the lip of the dock as if ten feet more might explain all this to her, and finally cues in that there's no construction going on in Terra Nova behind her. Like the second Thursday before July 4th is some kind of Idaho holiday? Not any one she knows about, and even if it were, the Founders would be paying holiday rates.

Where is everybody?

Jade shields her eyes and squints her vision better, can see now that the yacht's pulled right up to the jetty in front of Camp Blood, the one that used to be for kids to earn their diving badges off of.

This makes zero point zero sense. Jade looks around absently, finds the mailbox she's seen Dan Dan the mailman puttering across the lake for, and stuffs the pants and tape and pages into it like a bomb, just to complete her mission. Because now there's *another* mission, this one more recon oriented.

Twenty breathless minutes later she's on the chalky bluff back behind Camp Blood, peering down. Hardy's there, his airboat skidded up onto shore like he always does, and his two deputies are milling around with trash bags. But so are the state police, and some leathery rail of a guy in park ranger colors, and Letha is sitting on the jetty, wrapped in a blanket, Tiara hugging her from the side.

Jade leans forward, out over open space. She really did bury a heavy-ass double bit axe over here in junior high, "for future use." And also because it was stolen. But . . . no. Hardy wouldn't scramble all available units and rope in civilians just because Proofrock's high school drop-out of a janitor told him to look under the floorboards of cabin 6.

Would he?

Jade leans out over the open space even more, that soft chalky bluff crumbling down and down under the toe of her right boot, and . . . Letha, in that blanket. Her hated stepmom, consoling her.

Consoling her.

From what?

"The next kill," Jade says in wonder, and then in the same instant, she feels it: eyes on her.

She looks down, around, finally finds those eyes: Theo Mondragon in khaki shorts and an unbuttoned shirt, like he didn't have time to attire himself properly for whatever this is. Like he just ran out to whoever was screaming. Jade can almost see him powering the monstrous yacht across the lake, never mind checking depth or battening pitchers and glasses down in the state rooms.

He's out at the edge of Camp Blood now, cell pushed up against the side of his head, and he's looking up at Jade, her off-color half-bleached hair—all the purple's gone—probably an ash-blond beacon for him to fix on.

Jade steps back, tightropes it across the rail-less spine of the dam again, and runs all the way home, her chest heaving, spends the next hour coloring her hair black-black with *shoe polish*, which is all she can find. It's the hugest mess. The sink looks like a demon exploded in it, like this is a problem only Ben Affleck can solve.

Except Ben Affleck, as usual, isn't here.

Jade hauls out the cleaning shit, does janitor duty for the next hour, wiping up her *own* mess for once. By the end of it her hair should be dry, but it's all gummy and oily instead. She goes out to the yard, uses the hose this time, and vinegar, then rubbing alcohol, but some situations are just basically unsalvageable. Evidently deep black and the non-color her burned-out rat's nest of hair's been strained down to come together in a weird shade of orangey-brown, like . . . carrot with undertones of vomit? Leftover tendrils of black are shot through as well, and her scalp looks like the top of a scabby dress shoe, one cheap enough to have bubbled up in the sun.

Who cares.

The better to stare you down with, Jade hisses inside, her daily affirmation, and stalks into her room, ransacking it for whatever other papers she can slip to Letha, and then, and then—she has to decide what movie's going to be next in this Final Girl extension course, doesn't she?

She clamps her headphones on again, works her way through *The Slumber Party Massacre* and *April Fool's Day* and *Happy Birthday to Me* for the rest of the day, and somewhere in there she blisses out, only comes to when the screen fizzes its blue soul up. It's the same exact shade Casey Becker's television screen is early on in *Scream*. Meaning . . . does that mean that *her* movie's starting now, that Jade's Proofrock slasher is officially cueing up, the preliminary stages all checked off at last? And . . . and if she had the same stovetop brand of popcorn as Casey Becker, would it pop at the same rate? Does Casey's stalking and death move in real time or movie time?

It's worth investigating, even with just a normal bag of microwave popcorn. In the kitchen, though, her dad is cooking eggs, his whole face bleary.

He rubs his hand up and down over it, still trying to wake up all the way.

"Doesn't work like it used to," he says for Jade about his get-sober trick, and then smiles with the left side of his mouth, which is an invitation for her to smile with him about how much mornings suck. She almost does, just manages to look away instead, to the front door, cocked open to let the air in, which is something her mom used to do when she was up first, doing chores. For half an instant, Jade's ten again.

As if reading the moment right for once in his life, her dad, guiding his eggs from pan to plate, falls into a story Jade already knows, that he used to tell when she was a kid and the time before she was born was mythic, and the only reason her dad could walk across it was that he was a titan, ten stories tall.

"We used to hide under the pier on days like these, each of us with a sixer floating besides us," he says, miming the beer at chest-level.

"'We?'" Jade prompts, though she knows: Rexall, Clate, anybody else stupid enough to get roped in.

Her dad keeps going, says, "This was before Deputy Hardy had that swamp boat, see?"

"Deputy Hardy" is what Sheriff Hardy was back then, but it's also the only rank Tab Daniels allows him.

"Listen, I'm sure this story's going to be better this time, but I—" Jade starts.

"The department had that long bass boat with the twin Evinrudes," her dad says, scrounging in the cabinet for the pepper even though it's right there on the counter. "Could have pulled a house off its pylons if you tied the knot right."

"*And you would—*"

"And we would float there all day, our ski ropes tied to that boat, waiting for your mom or somebody to call in the emergency on the other side of the lake."

"Like on a schedule?" Jade asks. She's never thought to ask this question before.

"More like whenever she got around to it," her dad says, leaning back to fork his first runny bite of egg in. "Kimbat knew we were down there, would torture us by not calling in."

"Kimbat" is Kimmy plus Batman, because her purse was her utility belt, something like that, it's all dim and distant for Jade.

"And then the sheriff—" she says, trying to get this over with already.

"Deputy," her dad corrects, holding his fork up like to cross that T.

Jade makes her voice as bored and flat as possible, finishes his story: "He would blast off for the other side of the lake for this emergency call, and you and Rexall and Clate and whoever would come up from under the pier on those ski ropes, barefoot skiing until he looked back to see what the drag was."

"We'd have had cameras in our phones back then, there'd be proof," her dad says, bringing his plate up to his face because the yolks are just gelid enough to string. "Or if we'd have had phones at all," he adds with a smile-and-eyebrow thing that Jade would bet everything she owns is the exact same smile that lured her mom over to Camp Blood for a party one night, at the right-wrong time in her uterine cycle.

But it always starts like that, doesn't it? Some randy dude making eyes when he should be making tracks? Even when she dials up old Indian stories online, there's always some goofy old dude smiling exactly like Tab Daniels while he scraps the world together from goopy mud, making deals with muskrats and beavers, ducks and crows, anybody stupid enough to listen to him.

"You're saying a bass boat can pull three skiers?" Jade says to her dad.

"We were skinnier back then."

Jade shakes her head, narrows her eyes, and looks out the front door again, telling herself she's not doing this, she's not interacting with him, not even on accident. Because he can flip it all around on her in an instant.

"Why you telling me this story again?" she asks. "It was bullshit then, it's bullshit now."

Her dad forks another bite in, makes a show of savoring it, swallowing it down.

"You've got a mouth on you, you know?" he says.

"And a knee," Jade says. "A machete in my room."

Her dad smiles to show how little threat she is and rattles his plate down into the sink to either sit there for days or for Jade to wash it. And if she doesn't do it? Eggs are superglue after about half an hour. She hates when he's still in the house, can *hear* her doing his dirty dishes. But they don't have enough plates to let them sit, either.

"The ski rope's what I want you to pay attention to, there," he says at last, all the silence before it serving as emphasis.

"The *rope*?"

"How long they go, you think?"

"Why's it matter?"

"Seventy feet," her dad very clearly enunciates, reaching into his pants to scratch his hip bone but never breaking eye contact with Jade. "But let's say seventy-five, just to be safe."

"I don't know what you're talking about," Jade says. "And I don't care, either."

"You should," he says. "Seventy-five feet is as close as I need to be to the law, get it? It went for high school and it goes for now too."

"Thanks for the update?"

"And the street in front of the house here is a sight closer than that. Want me to measure it out?"

Jade dials back, translates. "This is about Sheriff Hardy dropping me off last night?"

"This is about you bringing the law to my front door. And how that's gonna be the end of that."

"It was just—"

"Any more interactions with *Deputy* Hardy, I'm gonna have to think my own daughter's a snitch."

"What am I going to rat you out about? Drinking on the job? Do you think that's some big secret?"

"Safer this way."

"What way?"

"Any more interactions with the law, you're out of here."

"You can't kick me out," Jade says, her eyes heating up. "I'm not eighteen yet."

"You're out of school. Might need to find your own place, like your mom there."

"Because I take up so much room here?"

"Because you're bringing the law to my *front door*," her dad says again, taking a step closer, putting himself in knee range as a dare, Jade knows.

"You shouldn't even be here right now," she tells him.

"My own house."

"Why aren't you at work, I mean? They giving Breathalyzer tests to cross the lake now?"

"Everybody go home, one of us Richie Riches bought it," her dad says like repeating an announcement, and then, so he can be the one to end this conversation, turns to the fridge, reaches in for milk, or a beer, or who cares, Jade's already stalking out, her heart thumping from anger, from fear, but mostly from what he just said: one of the Founders *bought* it?

In her bedroom she scrolls through her phone for whatever news blips she can glom onto, finally finds it out of Idaho Falls, which tracks since Proofrock doesn't exactly have its own broadcast: one of the Terra Novans has died in a "tragic accident," "stick with us," "more details as they surface."

No news on which Founding Father it is, but Jade knows it's not Theo Mondragon, anyway. She just saw him. Meaning it was one of the other four? *Are* there only five of them? Aren't there ten houses over there, meaning more moguls and tycoons coming in? But aren't they all waiting for their, you know, *homes* to be complete? This must be one of those ones who sniped in to breeze through, check on progress, be hands-on.

Still? *Letha* knows who it is. Because she's at the swirling center of it all. Because she's the focus, the star, the hero. As for Jade . . . this is what it's like to be at the periphery, she decides. She's safe, or safe-*ish*, sure, but it's like watching the story through a telescope.

Which is some bullshit for Proofrock's number one slasher fan.

Jade clamps a cap on over the greasy mess her hair is now, shrugs into her coveralls so Meg Koenig will know she's a county employee, and once it's dark enough, she shuffles down to the sheriff's office a full fourteen hours before she's due. Because she's such an eager beaver, yes.

For news.

SLASHER 101

Before I get started with this MAKE UP work for
40 PERCENT of my history grade, Mr. Holmes, let me
just say once again and in writing that a certain
Christine Gillette exclusive was NOT made up even
one little bit. Okay so there's no recording,
but that's just because I didn't have space on
my phone, but that doesn't mean she's making it
up. A broke clock is still right sometimes. But
don't worry, sir. I found another Stacey Graves
witness, surprise. I went to the most trustable
historical personage in town, if badges mean
anything.

I present now the honorable Sheriff Hardy, who
I'm transcribing FROM THE ATTACHED RECORDING, and
if the sheriff goes over the page limit then feel
free to give me extra points, I don't mind.

This is him now. You'll know me from my ALL
CAPS.

"Oh, yeah, Camp Winnemucca? Camp Winn-e-MUCC-a.
You've got to say it like that, kind of ramping
up at the end. It's an old Indian word, that's how
they talk. That's gamey stuff for a school paper
though, don't you think? Oh, wait. The 50 year
anniversary, right? You'll be, what, a senior then?
50 years, [expletive]. I was hardly even in long
pants. Don Chambers was still wearing the star.
That's Alison Chambers's dad? Didn't she teach you
all gymnastics?"

YOU CAN TELL I'M MUTING HIS CUSSING, SIR?

"Anyway, it only ran for that one summer. Nobody
had the heart to try it again after, well, [bleep],
after what happened. It was supposed to be haunted,
all that malarkey. 'We shouldn't have broke ground
over there,' blah blah blah, you know how people

are. But the name is from the Indians. Same as the
lake. My dad says when it was filling, all these
bow and arrow Indians stepped out of the trees
on the other side of the valley on their painted
ponies, feathers braided into their manes. The
horses AND the half naked bucks. They'd come to see
the creek they'd always known turn into something
bigger. That's when everybody started calling it
INDIAN Lake, not Glen Lake like it was supposed to
have been. And before you ask, no, there WEREN'T
supposed to be any Shoshone still going free range.
But Idaho's a big [bleeping] place, little miss,
pardon my French. There's like to be folks out
there haven't heard about the auto-mo-bile yet.
Any the hell way -- strike that, sorry -- I was
going to say about "Winnemucca," the word. It looks
good on a sign, don't you think? Like you're going
somewhere farther away than just across the lake.
Back into history, like. To when this was ALL
Indian land -- "

I MAY HAVE LAID SOME SLASHER LORE ON HIM HERE.
SUE ME.

"Sleepaway Camp, that's it. But yeah, that
article you found's on the money. 4 teenagers.
Let me see if I can get their names without
looking . . . Stoakes, Howarth, Walker, and . . .
TRIGO! And that's 50 years ago, little miss.
Winnemucca was a Shoshone though, bet that's
not in the article. Maybe your great great great
grandpappy could have told you that. The SNAKE
Indians, they were called back then. I don't
know that's exactly what they called themselves.
'Winnemucca' in English comes out to Bad Face.
Figure they named people different back then, don't
you?"

MY ANSWER TO THIS NOW AND ALSO IN MY HEAD THEN
WAS "YES," SIR. WAY DIFFERENT. STACEY GRAVES'S DAD
WAS "LETCH GRAVES," WHICH PRETTY MUCH SOUNDS LIKE

A BORIS KARLOFF CHARACTER ALREADY. BUT NOW WE'RE
SKIPPING AHEAD LIKE YOU SAID, FOR SALIENT DETAILS,
AND ALSO BECAUSE THIS IS SO MUCH REWINDING AND
TYPING.

"I mean, I was ONE of the camp counselors.
And I guess now I'm camp counselor for the whole
[bleepity beep] county, right? Funny how that
works. But the way they did it, each grade had
their own counselor. It was supposed to keep the
big kids from bossing the little ones around. So
none of those 4 were my watch, nosiree Bob. They
were 12, 12, 14, and 16, if I'm not mistaken. Well,
Jefferson came to camp 14, but he turned 15 the
second day of camp. That was the day we took the
canoes out. But he didn't die during that training,
just got wet. Like all of us. That was the real fun
of it. If you were wet at the end of that day, you
got your badge."

JUST SAYING, MR. HOLMES. YOU FIND ME ONE OF
THOSE BADGES AND THERE'S NEVER ANY HORROR PRANK
EVER AGAIN AT HENDERSON HIGH.

"But Jefferson Stoakes. None of us knew what to
make of . . . what can you even think, when a kid
you know turns up dead with a wasp nest not just
crammed into his mouth, but kind of in PLACE of
his mouth? And one detail Alison Chambers might
still know from her dad was that Jefferson was
floating on his BACK. In the WATER. And yellow
jackets, they'll avoid water. It gums their
wings up or something. Or maybe it's like those
baggies of water Dorothy puts up in the patio?
You know Dorothy? Dot's? You too young for coffee
yet? Give it a year. But we were all just stupid
[bleeping] kids back then too -- no insult. Now,
after Jefferson, it was . . . let's see. Howarth,
yeah. Crane Howarth. He had the prettiest goddamn
jump shot I've ever seen in real life. He just
would have sold insurance or drove a truck after

high school, I know. But watching him play, it was
-- I guess that's what people mean when they talk
about grace. He could rise up and have that ball
launched and perfect before you'd even realized
he'd stopped."

DOES THAT COUNT AS "LOCAL COLOR," SIR? SPORTSBALL
STUFF? IF NOT, THEN HOW ABOUT SOME ARCHERY.

"No, no, not arrows. It say that in that
article? No, Crane turned up at the bottom of
the bluff, must have been trying to climb it. It
was a . . . maybe don't print this next part?
Used to you'd climb the bluff, and one of your
friends would point out to everybody else that the
moon's just cresting, look how big it is, and when
everybody looked up you'd already have your pants
pulled down to show them the REAL moon -- I never
did that, though. And, after Crane, the bluff was
strictly off limits. Still should be, you ask me.
The whole place, I mean. Somebody's gonna get hurt
over there."

OR, YOU KNOW, CONCEIVED OVER THERE, MR. HOLMES.
BUT THE INTERVIEWER'S PERSONAL DETAILS AREN'T
SUPPOSED TO MATTER. I DON'T KNOW WHICH CABIN IT WAS
ANYWAY, SO CAN'T SAY THAT DETAIL. BUT I DID KNOW
THE NEXT NAME TO ASK THE SHERIFF ABOUT.

"No, it's Brockmeir, like 'brock' plus 'mayor,'
just you don't say the y-part as hard. But she
was . . . as far as we knew back then she was just
Remar Lundy's weird little niece. But I guess,
living back in the trees at their place, one of her
older cousins had maybe told her about the Lake
Witch, I don't know. And she took it to heart,
maybe. She wasn't right in the head, I'm saying. It
probably didn't help that all us junior detectives
around the campfire -- to us it was even money that
it was Stacey Graves who'd got Jefferson and Crane.
This was right after the big fire of 65, Bear teach
you about that? Good, good. Know your history,

don't [bleeping] play with matches. What I'm saying
though is that we were all kind of spooky already.
And it was kind of a thrill too, you know how it
is at camp. But yeah, before you ask, it was me
who ID'd her for Don Chambers when it was all said
and done. But that was after. I mean, that was 2
tragedies later, that's how I should say it. The
1st of those would be Anthea, Anthea Walker. She
was the 16 year old. But she was short, that's the
thing. Guess she had to be to fall into the big
cook pot. Except she didn't fall, we all knew that.
How do you fall into something you hardly even
fit in? We heard it was a dare -- that won't be in
your article there either. The story Midge and Gun
Saddleback -- they were the ones trying to make a
go of Winnemucca that summer -- the story they were
trying to get us to all buy into was that Anthea
pulled the short straw in cabin 2, so had to be the
1 to make the run down to the canteen, investigate
just what mystery meat was for lunch the next day.
But, Anthea -- we all called her Thea, kind of
like your old man's Tab -- she was friendly with
the Brockmeir girl, see? That's probably how Amy
Brockmeir was able to get behind her so close, push
her in."

BECAUSE WE HAVE TO PROVIDE CONTEXT FOR NON-
LOCALS, WHEN THE SHERIFF ABOVE SAYS THEY WERE
ALL SCARED OF THE "LAKE WITCH," THE STORY HE'S
REFERRING TO THAT YOU AND ME KNOW BUT NOBODY
NOT IN PROOFROCK KNOWS IS THAT A 100 YEARS AGO
SOME BOYS AND STACEY GRAVES THE 8 YEAR OLD WERE
PLAYING "WITCH" IN THE SHALLOWS OF THE RISING LAKE
AND THEY SWUNG HER AND THEN THREW HER OUT AS FAR
AS SHE COULD TO PROVE SHE WASN'T A WITCH, BECAUSE
WITCHES FLOAT, EVERYBODY KNOWS THAT, BUT SURPRISE,
THE WATER WOULDN'T LET HER IN, SO SHE FLOPPED
OVER ON IT, HUNCHED UP LIKE A CAT, HISSED AT THE
BOYS THROUGH HER CRAZY HAIR AND RAN AWAY ON ALL

FOURS TO THE OTHER SIDE OF THE LAKE TO FIND HER
MOM THAT HER DAD HAD PROBABLY KILLED AND HIDDEN
OVER THERE ALREADY, AND THIS IS HOW LEGENDS ARE
BORN, SIR.

"Well, yeah, that was Friday night. Saturday
night was -- [4 letter bleep] -- that was when I
saw what I saw, yeah. Which I don't know I should
be repeating, even for history. But . . . well
[same bleep]. I mean, Bear, your teacher, that's
his real name, he knows all this already. He was in
cabin 4, the 6th graders. So I guess it's okay. He
won't put this paper on the wall, I'm pretty sure."

AND HERE'S WHERE I WENT FULL GERALDO.

"You gonna believe an article by a reporter who
wasn't there or you going to buy the story of the
guy who WAS there? Nobody saw what I saw. It was
Amy Brockmeir, none of that mistaken identity bull
[bleep]. That's easy to say from the armchair, I
mean. But I was there, little miss, feet on the
ground, lump in my throat the size of a cantaloupe.
This was Saturday night, our last night there. I
don't know why we hadn't all gone home already,
with kids dying left and right. I'd got up to pee,
but the privvies, they were all the [bleeping]
way to the other side of camp. On the way over,
I rounded this 1 corner -- at first I thought it
was a badger, I guess. I can still see it, I mean.
You know how a badger, when it's eating, it kind
of bunches up in the middle, like it's humping
whatever it's eating? Strike that, don't write that
down, shouldn't have said it. But I think they eat
that way because of something to do with how their
throats are. Rolling at the spine, it forces the
food back faster than just an esophagus can."

IF YOU THINK I SAID ANYTHING ABOUT HUMAN
CENTIPEDE HERE, SIR, THEN THINK AGAIN. I DIDN'T
WANT TO STOP HIM.

"Trigo, that was her, yep. Number 4. She'd just

moved to Proofrock 2 weeks before school let out.
Her dad was the new dam keeper. This is 2 or 3
dam keepers before Jensen, who's there now. Being
the dam keeper, that's like working a lighthouse.
Don't know what her dad thought he was signing
on for. They were just over from Montana. She was
either Italian or Indian, olives or arrows, I never
knew. But you could tell she could scrap if she
had to. She had this way of looking at you, too.
I've only ever seen that look again once, across
all my years. The day my daughter was born. But
anyway, yeah -- with Stoakes it was wasps. Howarth,
a fall. Walker, a cooking pot. But now it's -- Amy
Brockmeir, she was EATING, I piss you not. And
then she looked up to me over the Trigo girl. What
was left of her, I mean. Amy's hair was matted up,
her nightgown all in rags. The lower part of her
face was all black with -- well, with what she'd
[serious bleep] been doing to the dam keeper's
daughter. I used to always imagine what if I'd ran
over, right? What if I'd tackled Amy Brockmeir
off her. She didn't die right away, either, the
-- the dam keeper's daughter. But she couldn't say
anything. Her throat was . . . it's why I was the
one who had to tell that it had been Amy Brockmeir.
That I'd seen her, that she was the only one at
camp with hair like that. The next night Mr. Trigo
locked himself in the control booth of the dam.
He was crazy with being sad, blamed himself for
bringing his daughter to this godforsaken place,
you know how it would have to be. That night the
lake came all the way up to the bank building
before Don Chambers shot out each corner of the
only window in that control booth. Lake came all
the way to that 2nd brick on the sidewalk. It was
the most amazing thing I'd ever seen, the water
sloshing up like that, to swallow us all. And when
I heard about Don Chambers shooting that glass out,

I think that was when I felt these 5 points on my
chest for the 1st time. He was Marshall Dillon, I
mean. He was Chuck Connors.

JADE WATCHES MOSTLY HORROR, THANKS.

"Before your time, before your time. And yeah,
that article's right about Amy Brockmeir. She ate
her blanket in the state hospital. I hear they
pulled 2 feet of it up her throat. Ask me, that
proves it. But, like I was saying, all we'd been
saying around the fire all week was 'Lake Witch,'
'Lake Witch,' so that was where my head went at
1st. Which is why I didn't run tackle her off that
Trigo girl. But [bleep], I was 11, and had, well,
had HAD a full bladder, right? [Bleep] straight I
got up on my getaway sticks, made for the water.
That was the 1 place we knew Stacey Graves couldn't
go, because of Ezekiel's holy singing being already
under there, and his tolerance for witches being so
famously low, so that was where I hid, and I never
looked around, kept my face down as long as I could
hold my breath, and maybe a little longer than that
even, but all that meant was that in my head I had
to see her scratching and clawing at the surface
of the water right over my back, not able to reach
into it. But like I say, I was 11. Stacey Graves
was just a story to get us home before dark. What's
worse in the real world are messed up kids like
Amy Brockmeir. Sorry to burst your bubble about the
Lake Witch, there, little miss. [bleep]. This badge
means I have to traffic with evidence, though, not
urban legend. And remember, eyewitness testimony
is only as good as the head behind those eyes, and
I was just a kid then, only 11. But Don Chambers
explained what I'd seen to me, and it made sense
the way he said it back, going slow through it so
I could hear it was important. When I heard him
telling my story back to me, I mean, even I could
hear it for the campfire story it was. There were

some facts in it he could use, though, like the
crazy hair, the nightgown, and he used them to keep
us all safe, and that was it for Camp Winnemucca.
It's for the best, too. Bad memories over there."

    "BAD" IS A RELATIVE TERM, SIR.

    "You look like him, you sick of hearing that?
Something around the eyes, there."

    AND YOU WONDER WHY I WEAR SO MUCH EYELINER.

    "Yeah, yeah, I caught that. Guess the newspaper
didn't nail down just every detail, did they? Her
dad's name was Trigo, and of course hers was too,
and that's what everybody called her, I guess
because that's how Miss Spellman read her name
from the roll that first day. But her front name,
her first name . . . it was Melanie. Her name was
Melanie."

    WHICH IS A PRETTY NAME, SIR.

    A VERY PRETTY NAME.

DON'T GO IN
THE WOODS

In *A Nightmare on Elm Street*, Nancy's dad is a homicide detective, so she has pretty much unfettered access to the whole station, can waltz in and treat all the uniformed cops like Tatum treats Dewey, and they just have to fumble their papers and let her pass by.

Jade is no Nancy.

Meg stops Jade at her big L-shaped desk, which is pretty much the reception desk, won't let her back into the hall that leads to Hardy's office, to Records, to the Evidence closet, to the two holding cells, and to the only room Jade has access to, once every two weeks: Janitorial Supplies.

"Community service," Jade explains, trying hard to sound as unenthused as possible, like there's twenty other places she'd rather be right now.

"Community what, dear?" Meg asks, followed up by two quick bats of her fake eyelashes.

"For . . . you know," Jade says, and rolls the left arm of her coveralls up to show her angry scar that, earlier—oops—she'd drawn centipede legs coming off of, like suicide is a bug she can pass with a handshake.

Meg sucks air in through her teeth, has to look away fast. Jade can still hear her daughter Tiff throwing up in the tall grass. Like mother like daughter.

"He said you might have some filing for me," Jade explains, using her pleasant voice.

"During working hours maybe," Meg explains right back with just as much false cheer.

"*You're* here."

"Special circumstances."

"I can't go home right now," Jade says, covering the rest of *that* particular story with a "don't want to talk about it" shrug, a purposeful breaking of eye contact that can only mean it'll crack her tough-girl façade if she has to go any further into this.

Meg bites her top lip in then rotates halfway around in her chair, tapping the plastic button of her pen on the front of her top teeth, which Jade takes as a strong reminder not to chew on any pens in this office.

"Why *is* everyone here?" Jade's not physically able to keep from asking after a few slower and slower tooth taps. "Somebody die, what?"

Meg doesn't twitch a single muscle on her face, just keeps looking around for a menial enough chore. One someone with zero clearance can do, someone with *negative* clearance, which is to say: this one's got sticky fingers, hungry eyes, and a bone to pick with authority. Only trust her as far as you can throw her, and keep in mind that you don't have any arms.

"You wore your *other* work clothes," Meg says, holding the back of her index finger under her nose so Jade gets the drift.

"Laundry day," Jade tells her. Or, challenges her with.

"Are you presentable under them?"

"What do you—?"

"Do you have other clothes on?"

"What's wrong with being a janitor?"

"Too many pockets," Meg says, staring right into Jade's soul, "too roomy. An enterprising seventeen-year-old could smuggle a coatrack out in that."

Jade stands and slowly unzips, holding Meg's eyes the whole while. She steps out of the coveralls, rolls them into a ball, sets that ball on Meg's desk, careful not to disturb all the inboxes and trays and pencil holders.

What she's wearing now—what Meg can *see* now—is a shirt with a Raymond Pettibon gig poster silkscreen of a bare-breasted dead woman named Janie, and Janie's friend asking Jesus, also pictured, about why, if he's Christ, why oh why won't he raise Janie?

Meg's lips tighten with disapproval.

"I can put them back on," Jade says, taking a seat, slouching down in it like the criminal she is, "but who knows, I might steal all the staplers. Get a pretty good price for them on the street. Kids these days can't get enough office supplies, I'm sure Tiff's told you."

"You can stuff envelopes is what you can do," Meg says, standing with purpose, her posture prim and schoolmarmish.

"I live to serve," Jade says, and hauls her ashes up, follows Meg . . . all the long way to the next desk over?

"So I can keep an eye on you," Meg informs her.

"Wouldn't have it any other way," Jade says, and starts to take a seat in the empty rolling chair but Meg's already rolling it away, replacing it with a battered stool.

"Helps with posture," Meg says, reaching around behind Jade like to straighten her up but not going so far into legally fraught territory as to actually touch the temporary employee.

Jade allows her posture to be improved, straddles the little stool, and takes the envelopes and flyers Meg provides, enduring her walk-through as well: proper method, desired results, blah,

blah. The flyers are pale green, are for some referendum to restrict the airspace over Proofrock.

Hilarious.

"Sorry, Sherlock," she says, and licks envelope number one, starts her stack of done-withs, pulls up the second flyer in desperate need of a careful crease.

For the first forty or so of them, Meg watches, harrumphing at Jade's more sloppy attempts, humming conditional approval over the better ones. The sun goes down and the overhead lights become more important. Phones ring and radios hiss, feet scuffle, and Jade's shoe-polished hair, she has to admit, *is* letting off an acrid scent that she thinks might be either getting her high or dollying her up to some ledge she's meant to tumble off.

At the hundred and fourteen mark she nods forward, her forehead resting on the top of the desk for just a moment's peace, but Meg clears her throat in a wake-up way and Jade startles, leans back into it.

"How many hours is this so far?" she asks.

"You keep your own time," Meg says. "We'll just hope it matches the time sheet I turn in to the sheriff."

"Wonderful," Jade says, and accidentally-on-super-purpose rips the flyer she's trying so hard to fold just right.

"Recycling," Meg tells her, directing Jade to the bin across the room, by the copy machine—same model as the library's, probably the same purchase order—and by the time Jade shuffles back she knows it's not worth the pleasure of wasting paper if it means she has to get up each time to do it. Her back does feel better, though. Maybe stools aren't as evil as she'd always thought.

"What *is* that smell?" Meg asks minutes or hours later, interrupting whichever reverie Jade's jellyfishing through. "Did you spill gas on your . . ." She jabs the rolled coveralls with the button of her pen.

"I don't drive," Jade tells her, voice creaky at first. "And they don't trust me with the lawnmowers."

"Probably a wise precaution," Meg says as if to herself, and turns to some task on her computer.

A hundred and thirty stuffed envelopes later, the fourth pile of them teetering in most dangerous fashion, Hardy steps in as if through the batwing doors of a saloon.

"Megan, I need you to—" he starts, is stopped just as fast by Jade's presence.

"Sheriff," she says, repaying the jumpscare he gave her last night.

"What you doing here?" he asks.

"Community service?" Jade asks right back.

"She's stuffing envelopes, sir," Meg says, looking up over her glasses to show Hardy that he's making a nuisance of himself in the front office, when his job is obviously *not* the front office.

"I see, okay, okay," he says, rubbing his nose with the back of his hand, his six-hours-old five o'clock shadow raspy and loud against the stiff cuff of his shirt.

"Is everything . . . ?" Meg asks, completing the sentence with her eyes.

"Staties are here," Hardy says with a shrug, like he didn't want the dead-Founder case anyway. To show how all right he is with it, he hangs his brown coat on the *un*stolen coatrack, puts his flat-brimmed official hat on top of that, and then swings his belt off, crashes it down on a lateral filing cabinet hard enough that Jade expects the service revolver to fire into her gut.

"You don't have to stay," Hardy says to Meg. "Gonna be a long night."

"And miss all the excitement?" Meg says back with a grin.

"Don't know what I'd do without you," Hardy tells her, and, passing by her desk, works something stubby and black up from his shirt pocket, deposits it in a wire-screen pencil holder on Meg's desk, tapping the lip of the pencil holder twice.

"If anybody calls—" Hardy starts, "Route them through Dispatch," Meg finishes. "And then tell you who they are, of course."

"My Girl Friday," Hardy says, sweeping past.

Jade has no idea what kind of pornographic pet name that might be, and doesn't think she wants to know.

Hardy stops at the hall, loosening the brown tie she's only now realizing he's got on.

"You were supposed to start tomorrow," he tells her, his voice booming through the station.

"Early bird gets the maggot," Jade says, flashing an evil smile.

"Eat what you will, eat what you will . . ." Hardy says in farewell, fading down the hall, still working on his tie.

"Very proper for a young lady," Meg tells Jade without having to look over to say it.

"I'm a woman, hear me roar," Jade says back, and licks the next envelope with as much attitude as she can pack into it, imagining her tongue lacerated by a thousand cuts, her teeth coating in blood.

An hour later Jade's on stack seven of infinity, and every time she looks up, her vision is stained pale green. The corner in the wall over by the copy machine is actually a giant fold in-process, and Jade, inside that white envelope, has checkboxes for eyes. The stool she's stuck on has a sticky surface some greater tongue has already licked. Meg is a greasy black hair that's fallen into the works to mess everything up, one Jade can't quite pinch up or flick away.

She raises her hand and Meg calls on her.

"Yes?"

"Bathroom?"

"Complete sentence, please?"

"May I visit the single stall women's restroom whose toilet I know better than I want to already?" Jade says with full-on defeat. "The one I've been scrubbing already for the past—"

Meg chaperones her down the hall.

"Receptionista *and* ladies' room attendant," Jade says. "This is a full-service station, isn't it?"

"Feel free to wiggle out the window in there," Meg says. "It's rusted open."

"The night is an embryo . . ." Jade says, leaning in. Washing her hands, she catches a flash of herself in the mirror. "Nightmare Girl to the rescue," she says, "up up and—"

Meg escorts her back to her station that feels like a cell, in the town that's definitely a prison.

This is such a great plan for glomming onto information about whatever happened in Terra Nova, yes. But, on the sulky way past Meg's desk, Jade does at least clock that wire-screen pencil holder that Hardy deposited *some*thing into: TRANSCRIPTIONS.

Well well well.

"There anything else I can do instead?" Jade whines to Meg.

"When you're done with the referendums you can apply postage, yes," Meg says, her eyes holding on to Jade's, maybe to see her flinch.

"More licking, yay," Jade says, and takes her stool.

For the next two stacks she imagines going fast enough that she sweats, fast enough that she can rub the tacky backside of the eventual stamps into her swampy armpits before applying them to the envelopes.

Get your entertainment where you can find it, right?

For now Jade has to make do with the grey smudges her stained fingers are still leaving on the pristine white envelopes, which she guesses will make the people of Proofrock aware these are hand-stuffed, not machine-.

Like that matters. Like any of this does.

This time when Jade lowers her forehead to the desktop for just a moment's escape, she forgets that she's awake, so that when she comes to, she's all alone in the front office, like she's been sucked into some Freddyfied version of where she just was.

She looks to the doorway for a bleating lamb, to the other doorway for a bodybag sliding away, and then to the water cooler, to see if it's just water in there.

It is. For now.

Jade taps her right foot on the ground, testing it.

Not oatmeal. Same old floor.

Maybe this *isn't* a dream. Meaning . . . meaning Meg didn't wake her this time? Jade dials her hearing up, can just make out Hardy in lecture mode in his office, Meg's attentive burble filling in the empty spaces, and some quiet stretches between the two of them that's probably some official on speakerphone.

When Jade tries to glide over to the Important Pencil Holder on Meg's desk, she finds, moments too late, that her legs are asleep, so it's more of a stumbling lurch, one that dislodges an inbox of metal-case clipboards, sends them sailing over the edge.

Jade dive-falls, just keeps them from rattling to the floor.

She sets them gently back in their place, checks the hall again because Meg can appear at any moment, and then she's in Meg's chair, is fumbling for the digital recorder Hardy dropped in the pencil holder.

It smells like his breath, plugs into Meg's computer like it *knows* that socket, confirming for Jade whatever "Girl Friday" means. And now, of course—of *course*—Hardy's voice in his office is doing that rising thing that denotes the end of whatever session this is for him and Meg and the caller.

"Shit shit shit," Jade whispers, and jabs a tab open in Meg's browser, dials her school email up *and* logs in, jacking the password up not just once but two times, the warning flashing that one more failed attempt and she'll be locked out until tomorrow.

Making herself go slow, she enters the letters of "Haddonfield" backwards, replacing the vowels with symbols and numbers.

Her inbox pops on-screen.

She drags the only file off the digital recorder into a new message right as the door closes down the hall, Meg's shoes approaching at a painfully brisk clip. But the file isn't loaded yet, is too big, shit shit shit.

Jade sends it anyway, which at least minimizes that guilty window, and, making herself wait long enough that the file *might* have had long enough to get sent, she guides the digital recorder out of its socket—X'ing out the DEVICE REMOVED WITHOUT EJECTING error pop-up—sliding it over, over, over . . .

She can't lift her hand to get it over the metal lip of the wire-screen pencil holder, the TRANSCRIPTIONS to-do box. Not without announcing what she's just been doing.

Is this it, then? Is this where she gets busted, hauled into the place she already is, her mask ripped off?

Not if it doesn't have to be.

Not before she hears that recording, anyway.

Because she can't give herself away by raising the hand she has turtled over the recorder, she leaves it there beside the pencil holder and slumps forward as if exhausted, trying hard to sell that this is just where her hand got to *unintentionally*, ma'am, sir. Meg.

"And what are we doing here?" Meg asks, suddenly just there.

Jade fake-flinches, "roused" from a cat-nap on the clock.

What her mouse hand has opened just on reflex is the last email from Mr. Holmes. It's still the top message in her inbox. And now that it's open, it could have just been new.

"Just," Jade gulps, calling on her inner Billy, her inner Stu, finally saying, "Mr. Holmes." She leans back, holds her hand out, presenting the email for Meg to see. "My dad doesn't believe in internet," she adds, cringing from having to play a card this needy.

Meg just scans the email. It's about certain liberties she took with the bibliography of her last make-up paper, the biggest of those liberties being that there wasn't a bibliography.

"I'm . . ." Jade starts, starts again, fully aware she's the only one speaking here: "Ask Sheriff Hardy. It's a late paper he wanted me to still submit."

"The sheriff?"

"Mr. Holmes. For history class."

"Which you already graduated from."

"It's complicated."

"That part I do believe," Meg says, scooching in but not yet displacing Jade, a proximity Jade overplays her reaction to, jerking her left arm—and *hand*—such that that wire-screen pencil holder goes tumbling off the edge of the desk, the digital recorder swan-diving in right after it.

"Shit, shit, sorry," Jade says, standing so that Meg's rolling chair rattles back against a file cabinet.

"This is why we should all stay at our own stations," Meg tsk-tsks, collecting the scattered objects as if they're nothing. She holds up the recorder, though, says, "If this doesn't work . . ."

Jade nods, playing guilty. For just and only that, nothing else.

"Go on then," Meg says about the still-open email on her screen. "I don't want to stand in the way of academic progress. Reply. I'm sure teachers in the summer live for messages from students. Especially retired teachers."

Jade positions her fingers at the keyboard version of ten and two, makes her email as short as she can: *Just finished it this morning, will send it tomorrow by noon. doc or pdf?*

She sends it with a flourish, like tapping the final ivory key of a piano performance, and in getting that fancy, she manages to accidentally open the file already attached higher in that thread. For a bad moment she's sure Hardy's mumbled voice is going to come through Meg's speakers, but then the computer's two-bytes are just rubbing together in their digital way to open the word processor around this document.

"He wants hard copy too?" Meg asks, probably because, being Tiff's mom, she knows Mr. Holmes prefers paper over digital. Probably so he can stand outside and smoke while grading.

"Do you mind?" Jade asks.

Meg motions for Jade to continue being the burden she already is, so Jade hits print, and—*shit shit shit*, that's right. This is one of her lists, could be either giallos in order of descending title length or "Actors Whose First Role Was in a Slasher"!

Neither are her best side, she's pretty sure.

The printer spools up high, higher, and then starts spitting out not a single page, which would be the stack of giallos, but the three- or four-pager, with Tom Hanks and George Clooney, Jennifer Aniston and Daphne Zuniga probably so prominent that no way can Meg not say something about them.

Meg, reading a memo, wanders over, plucks the stack-so-far up, and gives it a cursory scan.

"Johnny Depp?" she says to Jade.

"Nightmare on My Street," Jade mumbles, sucking her top lip in.

Meg breathes in deep, blows it out slow, and walks the pages over to Jade, says, "Using office supplies costs fifteen minutes on your time card."

"Thank you," Jade says, and logs out of the computer much more carefully, spins around in her chair like a real long-time county employee, her coveralls magically in her lap already.

"And he is cute, I'll give him that," Meg calls after her.

Jade looks back, *He?* evidently painted on her face.

"Johnny Depp," Meg says, complete with playful eyebrows. "I used to have a poster of him on my wall."

"Brad Pitt was in *Cutting Class*," Jade throws out there.

Meg considers this, finally seems to decide she's not sure they're each in the same conversation, so ends it with, "It's between you and him of course. Mr. Holmes, I mean."

"And the school district," Jade adds, rolling her list of slasher debuts into a tube and popping it on the end, which is Meg's cue to usher her the rest of the way out of the front office, apparently.

"Has it been twelve hours already?" Jade play-asks, electing to push the door open before her rather than have her face smushed into it.

"Just wait," Meg says, sweeping the problem Jade is from her office. "When you're my age, you'd pay anything to have these hours back."

Jade chocks her coveralls under her arm with the roll of pages, and, maybe fifteen steps from the building, all her attention pouring into her phone, waiting for this sound file to load from her email, she hears the single worst possible sound to hear: a lamb, bleating from the darkness to her immediate right.

Jade gasps and gulps in the same instant somehow, which sends her coughing, ends with her bent over, hands on her knees so she can dry-heave.

The bleat comes again, maybe a touch slower this time, as if aware of the response it's provoking.

Her eyes adjusting to the night now, Jade can just make out a shape stepping forward out of the gathered shadows, and, because she is who she is and knows what she knows, she'd bet her last breath—which she just coughed up, pretty much—that that shadowy figure's about to go bandy-legged, its arms stretching out farther and farther from its sides, until the knives-for-fingers on the right hand can scratch into a wall, a tree, her throat, it doesn't matter.

"Whoah, whoah," this Freddy says, though.

Bit by bit, Jade assembles this voice into one she's known since kindergarten.

"Banner?" she says. Banner Tompkins?

He steps forward, flipping the hourglass in his hand, which . . . isn't an hourglass at all. It's a deer-call, one of those little cans with some air-driven mechanism inside that bleats out a deer call when you turn it over.

And—and Banner, he's got a rifle slung over his shoulder, warpaint under his eyes, hunting pants tucked into his boots.

"Jade," he says back, and then they both look up when the world goes halogen-white: two pickups screeching in, the lead truck hiking a front tire up onto the grass. The beds of both trucks are lined with more hunters.

"What?" Jade says, just in general.

"Bye now," Banner says, and touches the brim of his straw cowboy hat, vaults up into the bed of the lead truck, which is already peeling out.

"Who?" Jade says then, because her first question was so effective.

She steps out of the way for the trucks to barrel past, and the grim faces of all these high school graduates and their dads sitting across from each other in the beds, the butts of their rifles riding their knees, long barrels tilting into the sky—they're soldiers, aren't they? This is some kind of war.

Against what? The deer?

The last face Jade sees is Lee Scanlon's. He's looking back, his free hand clamped tight on the tailgate, his lips pressed together, his eyes for all the world pleading with her, as if he's being abducted, just needs someone to say something about it.

Jade tracks the taillights until they make a turn just short of the highway, to the right. Where there's only logging roads that all bottleneck at the Old Bridge, two miles down the creek. The bridge that only leads to . . .

Caribou-Targhee National Forest, on the other side of the lake.

"*Jaws*," Jade says at last, like making a late identification of those two trucks. This is that comic relief scene in *Jaws*, where all the boats are vying for space in the water so can they be the ones to haul the killer shark back to Amity Island.

It's not so funny in real life, though. That look in Lee Scanlon's eyes for the half-second Jade saw him, it was fear, one hundred percent. Not that there's any sharks up here in the mountains. And not like any motley crew of villagers ever actually kills the slasher—looking at you, *Halloween 4*.

Jade remembers that massacred herd of elk over in Sheep's Head Meadow on the other side of the lake, though. And elk are way tougher than people are.

For a moment she considers ducking back into the sheriff's office to have Meg pass word on to Hardy that strange things are afoot at this particular Circle K. Things that could get people hurt.

But, too, a slasher's gonna do what it's gonna do, right? You can't stop wheels this big and timeless from turning, from grinding over who they need to grind over. All you can do is keep your eye on the sky, for if one of those wheels is rolling at you.

Jade thumbs her earbuds in right then left, wobbles her head to make sure the cable's free enough, and Hardy's already droning through them at a steady mumble.

"—the one who looked like a young George Peppard, that one? Or's he too old for you, Megan?"

Jade sneaks a look behind her to be sure she's alone. With Hardy whispering right in her ear, she doesn't feel very alone. She does most definitely clock Hardy's use of past tense, though. Whoever he talked about *looked*, not "looks." Ding ding ding, give the man a headstone, he's dead.

No clue on "George Peppard," though she likes the way Hardy rides that last syllable. It makes her want to say it herself, except of course he's not waiting for her, is just droning on. Fast-fast, she pauses his dictation, image-searches "George Peppard," and, holy shit, Hardy was right: that *is* one of the Founders, right down to the rakish smile, the hair, the softness at the edges that means money.

Deacon Samuels.

To be sure-sure, Jade searches him up as well, tabs back and forth from Peppard, and, yep, it's like she did the same search twice.

Point for Hardy.

"Thank you, sir," she says to him, and unpauses his voice.

"He didn't exactly have permission, no, strike that, strike that, delete. I mean, I'd given him a warning already, that better? Yeah, looked like someone was shooting a Roman candle over there, just poof, poof, poof, these orange fizzing balls arcing up from the old camp, sizzling down into the lake."

"That was you, then," Jade says to Deacon Samuels, looking up as if she can see all the way to Camp Blood from here. But, if the Terra Novans are the ones using the old campground as a place to shoot fireworks off now, then where are the kids from Proofrock supposed to hook up, drink? More important for Jade: where's she supposed to hide out for a night or two when she needs a place?

"But it wasn't fireworks," Hardy's going on, talking quieter now, as if he's hiding under the monkey bars at recess. "He was— get this—he had a bucket of gas right there by him, in this little tee box where he'd cut the grass down so it wouldn't wrap the head of his driver up on the way down. A tee box is like, shit—sorry, sorry. It's like a batter's box had a baby with a putting green? That help? Anyway, what he was doing . . . I got to get the order down here, else his ass'll blow up instead of—but I'm getting to that.

"So he had good expensive balls down in that gas, Dixon *Fires*, no joke, and then he had a lit candle maybe four feet away—about as far as he could reach while keeping his feet planted, same position every time, so he could know what to adjust. You know what I'm talking about, Don plays, you've seen him swing into that net he sets up in his front yard. Anyway, what Samuels would do is dunk the head of his driver into that bucket of gas—and, no lying, it was a *Maruman*, Megan, hand-crafted out of Japan, by families who probably, I don't know, make samurai swords? And these are just as deadly. One of them would pay for *two* of my trucks, for half of my house probably, and he's dipping the head in gasoline! And, if anybody asks, that driver's in Evidence now. But let's hope nobody asks. You know how tags fall off sometimes, stuff gets lost. Small town, don't have the manpower to keep up with everything. It's still a good club, I mean, might get me ten yards farther, out of the rough for good. We're about the same height, me and Samuels. Or, we were. But I'm getting ahead of myself, sorry, sorry.

"Anyway, he'd fish down in that gas bucket with the head of his driver, and he'd come up with a dripping ball balanced right perfect on it, deadcenter on that logo, and then, no lie, he'd dribble it up and down just like a paddle ball, just like Tiger, except with a *driver*, not a sand wedge, which has that flat landing pad on top, not a humped back. Something to see, believe you me. When I puttered over there the first time, it about hypnotized me, that. I thought I was maybe in a commercial. That he was about to make me famous.

"Then though, he'd get that little Dixon going good and bounce it hard once, so it'd go up a touch over head-height, and he'd use that time to pass the head of that driver through the flame of the candle, and it would poof orange but wouldn't break his rhythm enough that he couldn't catch the ball when it came down.

"Still with me on this? Now the head of that Maruman's lit, sparking, and the ball catches fire too, is just going up and down, up and down. That first time I was over there, I expected to keep sneaking looks over at cabin five like always, you know, your dad probably told you about that, but anyway, shit, sorry, then I couldn't stop myself smiling over his little trick. You know he's on the cover of golfing magazines, right, this Deacon Samuels? Well, it's not because of his real estate. Some people just have it. Or, had it, yeah.

"Anyway, just like Tiger then, he'd dribble, dribble, becoming like one with the ball—Chevy Chase, you know that movie? Forget it. Before your time as well. But Samuels would bounce, bounce, his knees starting to go up and down with the ball, like, and then he'd draw the Maruman back and he'd slash it forward with the prettiest stroke you've ever seen, I promise, making that perfect little knock, and he'd hold the follow-through too, hold it in a way that told me he'd played some baseball as a kid, wasn't only a golfer.

"And that ball, Meg, hot damn. There'd be a crush of sparks each time he did it, each time he slapped it with the head of that driver, and then it would launch up *out* of that, arc high out over the lake like a meteor, and then plunk down into Ezekiel's Cold Box with all the other balls he'd already been hitting.

"I couldn't ticket him up for something that beautiful, Meg. Or for burying treasure like a whole bucket of Dixon Fires out there either—oh, shit, just hearing that, a Dixon Fire is *on* fire. But don't include that in the write-up. Just what we need. 'Sheriff shows favoritism to rich residents on other side of lake, can evidently be bought,' no thanks. I did warn him, though. And, if he let me hit any balls into the lake, then, well. Let's just say he didn't and leave it at that?"

Jade turns the corner by the drugstore, her shadow leaking out ahead of her from one of the two streetlights the bank had installed next door to protect its ATM. Because Proofrock is full-to-bursting with kid John Connors, yeah. Important, too, there's no golf course in all of Pleasant Valley. Even if there was, though, what Jade doesn't know about golf would still fill all of Indian Lake. All the same, though, her heart does kind of swell, watching those flaming balls arc out over the dark water and hang, hang.

Which is exactly how easy it would be to fall in love with rich people. With Terra Nova.

Mr. Holmes is right, one hundred percent.

And he's lucky one of those golf ball meteors never burned through the silk of his wings while he was up there, Jade supposes. But, not like he's not flying with a *lit cigarette*, either. And, now that Jade thinks about it, just who *was* it who called these fireworks in, and who in maybe-return for that warning asked for that airspace referendum?

She nods in solidarity with Mr. Holmes, bumps the dictation back twenty seconds and adjusts her left earbud, doesn't want to miss a word.

"*Any* the hell way, you can take it to the fucking bank that that's what Samuels was doing over there when he got his ass killed. The bucket was there, still sloshing with unleaded. The club was there in the tall grass, waiting to get tagged and bagged. The candle he'd been using was burned down, somehow managed not to light the whole damn valley up. No witnesses, of course. But it was that Mondragon girl that found him, you know the one—oldest of them all? *Black?* Looks like a model from a magazine?"

Jade makes a fist, shakes it. Of *course* Letha found the next victim. Final girls have an unerring sense, are forever stumbling on eviscerated bodies, decapitated heads. Each one is a stepping stone to who she's about to become.

"She says she went out there when the fireballs stopped happening. She made the two girls she was sitting on the dock with . . . let's see, I wrote them down. Yeah, the Baker twins, I guess the Bakers left them there for the week or something. Or maybe Samuels trucked them in when he breezed into town, they don't tell me anything. But, so the Mondragon girl, she made . . . yeah, 'Cinn' and 'Ginger,' that's it, those Baker girls, she made them stay there while she went to see if Samuels had blown himself up, was flopping in the lake trying to douse the flames. She didn't say 'flopping,' though, maybe make a note of that. And I take it 'Cinn,' which she spelled for me, is for 'Cinnamon.' It's not like they're real witnesses.

"Anyway, the Mondragon girl beats feet over there, it's only fifteen minutes if you hug the shore, even in the dark, and . . . she's probably going to need some therapy, Megan. Good thing her dad can afford it, right? Samuels, he was . . . I don't want to paint the picture in your head . . . let's just say that that bodybag I keep tucked in the boat, that I might or might not ice down for beers for the Fourth? It wouldn't do the trick. Had to ask the Mondragon wife, Queenie or whatever, to go into the kitchen of that big yacht, fetch us back some sandwich-size ziplock bags. It was while I was standing around waiting for them, taking a trip down memory lane, cabin five kind of pulsing in my vision, when I saw what was right before my goddamn eyes, Megan.

"A bear print, clear as day and twice as big, I tell you. Because the mud was wet, there were even claws scratched into the ground two or three inches past the pads of the feet. A big-ass boar, I mean, and, judging by Samuels's, um, condition, a pretty unhappy one. Rex Allen tried to make a joke about Smokey the Bear just doing his job, open flame and all, but I shut that down quick, got on the horn to the ranger station.

"Time their man got here—I'm talking about Seth Mullins here, that's two L's—they'd decided to let me in on the little secret that they've had a trash grizzly causing problems over towards the Wyoming line. These are those bears that start to like human food a little too much. And, know what? Right there in Samuels's golf bag was a paper sack of some sort of pastries. Smelled them before I saw them, you know how I am when there's a donut in the room.

"Anyway, I know it can get kind of stale around these parts, that a little mystery might juice things up nice-like, but all we ended up with, aside from a man getting stuffed in sandwich bags, was about five minutes of mystery, or however long it took me to walk from the remains over to the bear print.

"Only other tracks for the staties to find with their fancy degrees and thousand-dollar equipment were ours, and then the Mondragon girl left some bare feet tracks I guess, that's 'bare' as in no shoes, not 'bear' as in . . . you get it. So, not counting all the tracks we could account for, and taking into account the one track from a bear we now knew was a problem case for the federal Forest Service—police work really isn't that hard, is it, Meggie? Hard part's—"

Jade pulls the earbuds down, has to lean over she's breathing so deep.

So Banner Tompkins and Lee Scanlon and the rest of them are out after a rogue *bear*, then. A killer bear. A verified monster. "*Grizzly*, 1976, Alex," she manages to dredge up, spit out. "Sometimes called a slasher with a bear, but really just *Jaws* on land, minus Quint." Which is minus everything.

Still.

If it had been a Proofrocker getting portioned up for the freezer here, Jade would know that the prank that woke this slasher was some crime twenty years ago, maybe even Melanie Hardy's drowning, which would probably put Jade's dad on the victim list, which would be just fine, thank you.

What does it mean that an untouchable Founder had been killed, though? And, not just killed, but killed in a way that a bear could be framed? How long had it taken whoever was doing this to lure a *bear* in to cover their tracks?

More important, why? Is this some townie with a chip on his shoulder about who was pulling good hours at the construction site, who wasn't? Is Terra Nova messing up the back porch vista a certain someone had been counting on staring into for retirement? If so—if either of those—then why now instead of months ago? Had it been last night because whoever it was knew Deacon Samuels would be out there alone, since he'd been alone out there before?

"Who are you?" Jade says to Indian Lake.

It's a good reflective moment, and she's milking it for all the drama it's worth when her phone rings in her hand and she fumbles it away, drops her coveralls, tangles her feet in them and falls, her pages unrolling every which way at once, her elbow scraping on the asphalt so she can answer the phone with a sharp "*What* already?"

At first, nothing. Then, timidly, "Um, I think I know you from, from the ladies' r—"

"You got the package," Jade says, rolling over onto her back, the wash of stars opening up above her. "You found the—the . . . you found them both. The kid in the lake. The Foun—Deacon Samuels. You know it's really happening."

Again, silence.

"Do you need those pants back?" Letha Mondragon asks in a way that Jade can see her mouth, kind of smiling.

"There's so much I need to tell you," Jade says. "I'll be your . . . what's that Pinocchio dude called, with the love letters?"

"Cyrano de Bergerac?"

"Like, together, my knowledge, what I know, mixed with your . . . your everything."

"What are you saying?"

"Something's coming is what I'm saying. It's already here is what I'm saying. You've seen it yourself, the proof anyway."

Letha doesn't respond to this.

Jade goes on: "I didn't know it was going to cross the lake for . . . for Terra Nova, though. I'm sorry."

"I have so many questions."

"I'm the girl made of answers."

"The bench," Letha Mondragon says, and it takes Jade a moment to reel through all the benches in Proofrock, finally settle on the only one that could be considered the main one: Melanie Hardy's memorial bench by the water, just up from the pier. To Letha, arriving by *Umiak* every morning for school last semester, it's probably the only bench.

"Out in the open, good, good," Jade says. "You don't know if you can trust me yet. You've got to be careful, I might be the one doing all this. Shit, I should have thought of that."

"My dad says—"

"Parents in slashers are either drunks or they want to put bars on your bedroom windows. Sometimes both."

Letha breathes in and out, is maybe about to cry, here.

Jade is looking across the lake at the yacht, back at its mooring.

"It wasn't a bear," Jade says at last. "I think you know that, don't you?"

"Somebody pinched the candle out," Letha says, quieter, like this is just for Jade.

"It didn't just blow out?" Jade asks back.

Letha doesn't answer, and in that silence Jade stands and spins around, silently cussing at herself: whose side is she on here? Not her own, evidently.

"Never mind," she adds.

"Okay," Letha says back timidly.

Jade takes a step closer to the water, then another step, is standing in it up to her shins now, her printed-out pages floating around her.

"That candle being out could mean it's somebody from over here," she says, quiet as well now. "We've all been trained on not burning down the national forest since kindergarten."

"Then—"

"But nobody over there would want to burn down their new house, either," Jade says. "And . . . did the sheriff ask if you were wearing shoes when you—you . . . ?"

"He didn't ask," Letha says with barely enough air to activate her larynx.

"We can't do this over the phone," Jade tells her.

"Three o'clock?"

Jade counters with lunch, which she can sacrifice for this. A thousand lunches, even. All the lunches she has left.

"Which light is yours?" she asks then.

In reply, one of the thirty or so glowing windows over there blackens, then comes back.

"Noon," Letha says, confirming it.

Jade nods, hangs up without a goodbye, holding the warm face of the phone to her chest, her feet not even cold in the water. She tells the Mr. Holmes in her head that she's not falling in love with Terra Nova, sir, don't worry.

Not all of it, anyway.

SLASHER 101

So okay I know I said this sequel or part 2 of my 2
parter extra credit paper would get here, and here
it is, after what I guess we can call the Interview
Project Meat Grinder. But if "Soul Crusher" works
better then cool. I am still barely a sophomore
though anyway, so there's that. And it's lucky I am
too, since whoever it was that made a Leatherface
mask for themselves out of edible panties from the
truck stop and then ran down the hall doing boogity
boogity hands at everybody didn't escape down the
sophomore hall, but the JUNIOR hall, meaning it was
most definitely and undoubtedly for sure a junior.
And I might add that all so called evidence should
be edible.

But part 2 -- masks and cameras, which means
going to Italy.

While Psycho was getting its success and formula
ripped off all during the 60s, which I'm sure you
remember first hand, there was another tradition
cooking in the red sauce over in Italy's boot heel,
or maybe the leg part, this isn't Geography. I'm
talking about the Giallo, sir, which is a word that
means yellow and a name that means "trashy movie
with a bodycount." As you can tell, a Giallo is
like a proto slasher. It is to the slasher what
dinosaurs are to birds.

Why the Giallo is super important is that
it's where the camera technique was born that's
basically what Carpenter would do in 1978 for
Halloween. Killers in Giallos don't wear masks I
mean, sir. Or, they do wear masks, but they're HAND
masks. What's a hand mask you ask? That would be
a . . . GLOVE. Killers in Giallos all wear these
black gloves. Those gloves are like that Father

Death robe in _Scream_. They hide gender and race
and body type and marriage status and tattoos and
finger count and also knuckle hairiness, Pamela
Voorhees, ha ha. But the camera in the Giallo is
always looking down AT those gloves doing their
bloody work. And because everything is limited to
what those killer eyes can see, black gloves are
all the disguise that's needed to keep an identity
hidden as setup for the Reveal.

So to conclude already so soon, what was black
gloves in the groovy 60s became through John
Carpenter's director camera MASK eyeholes to look
through in the 70s, which is what we in Slasher
Studies call "SlasherCam," which for example
is Billy's starting out Point of View in _Black
Christmas_ or the shark's in _Jaws_, which isn't just
a monster movie but also a slasher, wink wink.

Never mind that that's Debra Hill's hands on
the actual knife in that _Halloween_ opening, not
Kid Michael's. What you need to pay attention to
instead is what those hands are wearing, which
proves my point that John Carpenter knew the
tradition he was using, the Italian bodycount
movie, the Giallo. Those gloves, sir, are WHITE.
This is Carpenter saying that, yes, he knows from
whence all this bloody business comes, but he's
doing the INVERSION of that, he's one-upping it
all, sir. This isn't the only reason _Halloween_
is and was great and forever will be, but this
is a 2 page part 2 so I can only talk about the
first 5 minutes. But I'll "BE RIGHT BACK . . . "
don't worry.

HAPPY BIRTHDAY
TO ME

Jade comes to all at once and dives for her phone, frantically changing her school email password to, to . . . . to "S@v1N!," sure, why not, doesn't matter. Anybody who knows anything about horror *or* about her could crack it third try, but what's important is that it's not what it was last night, this morning, whatever. Meg's browser at the sheriff's office might have lodged that one in its memory, giving her access to Jade's sent box.

Close one.

Jade lies back, her heart pounding, and watches the sun climb the sheet that's her curtain, calms herself down beat by slower beat with the knowledge that on one side of Indian Lake or the other, maybe halfway around at Camp Blood, this same piercing light is sifting down over the slasher as well, his mask of a face probably looking over to the glowing horizon right now, his eyes still locked in shadow.

Jade can't help but smile, and feel a certain spring in her step.

Two hours later she's using rubbing compound on the graffiti scratched into the main men's bathroom in the high school—so she *is* setting foot there again—four hours later she's across the hall at the SKANK STATION, applying eyeliner but also clocking the background of her reflection for if Rexall's got an eye in the sky, and then six hours after daybreak she's clocking out for lunch. Her make-up is good, her ruined hair hidden under a different cap, and—"*Shit*," she says, catching a wavering image of herself in the glass of the double doors she's about to push through.

Jade pulls her cap down lower, trying to get her hair under control, and knows full well she's stalling, that here in the middle of this unscary day, she's scared. Not of Letha Mondragon, but of . . . of *talking* to her?

What if she laughs about Jade telling her she's a final girl? What if she read that letter out loud to Cinn and Ginny over French toast this morning, the three of them laughing so hard they had to be excused from the breakfast table? Of course she won't have a taste for horror, final girls never do, that makes the horror coming for them even scarier, but . . . what if the prospect of a slasher cycle happening right here in Proofrock doesn't even track to her, just sounds like a weak attempt at a bad joke?

"So she'll feel sorry for me, then," Jade mumbles. Which isn't exactly better than being laughed at. It's kind of worse, even.

Maybe she just shouldn't go, right? If Letha's a real and true final girl, she'll rise when it's time to rise, she'll fight the good fight for all of them. Well, either that or she'll bounce down into the cellar to check out that weird noise, get gutted or decapped or bisected or flayed, and then—then Jade can't be sure: would Ezekiel have to come up from Drown Town to put a cap on this slasher cycle? Can an evil preacher count as good when he's stopping a masked killer from slicing a town open?

Jade shakes her head no, she can't let it come to that. Meaning she has no choice *but* to try to talk Letha into being the final girl she's meant to be. Everybody has a function, everybody in a slasher cycle has a role—isn't that a line from the Bible, even? Not the over-the-top violent one Craven and Carpenter wrote, with all the massacres and gore, but the *other* violent one with all the massacres and gore. The one where revenge comes not in a hulking shape lurking at the edge of the light but as a series of plagues that starts out feeling random, come to feel a lot more like justice, like the scales rebalancing.

Same thing, different church.

Jade pats herself on the back for that and takes the alley behind the drugstore because alleys are where custodians lurk, because alleys are where the horror crowd holds its dark masses. And because Hardy's white Bronco is at the bank.

Seventy-five yards ahead, Letha Mondragon is already on Melanie's bench, the *Umiak* bobbing by the pier. Meaning this rich daughter of Terra Nova gets to take it out on her own, is trusted with a three-hundred-thousand-dollar cigarette boat.

Jade wonders if a girl like Letha's ever even *had* to clean a toilet. Probably to the filthy rich, toilets are disposable. Mario and Luigi are always standing by to switch a new one in after each use.

"You're still stalling . . ." Jade tells herself.

She broaches a timid foot out into the gravel of the parking lot between her and the lake then steps in all the way, damn the torpedoes, whatever that means. The gravel holds her, lets her crunch across its warm back.

Letha is just sitting there staring across at, Jade guesses, her house coming together on the point over there? It'll just be a summer crashpad for her, though, most likely. A place to decompress between semesters. A place to throw epic spring break parties if her dad and stepmom are in Bali that week, or can agree to be.

Unless of course Indian Lake comes to hold bad memories. Which is pretty much a foregone conclusion. There's nothing to be done about it, though. It's just the way a good slasher cycle works: the first death or two are people way outside the final girl's periphery—a Dutch boy, a Dutch girl—but then the shadow starts to fall closer and closer to home. Deacon Samuels, just a hop and a skip from where Letha sleeps. And it'll get much closer than that. Before it's over, any cherished pets Letha has will definitely be history, and . . . Theo Mondragon? Tiara? If it's only one of them, then Tiara is both the intruder into the family unit *and* probably the most disposable to Letha. Factor in the added benefit that her getting the blade can draw Letha and her father closer, facilitate some healing, and, well: Tiara's got X's for eyes, pretty much. Jade hates it for Letha—you're supposed to have a mom—but it's not like she makes the rules. She just happens to know them all.

She shouldn't open with that right now, though. Coming in hard like that will scare Letha off. No, what you do with someone like Letha is lure her in like you do a bird in the backyard: with closer and closer pinches of a single piece of white bread.

And, though she wants to with every last fiber of her being, Jade doesn't look back to see if Hardy's behind the wheel of his Bronco yet, just sitting there watching one picturesque girl find a moment of repose on the bench he dotes over, another girl sulking in to shatter that peace forever.

Better than the alternative, Jade tells him. Anyway, wouldn't it be even crueler to let Letha just keep bouncing through her skippy-drippy unicorn daydream of a perfect world, not tell her about the shadow creeping in behind her?

"Hey," she says, catching her hand on the backrest of the bench.

Letha's eating from a baggie of baby carrots. Of course.

"Oh, good," she says, and makes a motion that means she's scooting over, but she's already left room, would never have sat down in a way that didn't invite company and conversation.

Jade takes her seat, tries to take a wind-reading to see if the harsh scent her hair's still manufacturing is going to waft left or right.

Blame it on the coveralls. Blame it on work.

"*Now* we can shake hands," Letha says, extending hers after wiping the idea of carrots from it.

Jade takes her hand, says, "Town reject, nice to meet you."

Letha's dimples suck in and she shakes her head no about that, sets her bag of carrots down on her other side, says, "Jade Daniels, the *legend.*"

Jade has to blink, look into her lap. At the leg suddenly so close to hers.

"Nice pants," she says.

They're the ones *A Bay of Blood* was wrapped in, the ones that were supposed to just be an excuse for making a delivery. On Letha, rolled up to just under the knee like that, they're cute and baggy, of course. On Letha, they're killer.

"A friend gave them to me," Letha says, patting the top of Jade's hand. "And . . . I don't mean this in . . . in any negative way either," she adds. "Really it only casts a negative light on me, or where I'm from, how I've lived. But, if I don't say it—you're the first Native American I've ever known, I think."

Jade breathes out, relaxes a touch. Somewhere in town behind them, there's the regular *thunk* of an axe into wood, because, at this elevation, winter is always coming.

"Indian dude backed his tow truck down that pier right there once," Jade says, proud.

"Relative of yours?" Letha asks, her tone glad to have elicited this reply.

Jade is studying the *Umiak* now. A umiak is an Inuit whaling boat, according to her phone's dictionary. To better hunt the giant catfish that's supposed to drift past the windows down in Drown Town, maybe.

"I got your letter, yes," Letha says, signaling to Jade that the bullshit's over.

Jade nods, is ready.

"I—" Letha starts, doesn't know where to go, how to finish. "Stacey Graves," she finally gets out, batting her deer eyelashes. "That was the paper you wanted me to read, right?"

"All of them can save your life," Jade mumbles.

"But that little girl," Letha says. "What I'm—why is she so important, I guess that's what I'm asking."

"Because whoever's doing this is probably dressing up like—"

"To you, I mean. I read your letter six times, standing by the mailbox. By the end I was crying."

Jade has to press her lips together to keep from smiling like an idiot. If you cry writing it, maybe someone will cry reading it. It's more than she could have hoped for, is all she was wishing for.

"That bargain bin in Idaho Falls . . ." Letha says, kind of shrugging with her voice.

Jade sneaks a look over at the carrots, can only see the top corner of the baggie. It's open, meaning the carrots are drying out right now. Proofrock is killing them.

"I read between the lines, I mean," Letha adds.

"Mr. Holmes makes us double-space," Jade says, not following.

"To what you were *really* saying," Letha says, her hand on top of Jade's again. "And—it can't be easy to ask for help, especially from a complete stranger. It's really . . . it's brave is what it is."

Jade sneaks a look up, hoping that Letha's face can decode this.

"When we first moved here, I didn't know why," Letha goes on. "It was my senior year, all my friends are back home—but I see now. I'm here for *you*, Jade."

"In that I'm part of Proofrock and Terra Nova and Indian Lake," Jade says. "Yeah. Final girls, they fight for everyone, and—"

Letha starts to reach a hand up Jade's forearm to be even *more* consoling but Jade shifts away, unsure what's happening here.

"I just wrote that because you have to know," Jade tells her, the truth of that so obvious. "I can—if you'll let me, I can walk you through everything that's coming, I can—"

"I can *help*, Jade," Letha says, which pretty much sets off every last one of Jade's alarms.

"No, it's me who can help *you*," she says. "I've been watching these movies since, since junior high—"

"Textbook," Letha says. "It makes perfect sense."

"And it's definitely you," Jade insists, trying to push through Letha's supportive tone. "Anybody who's seen any of them, even the bad ones, they can tell right off what you are—who you are."

"A *friend*," Letha says, pouring her earnestness across, the palm of her hand warm on Jade's forearm now. There's something so Sunday school about it that Jade can almost feel the black paint on her fingernails steaming away.

"Sure, yeah," Jade says, halfway trying to take her arm back but not making a show of it, "friends later, fine. We can—you and me, we'll come to the ten-year reunion for the sequel, how's that sound? That's when Ezekiel will finally be coming up from the lake. We'll stand back-to-back in the middle of the gym floor, crepe paper floating down all around us in slow motion, and—and you'll have the sword from the trophy case, and I'll have ripped the blade off the paper cutter in the main office, and we'll, we'll—"

"Don't hate me," Letha says, her eyes flicking up and to her right.

Jade can't help but follow them over to the sudden grille of Hardy's Bronco, maybe six feet from the bench. Its tires had to have announced it crunching in, but Jade must not have been checked in to her surroundings. Real good, horror girl. Shit.

As if on cue, like this has all been rehearsed, Hardy steps heavily down from the driver's seat, the night's lack of sleep weighing on him, it looks like. He peels out of his chrome aviators, blinks against the new brightness, then fixes his eyes on Jade, studying her for the first time all over again, it feels like.

"What is this?" Jade says to Letha, fight-or-flight kicking in.

Letha's non-answer is answer enough. That and Mr. Holmes, climbing down from the passenger side of the Bronco.

Jade stands, looks back and forth between them, then to Letha.

"You, *you*—?" she manages to get out.

"I had to report it, Jade," Letha says, pushing her lower lip up like explaining how this is for the best, really.

Jade turns to run but one of her boots is already back to its natural state, so the dragging laces tie her feet up right when she's trying to find that hyperspace button. She faceplants, the heels of her hands instantly raw and dented from the gravel around the bench.

Letha is there to hold her by the shoulders, make sure she's okay.

"You *showed* it to them?" Jade says, hoping her voice isn't shrieking like her head is.

"Them?" Letha says with concern, looking up, taking stock.

"Them," Jade confirms.

Hardy is running the pad of his index finger along the top of the backrest of his daughter's bench, looking at that instead of Jade's current indignity, and Mr. Holmes is just standing there, the end of his brown tie flapping in the wind, his flinty eyes fixed where they always are: across the lake.

"No, no," Letha assures Jade. "I just—I read it to him over the phone, the *sheriff*, to . . . to show. To prove. So he could help."

"But the cops are always useless in cases like this!" Jade says, struggling to stand.

"I know it feels like that," Letha says. "But you've lived alone with this for too long. How could I go out into the world knowing I'd walked away from—from someone asking for my help? Someone *brave* enough to ask for help?"

"It's not *me* who's gonna have to be brave!" Jade says, her voice panicking.

"This isn't easy for any of us," Hardy says, wading into this.

"Jennifer," Mr. Holmes says in what sounds like the most reluctant, apologetic greeting.

"Jade," Jade corrects, on automatic. It's the call-and-response they've been flailing through since freshman year.

"Ms. Mondragon here was only doing what she thought best," Hardy explains, his hat in his hands for some reason, even though he's mostly bald and the sun's shining.

"It's just a—a personal letter and my old history papers," Jade says. "I don't know what you think—"

"Jade," Letha says in a way that Jade has to look back over to her. "*Tell them*," she pleads.

"I did," Letha says.

"She did," Hardy confirms.

"Then we all know, right?" Jade says. "Good, good, might as well have it all out in the open, why not. Not that that'll change anything. She's the final girl, yes, and there's a slasher around here somewhere, and, I don't mean to speak bad of anybody, but after Deacon Samuels, it's more than likely someone from over on the other side of—"

"*Under* that," Letha says. "*Before* all that."

"Okay, okay," Jade says to Hardy. "What you caught me printing the other night at the library."

"The extra credit?" Hardy says, scratching his head.

"I'm sure Mr. Holmes has already told you I was lying about that," Jade continues, "because why wouldn't he. Not like I can get detention anymore. That wasn't a late paper for history. Mr. Holmes is retiring, doesn't want to read any more of my bullshit. Which is fine, whatever, really. But—I had to tell Letha what was coming. I was trying to protect her. It's no crime to try to keep someone safe. I can pay back for the paper, and Connie might not even care—"

"Connie's known you do your schoolwork afterhours there for three years," Mr. Holmes says, pursing his lips after saying it, and holding Jade's eyes.

Jade opens her mouth to keep going, finds there's nowhere to go.

So . . . so Connie the Librarian's always known Jade's hiding just on the other side of the audiobooks aisle after lights out?

And then Jade sees what everybody else here has already seen: now that high school's over and she can't tell Mr. Holmes all her slasher theories, she's trying to find someone else to latch onto, impress with her slasher Q.

"No, no," Jade says, backing away from all three of them, which is just going to land her in the lake. "That Dutch boy she found in the water, he—him and his girlfriend, and . . . they were the *blood sacrifice*, see? They were the first ones, the proof, the promise of more to come, the appetizer that comes before the meal. That's how it always works. They trespassed, were somewhere they weren't supposed to be, so they paid the price, the ultimate price. That's how it goes, sorry. Then—that Founder, Deacon Samuels. He—this proves that this is really happening, can't you see?"

Hardy's fingers worry the brim of his hat. Finally he looks up, says, "Are you saying the bear—"

"It wasn't a bear, Sheriff," Jade tells him, tells all of them. "Bears don't have revenge arcs. The bear's just being framed, but nobody's going to believe that until—"

"A party," Letha offers, meaning she's read at least one of the papers.

Jade holds Letha's eyes, nods slowly, asks her back, leading her so slowly, so carefully, "And . . . what's the big party here every year?"

When Letha doesn't answer, Jade turns to Hardy, to Mr. Holmes, says, "She's not from here, she wouldn't know."

"Independence Day?" Hardy says with a shrug.

Jade fingershoots that *correct*, says, "Even in the form of a question."

"July Fourth?" Letha says all around.

"You'll see," Jade tells her.

At which point Mr. Holmes wades into this debate, directing himself to Jade: "And so it was this, this *slasher* that killed that herd of elk over in Sheep's Head, then?"

"Sheep's Head?" Letha says.

"It's what the old-timers call that meadow," Mr. Holmes says with a shrug, like that isn't the important piece of what he was saying.

"I told him he shouldn't have showed that to you all," Hardy says. "It's exactly the kind of thing that can add fuel to an over-active imagination."

"No need to use *names*, Sheriff," Jade says, pointing at her own temple, the overactive imagination in question.

"Independence Day," Letha repeats softer, which makes it somehow louder.

"I know you thought you were helping," Jade tells her, flabbergasted to the point of no return here. "But, and you couldn't have known this, authority figures—cops, teachers, parents—it's not *possible* for them to believe, not until it's too late. But your impulse to get help, to fight back, to stop this, that's what we can take from this, that's what we can weaponize, that's what we can—"

"But we *can* stop it," Letha says.

"You can, yeah," Jade tells her back.

"That's why I called Sheriff Hardy," Letha says, again with that apologetic tone.

Jade turns to Hardy about this.

"I pulled in Mr. Holmes because I—" he says, fumbling a bit, which isn't his usual way. "I know he was your favorite teacher. Is, *is* your favorite teacher."

Jade levels her imploring eyes over onto Mr. Holmes.

He shrugs, toes at the gravel with his loafer, says, "I confirmed that you're crazy for this subgenre of movie. For these type of horror movies. These . . . slashers."

"Thanks?" Jade says.

"Just . . . and this is on me," Mr. Holmes says, spreading his fingers to touch his own chest, indict himself. "I never saw it like Ms. Mondragon is . . . I knew you didn't want to write about history, but I never suspected it might be your own history you didn't want to talk about. So all the papers on horror—"

"About slashers."

"Complete with boogeymen," Mr. Holmes adds.

"He shouldn't have fostered that kind of speculation, he's saying," Hardy says, his tone getting across that he's sort of speaking *for* Mr. Holmes here, saying what Holmes can't say himself.

Still, "I think you mean 'foment,' Angus," Mr. Holmes snaps back to Hardy.

"That's Sheriff," Hardy says.

Mr. Holmes shrugs, and Jade can tell he's here against his will, somewhat.

Not that that helps her even one little bit.

"This isn't about me," she tells all three of them, *her* tone ramping up into a plea, which she full-on despises. "This is about that dead kid in the water, this is about the Founder who got killed with that fancy golf club—"

"With?" Hardy asks.

"Alongside," Jade corrects, brushing the clarification off. "This is about who might have gone to the dollar store specifically to buy a long black wig, and *why* they needed to look like that, and how they're, I don't know, pretending to walk on the water—maybe they're tying Jesus lizards to their feet—we don't *know* yet!"

"But, in your estimation, someone *is* dressing up like the Lake Witch and playacting a horror movie," Mr. Holmes clarifies.

"A slasher," Jade clarifies right back.

"To use your chosen subject matter," Letha says, taking Jade's hand from the side, "yes, as Mr. Holmes was saying, this *is* about the boogeyman, one hundred percent."

Jade jerks away, holds her hand in her other hand as if it's burned. She tries to smile these accusations off, to make a display of how preposterous all this is getting, but knows full well her smile has to look mechanical and scary to them, like if Michael Myers ever tried a grin on in the dayroom for Loomis. So she gives up, knows she can't convince all three of them. But . . . maybe just one? The important one? She turns to Letha, says, "Listen, if you care about your family, about *Terra Nova*, I need you to—"

"I read between the lines, Jade," Letha repeats slower, like that's going to make Jade finally hear what she's saying. "You were dressing it up as best you could, trying to hide, even hiding it from yourself, but—here, I've got it highlighted." She extracts Jade's printed-out letter from the back pocket of the pants that used to be Jade's, holds it up, flips to the page she wants, and: "'A doctor's appointment I couldn't do in Proofrock.'"

The silence after is as wide as the lake.

"That was—" Jade starts, starts over: "My mom, she didn't want Doc Wilson—"

"Because he was local?" Letha asks.

"No," Jade says, taking a step back, casing all three faces of her little make-do jury, here. "I was just—I was telling you where I found *Bay of Blood*! Every slasher has an origin story. Jason, Freddy, Michael, Chucky, but every slasher *movie* has an origin story too. The first time you saw it. Where you found it. That's all I was—that wasn't about *me*, that was about *Bay of Blood*."

Jade looks to each of them in turn again, waiting for the obviousness of this to register. For any of them to hear the logic of it.

"'My mom was having a conversation with herself in the car about will she, won't she,'" Letha reads this time, since that's a lot to recite.

Jade just stares at her.

"What are you saying?" she says at last. "This is—I was at a random gas station, I happened to look into the bargain bin—"

"You were at your most vulnerable, your most broken," Letha says, about to cry. "And you reached out for the first thing you saw, held it as close as you could, like armor. Like it could protect you. And it has, hasn't it?"

"*A Bay of Blood*?"

"Slashers," Mr. Holmes says.

"She's kind of been hiding in bad behavior too," Hardy's compelled to add.

"What—what—" Jade says, her thoughts swirling, only some of her words finding her mouth. "What are you saying? My mom *did* something to me?"

"Your dad," Letha says, barely loud enough to register.

"My *dad*?" Jade blurts out.

"Happens more than it should," Letha says. "And among Native Americans, the percentage is even—"

"You think he's why I was at the doctor in Idaho Falls?" Jade asks all of them, polling this jury now.

Yes, none of them say out loud.

Jade closes her eyes in pain, slams her fingers into her gunky hair and pulls, turns around on her combat heels, giving them her back, and—she doesn't want to do this, doesn't want to have to deploy the nuclear option, but what else is there?

"You're a father, Sheriff," she says, no louder than necessary. "Would you have ever done this to your daughter? To Melanie?"

"Jennifer," Mr. Holmes says sharply.

"*Jade*," Jade spins back around to hiss at him. "And aren't you always the one saying read between the lines, sir? Try this on, then. All this . . . all these accusations, all this textual evidence, whatever. Who's to say I didn't pack that in intentionally? Why would a girl like Letha ever give me the time of day if she wasn't feeling sorry for me? Maybe I wrote it like that to tug on her heartstrings, make her worry about me. Whatever it takes to get her here, talk her into my harebrained scheme about slashers and final girls."

Mr. Holmes just stares at her about this.

"What was your mom arguing with herself about in the car that day?" he says at last, super calmly. "Don't think, just answer."

"What was she—?"

"'Will she, won't she?'"

"Will she leave my loser dad, won't she leave my loser dad," Jade says without missing even one single beat.

Before Mr. Holmes can press her on this, she spins around again, glares out across the glinting water, arms crossed.

"Apologize to the sheriff," Mr. Holmes says.

Jade lowers her head, closes her eyes, says, "Sorry, Sheriff. That was out of bounds."

"You were scared," Hardy says back, and Jade closes her eyes harder, because she knows not to take this bait. If she nods yes to this, then the next question will be Scared of what? The truth? And if she says she wasn't scared, then what she did to Hardy was just cruel.

There's no way to win. Same as ever.

Why she even gets her hopes up anymore, who knows.

"We're just trying to help," Letha says.

Jade opens her eyes to the brightness and tears spill down both cheeks. Tears she fucking *hates*.

Instead of wiping them away, she slashes her right hand back in the direction of Mr. Holmes, because she can smell his nicotine on the air. He slips the butt between her waiting fingers.

"It's not your fault," Letha says again, still right there.

"No," Jade says again, breathing smoke out, finally turning around so they can see her wet face, see what they're doing to her here. "It's not what you think. Fathers don't do that to daughters, not even fathers as sucky as mine, as *Indian* as mine. I would say you've seen too many Lifetime movies, but if you've seen too many movies, what does that mean about me and my slashers?"

After maybe three seconds, Letha has to smile about this. Jade grins with her, takes another long drag, handing the cigarette back to Mr. Holmes before exhaling.

"Just saying," Hardy says, getting his own cigarette going, having to lean down into his cupped hand the way cowboys in westerns always do, "it would explain an awful lot. Your—all this gothic stuff, the way you dress, your attitude, the trouble you're always—"

"That's just me," Jade tells him, blowing her smoke out now, as underline. "Horror's not a symptom, it's a love affair."

"Are you saying—?" Letha starts, and Jade finishes for her: "I'd be like this anyway, yeah."

It's only when she looks up to Mr. Holmes that she hears what Letha tricked her into saying. It's the same story you hear about drunks on a traffic stop, arguing how they can't even say the alphabet backwards when they're *sober.* Meaning what Jade just said to all three of them was: Even if my dad *hadn't* done that to me when I was eleven, I still would have fallen hard for horror.

And trying to backpedal would just be protesting too much, she knows.

"Ask my mom, then," she says, just plucking the idea straight from the air without running it through the fire first.

"Kimmy?" Hardy asks.

"She's at work," Jade says, pointing with her lips down Main, to the dollar store.

All three of them look, and in that moment Jade knows she can run, that none of them can catch her, untied laces or no. As full of hatred as she is now, she could probably even run on top of the water, because no way would Ezekiel let her pollute his lake.

But her mom is her ace.

"She's got no reason to lie for him," Jade adds, to sell it. "Tell me I'm lying."

Hardy just keeps looking up Main.

"She's got a point," Mr. Holmes says. "The mom would know."

"It's a small house," Jade says. "And it was back then too. You hear everything."

"I don't like this," Hardy says, coming around to the three of them. "She can—she can warn him. Kimmy, I mean. She can warn Tab."

"Tab?" Letha says.

Nobody answers her.

"Just because he's Indian doesn't mean he can turn to smoke," Jade says. "If anything, he'd turn into a puddle of beer. But there won't be anything to warn him about. Just false accusations."

"If it matters, I don't think they talk anymore," Mr. Holmes adds, just to Hardy.

"All you have to do is admit it for the process to start," Letha says, like reading from a pamphlet.

"I know you're trying to help," Jade says, studying the gravel between her boots now, "and I thank you, really. I'm a stranger, I'm nobody, I'm the town reject, the weird girl, the walking sui-cide, the Indian who shouldn't even be alive, and you're—you are who you are, what you are. But you've got this all wrong, trust me."

"There are tests," Letha says. "Kits, the hospital can—"

"Test if I'm a virgin?" Jade scoffs. "Do you really think anybody in this town suspects that the custodian with different hair color every week has been able to keep her legs closed all these years? That she's even tried to?"

Neither Hardy nor Holmes can push back against this.

"I asked around," Letha says at last, like a card she didn't want to have to play. "You've never dated, never had a boyfr—"

"Maybe I'm not into guys," Jade cuts in.

"It's not about—" Letha says, trying to start this whole line over. "It's perfectly natural for you to want to defend him, it's the . . . it's like you consider yourself an accomplice just because you were involved. But your involvement wasn't complicit, wasn't voluntary, it never is, it can't be, you don't even *know* you can say no to a parent. Parents are good, parents are shining and right, they're the gods of our world, so whatever they do can never be wrong. It must be your *feelings* that are wrong. Their mask is that they're parents. Some of them are more, though. Some of them are monsters. But now, all these years later—"

"'*Our*'?" Jade says.

All eyes shift to Letha.

"We all think our parents are perfect," she says, blinking a touch faster than she has been, a tell Jade logs. "They feed us, clothe us, keep us safe—"

"Bring in another mother when the original's . . . ?" Jade says, leaving that blank for Letha to fill in: *Just what happened to your mother, final girl?*

Letha's own face becomes a mask then. Nothing changes about it exactly, just, now she's hiding behind it. But she can't be owning up to all this yet either, Jade knows. There's a time and a place for everything. *Both* bibles agree on that.

"Family Dollar," Jade says, letting the pressure off. "Her break's in ten, so we might want to get there."

It's a lie, of course, but the best kind, in that it's the last question Hardy will ask, standing at the register of the dollar store in an official capacity.

"We'll take my—" he says, reaching back to pat his hood while clamping his hat on, but Jade's already brushing past. Letha falls in, and then Jade hears Hardy and Mr. Holmes crunching through the gravel as well, and suddenly it's like the four of them are doing some epic walk down to the OK Corral, Jade's eyes slits to shoot arrows through, Hardy clamping his hat on tighter, Letha's hair bouncing with her every step, and Mr. Holmes's tie trying and failing to blow back over his right shoulder, his eyes both grim and, at the same time, amused, too aware of the absurdity of all this.

Jade does okay with the walk until all the eyes on Main could be clocking them through the plate glass windows. Like every time she's ever been the center of attention, her legs go robot, so that she's now having to give precise mechanical instructions to her hips, her knees, her ankles and feet, even to her arms that don't know how to swing anymore. How does Michael do it, his Panaglide walk? He's so inexorable, completely unstoppable, never wavering, always taking the most efficient line.

Jade decides that the reason he can do it—*walk*—and she can't, not without practically having a seizure from all the brain activity required, is that he has that singular focus: the next baby-sitter. Whereas what Jade has is . . . it's all the usual shit she drags with her, that she doesn't want to think about, but now there's even more tin cans dragging behind her: Letha's sincere but misdirected pity, Hardy's shrugging suspicion that Letha might be right, and Mr. Holmes's not even remotely wanting to be here, just wanting to please be retired. And, worse, a complete blind-side, does Jade feel responsible here? For all the lives this slasher can take, and how many more it can take if she doesn't get Letha prepped right?

That's the part that's not tracking for her: she should be thrilled about the prospect of necks being opened, limbs being hacked, guts spilling their steamy delights.

Proofrock deserves it.

But Letha doesn't, she decides. And, who knows, right? Maybe every final girl in the history of final girls has had a horror chick whispering to her from just off-screen. Maybe this isn't a devia-tion but the usual build. Just one nobody ever knows about until they're smack-dab in the beating heart of it.

Jade nods, likes that.

It's best she's behind the curtain, too. Unless the play she's in can be about robots, in which case her arms and legs have already got that *down.*

Thinking about what she must look like, walking like this, doesn't help at all, either.

And—and the pressure building around them, around all of Proofrock. It's like they're trying to cross from one side of an in-flating balloon to the other. But Jade knows the pressure-relief valve: the front door of Family Dollar.

She flails her arm ahead to haul it open, stop this moment from lasting any longer, please, but . . . Hardy has his meaty paw on her shoulder, is keeping her from pushing through, into the store?

"Excuse me?" Jade says, spinning away from his hand, probably making it more dramatic than it needs to be.

"Stay here with your favorite history teacher," Hardy grumbles, not a hint of give to his voice, and then he's barreling through the door alone, on a mission, only reaching back at the last moment to hold his cigarette up for whoever wants it.

In solidarity or at least an attempt at it after her betrayal, Letha slides in before the door can close, nodding to Jade on the way like she's going to make sure this is all legit, that she *isn't* going to let Jade fall through the cracks.

But the cracks are where bugs like me live, Jade wants to tell her back, and then have roaches spill from her mouth and eyes. Instead she brings Hardy's cigarette up in frustration, draws deep on it, and turns her head to the side to blow a clean, pissed-off line of smoke. When Mr. Holmes is just standing there awkward and unsure, she offers him a drag.

"It's not against the rules now," she says about the cigarette. "You're not a teacher, I'm not a student."

He looks away, down Main and across the lake.

"You really hate it, don't you?" Jade says to him. "Terra Nova, I mean."

He shrugs a noncommittal shrug.

"What's the history there, teach?" Jade asks.

"No history."

"There's always history," Jade says back. "A certain somebody might have impressed that upon my just-forming psyche once upon a freshman year. Nothing just pops into existence. Everything comes from somewhere. It's all got a story. Just a matter of if we're committed enough to dig it up."

Mr. Holmes shakes his head in amusement, genuinely impressed for once, it seems.

"Won't say you were my best student over all these years," he tells her, measuring his words. "But you are the one I'm going to remember."

"Voted most likely to die in a horror movie, right?"

"And I apologize for not—for not realizing what you were really saying, Jennifer."

"Jade."

"I should have, I mean. I could have helped stop all this from—"

"History needs *documentation* to be history," Jade cites back at him, her eyes flashing. "Documents, testimony, artifacts—the holy trinity. Otherwise it's just a pretty story. Compelling but empty, that's what you said, isn't it?"

"We haven't questioned *him* yet," Mr. Holmes says right back, licking his lips at the end in what Jade thinks could be anticipation, which she reads as him wanting to protect her from the "him" in question: her dad. It almost makes her feel something, but she can't allow that.

Instead she breathes in, says, "You haven't asked why this princess of Terra Nova is all bent out of shape by the possibility of a father going Chester the Molester over here in Proofrock. Or, in our case, all Rexall the . . . the—"

"Guinea pig," Mr. Holmes fills in. "It's an Italian slur. What they used to call him in high school, because of his weight."

"It's not his Italian-ness that makes my skin crawl. It's his *Krug*-ness."

"Are you talking your *Nightmare on Elm Street* or that one, the . . . *Last House on the Left*?"

"Good old Springfield Slasher his wisecracking self," Jade says, surprised Mr. Holmes has kept all those titles in his head. "Fred, Freddy, the Mr. Rogers of Elm Street. *He* was the one into kids."

"But the other one was a rapist, right?"

"Not a lot of nice bad guys in horror, no."

"And you say you recognize Rexall for being like that," Mr. Holmes says with a shrug. "Must we then ask why *your* senses are dialed in in that particular way?"

"I can't say anything to make you believe, can I?"

"To get me to *dis*believe?" Mr. Holmes asks back. "Ms. Mondragon in there makes a good case, a strong and telling textual analysis. All the symptoms and characteristics are there, Jennifer."

"Not everything with spots is a leopard," Jade says. "Now where did I hear that particular nugget?"

"I wouldn't be here if I didn't care."

"Rather be flying," Jade says. "I understand."

Mr. Holmes snickers, caught. Says, like finally giving up, giving in, "When I was a kid, we had a fort over there."

He tosses his chin across Indian Lake, to Terra Nova.

Jade takes another drag and holds it, not wanting to wreck this moment.

"We built this raft, had a pirate flag and everything," Mr. Holmes goes on. "We'd meet on this side at the new pier—it was new then— we'd meet at midnight, have candles and everything, our parents asleep, and we'd paddle across to our secret clubhouse."

"So they're messing with your childhood by building their fancy houses, that's it?" Jade says, turning her head again to exhale.

"Clubhouse was long gone by the time Theo Mondragon and his . . . his lords of what counts as industry got there," Mr. Holmes says. "I mean, childhood, sure, that's gone before you even realize it's slipping away, blink and you've got a mortgage. But the fort was long gone as well. Burned."

"The fire," Jade says, ashing between them discreetly, just tapping the cigarette with her index finger the way people in movies do. And in real life.

"How about this?" Mr. Holmes says, looking up to catch her eye, let her know this is for-real, not just their usual parrying and thrusting. "I'll trade you. Honesty for honesty. Nobody knows this anymore except—"

He hooks his head behind them again, meaning Family Dollar. Meaning Sheriff Hardy.

"*He* was in your pirate club?" Jade asks.

"That fire was . . ." Mr. Holmes says, his mouth and neck contorting to finally be saying this out loud after all these years, "it was us. Our campfire that night. Burned for nine days. Two campers from Kansas died. One firefighter from here—his uncle."

Jade widens her eyes, seriously impressed.

"You old scallywag," she says. "So, by slasher logic, which is, you know, *the* logic, then one of the Founders, these lords of industry, should have been a Proofrocker fifty years ago, and a pirate too. That's probably how they all heard about that virgin shore over there—no, no. One of their *dads*, right?"

Mr. Holmes shakes his head, says, "You never stop, do you?"

"That doesn't sound like a no."

"Your turn now," Mr. Holmes says, reaching across to take the cigarette from her, guide it shakily up to his own mouth.

He cashes it, grinds the butt under the sole of his loafer longer than he needs to to rub the cherry out, but about the right amount of time to memorialize the monumental confession he just made.

"My turn to what? Turn in another paper?"

"You can play dumb with him," Mr. Holmes says. "You can play dumb with everyone, doesn't matter to me. But I know, Jennifer. You're not dumb."

"Thanks, I guess?"

"I told you some painful truth, now you tell me some."

"Quid pro quo," Jade says with a snicker.

"Latin," Mr. Holmes says. "You never fail to surprise, Jennifer."

"Or disappoint," Jade adds. "And it's Jade, thanks."

"It's your turn, I mean."

"I haven't started any fires visible from space."

"On the walk over, it hit me," Mr. Holmes says. "The one horror genre you never broached in your papers and essays and creative pieces. How it was no accident that you avoided it."

"I do slashers, you know that. All kinds of subgenres I haven't written about. I mean—exorcisms are boring, just confirm western religion, and vampires and werewolves have so much lore they're practically fantasy, no matter how many throats they rip open, and haunted houses are just stand-ins for—"

"I'm talking about rape-revenge, Jennifer."

"That's not my name."

"Why'd you never delve into *that* subgenre?"

Jade lets her eyes unfocus so she can burn through what he's asking: rape-revenge is where a raped woman is left for dead but climbs back to life to take brutal revenge on her attackers, often using poetic justice, and usually a lot of primal screaming.

"Okay, so . . . if rape-revenge is going to be slasher-*adjacent*," she says, figuring this out as she goes, "then you're saying the rape is the prank, right?"

"You tell me."

"And you're saying that this woman, she *becomes* the spirit of vengeance personified," Jade says. "All that's missing is . . . is a mask—"

"She doesn't need one," Mr. Holmes says. "She's supposed to be dead. And the rapists weren't exactly interested in her face anyway. Or maybe their violence *gave* her a mask? The bruises, the black eyes, the fat lip."

"Okay, okay," Jade says. "But this is usually the same weekend, too, right? Raped on a Friday, killing all through Saturday and Sunday? There's no five or ten years where the pranksters can forget their crime even happened."

"They forgot her the moment they were done with her," Mr. Holmes says, seemingly ready for whatever Jade might have. Meaning his silence earlier was really thinking. Preparing. Scallywag indeed.

"Okay, I'll give you that," Jade says, though she knows this is a trap.

"But if you elect to exclude it from being one of your slashers," Mr. Holmes goes on, "if you say it's from a different shelf altogether, then you're saying that the crime itself doesn't warrant revenge, aren't you? That rape gets a pass. That sexual violation isn't beholden to the scales of justice you're always talking about, is somehow outside its purview."

Jade just stares at a bird prying something from a sewer grate.

"Either that or you're acknowledging that a minor can't *take* that revenge," Mr. Holmes adds, quieter. Because this is where he was going all along.

Jade kind of hates him right now.

It doesn't mean he gets to win, though.

"The reason rape-revenge isn't a slasher is that the slasher and the final girl would have to be the same person," she says, pushing off the front of Family Dollar with her butt. "Problem with that is that the final girl and the spirit of vengeance are forever locked in *opposition*, not the same jumpsuit. That'd—that'd be like Batman peeling his cowl off and being the Joker. Would that even *work*?"

Mr. Holmes is just watching her.

Jade shakes her head, says, "But really, is there anything I could say right now that might make you believe she's wrong?"

"She being her," Mr. Holmes says, tilting his head back to the store, to Letha.

"She not able *not* to be her," Jade says with a snort.

"There is one thing," Mr. Holmes says after a long consideration. "You were asking about documents or PDFs in my inbox? Well, when I got my degree in education, the final hurdle I had to clear to get my diploma was my orals. The *out-loud* part of the test."

"I was listening in class, I promise, but I can't remember all the dates."

"Just one question. No dates."

"So you're holding my diploma hostage," Jade says after thinking this through.

"That would be unethical," Mr. Holmes says, pushing away from Family Dollar now as well, and stepping out to study the street, his hands behind him, which means he's back in teacher mode. "But you have been petitioning for me to allow you to make up for your eight weeks' absence."

"I meant with more papers."

"About slashers."

"This a trick?"

"It's a gift."

Jade breathes in, shakes her head no about this—it's not a trick, it's a *trap*—but . . . just one question, and she graduates?

"Shoot," she says.

"You've got to be honest."

"Swear on my father's life?"

Mr. Holmes chuckles, asks the question: "Will she or won't she what? Your mom, I mean. Down in Idaho Falls that day, when you found that videotape in the clearance bin."

"*A Bay of Blood*," Jade fills in.

"That's not the answer I'm looking for," Mr. Holmes says.

Jade looks at him with just her eyes, weighing this all out in her head, full-on hating being in this corner, in this discussion, in this *day*, and then, before she can make something up, "sell him a bill of goods" as he wrote in the margin of one of her papers once, the glass door of Family Dollar opens all at once, spilling Hardy and Letha and a long sigh of air-conditioning.

"So?" Jade says to Hardy and Letha. "I some posterchild victim in an afterschool special, or was I just born bad?"

"It's never that simple," Letha says, and that's all the answer Jade needs.

Hardy puts his sunglasses back on one leg at a time, says, "According to your mother, and she's promised to get me the papers on it, that doctor's visit in Idaho Falls wasn't for . . . what we were thinking, based on your letter to Ms. Mondragon. You were there for a private reason, yes, but that private reason was getting your stomach pumped, wasn't it?"

Jade swallows, the sound loud in her ears.

"Getting your stomach pumped isn't a pleasant thing," she says.

"This isn't over," Mr. Holmes says to Jade, *just* for Jade—meaning her one-answer out-loud test is still coming, and probably when she least expects it, so he can feel like he's getting a real answer.

"Not supposed to be pleasant," Hardy goes on, about the stomach-pumping thing, his eyes boring into Jade's. "It was, there'd be no reason *not* to eat a whole bottle of aspirin."

"It was cherry flavored," Jade mutters.

"So it was an accident?" Letha asks.

Jade swallows, the sound loud in her ears, and holds her suicide-wrist up like a badge. "You all thought this was my first time, didn't you?" she says with the most superior, judgmental sneer she can muster.

Letha's eyes are shiny wet, about to spill over with concern, Mr. Holmes is just staring in through the front door of Family Dollar, probably wishing he were two hundred feet up in the air right now, and Hardy's got his eyes behind chrome lenses, meaning he could be anywhere. A thousand miles away already. Skimming across Indian Lake, the hull of his airboat only touching water every thirty feet or so.

So this is what winning feels like, Jade tells herself.

Minus the jubilation and accomplishment and impulse to cry tears of joy, she guesses it's pretty much what she expected. Give her ten, twenty minutes of scrubbing cusswords from bathroom stalls and it'll just be part of the background hum, the usual suckage of Proofrock.

And no, this lunch hour hasn't gone exactly as planned.

Right now Letha's supposed to be slackjawed on the bench, one hundred percent believing that this slasher is real, that all of Indian Lake is in jeopardy, and that she's the one pre-ordained to stop it all. Instead she's standing there with her arms crossed, her right hand over her mouth, her eyebrows up in worry. About Jade.

But it's not Letha's fault, either. Jade should have anticipated this, shouldn't she have? Letha's a good-enough person—a pure-enough final girl—that if there's even the *possibility* that what she thinks about Jade is true, then she has to try to right it. Balancing the world and avenging injustices is what the slasher does, after all, always and only. Yes, the slasher is the governor on unfairness, but the final girl is the *governor's* governor, the one who puts a cap on the cycle once it threatens to bleed beyond its own initial scope, go full-on franchise. Which is to say: the final girl is all about justice as well, is all about righting wrong wherever wrong's encountered. Even if it's between the lines in a letter, if you squint just right.

"This isn't over," Letha says, somehow holding both Jade's hands like they're about to drift out onto a dance floor.

"You're right about that," Jade says, trying to make Important Eyes, except a crusty clump of black bangs is poking into her right pupil, it feels like. She bats it away, turns to sulk off but then stops, makes herself say it, to all of them: "Thank you. I know you're trying to help. But, really, I just like horror. Not everything has some dark reason behind it. And I don't even do pranks anymore."

"Except trying to convince us there's a slasher on the loose," Mr. Holmes can't help but say.

"That's no joke," Jade says right back to him.

"I'll give her a ride back," Hardy announces, breaking the tension, his cop hand already around Jade's left upper arm, so he can steer her.

Jade lets it happen, only looking back once to Letha, who's watching her retreat, her eyes all about how she could have done more, she *should* have done more, it doesn't have to end like this.

But it's only just getting started, Jade assures her, then shakes free of Hardy, pulls ahead, hauling the passenger door of his Bronco open before he can.

"I'm working at the high school this afternoon," Jade tells him once he's easing them from the parking lot.

Hardy stops the left turn he was making, hauls the wheel over the other way.

"Jade, never mind what your mom told us. If your dad has ever—"

"Letha Mondragon's the one with the overactive imagination," Jade tells him, using his own words against him. "Some mother hen complex where she wants to take care of all of us. And I'm the least likely chicklet to survive, so that means I'm the first she has to save."

Hardy sighs, says, "I think what you mean there is 'hatchling,' maybe?"

Jade slumps down in the seat, chocking her knees against the warm dash.

"And she's right," Hardy goes on. "This isn't over."

"I was just—"

"*I've* got some questions, I mean."

Jade looks over to him but he's watching the road with every last ounce of his remaining attention, as if he hasn't driven this stretch of Main ten thousand times. He switches hands on the wheel, nods to himself that it's finally right in his head, and says, "You knew about the Maruman at the old camp, meaning either you were there when or right after it happened, or you somehow got hold of Meg's transcription."

Jade doesn't say anything.

"And if you *were* over there," Hardy goes on, reaching into the backseat to plop something on the console between them, "I know what you were wearing."

It's her dad's muddy boots from the porch.

"I would shoot myself in the face before touching his boots," Jade says, elbowing them away to prove how gross they are to her.

"History of suicide attempts, yes," Hardy says.

Jade opens her mouth to ask him why doesn't he just haul her dad in, since they're his boots? But that would just be setting a red herring up, wouldn't it? Because no way could it really be Tab Daniels. Slashers, in their own way, are as pure as final girls.

"What?" Hardy asks, letting his foot off the gas so Jade can say whatever she was about to.

Jade shakes her head no, nothing.

"Anyway, that's not even the worst of it," he goes on, stopping in the hug-n-go lane of the high school with her for the second time this month. "You said there was a Dutch boy *and* a girlfriend. When we only know about the boy, whose dental work *is* actually turning out to be European, at least in the forensic report that just hit my inbox *two hours* ago. Leading me to think you have some knowledge that we don't."

"They travel in pairs," Jade tells him. "Common knowledge. Casey and Steve in *Scream*. Barry and Claudette in—"

"'They' being . . . the Dutch?"

"I only said that because he was blond. Like on the paint cans."

"So you were there."

"I was at the party, yeah. Can I not go to parties with my ex-classmates?"

Hardy doesn't like her answers, but neither can he take them out at the knees, Jade knows.

"Then I'm sure you know we made a list of everybody who was at the Tompkins place that night," he says. "I don't recall your name being on that."

"I left early."

"But stayed until the end, too? To see the color of that dead kid's hair?"

"Was on my way out."

"I'm sure the Koenig girl or one of the others can confirm this."

"Tiff's recall of that night might be . . . blurry."

Hardy shakes his head, impressed—he must know Tiffany K was sloshed—but still, "So either you *were* at the party or you . . ." he leads off, using his fingers to pick words from the air, it looks like, "or you have unlawful knowledge about the events that led to that kid being there. Same as the golf club."

"Would you believe a bus ran over my evidence, or is that too much like the dog eating my homework?"

"Excuse me?"

"*Third* option, I mean," Jade says, opening her door, hanging a leg out for solid ground.

"I don't—"

"I've watched too many horror movies," Jade says. "I'm just making shit up left and right, because my dad did some unspeakable shit to me."

Hardy just sits there, brake pressed in, eyes hidden behind chrome lenses.

"Are you saying that Mondragon girl was right about him?" he finally asks.

"I'm saying something's coming for us, Sheriff," Jade says, stepping all the way down now. "I don't know why, I don't know who, but I do know when."

"July Fourth," Hardy recites. "Speaking of that."

This stops Jade. Then she connects the necessary dots.

"You can beef up security all you want," she says. "It won't—"

"In hindsight, your letter is a credible threat to the proceedings that night," Hardy says, using the official phrasing. "If you show up and try to self-fulfill your little prophecy, then it'll look like I was negligent, just some country bumpkin law enforcement officer not paying enough attention."

"But—"

"What I'm *saying*," Hardy says, speaking over her, holding her eyes for this, "is that your presence will not be needed that night, Ms. Daniels. Rex Allen and Francie will escort you out if you try."

"But you can't. I've been waiting for this for my whole—"

"It's for the best," Hardy says, challenging her to tell him otherwise.

I've been waiting all my life, she wants to say, but can't.

All she can do is stand there on the front sidewalk of her exhigh school, her world crumbling around her, all of it just falling away. Hardy tips his hat bye to her and eases away, and Jade can't even think of anything sharp or cutting to say. She's numb.

"Went ahead and clocked you in," Rexall says in passing, carrying a crumbling pipe over his shoulder, both ends seeping unmentionable sludge. "Thank me later, yeah?"

Jade doesn't have any clever comeback for him either, a silence he's probably taking for acceptance of this deal—timecard-action for later, to-be-*ascertained* action . . .

That's all distant to Jade now. Happening to some other girl.

Thirty minutes later she's trudged back inside, is scrubbing profane words from bathroom stalls. By midafternoon, using her county razorblade, the metal wall by the urinals her dark blue canvas, she's carving her own profanity, each letter a foot tall and deep, going down to bare metal.

THE LAKE WITCH SLAYINGS.

That's definitely what they're going to call it the morning after, when all the bodies are floating facedown in the water, blood blooming out from their sides like wings.

It's going to be glorious.

SLASHER 101

What's lucky is that you can go on teacher vacation
for MY WHOLE JUNIOR YEAR but when you come back
all the same rules of the slasher genre still keep
applying, and we can now finish your education,
sir. Or should I say <u>Night Flier</u>. That's not a
slasher but it's still from the horror mind of
Stephen King, who has a high bodycount in his books
and movies but his Freddy Krueger is Pennywise the
Clown and his Chucky is Gage and his final girl is
Carrie and his Jason Voorhees is a dog, but none of
them are really slashers. Really if you want some
truth then if you compare Mr. King with a little
old lady then she's probably done more to give the
slasher legs and arms and a secret face than the
acknowledged king. That's right I'm talking about
Agatha Christie and the next important slasher
ingredient, which is the Reveal.

But first a reveal of my own if you don't
overmind. Since this is the 2nd week of class only
that means this 2 pager in your extra credit box is
me putting money in the bank. Because Halloween is
going to be here before we know it.

So, the Reveal in the slasher is when all will
be said out loud and made clear as to Who's been
doing all this and Why and also How. So when I'm
mentioning Mrs. Christie above what I mean from
the one book of hers I mostly read titled <u>And Then
There Were None</u> which has nearly as many titles
through the years as <u>A Bay of Blood</u>, where people
are dying and who's doing it, who's doing it, then
at the end, SURPRISE! It was this one dude all
along, and here's why, and he's showing his secret
true face at the end.

Or if Scooby Doo is more your thing then that's

the very same thing, sir. I know he's a hippie dog
to you but he also faces ghosts and werewolves who
all pull their masks off at the end and explain WHY
they were doing all this, which made great money
sense at the time to them even if it was a LOT of
trouble, on par with some of the Joker's schemes.

But in the slasher where there's real necks
getting the axe, how that works is, okay, pretend
all the people who have been killed in the movie
get to be alive again for five minutes in a living
room and then the slasher comes in and explains
to them why he did what he did to them and they
all look at each and nod and say that, Yeah, they
probably did sort of deserve this. It sucks that it
had to hurt so bad and it was pretty scary and they
really had other plans and their families are going
to be sad and who's going to feed their dog now,
but they should have thought of that before doing
whatever Bad Thing they did to someone who couldn't
protect himself or herself at that point, and for
sure wasn't even close to asking for it any way
whatsoever. At which point any good slasher will
unlimber his machete and kill them all over again,
just paint that living room red.

However note that this is only for slasher
movies of the mystery variety like <u>Scream</u> and not
the supernatural variety like <u>A Nightmare on Elm
Street</u>. <u>Scream</u> at the end has Billy Loomis giving a
lecture REVEALING why he's been doing this, while
<u>Nightmare</u> has Freddy giving his lecture through the
whole franchise with quips, because while Tina does
pull his face off, showing his animatronic skull,
Freddy's really only more of himself without it,
which isn't really a Reveal, just a magnification.

Though if we're talking Agatha Christie like
this then we need to talk about fish and fishing,
Mr. Holmes. Specifically, Red Herrings. Coming soon
to an extra credit box near you.

VISITING HOURS

It's not Rexall who fires Jade for leaving graffiti when she was supposed to be erasing it—that's Hardy's job—but she's pretty sure he's the one who ratted her out, either as payback for stealing his glory at graduation or because she never does slow-motion shirt changes under any of his spycams.

It's kind of too bad, though. The no more money thing, sure— that means no more phone, next billing cycle—but she also had big plans for one of Rexall's illicit recordings being instrumental in unmasking the slasher, or at least documenting a kill in grainy black and white.

But that's Letha's job, Jade reminds herself, staring across the lake while Hardy straightens his desk calendar and drones on about destruction of county property, broken trust, no more second chances, adult responsibilities, civic pride, misuse of cleaning tools checked out to her name, abuse of key privileges, Henderson Hawk school spirit or the lack thereof, and somewhere in there she unfocuses her eyes as much as humanly possible, wide enough to just float in some muted state of mind through the whole rest of her Sunday, wash up on the shore of Monday pushing slasher after slasher into her VCR, trying to find a line back to herself. She drifts off ten minutes into each, though. She tries to convince herself it's about finding the right movie for her mood, but how can none of them be right, when they've *all* been right before?

Then, "Tuesday?" she says, looking around. With no school and no job, the days don't really matter anymore, do they? She hides her head under her pillow, sleeps until noon, then sleeps some more. Well, stays in bed anyway, staring at the ceiling, wishing for a glass of water to ungum her mouth but not wanting it quite badly enough to actually go get it. Because, she hisses to Hardy, she's not a go-getter, right? Everybody knows that. She's a coaster, a rider, and where do people who go with the flow always end up? The drain, yes.

Specifically, that one in Janet Leigh's black-and-white shower.

It's a good enough comeback that Jade's finally able to sit up and take stock.

Her dad should be at Terra Nova for the day, and her mom—why is she even thinking about her? It's because of the debacle Saturday was, right? It is. It's because she had to see her mom through Letha's eyes, sort of: as the future Jade. As if. No way will Jade end up here—no way does she ever shack up with some version of her dad, no way could she endure that same question her mom must get fifty times a day: "But . . . isn't this the *dollar* store? How can this cost two dollars?"

One thing Mr. Holmes told the class one wistful seventh period was that nobody ever makes it past twenty with the same hopes and dreams and certainties they once thought so dear and vital and true at seventeen. *Nobody except me*, Jade had assured herself, but she'd also had to wonder if that was even a partially original thought—if every other student in history class that day wasn't thinking the exact same thing.

It doesn't matter. Come the very last day of July she's eighteen, will be out of the house. Hopefully Boise is ahead of her somewhere, but Boise, she knows, takes bus fare, and bus fares cost money, and now there's no more paychecks coming in, *shit*.

With that, Jade can't seem to muster the will to untangle from her sheets. She's most definitely circling that *Psycho* drain, is just sitting there ticking off the things she's not: a custodian; a high school graduate; a final girl; welcome at the big Independence Day party; any help to anybody at all, even herself.

It makes sense, she supposes. Has there ever even been an Indian in a slasher? In *Friday the 13th* Ned wears a war bonnet and claps whoops from his mouth, does his high-knee dance, but he's still the same idiot he was before. In *Halloween 5*, there's another war bonnet, but it's just skating past in the background. There is that one Indian dude in *Sweet Sixteen*, Jade supposes. Or, two, counting his grandfather. Along that same line, though: outside of *Leprechaun 6*, has there even been a black final girl before? Usually in slashers, the black girls are the friends—*Scream 2, I Still Know What You Did Last Summer*. And that they're in part 2's means they're a response, a bandaid.

She thumbs through her videotapes for something else that can count, that Letha could use as model, as guide, but there's nothing.

Which is why she needs me, Jade reminds herself.

Not that that compels Letha to listen.

This is the part in the movie where Jade's supposed to rally, she knows. She's not supposed to mope, she's supposed to be gearing up, pouring black powder into lightbulbs, hammering nails into the business end of a bat, that kind of stuff.

But there's no camera on her, she knows. And there never was.

It doesn't mean she's wrong about what's coming, what's already happening, but it does mean that now she can sit back guilt-free and just watch it all happen from her I-told-you-so place, right? Maybe that's why she couldn't get into any of her slasher tapes earlier. In comparison to the one she's in, they're kind of pale.

But she will be goddamned if Hardy can keep her out of the water on Saturday. She's gonna be there front-row, shoving popcorn in, maybe wearing a clear poncho and goggles against all the blood.

Just, what to do until then, right? When it was going to be her and Letha working together, the week couldn't be long enough for all the slasher ground they had to cover. Now, without that, and with no litter to stab, no hours to log, it looks to stretch forever.

"Meddling kids," yeah. More like a bothersome ex-janitor with big ideas.

Jade guesses she could always go in, try to complete her community service, but if Meg was watching her close before, now Jade's going to be under a microscope. Granted, that's better than Rexall's hidden fisheyes, but still, it's not the kind of attention she really wants.

To try to be part of the day, Jade makes a bologna sandwich with mustard—her dad's *fancy* mustard, that's supposed to be only his—eats it in her underwear in the kitchen, being sure to avoid all the reflections of herself in the oven window, the stolen napkin dispenser, the chrome faucet. Not everybody can be Julie James or Sarah Darling, at least not without a personal trainer, a nutritionist, and an airbrush. Sure, the Indian maidens on all the truckstop blankets are always swivel-hipped, stacked like a Disney princess, but Jade figures she must be from a different tribe.

Sitting at the sagging table in the kitchen, the sandwich on her right thigh, she leans her head back, stops chewing, wonders what it would be like to choke alone in the house like this—what regrets reel through your head?—and then jerks hard when the screen door rattles. By the time the front door swings open, Jade's rolled off the chair, is crouched by the fridge, sandwich in-hand, eyes wide.

Rexall belches into the living room. She'd know that burp anywhere.

"Dude," her dad says about it, his keys jingling into his pocket.

"That's nothing," a third voice slurs, one Jade doesn't know.

Fucking great. Her dad's *not* at Terra Nova for fifteen an hour, and Rexall, with nobody to supervise anymore, isn't working either. It's a drinking day. Another "high school never ended" day. Perfect. Wonderful. And the side door out of the kitchen involves the hallway, which is one of two directions these three can take, as the bathroom's that way.

The other way they can take is right here, into the kitchen.

Jade's heart hammers in her chest. Not only is she only wearing a bra and panties, but these aren't even good ones, are even particularly *bad* ones.

And the voices are getting closer. Meaning they didn't swing by to crash on the couch for an hour or two, watch one of her dad's old westerns. This is a pit-stop, a refuel. They won't be staying in the living room, are definitely coming this way.

But, *which* way?

Or, which of them is going to find Jade crouched in her underwear by the fridge, holding half a bologna and mustard sandwich, her eyes wide, pasty black hair everywhere?

Shit. Shit shit *shit*.

Jade takes stock again, clocking both doors, and then . . . no, she can't.

The back door?

When footsteps start both crunching up the hall *and* resounding on the hollow part of the living room floor that leads to her, there's no choice: still crouched, she scurries for the back door, twists the weak deadbolt over and falls out as quietly as she can, pulling the door shut softly behind her.

Voices in the kitchen now.

Two beers cracking open, then a third.

And—no, no, no: the door handle Jade's still gripping, it twists under her hand.

She swings with it when the door opens, is dangling over the open space past the cement block under the door, is trying to flatten herself to the side of the house, and then has to hold that trembling position while one of them pisses a pale yellow line out into the grass already burned by a thousand other pees.

Jade risks a look up through the back door's window and . . . Clate Rodgers? Would Hardy let her have her mop back if she called in, whispered that his daughter's killer was back in town again? Or does Hardy's skin crawl all on its own every time Clate steps over the county line?

When Clate finally dribbles down, grunts through his shakeoff, and hauls the door back over, Jade lets go, falls into the sharp weeds that grow by the house, and makes herself as small as possible, hopes nobody across the way's looking out their window.

Two seconds later, footsteps still crunching in the kitchen, the window over the sink opening to blow cigarette smoke from, Jade sees her salvation billowing on the laundry line: the coveralls Hardy didn't think to ask her to surrender. Unlike Michael Myers, she won't even have to kill a mechanic to step into them.

Pulling them on in the shade of the house, she falls down like a boneless thing when a little brown bird explodes up from the leg. It's so close to Jade's face she feels the air from its beating wings, her hand coming up hours too late to protect her eyes. She pats down the arms for if this was a flock, then pulls the coveralls the rest of the way on and creeps around to the front, lifts her dad's backup muck boots from the bed of his truck, which she bets Hardy would just love to hear about.

A block down, almost to the lake, she realizes she's still holding the bologna sandwich. She takes a bite but her dad's mustard is too sharp, too warm. She tosses the sandwich in front of her, steps purposefully on it, mashing it into the concrete, and then shimmies through the gym door of the high school, which Hardy explained was strictly off limits to her. Forever.

Like he didn't know that was an invitation?

Jade goes through Lost and Found for mismatched socks, a confiscated t-shirt—green, a seventies Corvette dramatic on the chest—then does her make-up as best she can in the usual mirror, but only after roundly flipping Rexall off.

"Go ahead, turn me in," Jade tells him, enunciating clearly in case he's having to lip-read. "I'll just ask Hardy how he thinks you knew I was here."

She puts her eyeliner on thick as hell.

The next three hours she spends stalking the halls, playing *Slaughter High*. At least in her head. But she finally ends up being John Bender, escaped from detention in the library, using terrible form to shoot some hoops in the gym.

And then it's Mr. Holmes's old history classroom.

It's empty now. Empty of him. His corny posters, the part of the chalkboard he had marked off for that day's bullshit quote. The drawers of his desk are all stray paper clips and leftover staples.

Jade sort of wants to cry.

"Fuck you," she says instead, and leaves not by the door she used to get in but by throwing a trashcan through the glass of the front doors, ducking through that crashed-open hole.

This is graduation, she tells herself, crunching through the glass like the four misfits on the cover of her *The Craft* videotape. All the ceremony she needs.

It's night now. Pretty soon the streets of Proofrock will roll up, dousing all the lights. Jade cocks a hip out, glares down the empty streets. She's not worried about dying and going to hell for all her sins. She's not worried because she's been living in hell for seventeen years already.

She pushes through the darkness, her hands deep in the pockets of her coveralls.

It was worth it, she decides all at once. Getting fired. Getting fired for memorializing this slasher cycle on the bathroom stall.

Somebody had to, right?

Anyway, "The Lake Witch Slayings" *is* a killer name for what's going on, and what's still going on. She has to smile about that, which makes her . . . yes: there *is* a pack of cigarettes in the chest pocket of the coveralls. Fucking salvation. Thank you, tiny brown sleeve birds.

Jade fires up in the alley behind the drugstore. Through the smoke she can just see the *Umiak* bobbing at the pier, dwarfing Hardy's little airboat, two of the Founders in town, it looks like. They're stepping off the pier like just ferried across, anyway. Letha and Tiara are up at the boat cockpit, whatever it's called, Tiara even wearing a captain's hat like she's in a *Playboy* spread. But Jade only has eyes for these two Founders. Is this the closest she's actually been to them? It's hard to look away. The way they move—"fifty" doesn't mean the same thing at their tax bracket as it does in Proofrock. There's actual spring in their step, and they're yoga-limber, almost svelte, even, like they didn't just step down from a cigarette boat but up from the pages of a magazine.

Jade leans against the back of the drugstore, takes the most slit-eyed, noirish drag she can, and watches them walk to the Porsche, the Range Rover.

Neither of them are Theo Mondragon, she can tell, he's got those football shoulders, those dodgy hips. So . . . it's Mars Baker, right? The other one's either Ross Pangborne or Lewellyn Singleton, she can't really tell those two apart so well at distance. They're supposed to be grieving for Deacon Samuels, that's got to be why they've converged on Terra Nova, but they're not stooped with grief, they're not dragging, they're not sad and broken. That bounce in their long strides, really, it's almost like they're thrilled it wasn't them.

"But it will be," Jade says to them, and blows smoke out, spins away fast, trying not to let herself get caught up in their shine, their polish, their remove from real actual life.

Walking purposefully away from the road out of town to pay a visit to Camp Blood gets her going alongside the Terra Nova staging area again. She checks both ways and then, on impulse, why not, she steps in through the laid-over fence panel, walks fast in among the big equipment, the dozers and front-end loaders. Another time she might climb those big tires, sit in the cracked vinyl seats, pretend she's Godzilla'ing down Main on a righteous rampage.

She has adult responsibilities now, though, doesn't she, Sheriff? Civic pride, all that bullshit. To prove it she drops her cigarette, grinds it out under her boot like a proper citizen, and keeps stepping, trying the door of one of the storage sheds—padlocked—then cutting across a pile of junk to a more likely shed, just on the chance she can get eyes on whatever bladed weapon or chainsaw is probably going to be in play on Saturday. Halfway across the pile of junk, though, headlights stab on right beside her. She freezes, telling herself that if she can be still enough, then she's just another broken pallet, just another torn-off pull of shrink wrap.

But then the driver's door opens, and she realizes two things at once. The first is that this isn't Hardy's Bronco or some rent-a-cop the Founders have hired to patrol their lot. If it were, a dummy light would be pinning her in place right now, or at least a Maglite.

The second realization is that she's *been* in this particular car before.

"Um, need some help?" Shooting Glasses asks. He's the timid silhouette standing up behind the blinding glare.

"This where y'all keep the explosives?" Jade asks back, shielding her eyes as best she can. "Or, no. The candlesticks, the lead pipes, the daggers?"

"Who you looking to kill this time?" Shooting Glasses asks.

This time. Because "last time" was herself.

"Everybody?" she says, clambering down and out as best she can, without *quite* puncturing an ankle, or falling into a needle bath.

"Think they'd notice if you did?" Shooting Glasses asks, reaching in to dial the lights down to just the orange ones.

"*Dead & Buried*, 1981," Jade says by way of an answer. "Whole town of dead people who don't know they're dead. It happens."

Shooting Glasses makes a show of aiming his finger down to the door panel and punching the unlock button.

Jade steps around to the passenger side, says, "There's this other movie called *Children Shouldn't Play with Dead Things.* If there'd been a sequel, it might should have been 'Children Shouldn't Get into Cars They Know Are Stolen.'"

Shooting Glasses folds in behind the wheel, says, "Another of your slashers?"

"I wish," Jade says, settling in. "The director did go on to make *Black Christmas*, though, so maybe there's some genealogy there, if you squint right."

"Everything eighties with you, isn't it?"

"Those are both dirty seventies," Jade tells him, tracking the dim headlights prowling along the staging area's fence line. "But the eighties were great, that's why. They—"

Shooting Glasses interrupts by starting the already-started car, which results in metal screeching, parts grinding, and—more important—the brake lights of that car trolling by.

"That was pleasant," Jade says to Shooting Glasses without looking at him. Just waiting for that car to move along, move along.

"It's so quiet I can't ever tell if it's going or not," Shooting Glasses says about the car.

"But the eighties," Jade continues, since someone finally *asked*, "they're when the slasher was at its purest. Which is to say its dirtiest, its cheapest. Low production values, throwaway dialogue, nobody actors, recycled premises—all about making that quick buck. But that's what makes it the Golden Age, when Jason was born, Freddy was born, Chucky was—well, when Chucky was bought, anyway. But every Friday there would be either a new slasher or two, or there'd be the same ones from a few months ago, with new titles. It must have been amazing. And I was born too late for it."

"That's what Cody's always saying," Shooting Glasses says, nodding to the taillights finally weaving away into Proofrock.

"Cody?" Jade has to ask, then, "Oh, yeah. The anyflavor Indian?"

"He says he was born too late too. That if he'd been born a hundred years ago, things would be different for him."

"Good for him," Jade says. "Don't think it'd work for me, though."

Shooting Glasses cuts his eyes over to her about this.

"Some boys from town would play a trick on me," she says like the most obvious thing, "they'd throw me out on the water, and I'd run away into legend."

"Don't take this wrong," Shooting Glasses says, "but I don't think I've ever talked to anyone like you."

"Y'all almost done building Camelot over there?" Jade asks back, throwing her chin across the water.

Shooting Glasses backs the car up, repoints it so they're looking through the lake side of the staging area's chain link fence. Past it, there's the lights of Terra Nova.

"Foundation problems now," he says.

"It's rocky over there," Jade tells him. "That's why the cemetery is on this side, yeah? Only thing over there are old mine shafts. My history teacher says it's all pockmarked with caves, too. And"— Jade closes her eyes to get it just right—"he says that, before the lake, when Drown Town wasn't drowned, that at night you could see the sparks from the pickaxes over there. Everybody trying to strike it rich."

"Did they?"

"What do you think?"

Shooting Glasses pulls a Dr Pepper can up to spit into, being sure to break the saliva string off before guiding the can back to the cupholder.

"I like how your eyes squint right when you're spitting," Jade tells him. "It's like you know how gross that is."

Shooting Glasses turns the parking lights off, stranding them in the darkness. But it does make the fence go away, which is pretty cool.

"So why do you want to kill everybody?" he asks.

"Some more than others," Jade tells him.

"No names, no names."

"Said the car thief."

Shooting Glasses grins a guilty grin.

"You know that kid they pulled from the lake last week?" Jade says, patting the dashboard lovingly. "Bet his prints are somewhere in here. Hers too."

"Her who?"

"His girlfriend," Jade says. "She's dead out there too. Probably sunk, down in Drown Town."

"That's the old town that the reservoir—"

"Lake," Jade says. "Yeah."

"I heard one of them over there talking about it," Shooting Glasses says. "The—that astronaut one?"

"Mars Baker? He's the lawyer one, I think."

"He said he's going to take a remote-control submarine down there, get some video."

Jade looks into her lap, both amused and disappointed.

"Some things should probably just stay buried," she says.

"You saying you wouldn't watch that video?"

"I'd watch it until that girlfriend's decomposed face bobbed into the camera's eye, yeah."

"That's from *Jaws*," Shooting Glasses says, checking her eyes to be sure he's right.

"Good enough for Spielberg, good enough for me," Jade says back.

Shooting Glasses just sits there. Which is to say, he's not leaving, not sloping off to whisper to his buds about how weird this girl is with all her throwback references, all the horror, all the gore. Jade's face heats up, and, praying her voice won't crack, and only saying it after she's gone over it and over it in her head, she says, "I could like you, I think." When Shooting Glasses looks over for more, the Dr Pepper can to his lower lip, she adds in quick, "As somebody to talk to, I mean."

"Where was I your last four years?" he sort of quotes.

"Why'd you come over, shine your headlights like that?" Jade asks. "Did you know it was me?"

"There's supposed to be a bear around. Bears like trash."

"This one likes human innards, supposedly."

"Supposedly?"

"It's all setup, distraction, red herrings."

"Thought there were just trout up this high."

Jade has to grin a tolerant grin about this.

"I'm not supposed to be there on Saturday, even," she says all wistfully, changing direction.

"Independence Day? The movie on the lake thing they do?"

"*We* do."

"You do."

Jade can feel Shooting Glasses's eyes on her again. "Lot of people are going to, you know," she says, looking up to see how he takes this: "*Die.*"

"Said the girl looking for murder weapons in the junk pile."

"No, you're right," Jade has to admit. "I'm definitely a suspect, the reddest herring."

"Better than being a trout."

Jade hits his arm with the back of her hand and he rolls with it into his door, making a show of keeping his spit can level.

"You told that old sheriff about this big wilderness massacre only you know about?" he asks.

"Doesn't believe me."

"Because of your hair, your . . . *history.*"

"Among other bullshit reasons."

"Your taste in movies?" Shooting Glasses guesses.

"My *good* taste in movies," Jade says, flashing her eyes at him and also, for a snapshot of an instant, seeing the two of them through the windshield: two kids playfighting, making eyes behind the feeble jabs.

And she doesn't even know his real name.

Shooting Glasses holds his hands up in surrender.

"But if it's *not* you," he says, running with this just to keep her talking, it feels like, "then who? Is it that . . . who were you talking about? That janitor who caught fire? Cropsy?"

"Cropsy's strictly Staten Island," Jade says. "That's New York City."

"Jason, Freddy, that other one?"

"Michael," Jade fills in, shaking her head no. "I already—"

"No, the one who eats people."

"Leatherface. *Bzzzt*, not a slasher, sorry. It's not about revenge with him, just—there's nobody to get revenge *against*. Who's he supposed to come after, the Texas economy that forced his family into cannibalism?"

"Other one who eats people, I mean," Shooting Glasses says.

"Hannibal Lecter," Jade fills in. "*Bzzt*, not a slasher either, but partial credit because he also wears a face of human skin. He just likes how people taste, right? Anybody else before we move on? *Terminator, Alien, Fatal Attraction*?"

"You can do this all night, can't you?"

"What I was *saying*," Jade tries to continue, "is that I already explained all this slasher stuff to who needs to know the most."

"Did he buy into it?"

"*She*." Jade shakes her head no, sadly, Letha didn't. "Wait, though. I think it's gonna be someone dressing up like our local legend, Stacey Graves."

"Good name," Shooting Glasses says, having to rush the Dr Pepper can in to wrangle a grainy line of spit that won't break.

"Speaking of good names . . ." Jade says, looking past his current situation with the can to his yellow-tinted eyes.

He gets it, smiles, says when he can, "Greyson?"

"Greyson Brust," Jade completes, showing off that she still has that rattling around in her head. "I never heard the end of that story."

"I told you the beginning?"

"Never heard *any* of it."

"Because you . . . jumped out of the car?"

"Had to," Jade tells him. "You were about to spill, and I couldn't know this particular backstory yet."

"Because it matters?"

"At this stage we don't know what matters."

"But you think what happened to Greyson does?"

"I think you're stalling," Jade says. "What happened to him? There any reason not to tell me?"

Shooting Glasses looks down into the crusty mouth of his Dr Pepper can, kind of shrugs, says, "Sort of?"

"Meaning?"

"Meaning that one way to look at it is that—it's that we sold him, I guess."

"How much?"

"Eight hundred each. That church guy, he counted it out in cash. We had to sign the accident report the way he wrote it up."

"*Church* guy?" Jade has to ask. "Old-timey preacher, white hair and crazy eyes, big-ass hands, name rhymes with Bezekiel?"

"What? No, no—the . . . his *name*. That one the bear—"

"Deacon Samuels," Jade fills in. "The church of the flipped house."

"He paid us off. Now if we say anything, it's like perjury."

"Not sure that's really how it works."

"That's how he'll *make* it work."

"He told you this?"

"Didn't have to."

"But he's dead now."

"And my signature's still on that report," Shooting Glasses says, leaning forward to rest his chin on the top of the padded steering wheel.

"So the report's a lie, I take it."

"It wasn't supposed to matter," Shooting Glasses says. "We thought he was gonna be dead on the ambulance ride, I mean. But Greyson—"

"I really do like that name."

"You can have it," Shooting Glasses says, leaning back and looking out his window, his face right there in the reflection for Jade. "He's pretty much done with it."

"This is the part where you tell me," Jade tells him.

"What, am I hypnotized?" Shooting Glasses asks.

"I'll trade," Jade hears herself tell him back.

He looks over to her, says after a beat, "Trade what?"

"Not what you're thinking," she says, sure to hold his eyes for that. "Ever since . . . since we first met. That night. You've been wondering why I did it."

"You don't have to tell me," he says. "It's—I know there's never just one reason, I mean."

"Try me."

He considers this, considers it some more, then nods to himself, spits again, taking his time with it, and starts: "He could have been any one of us, right? Greyson, I mean. It was—we were leveling that lot on the point where the big house is going in. The dragon one."

"*Mon*dragon."

"Mondragon, yeah. One where that—I mean—"

"Where the hot girl's gonna live and take long naked showers," Jade says for him.

The dimple in his cheek gives away how right she is.

"You can pour the concrete so the top's level," Shooting Glasses continues, doing his hand left to right in case "flat" is a new concept to her. "The base, not so much. It doesn't have to be so flat, I mean. But you do want to dig down to pour. Bedrock works best, and like you were saying, it's shallow as shit over there."

"The bedrock you mean," Jade says.

"Yeah, what—?"

"The *lake* is deepest over there, because that side of the valley's steeper than over here. Forget about it, sorry."

She Theo Mondragons her hand for him to go on, and he does: "I wasn't running the backhoe, Telly was. Just scraping back and forth with the boom. He'd loosen a big rock then push it out of the way. One or two of them caught the slope, went all the way down to the lake. It was like a game. Anyway, we had this leaf blower, I guess.

It was so one of us could blast it around after Telly'd scraped an area pretty clean. So we could know what there was still left to do."

"Where'd you plug it in, this leaf blower?"

"It was gas."

Jade nods, chides herself for stopping him *again*.

"Anyway," he says, "Greyson had his safety glasses on, would step in right after Telly lifted out, and he'd—" In the confines of the cab, Shooting Glasses mimes sweeping a great windy nozzle back and forth at foot-level, like herding mice with air. Jade almost has to grin, the picture's so clear. "I was standing right beside his dumb ass, right? But I had my eyes closed, because Grey was spraying my legs. It was hilarious to him, I guess. He was always screwing around, was an accident waiting to happen. But I had to like close my eyes from it, all that little shit blasting up. Then my pants legs just went still. That was the first way I knew something had happened. At first I thought he'd maybe run out of gas."

"And this is in the *day*time?" Jade asks, hardly believing any slasher could be so brazen as to take someone with the sun shining down on them, people all around.

Shooting Glasses nods like that's not the interesting part. "He'd fallen *through*," he says. "I guess—I guess we were on top of a cave? I don't know how Telly's backhoe hadn't crumbled it all in already. But Greyson, man, the leaf blower was still there, wedged across the crack like he'd tried to hold on to it. It was still running. But he was gone, man. Fucking fell his ass all the way in, whatever."

"One of you go down there for him?"

Shooting Glasses winces, having to be there again.

"We dropped a flashlight down to him," he says. "Fifteen feet? Probably not even that. It wasn't a big-ass cavern or anything. Just a little hollowed-out place, maybe fifteen by fifteen. Your history teacher's right about it being all caves over there. Like fucking Swiss cheese."

The reason there's pockets of air in Swiss cheese, Jade knows but doesn't say, is that there's corruption in there, eating all around itself.

"But you got him out," Jade prompts.

Shooting Glasses nods.

"How?"

Shooting Glasses huffs air through his nose in a sick laugh. "We had to loop him like a goddamn pig," he says, wiping his lips with the back of his sleeve. "He kept—he kept running away from the light we'd shine down. Like, running on all *fours*, like he'd forgot he was even a person."

"Head injury?"

"Finally we shined all our lights into this one kind of corner he kept running to. So he had to cross under the hole to get out of the light, right? We dropped a cargo net on him, and when he tried to fight out of it, it tangled him up. He fought it the whole way, was making these . . . these like *noises*, I don't know."

"Had he been bitten?"

"What? No. I don't know, shit. By what? He couldn't breathe, though. Like, hypo—no. What do they call it?"

"Hyperventilating."

"Yeah, that. Rabbit-breathing, the kind where your heart's about to explode. And he was all curled up, kind of spasmy, his fingers crooked but not really broken. I don't think they were broken. You don't remember the day the ambulance came?"

Jade shakes her head no, she doesn't.

"When was this exactly?" she asks.

Shooting Glasses shrugs, says like dredging it up, "It was before you . . . that night, I mean."

"*Right* before I cut my wrist out on the water?"

"The weekend before?"

"You found this car the morning after?"

He looks across at her like how could she know this?

"Finish," she tells him.

"What?"

"Greyson Brust. Where'd Deacon Samuels hide him?"

"Hide?"

"Stash, store, house," Jade clarifies, not sure how else to say it.

"That—the old people's home over on—"

"Pleasant Valley Assisted Living."

"When we went to see him that . . . that night, he—god. He was still walking on all fours, right? Like he was thinking like a bug or something."

"That night?"

"Night we were burning the trash? You gave us that big lecture on . . . whatever?"

"Slashers."

"He'd like stop when you talked to him, but it wasn't the words he was hearing. I don't know what the hell he was hearing."

"Greyson Brust," Jade says, trying that name on again in all its glory.

Did he—did he get bit by something or some*one* in that cave, get infected, and now was sneaking out his window at Pleasant Valley every night, killing elk and people the same? *Was* this a supernatural slasher, even though it's so long after the Golden Age that it might as well be Bronze? Jade's heart thumps with possibility.

"You think it's him?" Shooting Glasses asks.

"I need to look at his feet," Jade says. "Did you have to sign the visitor log thing to see him, do you remember?"

"Not anymore."

Jade lets her thoughts keep rolling—Greyson Brust howling at the moon, his maw bloody, fingers sharp and violent—but then: "Beep, beep," she says, backing up. "What? Thought you said he was walking on all fours when you went to see him that night?"

"That night, yeah," Shooting Glasses says. "In March. He passed in April."

"What from?"

Shooting Glasses shrugs like *Does it really even matter?*

Jade supposes it doesn't.

"Eight hundred dollars," Shooting Glasses says again. "That's what we sold him for. Eight hundred fucking dollars each."

"What did Deacon Samuels say?"

"About Greyson?"

"About all of it."

He kind of squinches his face up, says, "He told us not to tell that other guy."

"Theo Mondragon."

"It was the foundation for his house," Shooting Glasses says, his tone suggesting this is obvious to him, anyway. "Mr. Samuels, he—he said every house has a story, right? That it's not always important that everybody know every little part of it. What you don't know, it doesn't matter so much."

"What happened to the cave?" Jade says.

Shooting Glasses pulls the parking lights back on, washing the galvanized chain-link diamond lattice in front of them pale yellow. "We already had the rig and the framing out there to pour the foundation later in the week," he says. "It was easy. We just—" he mimes directing a crusty-grey tube into a crack in the ground, cement slurping down. The exact same motion Greyson Brust must have been doing with the leaf blower. Except now they were blowing stone.

"You *filled* it?" Jade says.

"You can't lay a foundation over that kind of hollowed out space," Shooting Glasses says.

"It could be him, then," Jade says.

"Greyson?" Shooting Glasses says. "Told you, he's—"

"Dead, yeah," Jade says. What she doesn't say, at least out loud, is *Theo*. Because she doesn't want to mess this up. But it is *him* who was wronged, here, whose house is now built on a shaky foundation. It is *him* who had a score to settle with Deacon Samuels. Yeah, "Greyson Brust" is pretty killer for a slasher name. But "Theo Mondragon" definitely has that ring, too, doesn't it? And, if it's him—*when* it's him—there's that added twist of the boogeyman being the final girl's own father, which is perfect for a mystery slasher, no Golden Age supernatural shit necessary.

It's not as grand, is even kind of grubby, but it's pretty perfect, too. Especially since Jade had been right about him from the get-go. It *hadn't* just been paranoia. He wouldn't be the first Black slasher—Candyman, Jimmy Bones, Machete Joe—but he'd be one of hardly any, anyway.

"You gonna breathe?" Shooting Glasses asks from his side of the car, which is approximately fourteen miles away at the moment. And Jade isn't sure she can breathe right now, really. She's spent the last couple of days feeling sorry for herself, not sure what to do now that Letha won't accept she's the final girl. But this washes all of that away, doesn't it?

Saturday's three days away now, leaving her one day for reconnaissance, one day to sneak over to Terra Nova, get a sight line on Theo Mondragon, see if he's sharpening a blade or not, and one day to show that blade to Letha somehow.

It feels good to be back on track.

It sucked getting banned from Saturday's big party on the water, yeah, and she felt like a traitor, not being able to sit all the way through any of her slashers, but that's just because she's in an *actual* hand-to-God slasher. Not at the front, but not in the final tally yet, either. Just hanging around in the between-parts, which is right where she wants to be. With all her viewing, all her self-assigned homework, all she's ever seen with slashers is the main part of the story, right? The part everybody knows, the final cut. But now she's moving through the hidden parts, the connective tissue. The real guts, the *actual* terra nova.

"Watch a few movies, take a few notes," she says in her best Stu.

"You okay?" Shooting Glasses asks.

It's the same thing he asked her last time, right before she bailed. And now she's got her finger on the door handle again.

"I didn't do it because I wanted to die," Jade says, the rise of scar tissue on her left wrist practically glowing in the sleeve of her coveralls. They're watching ghost-versions of each other in the windshield now. Ghost versions that can waver away with one wrong breath. "I did it because I wanted to be part of the movie. Part of all of them. What was the day that it happened, you remember?"

"Friday, we were just off work."

"Date, I mean."

"March?"

"The *number*."

Shooting Glasses squints, trying to dredge it up, finally gloms onto it, says, "Friday the thirteenth, yeah. Radio kept talking about it."

Jade nods once, says, "Jason was supposed to rise up behind me, pull me across to Crystal Lake. Things make more sense there."

"That's that old camp?"

Shooting Glasses chin-points across the water.

"Pretty much," Jade says.

"But everybody *dies* in those movies . . ." he says, pulling the headlights on now, blasting white out across the water.

"But they really *live* first," Jade says, popping her door open to fade into the night. "Now, remember what I told you, be somewhere else this Saturday, cool?"

"What about you?"

Jade presses her lips together and stands from the car, is about to shut the door on this, which feels one hundred percent like the perfect gesture, like what would happen in a movie, but then she flinches halfway around instead.

It's not Hardy standing there—since the library, she's been spooky—but a long sustained *scream*.

It's not close, but it's close enough.

Shooting Glasses stands from his side of the car.

"They're playing my music," Jade says to him, and leaves her door open, is already running for the pier, Shooting Glasses's work boots pounding in after her. Behind the drugstore she smacks into her dad and Rexall, hustling the other way, eyes wide, Rexall still carrying a beer bottle, her dad's jeans wet, maybe . . . *all* of him wet?

The impact knocks Jade down but her dad doesn't stop, is already gone.

"Who—?" Shooting Glasses asks. She shrugs his helping hands away, wipes her dad's gross wetness off and gets up herself.

"Town drunks," she says, casting a single disparaging look after them.

Shooting Glasses turns to look as well, like there's anything to see—Indians really *can* turn to smoke—and Jade's already running again, is the first Proofrocker to get to the pier, though porch and window lights are glowing on up and down the shore.

Jade leans onto her knees breathing hard, taking in everything she can.

The *Umiak* is still there, too big to even really bob, and the screaming—yes. Yes yes yes.

It's Letha, not at the steering wheel anymore, but the back of the big white boat. Tiara's trying to hug her away from whatever's below them in the water but Letha's pushing her away, can't suffer contact right now. It's like she's trying to crawl inside herself, shut the world out.

Jade nods, gets it. In one of her papers for Mr. Holmes, she explained that the final girl goes from innocence and oblivious-ness into a series of staged confrontations with mortality, menace, danger—a funhouse of worse and worse horror—until she finally curls into herself to hide. But that's really a chrysalis. One she claws out of as an angel of death.

For Letha so far, it's been the Dutch boy in the lake, his skin sloughing off in her hands, and then Deacon Samuels, turned in-side out at Camp Blood, Letha probably stepping into him before even realizing what's happened.

"Don't forget the elk," Jade mumbles.

"What *is* that?" Shooting Glasses is asking beside her, stepping forward to see better.

Jade clamps onto his forearm, holds him back.

"This isn't for us," she says, nodding up to Letha, "it's for her."

Letha falls back so the short railing's hiding her. And now Proofrockers are arriving in robes and curlers, with shotguns, with fire pokers, with glasses of scotch they forgot to leave behind.

"Now he'll believe you?" Shooting Glasses says to Jade, about the thick red blood churning in the water, under the *Umiak*'s harsh lights. "The sheriff?"

Jade can only shake her head slowly, *no*.

Somewhere up on deck, Tiara, in her joke of a captain's hat, finally thinks to turn the propellers off. The *Umiak* sighs back into the pier, the one taut line going slack, and then Jade gets it: her dad and his idiot friends, still in high school, the three of them bobbing under the pier, waiting for the ski ropes they've tied to the boat to tighten, pull them up onto the surface of the water.

It was worth all the nights in jail, supposedly.

Until now. Until they tried to hook onto a much bigger boat, one with a whole rack of propellers back there to suck them in. Still, if it hadn't had that one line moored, it might have worked, right?

Would Letha have forgotten to cast off, though? Would Tiara? Had they ever forgotten just one single line? When they only had one line tied in the first place? And—why had they even tied-off at all, if they were just dropping a couple of Founders off?

"Who is it?" Shooting Glasses asks.

"Who *was* it," Jade corrects, backing the two of them out of this gathering crowd. "Pretty sure it was a guy name of Clate Rodge—"

She stops when she clocks a bulky shadow coming in from just behind them, where nobody should have been, where there's nothing, just . . . just the memorial bench?

"*No*," Jade says, her whole body going cold. Not because she's not supposed to be the one seeing some Scooby'd up Stacey Graves, but because . . . because there's no stringy black wig, no rotted gown. Just a wall of khaki.

She grabs on to Shooting Glasses again, to keep from falling down.

Sheriff Hardy must have been sitting there all along, smoking the night's last cigarette on his daughter's memorial bench, like every night.

"Who you say it is, there?" he asks over-innocently, his eyes flicking up to Jade's for a moment then away before she can register anything.

"N-nobody," she mutters.

He rubs his cigarette out between his fingers, deposits the butt in his chest pocket, then pats it like telling it to stay put.

"What the hell was that about?" Shooting Glasses asks once Hardy's stepped onto the pier.

"*A Bay of Blood*," Jade says, chest heaving, mind reeling, face numb, and because they're off to the side now, she knows Shooting Glasses has to be able to see what she's talking about: Clate Rodgers's frothy blood lapping up against Hardy's hull, some of the chunks adhering to the fiberglass. Not quite as high as the little airboat's name, *Melanie*, but when Hardy passes by, the water laps up a few inches, baptizes those eight letters in what's left of the boy who was with her the day she drowned.

SLASHER 101

Okay, before we talk Red Herrings in the slasher
even though it's official turkey season not fish
season, first, it's ALWAYS slasher season, as
there's plenty of <u>Blood Rage</u> around the dinner
table of <u>Home Sweet Home</u>, especially from the
<u>ThanksKilling</u> turkey itself, but second, HELLO,
MR. HOLMES! I never thought I'd miss 7th period I
mean. And since I've already done my time, this
time I can just say it out right that cutting
the fingers off my VERY FAKE glove, or, it was a
real glove but not my fingers inside just green
slime aka nightmare fuel aka Freddy blood, I
should really get a science award for that, not
suspension. Ever heard of a senior prank? I'm a
senior. That was my prank. And it's not my fault
Tiff did her big faint routine and broke her phone.
Probably it was broke already and she just wanted
someone to blame for it.

Enter me, sir. I always did it. And her mom
already bought her a new and better phone anyway.

But nevermind all that. Something's fishy here,
isn't it? It's the Red Herring in the slasher
movie. The origin of this is how when you're
running from dogs that are trailing you by smell
you can put a dead fish on your trail and that like
blows the dogs' noses up pretty much. For Agatha
Christie the Red Herring was the person all signs
and clues SAID was doing all that killing, but
really that's just Mrs. Christie being a magician
and shaking this hand so you don't watch the other
one.

Wes Craven does the same magic trick in
<u>A Nightmare on Elm Street</u>, where Rod is the obvious
killer to all the cops and parents. At least until

Freddy kills him, which is usually the way it goes
for stinky fish on the trail. And what's weird
is that for the 1st time in slasher history ever
probably, in <u>Friday the 13th: A New Beginning</u>,
which is part V, meaning "5," halfway to "X,"
Jason Voorhees HIMSELF is kind of the Red Herring.
Everyone thinks the killer is him, when surprise,
it's far less exciting. Even Randy in <u>Scream</u> SAYS
he himself is the obvious right suspect for Casey
Becker and Steve, his tastes all being in the
horror aisle of the video store, but this is AFTER
Billy and Stu have already fake set Billy up into
Red Herringhood.

What to notice here is the magic trick happening
before your eyes, sir. Agatha or Wes are just
shaking this hand around to distract your nose
if you were a dog, but it's all so this real and
actual blood soaked party can creep past into non-
suspicionhood. And while sometimes the way they
be fair is to say "LOOK, he's doing all of this,
can't you see?" we've been burned so many times by
exactly this that we know that can't be true, so we
keep on looking the other way.

What the slasher does I mean is turn us ALL into
the cops and parents who 100 percent know it's
Rod who killed his girlfriend Tina, who KNOW it's
Jason in <u>V</u>, and that's when it has us right where
it wants us, since cops and parents are less than
useless in the slasher.

So are we, I mean, except as carving dummies,
which isn't like carving a turkey, except for the
end result, I guess.

Enjoy your meal, Mr. Holmes.

STAGE FRIGHT

It's four in the morning and Jade's standing half-in, half-out of the front door of her father's house, not sure if she should take that next step or not. On the couch and in the chair are her father and Rexall, in the same places they were for what she guesses she should be calling The Night of the Carrot—her dad's joke about her orange hair. They're already passed out this time, though. Passed out and slobbering, snoring, twitching, Rexall hugging a pillow.

Jade gives her foot some weight, praying for no creak, and for once her prayer is answered. If they didn't wake from her hauling the door open, though, then that means they're really and truly conked, right?

Surely.

Where she's coming in from is the staging area. She sat there with Shooting Glasses until the next Terra Nova shift started to sift in. He'd cracked his can open for a morning dip then opened his door, nodded bye to Jade.

"Won't you be tired?" Jade asked him.

"Sleep when I'm dead," he said around his first gush of spit, spinning around on his heel to shoot her with imaginary sixguns. "Sam Elliott, *Road House*, 1988."

"1989," Jade didn't have the heart to tell him, just launched her fingers off her forehead in goodbye, sloped home with her hands deep in the pockets of her coveralls, her shoulders up by her ears, a sort-of smile on her face. The whole night, her and Shooting Glasses had just talked about nothing, not one single real thing. It was stupid, would be a boring art house film were it on-screen, two kids mumbling in the afterglow of a killing because they're both too shy to hold hands, but it had been pretty perfect too.

Its opposite, pretty much, is her dad groaning on the couch now, and scratching himself, doing that kind of shifting and flopping that means he's about to crack an eye open. Jade stops breathing, doesn't know whether she's hitting the floor to be below his blurry line of sight or if she's stepping cleanly back out the door she just walked through. But no way will she be making eye contact with him when his hands are down the front of his pants.

He snorts, nuzzles his face deeper into the couch cushion, and drops back into what she hopes is a falling dream, so she can watch his clothes flatten out when he hits bottom. When that doesn't happen and then doesn't happen again, she finally allows herself to breathe, and imagine what if . . . what if she *were* the slasher here? What if she had been raised by Ezekiel, attended all his black masses, learned all his lessons before she was swapped for a baby in Proofrock? If she were that slasher, then she would know to straighten a coat hanger out, creep up to both of these rejects, and drive that sharp point into their ear all at once, then wait around to dab up any blood that dribbled back out. Hardy probably wouldn't even have any autopsies run, as this would be good riddance to shitty rubbish.

It would be so easy.

Jade opens and closes her right hand, going through the motions, licking her lips with anticipation.

Except . . . she'd sort of thrown up just from stabbing that dead bird with her litter stick, hadn't she? Wouldn't pushing a coat hanger into a human ear require her to muscle through some membrane or thin bone or something, to get to the brain?

She's a gorehound, a horror fiend, the more brutal the better, bring it on, faster, pussycat, kill kill kill, but that's all on-screen. And at some level she never forgets that all the blood's corn syrup.

Still, she tells herself, she *could* do it.

Just, not tonight.

Rather, some other time when her alibi is bulletproof. And maybe not both at once, maybe not even Rexall at all, since he's no more aware of being alive than a jellyfish or mushroom. And, just one of them doesn't draw the same suspicion, does it? Especially when that one's whole life since his car wreck in high school is time he's been stealing. This is just *Final Destination*: Death, calling in its marker. That coat hanger in the ear would be more just a function of nature, wouldn't it?

Jade nods to herself about all of this, part of her fully aware that she's made this same plan twenty times before. Fifty times. Ever since junior high, really, with all manner of household implements, with every last screwdriver in the toolbox, with all the rakes and shovels and hoes in the shed.

This time she means it, though.

"Bang," she says, looking down her finger at her father, but she also sort of sees herself standing here, adopting that pose—sees herself as Hardy would, as Mr. Holmes would: another teenager who hates the parent she's stuck with. And that's the only way they *have* to see her, too, which is the catch-22 bullshit of it all.

Still, Jade angles the barrel of her finger over, drills a bullet into Rexall as well, just for good measure, and then freezes when Rexall hikes a leg up in an obscene pose, almost in response.

Jade angles her face up to stare through the ceiling, away from this moment, only slowly realizing she's listening to something. She cocks her head over to let the sound drain in better: somewhere far above Proofrock, Mr. Holmes's tiny rotors are whapping at the air. Either him or that's another LifeFlight up there, and, if it is, then who for this time? Who for and how late?

Let Letha handle it, though. Which means: let Letha *witness* it. Let it all stack up in *her* head, because she's the one who's going to need it as fuel for her big turnaround.

What Jade needs is . . . sleep?

Except, as much as she hates it, here in her living room are two survivors, two witnesses to what happened to Clate Rodgers. Two idiots who could tell her if the *Umiak* had been tied to the pier or not. That her father was wet in the alley meant he had to have been the one wading past the crusty pylons to find a latchpoint on that sleek white hull, Rexall high and dry playing lookout, Clate bobbing under the pier, psyching himself up. Well, shotgunning another beer anyway. Same difference.

Problem is, asking Tab Daniels for a version of this will be putting him up on a throne for as long as Jade needs that answer, won't it? When she's promised and sworn and vowed to never ask him for a single thing again, no matter what.

Jade comes back to her father's sleeping face. There's a beer in the crook of his arm, its longneck nestled in his armpit. When he shifts, it starts to seep into his pearl snap shirt, a slow flower of darkness to match all the faded-out flowers in the print. Jade watches it bloom as long as she can, finally has to ghost forward, tiptoe between, sneak the bottle up and out. What she tells herself is that she's Ripley, crawling over a sleeping alien. She's Sidney, squirming over an unconscious Ghostface. But really she just doesn't want her dad feeling that wetness and waking.

Much better to let him sleep on.

Instead of taking a swig of the warm beer, she settles it onto the taped-together coffee table with the other empties. That's another thing she's promised and sworn, mumbled vows about: never to drink beer like him. Cigarettes, sure, smoking doesn't make you stupid, just dead. But if she ever drinks, then that opens the door on a future where she someday shares a beer with her dad, and that's not a door she'll ever let life drag her through.

She could nudge Rexall awake, she supposes. Tricking him into telling her about what happened to Clate would be cake, *less* than cake. Except . . . talking to him would mean *talking* to him, and she's not that desperate. Even at four in the morning.

But what could Rexall *or* her father tell her about Clate Rodgers that would even be useful, right? Doesn't she already know?

This is always her favorite part of any slasher. It's already been established, thanks to the bodies stacking up, that somebody thinks they've got a good reason to be doing this, however it is they're doing it. Now the push is to figure out what the dead might have in common, where their paths might cross. After that it's just a matter of thinking back to who was where when a prank or accident went down. Who had stepped out to powder their nose, see a man about a horse, make a call?

Or, before *Scream*, anyway, that's how you used to be able to figure a slasher out. Until it was either Billy *or* Stu who had to be gone from the room long enough to don a certain mask.

But, it was just and only Hardy ambling down from Melanie's bench, wasn't it? Cashing his last smoke and then moseying down to what was left of the idiot that let his daughter die.

So it's him, then?

He is as good a candidate as anyone to bring Stacey Graves back. Except for Christine Gillette—his *aunt*—he's the only one Jade knows to have actually seen Stacey Graves. And, what a *Prowler*-y rush if the slasher's a law enforcement officer, right? That would . . . it would be like Nancy's dad in *A Nightmare on Elm Street* feeling so much guilt about breaking the law to kill Freddy that he ducks into the crusty fedora himself, doses the kids with something to make them think they're dreaming, and goes about punishing the whole block for their big crime.

As for how Hardy could have done Clate Rodgers: with his air-boat tied to the pier, he had every excuse to be ambling past the *Umiak* for whatever he forgot—his lighter for that all-important last cigarette, probably. And if Letha or Tiara called down to ask why was he tying them off, he could just say he didn't know any-body was aboard, he just didn't want it drifting away, a big pretty boat like that. What he *wouldn't* be saying would be that, when you have the chance to dispense with the grown-up version of the kid you blame for your daughter's drowning, you do that, even if you're already involved in something larger.

When the bodies are accumulating, there's always room for one more, right?

Jade nods, says it aloud in the living room, like a test: "Right."

Neither of the sleepers objects. Which she takes as permission to go on with this line of thinking. With . . . maybe one last smoke to keep her company.

She palms the half a pack of cigarettes from under the lamp and steps out onto the back porch, sits in the open door and chain-smokes two, then one more for good measure.

The plan, she's pretty sure, should be to sneak over to Terra Nova tomorrow—*today*, actually. It's after midnight, right? Any-way, before Clate Rodgers burbled up from Indian Lake in chunks and smears, it was a lock that Theo Mondragon had to be the one behind all this. And he still could be. She could have Hardy all wrong—Theo Mondragon could have stowed away on the *Umiak*, been setting a death trap for someone else, for one of those two Founders who were going to have to be picked back up, and Clate just happened to get literally sucked into it. That Hardy didn't stop it doesn't mean he actually *did* it.

Theo's got the more immediate motivation, anyway—his house, his literal castle—and since it's not the millennium, motivations matter. Motivations are everything. Hardy has his daughter as an excuse to let Clate Rodgers get pulled into those whirling blades, but his motivation for Deacon Samuels is a harder nut.

Oh: unless he wanted a certain golf club, Jade remembers. Do people really kill for golf stuff, though? She wants to say no, except . . . Jason did kill that one guy for littering, right?

But if greed or envy or gain is the motivation, then this is a giallo Proofrock's in, not a revenge-driven slasher, and since this isn't Italy in the sixties, she has to suspect there's some other motivation, one that feels a lot more righteous.

And? She's not *supposed* to have it all figured out yet, is she?

Doesn't mean she can't be trying, though.

Like she can help it.

So the plan now is to conk out for a few hours then hike around the lake to Terra Nova, maybe stop to wow over the Deacon Samuels stains behind the fluttering yellow tape at Camp Blood, and then she'll either figure out she's right, it's Theo, or she'll exclude him, easy as that, one-and-done.

Jade blows a clean line of smoke up into the night and cashes her butt on the sole of her boot, keys on another paper she wrote for Mr. Holmes, about how the reason final girls fall so much when running away is that they're like those mother birds who flap away from their nests like they're hurt, so as to draw the predator off of their babies.

She never turned that one in, though. She burned it half-written and flushed the ashes, because no mothers are actually like that.

What about Letha, though? Will she continually fall down on Saturday, so as to draw the slasher away from the floating masses? There will be lots of kids in the water that night, Jade knows. Lots of innocents.

She turns to go in, spinning at the last moment to catch the screen door, keep it from waking the living room, but then she stops: the smallest, saddest bottle rocket is tumbling down out of the sky. Which is to say: a lit cigarette.

"I'm telling your wife," Jade says up to Mr. Holmes with a smile, and, when the cigarette spools a trail of smoke up out of the tall dry grass, she steps over and stomps it out, saving the whole town, probably. "And that's how you do it," she says to the idea of Letha, and then leaves Mr. Holmes up there to court lung cancer and fight bats.

The kitchen is empty, the living room still asleep.

Jade pads through to her bedroom to cue something up and crash, and—

Shit. Really?

All her videotapes and clothes and posters are in two black trashbags on her bed.

Jade just stares at them, stares at them some more, and finally comes up with the only possibility: her dad heard about her OK Corral walk down Main with Hardy.

"But I didn't bring him *here*," Jade says, picking through the jumbled tapes, finally lucking onto *Just Before Dawn*. She can't carry the whole bag around the lake to Letha as one last lesson, but she can at least leave her with that one. Technically—chronologically—*Halloween* should probably be next in her education, and that's only if they skip over *Black Christmas*, but . . . this isn't the full course anymore, is it? This is a crash course, a late-night cram session. And if Letha's going to have to pick one final girl to follow, then don't pick the one who hides in a closet, don't pick the one who leaves the killer's *knife* behind, don't pick the one who has to get saved by a dude with a gun at the end. Pick the one who becomes rage, the one who climbs the front of that hillbilly slashing machine and jams her arm down his throat up to her fucking elbow, looking him in the eye the whole time.

Just Before Dawn, then. That and . . .

Jade reaches around under her bed, frees up the machete weaved into the mattress's undercarriage. It's from the flea market in Idaho Falls, still has the factory edge. Jade looks around for what else she might need, finally decides to change everything she's wearing under her coveralls. Because who knows.

Instead of throwing the dirties in the laundry corner, she stuffs them back in the bag.

After that, the only thing left is to dig out the food coloring in the kitchen, dye her hair one last time in the sink, being sure to lock the door first.

The food coloring's dark green, the result more aquamarine shading into turquoise, and temporary as hell. Still, it's something, right?

On the way out the front door, a fresh sandwich in each pocket, two garbage bags glistening over her shoulder, she flips the living room off roundly, walks backwards off the porch still doing it.

School's out *forever*.

Instead of trying to brave the trees and the muck in the pitch black—there *is* a rogue bear out there somewhere—Jade asks Terra Nova to wait until the light of morning, please. Maybe she can crash out in a storage shed in the staging area until then? Except, on the way there . . . of course.

The screen for the big July Fourth celebration is already inflated, for everybody to watch from the lake. They do it early like this now, since the time in sixth grade when they did it the afternoon-of, and had to keep the compressor running all through the movie because of some new holes in the vinyl, which kind of killed the whole "movie on the lake" charm. It was more like "movie nobody can hear over the air compressor."

Jade doesn't key on the screen just because it's *up*, though. It's also glowing.

On-screen is the giant version of someone's laptop screen, it looks like. Mac, not PC. Jade steps back into the shadows to watch, cues in that the two Founders who were getting dropped off earlier, they're back on the deck of the *Umiak* now—probably with whatever cable or adapter they needed for the projector, it being a few years old, their ports all next-gen.

It is Mars Baker, and, Jade finally decides, Llewellyn Singleton. Their little laptop screen is glowing onto their faces, and they look for all the world like two twelve-year-olds hunched over a video clip between classes. Hanging a few feet back from them, hands on the rail, is Letha Mondragon, her eyes cupped in the Jackie O sunglasses and pale wrap pretty much mandated for someone who's now found *three* dead people since moving to town.

When you're mourning, grief-stricken, shell-shocked, sunglasses at night are cool. And . . . does Letha see Jade? Jade backs up farther, dropping her bags into the bushes, only keeping the machete, but hiding it along her right leg like's proper.

Finally Letha's black lenses move on to Main all at once, Jade's eyes going with whether she wants to look or not. It's just a cat crossing under the streetlight, but is there anything more perfect to spook things up?

Jade nods thank you to Letha for directing her to this next Jonesy, and then whatever Mars Baker and Lewellyn Singleton are trying to magic onto the big screen finally pops.

"Hunh," Jade says. Also: *of course.*

It's a slideshow of Deacon Samuels's life. There he is in a silver hard hat, cutting a ribbon for some groundbreaking event. There he is on the cover of *Golf Digest.* There he is in a candid shot with Lady-bird, his wife. There he is having fun in the swan boat, Indian Lake all around him like the place he's been looking for his whole life.

The reason they're testing this now, Jade figures, is that this is going to play before the movie on Saturday, right? It's easier than inviting the whole town over to gawk through Terra Nova, breathe all the clean air up.

It's funny, too: the *Umiak* right under these Founders, and part of the pier is cordoned off with Hardy's yellow tape. Because the fish probably haven't eaten all of Clate Rodgers yet, have they? The bigger chunks of him had probably been the work of a few min-utes: plunge an official fishnet in and back a couple of times and he's gone, in a bucket, in cold storage, a big "do not drink / not margaritas!" sign taped on it.

And now the slideshow's over and . . . another no-surprise: it's a video of the remaining Founders. They're down in some ma-hogany part of the yacht, it looks like. Lewellyn Singleton, Mars Baker, Ross Pangborne, and the chair of the board, farthest from the camera—meaning the center of the shot—Theo Mondragon.

Jade tries to look past the screen, past the *Umiak*, all the way over to the actual yacht, but comes back to the screen when who-ever's holding the camera moves in on the Founders.

Instead of the suits or high-dollar casual wear they're usually wearing, all four look to be just in from a swim. Towels around the necks, either actually or artfully mussed hair, and wearing . . . not "trunks" exactly. More plum-smuggler cycling shorts? Not banana hammocks—there's legs to them—but not board shorts either.

And? They can each pull off shorts that tight, that unforgiving. Mars Baker, even, when he coughs into his hand, has a six-pack or thereabouts, and Theo Mondragon looks pretty damn sculpted, Jade has to admit before looking away.

Of course they'd turn the memorial for their friend into another way to lord it over the common folk, remind them of the pecking order.

This slasher can't come fast enough.

Jade starts to turn away, not be drawn into the practice run for this spectacle—thanks for the warning, Mr. Holmes—but then the speakers crackle. Jade stops, her hands clenching into fists, but she's listening now.

Sorry, Mr. Holmes.

Jade looks back over her shoulder and the memorial slideshow's still over, but now what Mars Baker and Lewellyn Singleton are playing on the inflatable screen is an actual recording of Deacon Samuels. A Skype session that somebody apparently hit "record" on. Deacon Samuels has his golf cap pulled down low like the frat boy he must be, and he's just lowering a disposable plastic cup but savoring whatever's in it, meaning this is maybe the end of the day, except . . . is that trashy wood paneling behind him? Is that dim light hanging on a fake brass chain familiar?

Jade turns all the way around, steps closer to be sure, then nods.

Deacon Samuels is in a room of the Trail's End Motel just off the highway, three hundred yards from where Jade's standing right now. To be sure, she turns, uses a tree to help tippy-toe, and, yep, there's that big dying Indian sign that's supposed to lure travelers in and, in the same way you warn coyotes by hanging their dead brethren on the fence, keep Indians out.

He stays *there*, though?

"And I just had this long wonderful conversation with the gentleman who runs the gas station, I believe his name was . . . Lonnie, yes. Apparently his family has been here since before electricity, that's the way he put it."

Jade's eyes skate over the water where the crowd will be bobbing on Saturday and she has to press her lips together, happy for Lonnie in his innertube, his name coming through the speakers. What Deacon Samuels isn't saying anything about is Lonnie's stutter, which would have made their conversation at the gas pumps . . . something a person on the cover of golfing magazine could be poking fun at. But he isn't. He isn't even mentioning it. And everybody watching this Saturday night is going to lift their beers to Lonnie, and there might even be a swell of applause for him, probably his first one ever.

"And then, do you know what he *did*?" Deacon Samuels says. "I'd forgotten the world could work like this, that it had ever been this small. He—he stepped out into the street and waved at someone having coffee at this perfect little diner, Dot's"—another round of applause here, surely—"and who he was calling over was a realtor, a Mrs. Christy."

Misty Christy takes a bow here, from whatever float she's on.

"And, and of course there's plots of land available here, but that's not what I'm talking about. What I'm talking about is . . . it's the clarity of the water, Theo. This isn't like Boston Harbor. And, Lew, the air here, I think it'd be good for Lemmy. Mars, I know Macy likes to birdwatch, doesn't she? And aren't the girls on the swim team? And Galatea, Ross, there's so much up here for her to photograph. But it's not just what to do, you can do stuff anywhere, it's . . . it's like, do you remember that old movie *The Land That Time Forgot*? Theo, I know you do, I think you own it now. This is like an idyllic little part of the world that's stayed safe and pristine, that hasn't been touched. And, I don't want to presume, but I think if we were to pool our resources and connections . . . Mars, this is more your domain, but we could—"

Jade's face is slack now.

This is Deacon Samuels, out driving across America, and stumbling into Proofrock, and falling in love with it, and trying to . . . not to *sell* it to his friends, but to get them to see it as he does.

He's a realtor, a salesman, Jade reminds herself.

But still.

"How could we have said no?" another voice comes in now.

It's Lewellyn Singleton, the banker. He's stepping out from the mahogany locker he was sort of leaning against, and the camera's close on him now. His hands are working the twisted ends of the towel slung across his neck.

"This place was and is everything Deacon said it was," Lewellyn goes on, "and more. Yes, this high mountain air has done wonders for my son's lung condition. Who'd have thought that a nineteenth-century cure would still work in the twenty-first century?" He smiles, shrugs. "But it's been good for me, too. I feel like I've finally found home, which I know has to sound like . . . most of you have been here your whole lives, it's *your* home, we understand that. But"—he rolls his lips in, looks away like trying to keep his eyes busy—"I don't know how you define 'home,' that's . . . I know interest rates and long-term this and that, it doesn't matter. My little dog of fourteen years, though, Princess Leia, we brought her with us last time we were here, and—and now she's buried over here in Terra Nova. That's how *I* define it, that's how I define 'home.'"

He shrugs, steps back, and Jade's arms are crossed now. Because she's trying to resist this.

"Hi," Ross Pangborne says, raising his hand and stepping forward, then evidently taking direction from whoever's behind the camera. He steps over, more into the center of the frame, waves all over again. "First, let me say that I'm not reading any of your direct messages," he says with a guilty smile, referencing a recent privacy scandal his social media empire just went through. Jade can't help it, has to smile with him here. He's so awkward, so vulnerable, so *not* the raging, power-mad tycoon. "Second, and much more important, I want to thank you for welcoming us not just into your beautiful town, but your lives. And I want to personally apologize for the—the process of building across the lake, here, which is leaving industrial scars, I know. But we want you all to know, and this is a promise, there's going to be a park there next summer, and it will be fully accessible, and the—the county won't have to support it. That's going to be our job. You'll see one of us out there every weekend, collecting any gum wrappers, any soda bottles. That's our guarantee. Thank you."

Jade shakes her head no, this isn't happening, this can't be happening.

Mr. Holmes was *right*. He has to be. The Founders are evil, they're capitalism in human form, they're only in Proofrock because mountain towns are in style for their tax bracket this year.

"And don't worry, I'll make sure that's all legal and proper," Mars Baker says with a smile he can't quite swallow. This is the point in their pre-movie show where everybody in the water laughs, Jade knows: the high-dollar lawyer reminding them that he can get down and dirty with a contract. "But seriously," he says, already making his closing argument, "I know you can't see it yet, but we've told the teams putting our homes together that they're not to cut down even one single tree. And we're not allowing any fences over here, either. To us, this is still going to be national forest land, and before that, the traditional homeland of the Shoshone, a fact we should all keep in mind. Ownership in these mountains is a recent concept. The one we prefer is *stewardship*. When the deer come in and nibble Macy's garden down to nubs, then, well, we'll just come over to Dot's, order a salad, right, Ms. Dorothy?" Then Mars Baker steps closer, says behind his hand, "But don't tell Macy, her squash and black-eyed peas are already all she talks about . . ."

Jade looks up into the sky, reminds herself that Macy Todd killed a boyfriend in a hotel once upon a time, and then rented two days' worth of movies.

While she's staring up, Theo takes the stage. She can tell from the silence. The media mogul knows how to work a camera.

"As many of you know, my daughter will forever be a graduate of Henderson High, class of 2015!" He pumps his fist and then holds it there, like congratulating Letha. Like congratulating all of them. Then he opens that hand, massages Lewellyn Singleton's shoulder, his eyes still staring right into the soul of the crowd. "And I don't know what I can add that these fine gentlemen"—Ross Pangborne pushes him, as if "gentlemen" is an insult, a joke, but the effect is that they're just boys in a locker room. That they're just like everyone bobbing in the water, soaking all of this in—"that they haven't already said, and said so much better than I ever could. We do, we love it here. This isn't a refuge from the modern world, we wouldn't use your town, your lake, your valley like that. This is a place we want to put down roots, a place we want to watch our children grow, and their children's children. But shh, shh, we don't want to tell anybody else about it either." Laughter here, Jade knows. She knows because she almost burped a laugh up herself. "Where else in all of America can a town come together to float in the water and watch a movie about people in the water!" Theo says, louder now, and Lewellyn swims a rubber shark in behind him, Theo unaware of it. "And yes, a hundred times over, we miss our friend Deacon." The shark lowers. Theo's face lowers. "He was the best of us. He was the one who found this place. He's the one who should be here saying all this to you."

The mahogany locker room of Founders dissolves then, replaced by . . . shit.

It's the snapshots Deacon Samuels took of Indian Lake and Proofrock, the first time he swung through. In some of them he's running to try to be in the shot, but he never quite makes it, and that makes it approximately one thousand times more endearing.

Finally it holds on a selfie he took, him and Lonnie at the gas pumps, Lonnie's lips pressed tight together like he always does because he doesn't want to stutter, Deacon Samuels smiling full-on into the camera, his sunglasses in his right hand, his eyes crinkling into crow's feet from all his hours spent on the links.

When that image is finally burned in, faded away, Theo Mondragon is there in that mahogany locker room again, Lewellyn Singleton and Ross Pangborne and Mars Baker all crowded in like groomsmen. Theo Mondragon takes a sip from his plastic water bottle, looks camera right, then leans in, says, "But we've got to be part of the community, we want to be part of the community here. Ross, weren't you saying that? We can't just invade the place, we've got to . . . we should prove ourselves to them somehow, don't you think? That we're committed, involved?"

It's obviously scripted, and Jade's pretty sure Theo Mondragon is being a worse actor than he really is, which takes some real acting chops, but still, it works.

"And, just so you know," Theo says, "this wasn't our idea. This is all Deke—*Deacon*, I mean. He didn't want to be a siphon on the community, but a reservoir the community could draw from."

"He wanted to pay back into this place," Lewellyn Singleton, the banker, says.

"His testimony about Proofrock sealed the deal," Mars Baker, the lawyer, says.

"He clicked 'like' on every person here," Ross Pangborne adds with a smile.

The four of them lift their water bottles in toast, and, come Saturday night, all the beer cans come up in response, Jade knows.

"In the spirit of that," Theo says, "we propose a standing offer to every graduate of Henderson High starting next year." He looks around solemnly to the other three Founders, as if confirming this crazy idea. When there's no takebacks, he looks back into the camera, says, "We propose to establish a scholarship fund that will pay for four years of college at any state university."

"To every graduate!" Mars Baker adds.

"Just *state*?" Ross Pangborne says to all of them, the most scripted line so far, and Pangborne oversells it by a mile, but this is the "all in good fun" part of the programming.

"*Wherever* they want to go!" Lewellyn Singleton adds, like what the hell.

"The Deacon and Ladybird Samuels Memorial Scholarship Fund," Theo says as farewell, and, because they can't take it any higher after that, that's when the Founders freeze-frame, arms over shoulders, smiling lopsided smiles, fizzing black and white, and THE DEACON AND LADYBIRD SAMUELS MEMORIAL SCHOLARSHIP FUND burns in over them in a tasteful, dignified font.

This is how you buy a town in the mountains.

It's gonna be a drunk night, Jade can already tell. More than usual. All those college funds will be getting turned into boats, into trucks, into vacations. Jade hates it, but, standing alone at the front edge of the trees, she has to blink away tears herself, even. Not of happiness, but of having been born too late: this starts with the class of 2016, not her and Letha's class.

Jade laughs a sick laugh and shakes her head in disgust, trying hard to be bitter against all the Hawks just a year behind her, who now have access to the world. But some of that disgust is also for herself: this was so much easier when she could hate all of these Founders *righteously*, like Mr. Holmes. Now it's . . . it's complicated. It's bullshit.

Worse, what she has to take into account now—to use a Lewellyn Singleton banking term—is that one of these rich goofballs is the slasher? In theory, it's great, it's ironclad. Of course it's one of them. In practice, though, after having actually seen them, heard them . . . no way could it be Ross, and not Lewellyn either. They could no more lop a head off than Bill Gates could. Any violence they do, it's with keystrokes. It still could *possibly* be Mars, she supposes, but that's just because he's a lawyer, has to have a black heart, a hidden agenda, and the ability to think fourteen steps ahead. And the only reason Theo Mondragon would still be in the mix is that he makes the cycle so neat, so contained, so elegant—all in the family.

She'll just have to go over there, see. And if it's not Theo Mondragon? Then . . . Rexall? Except he's always fourteen steps *behind*. It could always be Hardy and Holmes tag-teaming it Billy and Stu–style, she supposes. Or even her dad, out killing between beers, and then popping a beer to celebrate each death, and then probably sneaking a nip or two in the act-of. And of course there's always Deacon Samuels. He was collected in bags, right? Meaning he was mostly identifiable by his golf clubs, so, if he could stage a body double for that bear, maybe to avoid the SEC or something, he could still be out there, could be the one doing all this.

The suck-thing about all this, of course, is that if Jade's wrong about the Founders, then who else is she wrong about? It's like on cop shows: when the prosecutor turns out to have been bad, then all the people they sent up get released. Is Jade that prosecutor now? Does her mom deserve a second chance? Her father? Is *she* the one with Michael's babysitter goggles, except, for her, "babysitter" is *all* adults, and since she doesn't have a machete in her hands, she uses her tongue, her accusations, her suspicions?

"But I *do* have a machete," Jade hisses, and thunks it hard into the tree beside her, which makes her general area go halogen-white. She threads her sticky bangs out of her eyes to study the top of the tree, see if this is actually a streetlight. When it's not, she leaves her hand as visor, and peers around to the dummy light pinning her in place.

Hardy. Of course. In his Bronco.

She's running before she even tells her legs about it, the machete still in her hand, the blade in the tree nearly pulling her shoulder out of its socket, both her boots actually airborne for a moment, like the cartoon she doesn't want to be.

"Jade, wait!" Hardy calls through his speaker, but Jade can't.

She falls ahead, the machete tearing away from the tree with a distinct horror-movie sound, and it's all downhill from there. The slope to Indian Lake lets her be faster than she is, faster than her own thoughts: What's she going to do, swan dive off the pier, swim to Camp Blood? Ask Letha for asylum on the *Umiak*? Hope Hardy gives up, which is exactly what cops do when perps holding deadly weapons run?

More important, why is she even running? It's Hardy, isn't it?

Shit. Shit shit shit.

She wants this to be *Scream* so was trying to pair him up with Mr. Holmes, but the feeling she can't shake is his voice coming out of the darkness outside the library the other night. His shape walking in from Melanie's bench, sparks trailing from his hand, Clate Rodgers a red smear on the surface of the lake. And he does have that backstory with his daughter dying probably fifty yards from where they are right now, and *with* someone Jade's dad used to drink with, and he does have a brush with Stacey Graves, he did grow up with his aunt telling him that rhyme, he did find Deacon Samuels, he did set a fire that killed his own uncle or whatever, and with that airboat, he can skid up onto shore wherever he wants, be gone in an instant. Or, if you're out on the water, he can be right there beside you before you know it, hardly even dragging a wake, his big fan turned off a hundred yards back, so he just coasts in, the only sound the soft *whop-whop-whop* of his blades spinning down.

On the other hand, he did save Jade when she was bleeding out, and he did get her the custodian gig after freshman year, and he does run her dad in whenever he can—could the enemy of Jade's enemy even *be* a slasher?

Jade doesn't know, but what she does know is she can't stop running. The slope's got her now. All she can do is . . . is sling the machete as far out into the water as she can, dispose of that evidence, not give him a reason to take her in. Never mind that there's nowhere to go after she does, nothing to do, no way to hide.

Halfway up the pier she catches on that Letha's leaning over the rail, is watching this hopeless little effort.

Jade changes her grip on the machete so slightly, but it makes all the difference.

"Letha!" Jade yells up to her, and Letha cocks those bug-eyed shades up on her forehead, which is all the invitation Jade needs. She stops hard, her combat boots finding traction for once, and turns all that momentum into one desperate throw.

The machete goes twirling up into the night, Mars Baker turning around to track it, Hardy's tires screeching, all of Jade's hopes and prayers in that spinning blade, now.

It climbs, it climbs, and, just when it should be lodging in Letha's chest, instead her hand stabs out as only a final girl's can, and catches that machete by the handle as perfect as anything, so perfect that Jade hardly even feels it when Hardy tackles her.

SLASHER 101

So for a slightly late Christmas present, sir,
please accept this gift of a last ingredient of the
slasher, whose season will be upon us again soon
in only 10 short months, by which time you'll be
having to get your slasher information from some
other horror fan, since this girl will be graduated
and GONE.

   And you would never guess it in a 100 years
unless maybe you were Clear Rivers from the
<u>Final Destination</u>s, but this ingredient is tied to
the incident in the cafeteria just before winter
break. But in my defense though Manx wouldn't
believe it, I really was projectile puking from
sudden onset sickness. This wasn't my attempt to
spit pea soup like Regan in <u>The Exorcist</u>. And also
it wasn't a prank, sir. I think if anyone else had
been sick then the cafeteria monitor would have
made tracks to get that student to the nurse's
office instead of sending her to the principal's
office based on only past History of trying to make
high school a fun or just less terrible experience.
But that was last year as they say. Well, as
everybody says except Billy Loomis, or in 1958,
Pamela Voorhees.

   You'll also have to start getting excellent
jokes from somewhere else, sir, sorry about that.

   But, since we're already talking puking, that's
what final girls are all better than me at not
doing in the Third Reel Bodydump. There aren't
autopsies to prove this but I think final girls
must have an extra valve in their esophagus that
keeps them from upchuck city, sir. How else to
explain them not losing their lunch when, about
2/3rd's or even 3/4th's through the slasher

movie they're in, suddenly they stumble upon
the dead and necrogymnastic bodies of their
friends and families? Think Laurie Strode in
Halloween for example, finding so many of her
friends surprisingly dead and suspiciously posed
in that bedroom across the street, which would
become the basic model to repeat not just for
the Golden Age, but all the way to now, sir, which I
won't walk you all the way through since you always
mark all of them out as extra like that swimming
pool of bodies in House on Sorority Row, which
I'm not even mentioning. This Third Reel Bodydump
though is a most important part of the final girl's
development. Or instead, being faced with all this
definite PROOF of what terror she's up against is
carving away of the rules of her once sane world.
It pushes her over the edge, and when she climbs
back up again, she's different and more dangerous.

The question that's never answered here though
is why the slasher DOES this, which I'm sure you're
right now asking out loud at your desk. Well, WHY
he does and HOW he learns all these knot tying and
spring loading bodies from ceilings tricks, but
if you start thinking like that then Michael Myers
would never have learned to drive the car he steals
to get back to Haddonfield, and nobody wants to
have to think like that, sir. Especially not Yours
Untruly.

But there is a reason the slasher does this
kindness, sir, but since I'm nearly at my 2 page
limit here I'll save that for a My Bloody Valentine
to you, I think. But don't feel cheated either.
Really, I've put my own beating heart into every
one of these already.

DON'T GO IN
THE HOUSE

In *A Nightmare on Elm Street*, after Rod's been jammed up for Tina's murder, he doesn't know not to fall asleep. So, when he does, Freddy's able to twist a sheet into a noose and hang him, make it look like a suicide, which is pretty much an admission of guilt as far as the cops and parents are concerned.

Nancy knows better.

So does Jade.

All night in her cell, each time her head started to nod forward into sleep, she'd jerk awake, check the bars and cinderblocks for a hidden face, watch the drain in the middle of the floor for blade-tips reaching up. And it's not just Freddy to watch for in a place like this. Wishmaster could step into the passage between the two cells, use his drug dealer voice to ask her if she'd like to walk through these solid bars to freedom, and if Jade was tired enough, she might not remember to word this wish with utmost care, and end up being pulled like taffy through the steel bars.

No thank you.

It's so hard to stay awake without a phone, though. Without a spear to stab trash with. Without Holmes sad-ranting about Terra

Nova. Without a videotape playing. Without Fugazi leaking into her ears. Without Letha screaming to fill the night.

It had been glorious, though, hadn't it? And—the way she stabbed her hand up, plucked that machete down from the heavens by the *handle*. If she's not a final girl, then there never was a final girl, and Jade's wrong about everything.

But no way is she wrong.

Jade stands, paces the meager length her cell affords, tries to grim her eyes down like a real convict but it's hard to maintain while doing the pee-pee dance. There are no facilities in the two cells, just a chamberpot from, she's guessing, 1899. Henderson and Golding themselves probably took turns pissing into it.

So far, Jade's been granted access to the ladies' room up front. But that was only one trip, and that was a lunch tray ago, which included two boxes of apple juice.

More pressing, if it's halfway through Thursday afternoon— and she's pretty sure it is—then that means the massacre is seriously looming.

"*Sheriff!*" Jade yells, and it's like she's yelling into a megaphone while also being *in* that same megaphone. Before the first call's even echoed away, she's saying it again, and again, louder and louder, until a key announces itself in the lock, giving her a chance to stop before the door opens.

Hardy saunters in, one side of his face printed with the ghost of a backwards "4": he was asleep on his desk calendar.

"I'm thinking you need to charge me or let me go," Jade informs him, digging hard in her *Law & Order* dictionary.

Hardy breathes in deep, lets it out slow.

"How was the bologna?" he asks, then before Jade can get a comeback together, he's already following up: "There's an old song by Tom T. Hall about getting hot bologna every day of his stay here in the greybar hotel." Hardy pats the cinderblock up high as if confirming its solidity. "He comes to like it."

"What am I being charged with?" Jade asks, trying to lock him in her glare.

Hardy chuckles, strings his keys out from his belt, hauls Jade's door open, grandly presenting the outer world to her.

Jade steps through, not trusting this even a little.

Hardy rubs his mouth so he can smile behind his hand.

"This is for your own good," he finally says.

"Being locked up?"

"Your dad let me see your bedroom."

"What? He let you in the *house*?"

"Why wouldn't he? But it's official now, Jade, sorry. You're a runaway."

"I'm almost eighteen."

"Which means . . . let me do the math here, let me do the . . . does that mean you're still *seventeen*, and subject to a whole different set of laws?"

"I'm not running away," Jade tells him.

"To say nothing of your attempt on Letha Mondragon's life," Hardy goes on, moseying ahead of her to the front office.

"I was giving her something, not trying to hurt her," Jade grumbles.

"And if she hadn't caught that something?"

"I knew she would."

"More like you're lucky she did," Hardy says, presenting the hall to her.

"Bathroom?" Jade has to ask as it's sliding by.

"In a moment," Hardy tells her.

"Cruel and unusual," Jade says.

"Shit, don't get me started," Hardy says back with a chuckle, offering her the perp chair on the other side of his desk and not taking a seat himself until Jade settles in. Her phone is plugged in on the edge of his desk, is pretty much the only thing she can see anymore.

"I really do need to pee," she says.

"If you'd just used the thunder pot in there, we could avoid these little discussions," Hardy says, taking a fancy silver pen up from its holder, rolling it across the back of his knuckles. "But— kids these days, right? I mean that too, *kids*. You are still seventeen, little miss. And you were running away. I found your bags back in the trees. Much as this might seem personal, I do have a duty here."

"Then this isn't about . . . about anything I might have seen the other night?" Jade asks, careful with her phrasing.

Hardy creaks back in his chair, studying the much-studied ceiling, it looks like.

"And what do you think you might have seen?" he says. "You want, I can get my recorder from Meg, you can give a statement. Or, no—you can get it. Know right where it is, don't you?"

He angles his face down to hers, rubs his lips hard against each other like he just glossed them, is trying to spread it around, get it worked in proper.

"Nothing," Jade finally says. "Didn't see a thing, Sheriff."

She's not sure whether she hopes that's the exact wording thirteen-year-old Clate Rodgers used once upon a time, or if lucking into that would be the worst possible mistake.

"Seen more deaths here in the last couple weeks than in the forty years previous," Hardy says, leaning forward now, his elbows finding the desk. "Then I find the local horror fan running around at night with a machete that's got a name scratched into the blade?"

"Jamie Lee Curtis."

"*Blue Steel*, yeah. Don't think Bogey's in that one."

Jade takes this, tries not to let it show.

"She's kind of a final girl in that one too, you know?" she says, trying to keep it casual now. Just talking movies, not passing index card after index card of subtext back and forth, because pretty soon one of those index cards is going to have something to do with what she said to him the other day, about Melanie.

Hardy just watches her, probably waiting to see if she's going to go on about JLC being forever the final girl.

That would be too easy, though. And she's still got to pee.

"So that's what you're jamming me up for?" Jade says instead. "A weapon? Thought I was running away."

"Not supposed to run with scissors," Hardy says. "Think that goes double for machetes, don't you?"

"You'll be glad I gave it to her."

"Because of . . . what were you saying?" Hardy asks back with a patronizing shrug. "Bear sketched it out for me a bit, yeah? Something about . . . Scooby-Doo?"

"It's a Scooby-Doo *build*," Jade spits back, disgusted. "Someone in a mask. Probably her dad, okay?"

"Her being—"

"Letha."

" 'Saturday,' " Hardy says, holding Jade's eyes.

Jade spins away, stares out across the lake. Mr. Holmes is bucking the wind in his ultralight. "This is where I'm probably supposed to tell you to close the beaches," she says.

"That's from *Jaws*."

"There's gonna be kids in the water, I mean," Jade goes on.

"They see worse on their videogames."

"You know what I mean."

"That they're in *danger*."

Jade comes back around to him about this but Hardy's already staring into her soul.

"Bear also took me through what he says is probably your reasoning for . . . for Saturday."

For the first time, Jade really hears that: "Bear."

A bear was supposed to have killed Deacon Samuels.

"I know this is all very real to you," Hardy says, standing, taking a step over to the window, to what she guesses is his usual place, like he's standing sentry over all of Fremont County.

"It's bigger than me," Jade says. "There's . . . those two kids in March—"

"Of which kids we have to take your word about the second."

"There's Deacon Samuels."

"Animal attack."

"Clate Rodgers."

"Boating accident."

"'Boating accident,'" Jade repeats before she can stop herself.

Does Hardy's back straighten a little, though? Has he drawn some breath in that he's not releasing?

"But he had it coming," Jade fumbles in, standing now as well. "He's probably not even part of the cycle, actually. Just an add-on."

"That a thing?" Hardy says without looking around. "Add-ons?"

"The slasher gets blamed for all of them, yeah," Jade says. "Winners write the history books, and the slasher's never the winner."

"Doesn't do much writing," Hardy adds.

"Signs all his kills in blood," Jade says right back.

Far out over the lake, Mr. Holmes's ultralight is nearly skimming the water now.

"That's how he gets out of the wind," Hardy says, chucking his chin to Mr. Holmes. "Wonder if the fish think his shadow is the mother of all eagles, that him swooping down like that is the end of the world?"

He turns to her then, his face easy, says, "Somebody threw a trashcan through the front door of the high school, hear about that?"

"School's out for summer," Jade singsongs.

"Thing is," Hardy adds, "all the glass is out on the sidewalk. Not in by the trophy case."

"Not my concern," Jade says. "I'm not the custodian anymore."

"Just saying," Hardy says.

"Just listening," Jade says. "Not that I know why."

Hardy shakes his head, impressed it seems.

"Your dad started out just like this, once upon a bad afternoon," he says. "Sitting right in that chair when he was eighteen. I told him he could either—"

"I'm not my father," Jade cuts in.

"You don't have to be, no," Hardy tells her. "You should have seen him when he was a yardegg, though. Always underfoot. Everybody wanted him to play cowboys and Indians with, you know that?"

Jade's just staring out through the window, trying not to move even one single muscle on her face. On her whole body.

"Because he already *was* the skin," she finally says, obviously.

"Because he was always carrying a shiner, a busted lip," Hardy says back—where he was leading her. "Thing is, it would look like the cowboys had beaten him up."

"I supposed to care about this trip down memory lane?"

"Just saying," Hardy says. "I told him before you were born, I told him he lays one hand on you, just passing down what he'd got, that I'd be all over his ass."

Jade swallows, blinks, says, "I see Letha got to you too. Good to know."

"I—"

"He's never hit me," Jade says, "you saved me, Sheriff, thank you from the bottom of my heart."

Hardy just stands there, lets Jade stew in her own juices.

"So when's dinner around here?" she finally has to say just to move them ahead, out of this hole she's dug. "And what is it? More of that hot bologna?"

Hardy doesn't answer, is tracking Mr. Holmes now, it feels like. He's buzzing Terra Nova. Just a small angry fly, banking high against a gust only he can feel.

"They hate it when he does that," Hardy says, tossing his chin across the water. "Just wait, my phone's about to ring."

"And he hates them right back," Jade says. "All balances out, doesn't it?"

Hardy plunks down heavy in his seat, creaks it back again, regards Jade over his steepled fingers.

"So you hoping you're right about all this, and a lot of people die, or is it better if you're wrong?" he asks.

"People are already dying," Jade tells him. "Doesn't matter what I do and don't hope. I'm not part of it, am just, like, calling it."

"Good answer, good answer," Hardy tells her. "But here's mine. I'm concerned that if you're not locked up in back, here, then you find a way to ruin Saturday for everybody. Or at least for me and my deputies."

"Sheriff, you can't—"

"I know, I know, charge you or set you free. Turn you over to Child Protective Services or . . . or don't. But I've got forty-eight hours to decide, too, don't I? Don't answer that. I do have forty-eight hours where I can know exactly where you are the whole time. And, the way I tally that up, that clock started last night on the pier. So your forty-eight hours will be up about ten o'clock Friday night, which'll be well after working hours. Meaning you spend the weekend here, Jade. You miss all the festivities. Sorry."

"This is bullshit."

"Sir?"

"This is bullshit, *sir*. You can't—"

"You're right, you're right," Hardy says. "Your mom or dad comes down, sits where you are right now and pleads your case, I'll probably have to listen, won't I?"

Jade just stares out across the lake.

Mr. Holmes is barreling back to Proofrock now, is like a bobsled racer in the air, scraping down some frictionless channel, rocking back and forth from side to side, goggled eyes fixed on home.

"If I was eighteen—" she says, not sure where to go with that.

"This is for your own good," Hardy tells her. "And for the good of the town."

"I'm not the killer here, Sheriff. I'm no slasher."

"But you do want him to ruin the big party, don't you?"

Jade tries her best to make her eyes go dull, film over. It's the only armor she has.

"Do I get a phone call at least?" she asks, starting to reach for her phone, but then something keeps her fixed on the . . . lake?

Growing up, staring out over the water, what she'd always imagined was some monster of a fish spurting up through the glistening surface, snatching a bird or three, then splashing back down. Anything to break the boredom.

Not this, though.

"*Sheriff!*" Jade doesn't just say, but shrieks, just like the stupidest most bouncy cheerleader.

Hardy stands fast, his chair crashing back behind him, and he's fast enough to see the very end of it: Mr. Holmes's ultralight, not skimming the lake anymore, but skipping on it. Once, twice, and on the third time it sticks, Mr. Holmes's small body crashing through one purple wing and floating through the air, floating, then cartwheeling across the hard-hard water.

Hardy's gone faster than a sixty-one-year-old man should be able to be gone, actual papers drifting in the air behind him.

Because that's the last member of his old pirate band out there sinking in the lake, Jade knows.

"Go, sir," she says, quietly pocketing her phone and the charger then touching the glass of the window with her fingertips, which is her version of a prayer for Mr. Holmes: the longer she keeps her fingers there and perfectly still, the better chance he has.

By degrees, then, she realizes she's . . . alone? unmonitored?

She turns in wonder and Meg's standing in the door, waiting to be seen.

"I'm to deposit you back in 1A," she informs Jade.

"But Mr. Holmes—"

"The sheriff is on it, dear."

"I can't—"

"You have to, I'm sorry."

Jade shakes her head in disappointment, regret, and sneaks one last look out the window on her way out of the office, for Hardy's airboat, the throttle pulled back to 11.

Not yet.

"Can we just wait and see if he—?"

"I have to call emergency services, I have to call—"

"Okay, okay," Jade says, and slips past Meg into the hall.

"We all told him to be careful in that death machine," Meg says behind Jade, as if she's talking to herself, is actually flustered for once. In the front office, at least two phones are ringing, meaning Jade wasn't the only one to witness the crash.

"Oh, oh," Jade says. "The sheriff—I have to pee, and I can't, not in that—Sheriff said I could use this one again."

"I don't have time for this, Jennifer."

"Please."

"You can hold it."

"I've *been* holding it."

"Just—"

"Could you, in that thing?"

"Fine," Meg says, and holds the door to the bathroom open.

Jade steps in, Meg of course *not* letting the door shut, and Jade makes a production of the complicated mechanics of her coveralls, pretty certain Meg is fully aware of what she said last week, about the window in this bathroom being rusted open.

But then the cowbell above the front door jangles and Lonnie's trying to get his words out, is trying to tell someone, anyone, what he just saw out on the water, but he keeps sticking, can't get it all the way out, and—

Jade pulls the stall door closed, loudly runs the slide bolt home, and then every iota of her awareness is focused on the line of shadow she can see through the crack of space between the stall door and the stall. That line is the leading edge of the door Meg is holding open. And the sound is her toe tapping.

Both fade, the tapping first, turning into quick footsteps, then the shadow, slowly blurring as the door sighs in, so she can hustle up front, talk Lonnie down.

Jade zips up much faster than she unzipped, steps out, and is up and through the window before Meg's even told Lonnie that the sheriff's on it, that this is being handled, *thank you*.

It's trees and trees behind the sheriff's office.

Jade crashes through them holding her arms in front of her face, and wonders if that's another part of why slashers are so into masks: to avoid scratches. Five minutes later, when she can't hold it anymore, she has to step behind a tree, pop a squat. Because she wasn't lying about needing to pee in the worst way.

Five minutes after that she's standing on the shore over by Banner Tompkins's, her right hand opening and closing. All the boats that could scramble are out on the lake where Mr. Holmes went down, meaning . . . meaning what? Why do they *still* need to be out there? Jade's heart sinks, then rises back into her throat, her eyebrows doing that stupid V thing she hates.

"*No*," she says, a hundred seventh periods reeling through her head, "not him too, please, he's not part of it," and then claps her hand over her mouth when, just to make the nightmare complete, there's a mewling sort of animalish *creak* over to her right, on shore.

Slowly, still holding her hand over her mouth, she cranks her head over.

It's—it's . . .

Jade can't breathe anymore, maybe can't breathe ever again.

It's a shadow on four legs, tumbling after a shopping bag, a small shadow, a—

Not a dog, not a cat.

Jade feels a smile spread across her face by degrees: it's a bear cub.

It's just playing.

Jade shakes her head, impressed with the world for knowing just how to give her a heart attack.

When the shopping bag snags on something in the gravel, the bear cub's moving too fast, slides past, reaching back to try to bite it, its effort the cutest thing ever, pretty much. Even to a horror chick.

"Go," Jade says to the little bear. "Go find your mom, snuggle up close. There's a scary bear out there somewhere, the kind that eats little guys like you."

The bear cub stills, having heard her voice, Jade guesses, and she starts to step out past the trees, maybe snap a picture of this, but then she stops herself.

She's a fugitive now, isn't she?

She steps back into the deeper shadows, feeling for dry branches before giving her foot any real weight.

She still has a good line on the lake, though. On the part of the lake she needs to be watching. One of the boats' lights are just coming on, in anticipation of dusk, and Jade shakes her head no, runs through Idaho state history dates in her head, on the idea they can somehow help Mr. Holmes: Nez Perce in the north, Shoshone in the south; Lewis and Clark, 1805; Oregon Trail, 1846 through 1969—no, *1869*, shit; gold in the hills, 1860s; Henderson-Golding, 1869; Chief Joseph, 1877; becomes a state in 1890.

"I know them all, sir," she whispers.

The lights out there just keep on, though, and none of the boats are buzzing back to Proofrock yet, and that can't be good, can it? Keeping to the trees and watching for baby bears—for *any*thing, anyone—Jade slips through town, her lips pressed together in an attempt to keep her eyes from crying for Mr. Holmes.

Stupid *idiot*, she tells herself. Senior citizen high school teacher flying a sky go-cart just so he can smoke cigarettes his wife won't know about? What the hell did he expect? Except she already knows the answer to that: *to get away*. And, yes, okay already, she does it with slashers a little just the same, so what. And for Hardy an airboat is what he uses to get away, isn't it?

Before she can stop herself, then, she's answering for her dad, too: beer, and reliving high school. For her mom, though? What does her mom use to check out?

"Dollar store customers," Jade mumbles, trying for a smart-ass grin but probably easing more into the "constipated grimace" category.

She hates herself more than a little for giving that voice, and slips through the staging area's fence for a third time. There's bodies lumbering back and forth, calling orders and stacking things, rounding out the day's work, but they're on the other side of the lot, the active side. Over here on the dead side, Jade's alone.

She chooses the least-used storage shed, the one with pallets teetering in front of the door so she has to slide sideways to get in, and with her phone light she inspects her new home. It's just junk sheathed in cobwebs. But some of the junk has a crackly-stiff tarp over it, who knows why. Jade peels the tarp, folds it into a sleeping pad of sorts, and nestles into it, not letting herself sniffle, not letting herself think of the way Mr. Holmes would look up when she was late again, and then pretend to count her tardy. Except those tardies never quite added up to detention, did they?

Goddamn him.

But at least there's no windows in here. And, really? It's a shed, sure, but that's a skip and jump from a shack in the woods. All she needs now is Pamela Voorhees' head in a tableau of flickering candles on an upturned spool. Or, you know: her father's. If you're gonna dream, right?

Anyway, at least now she knows Mr. Holmes wasn't working with Hardy to drive the Terra Novans away. He had the hatred, though, didn't he? He needed the revenge, had the investment in the community, and there's probably some personal history Jade can't even guess at.

"Unless I was right all along," Jade says to herself, sitting up in the darkness. Maybe Mr. Holmes's plane wreck was staged, is supposed to remove him from suspicion. Maybe this is just another cog of their plan, part of the setup for Saturday's Grand Guignol, Proofrock's version of *Demons*.

"You wish," Jade says into the tarp.

Except it might explain why Hardy let her keep the sandwiches in her cargo pockets, that are pretty well flattened in their baggies now: because he knew she was going to run, and figured she might need some calories to get her through to Saturday's big party in the water. Because . . . because he needs her there? They both do? To, what, frame her?

Jade has to call bullshit on that.

Though, at the same time, was it really any accident that she got that pink phone right when it could convince her all of this was real? And, aside from her, who else in Proofrock would know the slasher any better than Mr. Holmes, who took Letha's final girl crash course over the last four years?

Jade doesn't know which version of Mr. Holmes she wants to believe in, the one who died out on the water, or the one with a score to settle, and a blade to settle it with. And . . . and she doesn't even know what color this tarp is, does she? It can't be "dust-colored," even though that's what it keeps sighing up, coating her with.

Whatever.

She zones out not by listing giallos in her head like usual but by pretending she can hear the kids playing on the park that's going to be here someday. By imagining what it would have been like to have had a park like this when she was young enough for it to matter. But she would have still ended up sitting alone in a swing at three in the morning, smoking a cigarette, wouldn't she have?

"Run, little bear," she says again, into the dusty crunchiness of the tarp.

She wakes with the shift change at four in the morning but nobody opens the door to toss any cutters or pry rods in on top of her, and nobody needs the tarp to cover the equipment, and Shooting Glasses's radar doesn't lead him to her a second time. She's not sure what exactly she'd say to him if he did open the door, though. Probably bluster and lie, hide that she's homeless now—homeless, jobless, and escaped from jail, sort of.

Before dawn—"*Just* before dawn," she tells herself, patting herself for that tape, which is *also* still there—Jade is gnawing on the second sandwich (either the first was appetizer or this one's dessert) and moving through the dark trees for the dam, to tightrope across one more time. If she'd thought ahead she'd have a pair of binoculars and more cigarettes. If she'd thought even *more* ahead she would have just braved the dark, bunked in Camp Blood with the rest of the ghosts, and her stolen axe. Then she'd already be most of the way over to Terra Nova. Not that there would have been any electrical sockets to charge a phone with at the abandoned camp. Not that there were in the shed, either.

That's got to be the first thing at Terra Nova, then. Sneak in, find an unmonitored plug to juice back up, then scope the place out, get a line on Theo Mondragon.

Is she just stacking tasks in front of actually having to find him out, though?

Her big fear is that once she settles in to watch for the day, it's just going to be business as usual: yacht people doing yacht things, construction grunts grunting over construction, nature blasting out serene and pristine all around, Theo Mondragon walking the deck or the dock, having important phone conversations.

If so, then . . . what? Who's left that it could even be?

Jade walks and thinks, thinks and walks, and, even though there's warning signs and the chance of being spotted, still, she hops up onto the concrete spine of the dam, to balance across. But not before sparking a cigarette up to keep her feet steady and sure. There's no fence, no handrail, just nearly two hundred feet to plummet down on her left if she slips. And then about halfway across there's the control booth to shimmy around.

At least having to be sure about each foot placement, having to track each trailing boot lace, it keeps her from dwelling too much on Mr. Holmes. She focuses hard on each next step, dials down and tries hard to think about what she's *not* thinking about, as, in a slasher, that's usually key.

What she comes up with is *Cry_Wolf* and *All the Boys Love Mandy Lane*, which means admitting the worst of all possibilities: Letha herself. What if the final girl is finding all these bodies specifically because she knows where she's left them? Would that not be the best cover? What if Letha fought tooth and nail *not* to move out to the sticks of Idaho, and blames everyone in Terra Nova for her losing her friends, her social life, her favorite boyfriend?

Jade would allow this . . . except for Letha herself. Letha who made a hard phone call to Hardy to try to save the horror chick, the sad girl, the—the Ragman of Indian Lake, yes. *Trick or Treat*, 1986, Alex. Ragman's peers hate him, are always crapping on him, but so what, he's got metal, faster harder thrashier, and he finally wishes hard enough that he gets the slasher he so thought he needed.

And it tries to kill him too.

Figures.

But no, not Letha, not the final girl. There was a moment when the slasher was getting turned on its head like that, but that moment's over and done with. And Letha is pure, anyway—*too* pure. She's not going to be the so-called final girl Leslie Vernon's dreaming about, swinging her own panties over her head. No, Letha's bookish, she's virginal or close enough and she's got the long limbs of a girl meant to run through the syrupy colors of a Dario Argento sequence. Only, where she's running, it's right through the Golden Age, what she's vaulting over, it's the Scream Boom of the late nineties, and where she's coming down to make her stand, it's here, it's Proofrock.

She's a killer, yes, but not until pushed. Not until having her good-girl veneer carved painfully away.

Jade pads up to the control booth window, can't see through the dark glass, shimmies around anyway, and then hears the door shut behind her and has to run, run, no balance, all forward momentum, the sky all around her.

She crashes to her knees on the other side breathing hard but smiling big.

This is why she loves coming around the lake this way instead of walking two miles down for the bridge: it's always a close call, is always the best rush.

And, where she's landed, she's pretty sure, is in the last act, the third-reel bodydump. Somewhere out there Letha's probably screaming about a corpse unfolding from the ceiling, and another crammed into a cabinet.

It puts a pep in Jade's step, just on the off-chance she can see that from far way.

She keeps to the top of the chalky bluff above Camp Blood—no choice: it's not like you can get to Camp Blood without looping around almost all the way *to* Terra Nova. Two or three minutes later she can see the yacht at its usual mooring, and then the *Umiak* in its shadow, no longer in floating impound. Since it's the first boat anybody takes, Jade assumes the rest of the boats are in their garages, even though all the Founders are, for once, because one of their own fell, here.

The long flat barge the construction crew drinks their coffee on, crossing before sunup each morning, is already back at Proofrock, Jade imagines, taking up ten or twelve berths, Terra Nova just renting out that whole quarter-mile of the shore.

And the houses over here, goddamn.

Somebody's mixed some Miracle-Gro into those frames, those roofs, those driveways, all that landscaping. It reminds Jade more of a cartoon than a gated community: the outlines of the houses were there all along, all they needed was some great hand to tip a bag of ink over into the chimney, to let color leach down all the lines, find all the corners, fill in all the windows.

All ten are ready by August first, she has to imagine, and then realizes she's just standing there skylining herself like an idiot, practically *asking* to be called out, asked what she's doing over here.

Jade lowers herself slowly, tries to bore her eyes all the way across the lake to see if Hardy's glassing for her, but Proofrock's just shapes and shadows. Are students gathered at the flagpole in front of the high school already, for Mr. Holmes?

Jade closes her eyes, isn't going to think about that.

"Not everybody gets to live," she says to herself, confident that, at fifty yards, her whisper will dissipate before cranking anyone's head around.

Not that there *is* anybody.

Does that mean . . . has the crew moved on to doing the interiors of the houses now? It makes sense the insides of the houses would be last on the to-do list. You don't hang sheetrock until that sheetrock's protected from the elements.

Still: no one?

Jade pats her pocket for the second sandwich she knows is just as gone as the first. It's less actually looking for it, more showing the world that she's hungry, that it can deliver her some nuggets or a burrito or fishsticks if it wants. She won't tell anybody.

In lieu of food, she lights another cigarette, her fourth from last, and then smokes it lying on her back, waving the smoke to tatters, hoping none of the smell wisps down between the houses. But surely some of the crew burns em if they got em.

A harsh *clack!* rolls her over, gets her studying downhill again.

It could have come from anywhere.

Shit.

Is this what a stakeout is? If so, isn't there supposed to be coffee and pistachios? But it's not like Jade can just stroll in and start asking questions, either.

She rests her chin on her crossed hands, situates her frontside against the dirt and grass, and tells herself stories about the houses, how they're not mansions but cabins, how this is Packanack Lodge from *Friday the 13th Part 2*, just down from the original's "Camp Blood," ha.

She's Jason, looking through the one eyehole of her pillowcase. Watching the skinny-dipping, seeing seductive shapes through the gauzy curtains. Half the counselors piling into a car and a truck to caravan down to the local honky-tonk, the other half either already dead or in the process-of.

Over here *is* where all the bodies are buried, right? Mr. Holmes was always telling them. Before there was a lake dividing one side of the valley from the other, people who caught a bullet to the gut or a pickaxe to the head would usually end up over here, stuffed into a seam, a crevice, a crack. Which would have worked fine if not for the buzzards. According to Mr. Holmes, when Henderson-Golding was booming, that was the sheriff's main job: watch for buzzards.

Jade rolls over, cases the sky, the sun's position, decides she must have either slept or got *Fire in the Sky*'d.

Probably noon already, or one, shit.

She's like the police officer assigned to protect the final girl's house: dozing off on the job. Then, *Clack!*

"What is *The Nail Gun Massacre*, Alex," she mumbles.

It's where she knows that *clack* from.

Jade sits up and scooches forward, looking at Terra Nova all over again, this time with eyes pre-shaped for "nailgun." What she sees instead pretty much stops her heart, and answers every one of her wishes.

It's a tall male figure, moving like the Prowler from one nearly-complete house to the next one, never mind the daylight, or that it's not 1981. At first Jade thinks he's wearing a military helmet like the *actual* Prowler, or a motorcycle helmet covered in electric tape, like Bubba in *Nail Gun*, but it's just . . . a black golf cap turned around backwards? Strapped down over that cap is a full-face gas mask with two stubby, close-to-the-face filters coming down, angled away from each other, giving his head a kind of oblong, giant-mouse shape.

"No," Jade says, even shaking her head like to prove it. Because this can't be real and actual, can it? *Can* it?

He's carrying that heavy nailgun as easily as a pistol, too.

This is really happening. It's really *been* happening.

"Makes sense, makes sense," Jade tells herself about the nail-gun, her voice jittery. In—in *High Tension*, the chase runs through some road construction, so they come out with a huge and just massively dangerous concrete saw, which spins so much faster than any chainsaw. It stands to reason that this Prowler down there would pick up whatever's handy. Well, handy and deadly. But it's all deadly in the wrong hands, with the right intent.

Jade should be happy, too, she knows. This is proof, this is what she's always wanted. She fumbles her phone up to take a snapshot for Hardy, but by the time she gets her phone up from her cover-alls' complicated pocket, Terra Nova's still again, exactly like this Prowler had been a figment of her overactive, blood-soaked wish-ful thinking.

If she'd been making him up, though, then, first, he'd have had motorcycle boots on, most likely—those ratchet-buckles are so cool, so metal—and, second, there'd be a reason for the gas mask past just its essential scariness. In *My Bloody Valentine*, the gas mask is because this is a mining operation, and in the actual *Prowler*, the sheriff with the covered face is supposed to be a sol-dier who had probably had to deal with mustard gas on the battle-field or something.

Jade takes the best scent reading she can, identifies no foreign smells—no mustard gas, no horseradish—and finds herself both wanting this slasher to step out again, prove he was real, and also wanting him *to* have been all in her head.

She's caught between those for, by her best guess . . . *two hours*? Has any slasher ever moved this slow? Granted, movies probably compress events that would take a lot longer, but two hours is long enough for her to spin all kinds of excuses for whoever that was down there to have been wearing a gas mask, carrying that nailgun, and wearing that black hoodie in *July*. Which isn't the way to be ready, to be vigilant.

Then, finally: *Clack!*

Adrenaline floods all through her again, sharpening her senses. By the time it's washing out of her system, she's back to trying to make it all make sense. If this slasher were trying to nail someone running across the room, there'd be a barrage of *clacks!* This guy's more deliberate, though, isn't he? That game where two people hide on opposite sides of the same wall, each waiting for the other to burst out?

Evidently he's the more patient one.

Except . . . except this is too early, isn't it? This is supposed to be *tomorrow* night. Jade wants to stand, wave her arms for everybody to slow down, that they're blowing their wad ahead of time, aren't going to have any left when it counts.

She doesn't know how far a nail from a nailgun can tumble through the air, though.

She looks up to the flurry of motion to her distant right—the yacht.

It's Tiara Mondragon. She's in her black bikini, her sunhat and shades on, a book tucked under her arm.

Completely unaware.

She sashays down to the—to whatever the tower part of a yacht is called, kind of two-thirds of the way back. She disappears into it. Moments later she emerges on a higher, closer-to-the-sun deck, drink in hand.

Call Hardy! Call 911! Jade tries to brainwave across, straining so hard her head nearly *Scanners*.

But, call him to say what, exactly? That someone over here's wearing a gas mask all suspiciously? That their gait is all slashery? That—gasp—there's a super-dangerous nailgun over here?

All the same, Jade gets her *own* phone ready, except . . . she *did* really need to plug in last night. All the charge she got from Hardy is gone, shit. Jade shakes her phone like she can get the battery juice to an important place long enough for just one call, but that works about as well as it usually does.

It's all up to Tiara to save them now. Tiara who's just settling down onto the towel she must have spread while Jade was having a panic attack about her battery. On the deck Tiara was just on, though, one of the Founders—Lewellyn Singleton—is walking and reading a newspaper, his robe cinched loose. At the back of the yacht the two girls, Cinnamon and Ginger, mirror images of each other, are tossing bits of something over the railing into the water and giggling, and that short one whose head's barely taller than the railing must be Galatea Pangborne.

None of them know. Yet.

Including Letha.

"Where are you?" Jade whispers to her. More important, where is this slasher prowling around? *Is* he, even? Do slashers take naps too?

"Fuck it," Jade says, and stands.

Nothing happens. No nails whizz in, bury themselves in her gut.

"Well, let's get this party started," she announces, and walks downhill with long deliberate strides, all her pockets zipped, her lips set in a firm line. By the time she's twenty yards from the closest house, past the last of the trees the Founders aren't going to let anyone cut down, her lips feel more squiggly, more Charlie Brown. And she can feel his cartoon parentheses around her eyes, too.

Thing is, she's close enough now she can't see every exit, every entrance, and she's only eighty percent certain—okay, seventy—that this is the same house she saw the slasher walking away from. Meaning it could be one he's back inside.

Jade nods to herself for strength all the same, reminds herself that she *knows* this genre, and regrips her hand around her phone, blasts across the last of that open space, certain that if she turns around, that gas mask is going to be right there, and gaining.

She makes the door, it's thankfully unlocked—she hadn't even considered that it might not be—and she opens it both quietly and as quickly as she can, guiding it shut behind her.

The hall she's in is dark, but there's a light glowing in the . . . kitchen, it turns out. She pats her pockets for the charging cable she suddenly can't find, but knows that, because this is a slasher, any plug she finds in here isn't going to bring her phone back to life, isn't going to connect her to anyone who can help.

Instead of using it as a communication device, then, Jade holds her phone like it's the handle for her machete—the one she *gave away*—keeping it directly in front of her. She tunes in for footsteps, for breathing, for crawling, but she's really and actually alone, as best as she can tell, and as already suggested by the slasher striding purposefully *away* from this house. But it's these kinds of situations jumpscares are made from, she knows.

Moving room by room she clears the first floor, then has the choice of either going upstairs like Sidney says stupid girls in horror movies are always doing, or going downstairs, into the basement, which she's now insisting will just be that: a basement. Not a cellar, and definitely please not some *Evil Dead* fruit cellar, because there's only so much her mind can take.

"Shit shit shit," she mutters, looking up then down, up then down. And then she sees it: one golden-tinted nail standing up from the frame around the door to the basement.

Her face goes cold, her breathing deep.

She swallows, the sound a thunderous gush in her ears, and, keeping her right foot ahead like that matters, shuffles alongside the stairs, eases the basement door open, the whole while picturing a network of tunnels connecting basement to basement across Terra Nova, so they can scurry from home to home during the winter months.

Except, she reminds herself, it's rocky over here. *Too* rocky.

Meaning, of course, that if the basements do end up connecting, it's going to be by burrowing dead people, left-behind murder victims from the nineteenth century contorting around rocks, gathering in caves, turning their faces up to the hateful sounds above them.

"Shut up, shut up," Jade hisses to her brain, and takes the first timid step down, deciding at the last moment *not* to turn the staircase light on, as that would only announce her presence, which might then lead to her bloody absence. Which, to everyone across the lake, would be good riddance, the best riddance.

At the blind turn halfway down the stairs, Jade's ninety-nine percent sure anybody down there will be able to hear her heart pounding. When she's finally *down* there, she has no choice but to feel on the wall for the light switch. Either that or pull out her trusty Jame Gumb night vision goggles.

The lights come on and instantly she's blinded, is falling away, swinging her dead phone in front of her like that would do anything. Finally, after all these years, she understands Laurie Strode: you cringe, you fall, you shriek and you cry. Never because you want to, not because you intend to, but because it's scary shit. The body's gonna do what the body's gonna do, and screams aren't at all voluntary.

When she can see again at last, there's no furniture, just an endless tile floor, already-textured walls—the whole basement's finished out already. Up near the ceiling there's those short wide windows that mean this isn't completely underground, but it's enough underground to be that clammy kind of cool, and kind of muffled.

Any nails fired down here are probably not nails she heard.

Proof of that turns out to be on the wall behind her. Going from waist-high and up into the ceiling, maybe twelve feet in total, is a zipper line of nails, set close enough to be a stairway for an acrobatic mouse. Meaning, since they start in the corner, that the target was running the *other* way.

Jade listens hard for creaking above her head, peers as deep into the high windows as she can for gas mask eyes clocking her, and, though she's still not sure this is the best of all ideas, goes the direction the nails are telling her to go.

For reasons she can't explain even to herself, she's still being sure to lead with her right foot. Everything that made sense when she was *watching* slashers doesn't seem to matter just one whole hell of a lot while walking *through* a slasher, does it?

Worse, "It's July fucking third," she says aloud, like calling foul.

None of this is even supposed to be happening yet.

How many final rounds does *Scream 4* have, though, right? Maybe, since the slasher's been going for nearly four decades, the only way to still surprise is by breaking its own rules.

It's definitely working. Jade has no idea what's coming.

The next breadcrumb for her eyes is golden again, and nail-shaped again, and in a doorframe again. Either a closet or a bathroom. Or, this is a basement—maybe storage, then? Water heater, furnace?

"H-hello?" she asks.

No response.

She taps on the door with her phone, runs through a mental list of who's not behind the door—everyone she knows is in Proofrock, and everyone she just saw on the yacht is, you know, *on the yacht.*

"I'm coming in!" Jade announces as clear as she can, and, using her left hand on the knob, she swings the door out and hustles back into something like a defensive stance, spinning instantly around because how it always works is that the slasher's right behind you when you least expect it.

She's still alone.

Trusting neither the space before her *nor* behind her, she turns back to the door she just opened.

It is a bathroom, what she guesses is a "half-bath" over here in Camelot. For all she knows, her dad carted the tub down for somebody more expert to install.

There's a body in that tub, too.

His legs are cocked out over the edge, his arms thrown out to the side, and his eyes are open, but they're not seeing anything anymore.

"Cody," Jade whispers, in pain.

Cowboy Boots.

He's still wearing them, along with a golden nail between the eyes, a ribbon of blood unfurling down from it and curling across his face, tucking itself into his mouth at last instead of pooling in the hollow of his neck.

Jade spins around again but it's still just her in the basement.

Which is when the lights black out.

She nearly falls down from it.

All she can hear now is her breath. It's coming in hitches, in gasps, then not at all because she's listening.

"Cody," she says at last, "CodyCodyCody," but he's not answering. Which is surely for the absolute best, thank you thank you, Indians have to stick together. But still.

She was never Jame Gumb, she realizes. She's Clarice, feeling her way with wide-spread fingers.

The lights fizz back on.

Jade cringes back, sure that's just step one of her getting rushed.

But . . . she finally sees it: the light switch she flipped up. There's a motion sensor under it, to save energy. The lights go off when it thinks the room is empty.

Jade spins back to Cody.

Still there. Still dead.

Jade leans against the wall opposite the bathroom door and slides down.

"I'm sorry," she says into the bathroom. "I—I don't know why, man. You're not even part of all this, are you? You weren't, I mean. Until now."

Was it just because he was there? Is this target practice for tomorrow night? Cleaning house before the big party? What could he have done to have deserved a nail in the forehead, though?

"Nothing," Jade tells him.

Oh. Unless it's that he talked to *her* back in March? Which would matter to the slasher *why*? Does her knowing the genre and predicting the day and trying to pull Letha into all of this somehow mess things up for the slasher? And, how can she even be thinking rational thoughts, this close to a dead body? Just as important: it's *Letha's* job to find Cody, not Jade's. This could be screwing the whole process up.

"But I was never here," Jade says out loud, and stands, resetting the room as best she can: pulling the bathroom door shut, policing the tile for any mud she's tracked in, and, back at the stairs, flipping the light switch to *down*.

The next moment is when she realizes that lights in the high basement windows suddenly *not* glowing are like a flashing sign for the slasher. But it's daytime yet, probably not even four in the afternoon. Whoever's playing slasher out there would have to be watching these windows specifically to catch them going dark.

And, anyway: why stake out a room you've already killed in, right? That's no way to hit a bodycount.

"Sorry," Jade says one last time to Cody, and then slouches upstairs.

After watching through the window of the back door for what feels like twenty minutes—no one, nothing—Jade steps out, walks the same exact path the slasher did, going from this house to the next one over.

This time the first floor and the basement are empty, and the side door into the garage is yawning wide, the garage past it open. No nails in any doorframes, no blood misted on any walls.

Same for the second floor.

Jade steps into what she thinks will probably be a study in a month or two and positions herself just inside the broad window, enough so she can see out, not quite enough where she's a distinct form in the glass. Just an irregular continuation of the wall, she hopes. A half-assed drape—tarp or something.

From here she can see the yacht so much closer.

Tiara's swishing her hips along the railing, disappearing through a door. Nobody's reading a newspaper anymore, nobody's dropping flower petals into the lake.

Does this mean they've all been nailgunned in the forehead?

And then, finally, a flurry of fast motion.

It's Shooting Glasses. He's scrambling down a roof two houses down, is Jesse Pinkman'ing into what's going to be the front yard, and already rolling that impact away because it's the least thing he has to worry about. Jade watches the window he must have dove through but it's the front door of the house that swings open instead.

The Prowler, the killer, the slasher.

His chest is heaving, his face unchanging, still gas-masked, the nailgun heavy and deadly by his thigh.

Shooting Glasses looks back, shakes his head no, holding his hands up like to ward off flying nails, and he's saying something over and over but it doesn't matter.

His killer steps down off the porch, is already leveling the nail-gun.

"No, no!" Jade hears herself screaming, the flat of her hand slapping the glass of the window she's up against.

The slasher stops, turns around, settles his tinted eyes in her general direction but hopefully she's behind a glare, hopefully those tinted lenses aren't binoculars.

Jade backs a step up and the slasher has to give his attention back to Shooting Glasses when Shooting Glasses is up and running again. He falls twice on his way to the pier but makes it there fast enough. The slasher just steadily approaches behind the whole time, until there's nowhere for Shooting Glasses to go but into the lake, not so much a dive as a desperate jump, or a failure by the water to hold him up when he tries to run across it.

Right as he goes under, nails stitch the water all around him.

The Prowler wades in up to his knees, quilting the whole area with nails until his cartridge runs dry.

He looks at the gun and tosses it aside, lets it kerplunk down.

Now he's looking up, to the yacht.

Letha is up against the rail, calling down. Not shrieking, not screaming, not crying, not asking what or why.

"*T's napping!*" she whisper-yells, just loud enough Jade can make it out.

Below her, knee-deep in Indian Lake, Theo Mondragon peels out of the gas mask and hoodie.

"Did you get them all?" Letha calls down, apparently forgetting her injunction against waking Tiara.

Theo Mondragon shakes his head no as if disappointed with himself, then holds his forearm up as if for inspection.

"Do wasps bite or sting?" Letha calls down, leaning far out over the rail, completely unconcerned about gravity.

Theo Mondragon looks at his forearm, probably at a welt Jade can't see from this distance, and exaggerates his shrug.

"You should be careful!" Letha says, but is kind of thrilled too, Jade can tell.

Her dad was rooting out a wasp nest or two. Thus the mask, the hoodie. Just, he redefined "wasp" to include Cowboy Boots, and Shooting Glasses.

Mismatched Gloves?

Jade looks behind her, half-expecting him to be sitting in the corner with a bellyful of nails, his fingers moving over them like accordion buttons.

Why? Why would Theo Mondragon be going after his own workers?

It doesn't make sense. They can't be in the justice cycle, shouldn't be slasher vics at all.

But Clate Rodgers wasn't exactly supposed to have been, either. And Mr. Holmes was supposed to have been around to write the sad history of this all down.

And, really, if she's counting people who don't deserve it, the Dutch kids were sort of extra too, Jade figures.

Deacon Samuels may be the only actual *targeted* victim.

Unless Theo Mondragon saw Jade through the glass, that is. Unless she's about to be the next clean-up on aisle 9 of this wilderness re-enactment of *Intruder*.

Her insides clench, her airways constrict.

At least it won't be nails, when it comes. The nailgun's wet and buried.

And, like Nancy Thompson in *A Nightmare on Elm Street*, her chances go way the hell up if she can just keep from falling asleep.

Just, there's still the night to get through. And then tomorrow. If there is one of those.

"Here!" Letha calls down to her dad. What she's waving in her hand—offering—is a tube of something. After-bite cream, lotion, Jade can't tell.

Letha makes to lob it down once, twice, so Theo Mondragon can get in sync, and then she lets it drop, plummet end over tiny end. Theo Mondragon snags it from the air like the athlete he had to have been at one point.

He nods thanks, already applying the cream, and then Mars Baker is leaning out over the railing on the deck below her. With an over-under shotgun he's just now swinging shut. Letha leans out and over even farther to see him but he's not looking up at her, just down to Theo Mondragon.

"*This* is what you should have had," he says, snapping the shot-gun up so he can track a duck flapping low across the water. He fake shoots it, doing the recoil and everything.

"What's for dinner?" Theo calls up to them, as if he wasn't just on a killing spree.

"Not duck!" Tiara answers.

"Duck, duck, right," Jade says to herself, lowering herself down below the level of the window so Theo Mondragon won't acciden-tally clock her on his walk up the pier.

He hooks the gas mask on a rack, twists his hoodie around his neck after this hard day's work, and saunters up into the yacht like nothing's wrong with the world. Nothing at all.

Moments after he's gone and nobody's at the rail, Shooting Glasses's body doesn't bob up to the surface, perforated fifty times over, blood staining the water.

Probably because he's nailed to the bed of the lake.

SLASHER 101

Okay, for <u>My Bloody Valentine</u>'s or just even only
for <u>Valentine</u> but also to make up for my perfect
gag for the year book crew, which if you didn't
see it but only missed my presence, was 6 FAKE
hypodermic needles superglued to my forearm <u>Dream
Warriors</u> style, with each one labeled Algebra and
English and P.E. and the rest, including of course
HISTORY, but to make up for the quiz that day, I'll
pay you back and more with a little insight into
how there's not enough slow motion in the whole
world really for when the final girl finally stops
running and turns around to fight this unkillable
killer, and also WHY he's so nice slash mean to
her. Emphasis on the "slash" there.

First you have to imagine what's in her head.
She's been watching her friends and family and
pets all get killed, and THEN she has to run down
whatever hall it is they've all been put in in
various and many jack in the box contraptions.

At some point this final girl has to realize
that this is all about her, don't you think? That
her friends and family and pets would all still be
alive if this slasher had only STARTED with her
instead of cutting his way closer and closer to
her. So she feels guilty like maybe she's sort of
the killer herself, like this bodycount is maybe
HER bodycount.

What I'm saying here, sir, is that she's been
groomed to become her secret and best self. The
slasher COULD have started with her easy. The
slasher doesn't HAVE to start at the outside edges
but CAN just walk right into the center, apply
blade, deed done, go home now, story over.

But that wouldn't be enough. Not even close.

The slasher cycle is a dance, see? Imagine a
dance floor in a high school gym, the lights are
down, crinkled paper everywhere, spiked punch,
fancy handed down jackets and dresses, shoes
it's impossible to even walk in, I know you've
chaperoned some. Now who the slasher WANTS to
dance with is this one quiet girl way on the
other side of the gym floor, but he can't cross
to her yet, instead he has to work his way across
TO her, dancing with this person and then that
person, the back of his hand sometimes touching
the final girl's sleeve during a slow song, their
eyes locking like fate, but he's waiting for the
last dance, sir. The slow (MOTION) one. That's
the one that matters. You don't go home with who
you dance your 3rd dance with. You go home with
who you're holding hands with when the music's
over.

But it's not love, don't let me get you thinking
that. And it's not hate either. It's deeper than
both of those.

My theory or thesis from many viewings and more
knowing is that the slasher has the kind of eyes
that can recognize which girls have a final girl
hiding inside them, which is why he targets them
LAST. But is it really to kill them? I don't think
so, sir. I think the slasher's life of revenge is a
life of pain and misery, and the slasher knows that
no ordinary person can end that. Only a very very
certain kind of girl can. Only a final girl. But
not in her current state or form. No, the slasher
first has to help her TRANSFORM, which involves
killing all her friends and family and pets,
everybody except Dewey pretty much, because Dewey's
basically unkillable.

So that super slow motion moment at the end when
this bookish reserved quiet girl finally stops
in all the swirling madness and blood and tears,

turns around with a machete or a chainsaw or just
even only her hands like Constance from <u>Just Before
Dawn</u>, and she's screaming with rage, this is why
slashers really wear masks, sir.

It's so you won't see them smile.

FINAL EXAM

After a thorough search of her coveralls turns her charging cable up, Jade plugs into a socket, gets no little lightning bolt on her screen, which doesn't surprise her in the least. This isn't a romcom, after all. But then, on what feels like a lark, she unscrews the lightbulb in the sconce on the wall above the socket and hits the switch on the wall.

Magic. Juice starts pouring into her phone. While it's charging, Jade walks up and down the hallway of whoever's house she's in. Out in Terra Nova—over all of Pleasant Valley—dusk is coming in, the light going granular, the lake darkening to ink. Every few minutes she paranoids out, sure her phone isn't on vibrate, that it's going to ring with alerts and give her position away. And when it's not that, then she's just as certain that the front door's about to open, that Theo Mondragon's going to be wading in behind a weed whacker or jackhammer or even just a random board. A length of 2 x 4 would do the job on her just fine. Or even just a dry-cleaning bag pulled tight over her head, *Black Christmas*–style.

Speaking of: has there ever been an Independence Day slasher?

Yes: *I Still Know What You Did Last Summer*. And also *I Know What You Did Last Summer*. More important, why does the Fourth matter to Theo Mondragon? Jade knocks on her forehead with the knuckle of her thumb, tells herself to wait for tomorrow night, all will be revealed at the Reveal, dummy, it's not your job to figure it all out.

For right *now*, what she needs to concern herself with is not being seen, plain and simple. Which should be easy, with night falling. Just, the temptation to use her phone's flashlight is strong in this one.

"*Alone in the Dark*, 1982," she mumbles into the empty house, just to see if anybody gets it.

Silence. Good.

Jade promised herself to wait to use her phone until it hit ten percent, since under ten is when it tends to tank all at once, but she swipes into it at eight percent, dials before even checking the signal.

Her phone informs her that cellular data is temporarily unavailable.

"What the hell?" she asks, carrying her phone high to all corners of the room. Not even a blip, not even a thready iota of a dot that could stand up *into* a bar.

"Because this is horror," she reminds herself. Not that it helps.

She executes a neat flipturn at the end of the hall, just allowing herself a glimpse of the big second-floor window before removing herself from the chance of being spotted through it.

But . . . didn't she see Theo Mondragon on *his* cell over at Camp Blood? Didn't Letha call her from the yacht the other night? How do Founders on the Proofrock side of the lake even call across for a ride?

Jade studies her settings to see if she's the problem, but it's not her. She shakes her phone because that always works, then shakes her head at how stupid she is.

So she can't call the cavalry in. It would be a betrayal anyway, she tells herself. Indians run *from* the cavalry, not to them. But, were the Blackfeet the ones who scouted for Custer? Jade isn't sure, and of course can't look that up now.

That was a hundred and fifty years ago, though. This is now. And Jade can't stay up here all night. Staying put in a slasher is just setup for a blade coming through the door you're leaned up against, and splashing out your mouth.

Going slow, and knowing it's hopeless from the get-go, Jade takes the stairs down one at a careful time, finally stepping into the long-shadowed kitchen, checking every cabinet for some leftover lunch or a stashed bag of jerky, half a bag of chips that got hidden at a last moment. She drinks from the faucet, only realizing afterward that the spigot is actually pull-down, pull-out—whatever the term is for those ones that come off, have a nifty little hose, can point wherever. Jade detaches it from its magnet base, aims it here and there around the room, understands it's best she didn't grow up with one of these. People with these over their sinks must be naive, overly trusting.

She magnets it back to its home, pats it like a good dog, which is exactly when a determined silhouette crosses from one side of the kitchen window to the other, not bothering to look in.

If Jade had been holding coffee to her lips, that mug would be in pieces on the expensive tile floor now. As-is, she just stands there, and a second later she knows that's what saved her: she didn't burst into motion in Theo Mondragon's peripheral vision. She drops fast to her fingertips *now*, though, her legs gathered under her so she can explode whatever direction. When no doors creak open ten seconds later, then twenty, and when the air pressure inside the house doesn't seem to change, signaling a door having opened, and when her bat ears can't detect any floorboards taking on new weight, any rubber soles twisting for a better grip, she hustles into a room in the direction Theo Mondragon had been walking, just to confirm that he's still moving *away*, not closer.

Through the window she sees him stepping into the one house she's already been through.

Two minutes later he emerges, dragging Cowboy Boots—Cody, Cody Cody Cody—by his right heel, the rest of him wrapped in foggy plastic, Tina-style.

Theo Mondragon stands there casing the night for maybe thirty more seconds in which he pulls his own phone out, unlocks it, and stares into it, finally shaking it just as Jade did. His doesn't get a signal either. He smiles to himself about it, though, nods, slips the phone back into his pocket, and walks a straight line out from Terra Nova, a flashlight or headlamp coming on once he's in the trees. It dims a few steps later, then fades completely.

Jade wants to follow, wants to know, but her legs don't agree.

Instead she counts under her breath until he steps back into the clearing she *can* see: six hundred and forty-one. Which has got to be something like ten minutes, right? Does he know of a cave over here to stash a body in? Has nothing changed since 1872?

Jade steps back from the kitchen window, careful not to be a body-shaped shadow against the tall silver rectangle the refrigerator is.

But he's not coming for this house. Not even close to this one.

He goes to the third or fourth house back, his headlamp—she can see that now—a disc of yellow light against the windows from room to room until he steps back out onto the porch to turn the light off, his chest heaving, breath steaming.

He's just staring at the yacht.

When he's satisfied he's alone, he hauls Mismatched Gloves out through the front door. Unlike Cody, Mismatched Gloves is belly-down. It's because his back is bristling with dull golden nails. His face dribbles down the stairs, and when there's a snag in the forward motion, making Theo Mondragon have to chock up on a shin, it's because the top row of Mismatched Gloves's teeth have caught on a step.

Jade blinks her eyes against the tears trying to spill, hates herself for them.

What she knows but doesn't want to have to think is that Mismatched Gloves and Cody and Shooting Glasses shouldn't have sold their friend for eight hundred dollars each. That's got to be why Theo Mondragon's doing this, doesn't it? He found out about the accident, the coverup. So the first thing he does is take care of Deacon Samuels, who really should have known better. And now he's taking care of the only witnesses.

If nobody knows the story about your big wonderful house, then it can just keep on being big and wonderful, can't it? Kill the storytellers, kill the story.

Except Jade knows it too. Second-hand, but still.

"Sorry, Letha," she says, and then shrinks forward when the voice comes from behind her, crawling over every last inch of her skin: "For what?"

It's Letha, standing in the doorway by the refrigerator, cupping a Yankee candle at her sternum, the shadows on her face upside down, the wrongness sending a jolt up Jade's spine that she has to consciously not let show.

She does wonder if she maybe just peed a little, though. Or a lot.

"For trespassing," Jade pulls out of the thinnest of thin air.

Letha steps in, says, "What are you looking at?" in a way that can either be charged honestly and innocently, which Jade so wants to believe, or can be charged with that cat-playing-with-its-food way, which would mean that Letha completely knew her dad wasn't after wasps earlier. That she knew it was a different breed of pest getting taken care of. And yes, Mars Baker, a shotgun would have been more efficient. Good one, sir.

Shit.

"Looking for the bear," Jade says.

"It's still around?" Letha says in either real or mock shock, holding the candle away so she can lean over the sink and study Terra Nova in the dark, her dad's disc of light just barely gone into the woods. Or, if not gone, then she doesn't say anything about it.

"Don't know," Jade says. "That's why I'm, y'know, looking."

Every word that comes out of her mouth is stupider than the last.

"You're running away, aren't you," Letha says then, turning around to fix Jade in her hundred-watt caring eyes. "The sheriff called over looking for you." Letha sets the guttering candle down by the sink between them.

"C-called over?" Jade stammers.

"Um, yeah?"

"But—"

Jade pulls her phone out, like that proves the lack of signal.

"Oh, did he not turn that off?"

Letha gets her own phone up, shakes her head at how stupid this is.

"We—" she starts, then picks her words more carefully: "Some of the construction crew was spending too much time on their phones, and Instagramming stuff too. Mr. Baker said the floor-plans for some of our houses could be in the backgrounds of their selfies, so—"

She leaves that hanging.

"So?" Jade prompts.

"Mr. Pangborne had a jammer installed? The yacht's out of the radius, but all the houses are in it, or in them, however it works."

"A jammer," Jade repeats.

"Like an umbrella, except it blocks from the—"

"No, I get it," Jade says. "Is that legal?"

"There's no guarantee of service over here," Letha says with a shrug. "It's the wilderness, right?"

What do they call those jammers, though? She's heard it online. A . . . a rape tent, or something? At least when they're used to keep a victim from calling the cops.

Or, a potential victim.

"Hardy was warning you about me?" she says.

"No, no," Letha says, crossing to Jade to touch her forearm, swat that possibility away. "He was worried that you might be in danger."

"Figured he'd be busy."

"I mean, his office called."

"Meg."

"Tiff's mom?"

"You caught that machete last night," Jade tells Letha.

"T was behind me," Letha says. "It could have—she might have gotten hurt."

"It's for tomorrow night," Jade says. "Hardy didn't take it?"

"I told him my dad was putting it in the safe. He had to . . . you know."

"Take me to jail, lock me up for my own good, keep me from being a menace to society."

"He really cares, Jade."

"This too," Jade says, unholstering *Just Before Dawn*. "I couldn't throw it. That's . . . it's why I came over."

She holds *Just Before Dawn* across.

"A videotape," Letha says, like identifying a bug.

"Yeah, it's the only way—"

"We don't have a player on the yacht?" Letha says, kind of in apology.

Jade winces, says, "So—wait, does this mean you couldn't watch *Bay of Blood*?"

"*Bay of*—oh, oh, yeah. No, I'm sorry. But I've still *got* it—" She's walking and talking, Jade's wrist somehow in her hand now, like she's been arrested in the kindest way possible.

"No, we can't, your dad—" Jade starts, unsure how to say what she needs to say.

"He won't mind," Letha says, pulling, not stopping, "won't even know I've got someone over. The yacht's so crowded tonight, everybody's here for the Fourth! And for, you know, Mr. Samuels. Anyway, my dad's room's all the way in the bow, we'll be—"

"I can't, I've got to—"

"Walk around the lake in the dark with a bear in the area?" Letha asks, dragging Jade across the living room now. "I mean, if you *want*, I can call the sheriff, have him send a boat."

"Or, or. You could—"

"My stepmother won't let me drive the boat at night," Letha says with ill-feigned disgust. They're coming through the front door now, are on the porch.

Jade immediately clocks the inky black trees Theo Mondragon is about to come slouching out of in his burly-lithe way, the bulb in his headlamp off but still warm.

"Okay, okay," Jade says ahead to Letha, giving up this futile resistance, stepping in alongside so as to get up the pier and into the boat faster, please. If Theo Mondragon really doesn't know his daughter has a guest for the night? That can almost maybe work. Or, it can work one hell of a lot better than getting caught out in the open by him when his hands are still red.

"So where did you spend the day?" Letha asks in a making-conversation bid.

"Camp Blood," Jade monotones, looking behind them at the candlelight flickering in the kitchen window like a beacon.

"That old—?"

"Yeah."

"Isn't it scary over there?"

"You tell me."

"I know I'll never go there again," Letha says, doing a full-body shiver, the memory of Deacon Samuels apparently washing through her.

"I'm serious about tomorrow night," Jade says.

"The—the *slasher*?" Letha's lips are pressed together in a way that feels one hundred percent patronizing. "So from . . . from Camp Blood," she says, changing direction for them now that they're up on the pier, "from over there could you see . . . out onto the lake?"

The way she's picking through her words, Jade can hear what she's trying not to say, as she doesn't want to say it if Jade doesn't already know: "Mr. Holmes."

Letha looks over, her eyes blinking fast and tragic.

"It's funny," Letha says, then takes Jade's forearm in both of her hands, draws best-friend close, whispers, "not *funny*-funny, but . . . ironic, I guess?"

"What's ironic?" Jade asks, not sure she wants to know.

"My dad was always saying he wished he had a BB gun for him," Letha says, letting Jade assemble the rest in her head. But Jade has pieces Letha doesn't know she has: Mars Baker tracking that duck across the water for Theo Mondragon, saying he should have used a shotgun; Mars Baker saying that to a guy who just had a *nail*gun.

Jade looks back to the woods.

"The bear?" Letha asks, pulling Jade closer.

Jade shakes her head no. Well. The "bear" that killed Deacon Samuels, yeah. The one that, say, was out turning their handy-dandy jammer on when a certain history teacher buzzed over for the hundred and first time. No, Theo Mondragon *didn't* have a BB gun or a shotgun handy, but he *could* pick up the only gun handy: the one that spits nails.

Why not fling a golden nail up into the sky at the annoyance Mr. Holmes most certainly was? It's just a gesture. It's not like the nails are arrows, it's not like they're made for flying. It's not like they're meant to rip through a Dacron wing.

But what if one did, right? A one-in-a-million shot? Isn't that exactly the kind of shot someone like Theo Mondragon's been making his whole life already?

And what if, for sixty seconds after that, Theo Mondragon stood alongside three construction grunts and watched the little kit plane he'd just shot founder in the air, finally nosedive into the lake, launching its old pilot out into the water?

What if Theo Mondragon had just accidentally killed someone in broad daylight, and done it in front of three witnesses? Probably what he'd do then was what Deacon Samuels had already done: stuff those grunts' hands with cash, assure them it was an accident, it was just a joke that got out of hand, but someone of his station didn't need the kind of media attention this could bring, surely they could understand, couldn't they? And then . . . he probably didn't sleep on it, probably didn't sleep at all. Who would?

What he *would* do, though, what would make sense at two in the morning, would be to involve himself with the construction the next day, and maybe send everyone but those three back across the lake. So he, the quintessential businessman, taking risk analysis and cost-benefit margins into severe account, could take care of business. Nobody on the yacht would think twice about a nailgun going off in Terra Nova. Nailguns were always going off in the houses.

And—and from his angle, he'd have to do it, wouldn't he? If he didn't, Shooting Glasses and Mismatched Gloves and Cody could pull this whole enterprise down. Pull his whole *life* down.

"What is it?" Letha says, peering over into Jade's eyes.

"Just . . . thinking about that BB gun," Jade says back.

"He would never get one, though," Letha says. "He hates guns."

Of course he does, Jade answers inside. All slashers do.

She stands up fast when a light's bobbing through the trees. When Letha starts to look back to see what's got Jade's attention, Jade hustles them ahead.

"Hungry," she says. "Haven't eaten since, since . . ."

As if she could.

Except then she does, two plates' worth of smoked salmon and crackers and leftover potato skins warmed in the microwave, delivered back to Letha's room because Jade says she doesn't want to startle anybody in the tight halls, meaning: there are no other girls on this yacht in coveralls, with hair like all the crayons melted together at the bottom of the box.

The salmon is so good, too, and the potato skins themselves, being left over, have a sort of skin over them that's the most wonderful rubbery sensation to bite through. Each time it scrapes against Jade's gums, she almost has to wince in a delight so pure she feels guilty for it.

"More if you want it," Letha says in her jaunty, nonjudgmental way.

What they're drinking is sparkling grape juice. Only nonalcoholic beverages for final girls.

"What were you, um, doing out there?" Jade asks between bites and gulps.

Letha's nibbling at the one potato skin she has on her plate, which Jade's pretty sure she just forked over so Jade wouldn't have to eat alone.

"In the houses?" Letha asks, which feels like a stall.

Jade chews, nods.

Letha shrugs, studies the wall of her grand bedroom, and the way she doesn't answer at first makes Jade sure that she was part of the hunt, that she was flushing construction grunts for her father, that she was supposed to lure them out in the open.

"Looking for you?" she says at last, in a small voice, her shoulders up by her ears.

"Me?"

"The sheriff—he's worried about you, Jade."

"So he did call."

"It was Tiffany's mom the first time. I wasn't lying about that."

"He probably just thinks I'm a threat or something."

"You could never—"

"So you came out with a candle to look for me?"

"The houses aren't locked yet," Letha says with a shrug. "And . . . and you already left me those pants before?"

"So you . . . knew I could walk around the lake?" Jade says, following this logic.

"I couldn't sleep, thinking of you over here without a blanket, afraid, alone."

"Thanks?" Jade says, the word unfamiliar in her mouth. "Not really tired, though, I mean—"

"And if my dad saw you," Letha adds, no eye contact for this.

"He . . . doesn't like trespassers?"

"He's kind of really into privacy, I guess?"

"Hardy said someone was always calling Mr. Holmes's plane in, yeah," Jade says.

Letha tries to suppress her grin, ends up standing to take her earrings out at the dresser, tilting her head this way and that. "It was kind of pervy," she says.

"Pervy?"

"My stepmom . . ." Letha closes her eyes to get through the next part: "On the top deck, she'll—she'll lock the deck door and tan her . . . all of her?"

"No top," Jade fills in, and about Mr. Holmes, "that *dog*."

Letha's dabbing some solution or formula onto her eyelashes now, blinking fast from it. "She doesn't like tan lines," she says.

"White woman married to a black man," Jade fills in. "She's trying to catch up."

"She's white?" Letha says, lilting her voice up like she might really have not noticed.

Jade waits a beat then looks away, kind of impressed. "She doesn't want to peel out of her shirt in the bedroom and have *literal* headlights," she says, doing bright beams in front of her chest with her hands, Letha clocking that in the mirror.

"Stop!" she says, giggling, and Jade wonders if this is what it's like, having a best friend. One who's so unselfconsciously applying moisturizer to her face now that it seems Jade and her must have been connected at the hip since kindergarten.

But then, "What's that smell?" Jade asks.

Letha angles her head up to sniff, says, "Oh yeah—you're not allergic, are you?"

"To what?"

"Lavender and melatonin," Letha says, sitting down on her bed with one long leg folded under her. "A diffuser. Helps me sleep. It's on a timer."

"Flowers," Jade says, patting her pockets for the charger still up on the second floor of the last house she was in.

"The lavender," Letha says with a shrug. "Makes you think purple thoughts."

"You have a phone charger, maybe?"

Letha does, and of course her model of phone's generations newer than Jade's clunker.

"Want to ask Mr. Pangborne?" she says, standing to go do just that. "He's got every connector known to man, and some that aren't out until next year probably."

"Not important," Jade says, blinking against the sleeping pills misting through the air.

"I'll sleep on the futon," Letha says, gathering an extra blanket and pillow off the bed.

Jade tries to protest but Letha isn't having it.

"What time is it?" Jade asks, knowing full well it can't even be seven o'clock yet.

"We can watch a movie!" Letha answers back, and aims a remote at the flat-screen on the wall.

"What do you got?" Jade asks.

"Everything?" Letha answers, and, of course: her dad's the media mogul. She tosses Jade the remote, says, "Just say a title to it."

"To the remote?"

To remote, yes.

Jade looks down to it for a microphone hole, doesn't see one, finally just says timidly, to test Letha's "everything," "*The Dorm That Dripped Blood*."

The movie rolls up by its alternate title *Pranks*, the cursor blinking on the play button.

"What's it about?" Letha says.

"Kittens and rainbows, obviously," Jade says, and falls through all the video shelves in her head, knowing this is her one chance, that she has to pick one single movie that can show Letha how to fight, how to survive, how to win tomorrow night. And *Just Before Dawn* is practically spinning its two reel hubs in her pocket. But no. Even though it's 1981, it's still too seventies for a newbie. No, Letha needs something she can recognize herself in, something where the killer isn't a cartoon, something—

"*Kristy*," Jade says into the remote, with authority.

Which brings up all the actresses with that name.

"*Kristy*, 2014," Jade corrects.

Same result, different shuffle of faces.

"Who you looking for?" Letha asks, snuggled into her blanket on the futon.

"Different dorm that dripped blood," Jade says, scrolling through. "A Lifetime movie, actually."

"Like Hallmark?"

"More stalkers and psycho grannies."

Kristy's not there, though. Probably because the copy Jade watched was downloaded onto her phone a bit at a time over five nights, and had two stacks of different-colored subtitles on it, neither of which she could read, all of which were in the way.

It would have been perfect, though. Justine, the girl in *Kristy*, fights. It's probably more of a home invasion than a slasher, but Letha doesn't need to know motivations or builds at this point, or what can count as "home." She just needs to feel a girl insisting on her own life, and living through the night, and having that slow-down moment where she stops running, turns to face her attacker.

"Wait," Letha says, rolling off the futon, pulling her phone up, dialing before Jade can stop her. "Dad?" she says, and repeats the title and the year to him, adding a "Pleeease?" at the end, batting her eyelashes even though this is audio-only. "We really want to watch it . . ."

She sits up straighter from whatever her dad says back. Sits up straight and looks over to Jade like *oops*.

"Just—no, of course not, Ginn's scared enough already. I'm talking to someone on the phone, Dad. We want to watch it at the same time . . . someone from school . . . no, it's not . . . it's a Lifetime movie? Thank you, just check, thank you."

She hangs up, sits back hugging a pillow and making a face that Jade guesses means "parents," and then before Jade can even ask what exactly that was about, the flat-screen on Letha's bed-room wall fizzes, resolves back with what Theo Mondragon is pushing to it from upstairs, downstairs, "the bow," Jade has no real sense.

"Where is he?" she asks.

"They're probably up on deck?" Letha says with a shrug. "He sleeps up there sometimes."

Of course he does, Jade thinks. Because creeping out of a bed-room and down a hall can draw attention. Slipping over the railing when you're already on-deck is nothing, though. And he probably *does* use a little Zodiac boat with a trolling motor. Or, it's not like he can't swim the lake, or walk around it.

"How did he—?" Jade asks, about the shaky opening credits of *Kristy* starting up.

"Owns the network?" Letha says. "Parent company, I don't know. Doesn't matter."

"Hunh," Jade says, a little bit impressed. She settles back to watch, hugging the two-hundred-dollar pillow to her.

"Going tomorrow night?" Letha asks. "The movie thing?"

She's sitting up now like she doesn't want to, but there's one pre-bedtime duty left to perform: wrapping her hair up for sleep?

Jade doesn't understand, just answers the question instead: "Wouldn't miss it for the world."

Thirty minutes later Letha's asleep, snoring cutely into the futon's backrest, one of her legs hiked up around her body. Jade weighs waking her for *Kristy*'s excellent lessons against the final girl being tired for her big fight tomorrow night but decides sleep will be the best thing, as each minute in a massacre uses twice as much adrenaline as the previous minute, and it's probably even harder if you're having to actually *fight* the slasher, not just get away from him.

That doesn't mean Jade's tired yet, though. But, not like she can step outside and blow smoke up at the stars, either. Anyway, at this point in the game, standing alone in any dark place would be setting out a formal invitation for a beheading. Cigarettes are great and all, but her head staying attached to her body is even better.

Because her fidgety hands need to be doing *something*, she snoops through the shelf by the bed—Letha's sleepytime reading. Which are all the extra-credit history papers Jade hand-delivered. The whole sheaf is still folded in the middle. Jade opens them, is ready to be thrilled by all the highlights Letha has to have done, because final girls always do their homework. But these haven't been read at all, it doesn't look like. They're even . . . Jade checks every third page: yep. Except for the letter Letha evidently keyed on, they're in the same order even, from revenge and pranks to final girls, on through the big interview debacle of sophomore year, then adding it all together into *Jaws*: a whole slasher crash course in thirty pages. Just, a crash course Letha doesn't seem to have bothered with yet, as Jade's letter was, evidently, *so* much more fascinating, *so* much more "revealing."

Jade has to chuckle. The kind with no smile.

She weighs again the pros and cons of waking Letha to maybe do this Very Important Homework, but finally pulls her phone out instead. Letha wasn't lying, either: signal's fine, now. Three bars, same as Proofrock. Not that being connected does anything but remind her that her inbox has zero new messages.

Jade opens her photos, swipes up and up until she finds what she wants: a snapshot of a photograph from that paper they had at the treatment center down in Idaho Falls . . . *Post Register*, yeah. The story about Mr. Holmes. The one photo was of him in his ultralight, the sky clear behind him.

Jade touches the heart under the picture, so it'll be easier to find next time, and then she tries to blink away all the feelings trying to crowd in.

This isn't the time for that.

Instead, she catalogs the day's events, plugging them into and out of this or that slasher to see what might fit, and finds herself early on in *Scream* again. Not the Casey Becker kill, but the Sid-scare, where Sid shows the first glimmer of the survivor she is: when she can't call the police to her house, she uses her computer to get them there.

Jade's phone has battery and signal, though. Meaning—meaning she could just dial Hardy up right now, couldn't she? There *are* dead bodies over here. And she *is* a witness, at least to Shooting Glasses. She owes it to him to call Theo Mondragon in, doesn't she? But if she does, then tomorrow night doesn't happen like it's supposed to, either.

Jade studies Letha's memory wall, all the printed-out photos of her with friends. They're at dances, scaling cliffs, just walking down streets that don't mean anything to Jade, but probably mean everything to Letha. And of course there she is with her dad, with Theo Mondragon, both of them with scuba goggles cocked up on their heads, nothing but empty blue water behind them.

If Jade calls Hardy in, then Letha will be taking *that* photo down, at least. And blaming Jade for it?

Maybe, yeah. Probably.

A half hour later *Kristy* crescendoes in a beautiful necessary fireball—killing the killer feels so good—then scratches into the credits, and Jade salutes Justine, the bad-ass survivor girl, but all she can think about is *Didn't she have to pee at some point in all that running?*

Jade has to pee so bad she can't keep her legs still, which is only tangling her up deeper in the sheet, making this emergency situation worse.

Instead of jarring Letha awake by pausing the credits—ripping that sound away would have to startle her—Jade uses the remote to bump it back all the way to the pool scene, which gives her like forty minutes to pee. Which, judging by how the whites of her eyes are going yellow, feels like about how much time she'll need. And the bathroom, Letha was sure to say, is just down the hall to the right.

Jade pulls Letha's door in, chances a look out into this narrow little *Dead Calm, Donkey Punch* hallway. It's just as empty as she hoped, and Jade supposes that, all in all, being in a *Dead Calm* or a *Donkey Punch* at least means you're on top of the water, not down in all that *DeepStar Six, Leviathan* pressure. Though up here there's always *Triangle* and *Ghost Ship* and *Virus*. But at some point you just have to find something to pee in, too, ideally a toilet. Jade steps out into the tight hall, immediately feels too exposed. She ducks back into the room, steps out a moment later in Letha's Italian silk robe, a towel wrapped around her hair. Letha's tall enough that the robe covers Jade's combat boots. Score one for the good guys.

Jade speedwalks down to the first door on the right, ducks in, doesn't turn the light on until she's got the door closed again.

Right across from her is a gas mask.

Jade flinches back, not ready to die yet, but the mask doesn't shoot two arms out for her. It's just hanging there, along with . . . a full scuba suit, complete with goggles, a slicker and hat Creighton Duke would like, and . . . no hockey mask. No fedora. Just a rack of scuba tanks, which is a stupid thing to keep all the way down here instead of up on some deck, right? Unless . . . unless someone's *keeping* them hidden?

But why?

Oh, Jade realizes: because of Scooby-Doo. In the big reveal, there's always the careful walk-through of how the fake ghost or whatever was doing it, isn't there? These tanks are probably going to be part of that, aren't they? Someone, maybe Jade, will pull a holding strap and let the tanks roll out into the middle of the confession.

Jade should most definitely not be in here with them right now, though. It's too early. But still, and mostly just because she's seen *Scream 3*, Jade pushes her hand into the belly of each hanging outfit just to be sure none of them are going to reach out for her as soon as she turns her back. She turns the overhead light off, listens hard for footsteps or breathing in the hall, and steps out again, darts across to the bathroom, which is to the right *from* Letha's bedroom, but is *on* the left.

She's just done, is dealing with the many complications of coveralls and this impossibly soft robe, when she takes stock of the counter, and the beauty toolkit exploded all over it. No, this isn't a workbench, she decides, it's an artist's station. She touches a smudged sponge, runs her fingertip along the spine of a brush, and . . . what's this? Cylindrical, electric, surely not . . .

Jade picks it up as delicately as she can: Oh, clippers. Phew. Meaning . . . she stares at the door, is thinking about the halls beyond it, and all the rooms it connects to, and Letha saying the yacht's full tonight, because everybody's in town for Deacon Samuels, and for the Fourth.

This is a *dude's* clippers. She can tell because they're big to fit big hands, and don't have any feminine accents. And . . . the only one of the Founders with a roguish soul patch that probably needs constant attention is Mars Baker.

So: Mars Baker is close enough to *also* be using this bathroom.

Jade swallows hard, looks at herself in the mirror, and has to touch her hair to make sure it's real. It looks more like she smeared glue all over her scalp and thrashed her head around in a New Year's Eve dumpster.

Touching it just leaves her fingers oily, too. She's probably ruining Letha's expensive pillow.

"Fuck it," she says, and before she can think twice, she takes Mars Baker's clippers, peels the guard away, and stares herself down while shaving off hank after hank of hair. It's supposed to turn her into Ripley from *Alien 3*, when space lice were an issue, but she's really just a stubbly mess now, a slightly taller Tommy Jarvis, her scalp still unevenly stained from the shoe polish. Her head looks like a kindergarten class's pottery project.

"Well you asked for it," she tells herself, and runs the faucet to try to swirl all the hair down the drain. When it clogs, she has to reach into the mucky water, grainy with the spit-out toothpaste of probably ten people, and grab onto the oily clump of her hair, deliver it to the trashcan like the drowned rat it is.

Finally the water gurgles and burps down, leaving the rest of her split-ends all over the steep walls of the sink. Jade runs more water, guides those strays down as best she can, and almost has them all gone—no evidence—when the knob rattles and a shoulder thunks into the metal door.

"Um?" she says.

"*Hurry*," someone whispers—female, thank you, not old and male and litigious.

Still, someone's standing right out there now, waiting.

"Okay, *okay*," Jade says in her best Letha-sleep voice, which she knows can't be very convincing, because final girls don't let their frustration and grogginess make them snappy.

Jade runs water over her hands, pats them dry on her cloud-soft hips, wraps the towel back around her prickly scalp—a completely new sensation—and turns the light off. She breathes once, twice, and on *three* she spins out, keeping her back to whoever this is, stepping around them in a way that's also kind of pushing them into the bathroom they evidently need in a desperate way.

For a flash she sees that it's one of the twins, either Cinnamon or Ginger, which is the best she could hope for: kids. Not Mars Baker, not Ladybird Samuels or Macy Todd, not Ross Pangborne or Lewellyn Singleton, not Lana Singleton, not—not whatever Ross Pangborne's wife is named. Donna?

Lemmy, though, Lemmy Singleton would have been all right. Him or Galatea. Kids she can deal with. Kids she can bluff.

"Thanks," either Cinnamon or Ginger says to Jade's back, stepping into the bathroom, and Jade nods, keeps moving, the hallway surely free and clear all the way back to—

Facing her now is the *other* twin, either Cinnamon or Ginger.

She's looking Jade full in the face, not recognizing her.

"Who—who are *you*?" this other twin asks.

"Letha's friend," Jade mumbles.

"There's hair in here!" the first twin announces from the toilet.

"Does her dad know you're spending the night?" the other asks.

"He ordered us a movie," Jade says, turning sideways to slip past.

"The bathroom's not even steamy," this other twin says, which is the same as asking why Jade has a towel wound around her head.

Jade doesn't explain, just keeps on trucking down to Letha's room, ducks in breathing hard, feels exactly *like* Justine in *Kristy*, always hiding behind this door, in that locker room, certain death around every corner.

She feels for the lock on Letha's door, twists it over, falls back onto the bed.

Her heart thumps slower and slower, the adrenaline flushing out, and in its wake is lavender and melatonin to inhale. Jade fights through it as best she can, Letha's light snoring not helping.

"*Friday the 13th*," she whispers into the remote, and pulls up *The Final Chapter* which wasn't, hoping the carrot of counting machete-strikes into Jason's head at the end will keep her awake.

It's the scene she always imagined watching with a garageful of classmates, all of them chanting the numbers higher and higher, some of them acting it out, all of them killing Jason together, because it takes a village.

Jade makes it through, does the count alone in her head, then dials back to *Part III*, is in and out until the headstand, which she suspects is *not* actually part of sex, but when Jason splits that guy from crotch to head, one side of her falls away with him, and—because all the camera angles and compositions are built around 3-D—Jade tracks it down. To her phone, awake in her hand somehow.

No, not somehow. Very much on purpose.

This is the decision she's been avoiding, isn't it? Cutting all her hair off hasn't made her forget, though. Not quite. Even Jason hasn't distracted her enough.

She can save a lot of lives if she just makes one phone call, can't she? If she just touches one phone number?

It means . . . it means all her slasher dreams don't come true, but—if they do? Is it really winning if everybody dies? More to the point: if she'd have nipped this slasher cycle in the bud already, by turning that pink phone in, would Mr. Holmes have ended up dying in Indian Lake?

That decides it for her.

She calls Hardy's office. Not 911, where a dispatcher will answer, give her time to lose her nerve, but the actual office.

It rings three times, four, and on five—

"Fremont County Sheriff's Office," Meg says, as chipper as the day is long.

"Ms. Koenig?" Jade says, not speaking too loud.

"Um, who is this?" Meg asks back.

"I just want to report something."

"May I have your name, please?"

"I saw a—I saw someone die. I saw him get killed, I mean."

For a moment, nothing, then, so cheery, "And where are you, dear?"

"Across the lake," Jade says, obviously. "Terra Nova."

"And who is this?"

"It doesn't matter. It's . . ."—quieter, much quieter—"it's Theo Mondragon who did it."

"Excuse me?"

"He's the one who did it. Theo Mondragon."

"This is Jade Daniels," Meg says, switching ears it sounds like.

"I'm anonymous," Jade says back.

"We do have caller ID, dear."

Jade closes her eyes in pain.

"I'm sorry," Meg says. "But the sheriff left specific instructions for if you called. He said it would be your next . . . what was the word? Oh, yes. 'Gambit.' Your next gambit. That's like a gamble plus a ruse, it means—"

"I *know* what it means."

"Yes, yes, of course. Grady . . . he had said you have a vocabulary on you."

Grady, Bear, Sherlock, Holmes, pirate of Indian Lake, Night Flier—some history teachers have as many names as *A Bay of Blood*, don't they?

No: had. Some history teachers *had* that many names.

More important, "He talked to you about me?" Jade asks, fully aware this is giving away that it's really her.

"He was proud of you," Meg says, her mouth closer to the phone now, but all Jade can hear is that past tense.

"This isn't a gambit," Jade says. "This is . . . I *saw* it, you've got to believe me."

"Was it like a—a slasher movie?"

"Just because . . . that doesn't mean it didn't happen. If you don't—a lot of people are going to die tomorrow night."

"Sheriff said you would say that," Meg says. "Something about 'closing the beaches,' I believe?"

Jade lowers the phone to the sheets, watches her thumb end the useless stupid idiotic doomed call, and she decides to just count the seconds until her phone dims to half-bright, then completely blacks out: fifteen, then thirty. But to be sure she does it again, gets a count of fifteen and thirty-two, so has to do it again to be sure, but this time—or maybe the next?—when the screen goes dark, it takes her eyelids with it. As she's sinking, she tells herself it doesn't matter, she's safe. The door's locked, the yacht's still as a tomb, this blanket is soft and warm, the twins haven't rung the alarm, and, most important, you don't slash where you live. Theo Mondragon must know that, it's basic stuff. All she has to do is be sure and wake before dawn, sneak out through the tangle of halls, be gone before Letha can insist on a group breakfast up on deck.

Jade's first thought when she wakes back *up*, though, which feels like the same moment she was just in, is the thesis of another paper she wrote for Mr. Holmes: "The Strange Algebra of Horror." Her lead-in example, and where she got the title, was that hurting the leg of a slasher, instead of slowing it down, it actually makes the slasher faster, just, now it's got a scary limp. But her main push, with many examples, was that proximity to the final girl greatly reduces your likelihood of survival. Meaning a fly on the wall might just have a chance of slipping through alive—like, talking *Friday*s, Ted, the prankster in *Part 2* who kind of by convention has to die and die hard. Except he goes out drinking on the town, is safe from all the carnage specifically because he increases his distance from the final girl.

Instead of, say, sleeping right alongside her.

Jade yawns a long luxuriant yawn, her jaw nearly popping out of place from it, and apologizes in her head to Mr. Holmes, as that paper must have been wrong, since, right now, Jade's as safe as she can be. But . . . what was it that woke her up, here? A sound? Yeah, some sound, something jarring. A wrong sound. Her memory can categorize it as "sudden," just can't hear it again, quite.

She tunes in to the rest of the yacht as best she can, squinting to dial whatever it was in. Because she's listening so hard, the footsteps suddenly pounding past the door are absolute *thunder* to her. She kicks back into the corner of the bed, eyes wide, mouth instantly dry, muscles tensed and getting tenser.

Moments later the doorknob rattles violently and someone slaps the door high and to the side like a cop.

Letha squirms on the futon, shaken awake.

"W-what?" she says, not able to completely open her eyes yet, her lids probably gummed together with airborne melatonin. She reaches up to rub them with the back of her wrist, which is exactly when the wall maybe six inches above her head disintegrates with a blast that can only be Mars Baker's shotgun. One of the barrels, anyway.

Letha rolls away from the wall as if stung with shot. She spills onto the floor just as the next barrel unloads into where she was lying, leaving wisps of foam floating in the air. In the silence after the blast, a single flame flickers at the edge of the crater in the futon, and, through the hole in the wall, there's a scream, a gurgle, and then that gurgle's cut sharply off.

"*Macy?*" Letha says about that gurgle.

Jade's on the floor with her already, pulling her close, her breath fast and shallow, but when Letha sees her she pushes away, trying to escape.

"It's me, it's me!" Jade yells, running her hand over her scalp like that somehow proves she's the same, just, with less hair.

"Jade?" Letha says, slowly getting it.

"*We've got to get out of here,*" Jade hisses, fully aware her voice can now be heard through that hole in the wall.

"But—"

Letha's cut off by a hammering on her door. Not a slap anymore but the side of a fist, pounding.

"Where's the machete I gave you?" Jade asks, casting around. "Your dad didn't really put it in his safe, did he?"

Letha looks over to her like Jade's talking in possum, and she wants to watch her lips, see how an animal can be making human words like this.

Jade shakes Letha, says, "I know you're not ready, but you have to be. It's happening."

"But . . . this is—"

"I know, I know," Jade says. "I said tomorrow night, the party, but I was wrong, I don't know, I'm sorry, okay?"

"The massacre?"

"It's happening right now."

"But who—"

"You don't want to know," Jade says, standing, pulling Letha up alongside her. "Now where's that machete?"

Letha pans around the room, her eyes wide and dumb like a cow's—*I should have prepared her better,* Jade's chiding herself— then reaches over behind the dresser, unsheathes the machete from its excellent hiding place. She offers it to Jade but Jade steps away, hands high.

"This is all you," she says. "I take that, I die fast. That's Indy's whip, Thor's hammer, the Dude's housecoat. One user only."

She guides it back closer to Letha.

"I don't know how," Letha says, trying to figure where her fingers go, what the balance is, which is the sharp side. After snatching it from the air like a ninja chopsticking a fly in flight, yeah.

"You will," Jade tells her, and steps forward, hates that she has to but does it anyway: pushes the side of her head to the door, to listen. What she deserves for that, she knows, and would even cheer for, is Ghostface's knife plunging into the side of her skull, but the only other option is stepping out there without knowing it's empty.

"Clear," she says after maybe three breaths of silence, and snaps for Letha to come close, to be ready.

"Where are we going?" Letha asks.

"Off this boat," Jade hisses back, and hauls the door in all at once.

Ladybird Samuels is lying there eyes open, mouth doubly-open—no chin, no jaw, maybe no throat either, like the skin just kept holding on and holding on. Her bloody handprints are on the door right by Jade's face.

Letha screams until Jade turns around, covers Letha's mouth with her hand, bringing her eyes right up to Letha's, warning her to stop. After nodding to Letha and getting a nod back, she finally—slowly—removes her hand.

Letha draws in like to scream again, to tell the whole boat where they are, but instead she throws up her half a potato skin.

Jade doesn't hold her hair or pat her back. She steps into the hall.

"Which way is out?" she asks.

When Letha's just crying, probably replaying Ladybird Samuels in her head, Jade says it again, harsher: "Where *to*, Letha?"

Letha weakly points back the way they came, past the bathroom. Jade takes her by the wrist, then the hand, and leads her out, both of them stepping carefully over Ladybird Samuels.

"Who's doing this?" Letha says, unable to look away, or be helpful at all.

"You'll see," Jade tells her, and they make it all the way to the stairs before the next body confronts them: Ross Pangborne.

He's been ripped apart somehow, his torso up at the switch-back, his legs playing catchup, though they never will.

"W-what could do that?" Letha says, trying to fall to her knees, give up.

"Shotgun, chainsaw," Jade says, not letting Letha give up, just pulling her deeper into this.

"But what did he do to—to deserve this?" Letha asks, and Jade lets a grim smile touch her lips: if Letha's already seeing these deaths like that, as the consequence of previous bullshit, then there's hope.

Jade eases them around Ross Pangborne, trying not to step in the blood as that leaves red footprints.

"We can't just—" Letha starts.

"We have to," Jade completes, and then they're to the top of the stairs, in the tower part of the yacht, she's pretty sure, are having to step over a shattered shotgun to see—

Letha falls back shaking her head no, no, and Jade doesn't want to look, but has to: Mars Baker has been thrust headfirst through the big window, and his jaw has been pulled off too, so his mouth is locked into a forever scream.

Letha falls back shaking her head no, no, and now it's Jade's turn to throw up. Just into her mouth at first, but when she can't swallow that, all the salmon and potato skins and lavender and melatonin comes up and out, splashes her boots and Letha's bare feet, and it's not purple, and her eyes are hot and leaky so she guesses that means she's crying because there's vomit burning her nasal passage, and now more's coming up, and Letha's hand is on her back, the same as it was for Tiffany K, once upon a puking.

Jade reaches out, steadies herself on the thin blue knee of Letha's sleep pants.

"Who's doing this?" Letha says, a kind of checked-out quality to her tone now, her eyes practically flashing *vacancy*, *tilt*, like she's pulled some internal eject lever on this whole situation. Like she's reached the maximum amount she can sustain, so the rest can now just wash over her.

"Where's the machete?" Jade asks.

Letha looks down to her empty hand, and then they both hear it: scraping on the ceiling above them. Meaning somebody's a floor up in the tower.

"Dad?" Letha says, and leads Jade out onto the deck to look up to the top.

With both of them already straining to see, Tiara comes sailing out over the railing of the deck above them, pedaling her legs, waving her arms like there's anything to grab on to.

"*T!*" Letha screams, rushing the railing, slamming into it like if she could have just got there a second earlier, she could have reached out, snagged the hem of Tiara's shirt.

Jade tracks Tiara's ragdoll body all the way down to one of the posts built into this modular pier. The post isn't sharp, is flat and blunt, but all the same it plunges up and through Tiara's chest, splashes out the back, and when Tiara's face slams into the wood or plastic or plastic wood, whatever it is, Jade feels her own cheek tingle in sympathy.

"This can't be happening," Letha says.

"We've got to get off this boat," Jade says back, hauling Letha up and casting around for—for whatever's next. They have to get off this boat, right? Right. Jade steps to the railing, chances a look down to the lake side of the deck. It's dizzying. This yacht is a monster.

"How deep is it down there?" she asks.

"The water?" Letha asks.

"The water," Jade confirms, having to lead this final girl along.

"The valley is steep on this side," Letha pretty much recites from Mr. Holmes's rambling talks, "that means . . . that means—"

"It's deep enough," Jade says, and, steps up onto the rail, holding Letha's hand to steady herself.

"No, if we—"

"There's nowhere safe here," Jade says, pulling Letha up onto the rail, which nearly overbalances her.

Letha steps up in her dainty athletic way.

"My dad," she says, peering around from her higher vantage point to the deck Tiara was just launched from.

"I'm sure he's fine," Jade says. Not that she probably just missed him in the costume closet. "He'd—he'd want you to be safe. That would be his first concern, wouldn't it? Wouldn't he throw you over this railing himself if that's what it took to keep you safe?"

Letha looks down and down, to the water.

"If he were here, he'd tell you your first job is to survive, wouldn't he?" Jade asks, and before Letha can answer, Jade pulls her arm hard enough that it's jump or fall—also hard enough that she's committed now herself, is already tumbling, wheeling her arms, pedaling her legs just like Tiara was, breathing in as deep as she can with all the air sucking away from her. Once in the open, no footing, she loses Letha's wrist immediately, which she tells herself is probably for the best, as they don't want to come down on each other.

Seconds later she hits the surface of the lake with a thought-erasing *slap*, is slamming down into Ezekiel's Cold Box, all the breath she thought she was saving gone in an instant, the water around her thinner than makes sense—made of bubbles and speed and thrashing, but in slow motion too, like it's not a body of water Jade's fallen into, but a nightmare pool, the kind you can never surface in.

She hits the slanted bottom, her face scraping rock, and pushes up clawing for air, certain beyond certain that a large hand is about to wrap its cold dead fingers around her ankle. When she surfaces, half of her comes up out of the water, and she's not a human anymore, is a gasping machine. Five, six seconds later she's treading, treading, and, way above, can just see Letha, still perched on the railing in her clingy camisole and pajama bottoms.

Of course she was able to regain her balance. Of course a doof like Jade wouldn't be enough to pull a majestic creature like Letha Mondragon overboard. Now that Jade's free, though, Letha's just looking down at her, head cocked over like Michael's, like Jason's— like Jade's a dead thing, a dying thing.

It makes her spin around in the water for whatever's coming for her.

Nothing.

And then—no.

"Behind you!" Jade screams as loud as she can, pointing with both hands, which makes her face nearly slip underwater.

There's a head of long hair blowing in silhouette from the railing of the deck above Letha.

Synthetic hair, Jade wants to tell Letha, but in the moment it doesn't matter.

Ross Pangborne's dead, Mars Baker is dead, Deacon Samuels was dead before this night even started, and Lewellyn Singleton can't have enough backstory to be any kind of slasher, can he?

Leaving one man up there in a Norman Bates dress, a Samara wig: Theo Mondragon. Who else could get close enough to Tiara to toss her over like that? Who else would have that upper body strength?

"Jump!" Jade screams up to Letha, and, instead, Letha looks behind her, sees this mask-face from much closer, and this does dislodge her.

It's a fall that should crunch her ribs in on the railing of one of the three decks below, break her in half, ground her for life if she's so lucky, but Letha's Letha: one of her bare feet finds the solid railing she just slipped from and pushes out *hard* from it so Letha's no longer going straight down but is arcing out, her body stretching out into a dive so perfect Jade almost gasps.

Three seconds later Letha slips into the water with less splash than a dagger, porpoises up maybe twenty feet out, meaning she turned back for the surface the moment she broke it, to be sure not to mar her face against the stony bottom.

Good for her, Jade says inside. Smoke em if you got em, and this final girl most definitely does.

Jade slaps the water like a beaver tail to get Letha's attention and Letha clears her hair from her eyes, looks around, awake again. She takes a long, easy stroke Jade's way, then another, and, right before she's going to get there, Jade kicks away, going for around the front of the boat, for shore that doesn't involve the pier.

"Camp Blood," she manages to get across to Letha. "We have to—"

Letha stills, stops swimming alongside Jade.

"We have to," Jade says, swirling her hands to stay afloat.

"*No*," Letha says, and Jade can tell from the set of her lips that she's seeing Deacon Samuels all over again. At Camp Blood.

"But—"

"I can't," Letha says. It's not a plea, just a fact.

"*Shit!*" Jade says, slapping the water in frustration now, but then she turns back the other way, to the ass-end of the boat, where it's darker. Where they can hide better, if they can slip into the trees? Maybe bunk in the woods, take the long long way around to Proofrock, through the national forest? Show up sometime in early August?

"Where are we going?" Letha asks, having to swim slow to not pass Jade up.

"Land," Jade says, struggling through the water.

They're almost there when Jade's hair is sticking into her eyes in a way it hasn't been—at which point it registers that she doesn't *have* hair. And it's not hair anyway, but a thick coating on her whole face, chunky like canned dog food that's been poured into the lake and then let spread out until it's thin. She looks over to Letha, and the chunks on the pale shoulders of her camisole are red in the moonlight. Jade's next awkward stroke brings her hand into a warm cavity like a floating bowl of oatmeal, a floating bowl that's . . . Lewellyn Singleton's caved-in *face*? What, is this a Fulci film?

She spins away, swims *under* the floating body, no breath this time, hits bottom almost immediately with her fingertips. She pulls ahead rock by rock, finally stands in the shallows, well clear of any floating dead people.

Letha's already there, chest heaving, her eyes locked on Lewellyn Singleton's pale form.

"Is it over now?" she asks.

"Not even close," Jade tells her, and they trudge up into the mud and grass, then scramble for the trees hand in hand, groping through the darkness when the moon's gone above the trees, and . . . was this what it was like for Stacey Graves a hundred-plus years ago, when she made it across the new lake? Was she scared like this?

Except she was younger, Jade reminds herself.

And what she was scared of, it was herself.

More important, it's now, not then. And no, Letha, this isn't over yet.

"We've got, we've got to—" Jade tells her, pulling her away from the yacht, away from the yacht, that's all she knows right now.

"Um," Letha says back, in a way that makes Jade follow where she's still looking: a space between two trees, like trying to confirm what she just saw. Except why would what she just saw hang around where it just *was*? Jade looks two trees to the right from that, which is away from the lake, then three trees ahead, focusing on a jagged slash of moonlight, and—

A hunched shadow flits from one blacked-out tree to the next, as skulky and silent as any Ghostface ever was.

"He's coming," Jade says, Letha's hand in hers again.

"*He?*" Letha asks, panic rising in her voice.

"Run."

They do, Letha pulling ahead without effort, dragging *Jade* now, and . . . and this is what it's like for a final girl to save you, isn't it? Jade *was* at the periphery, watching this slasher happen on a drive-in screen she could barely see through the telescope of all her hopes and self-assigned homework, but now she's right at the center of it all. It's terrible because it means she can die at any moment, but here at the center of the hurricane, dead bodies down this hall, through that window, falling from the sky, it's kind of a goddamn wonder, too, isn't it?

Until the toe of her boot catches under a rock and her left leg stays in place while the rest of her tries to keep going. Letha loses her grip, falls ahead, has to touch her fingertips lightly to the dirt to keep from spilling. But she's already looking around, probably thinking a wall of fishhooks have slung forward to hook into Jade's face, pull her soul apart.

Well—no, Jade corrects. That's what the horror chick's thinking. The final girl doesn't know *Hellraiser* from *Hannibal*, and why would she.

"My foot?" Jade hisses, feeling down her calf with her hands.

It's not a root.

"Oh, shit," Letha says.

It's a bear trap. Of course.

"What the hell?" Jade says, trying to wedge her fingers in between the metal teeth.

"We thought the bear might come back," Letha tells her, taking a knee.

"To this tree?"

"All those dead elk?"

Jade looks ahead and nods, remembering them at last.

"My dad had some of the guys stack them up in a pile."

"Interesting," Jade says, meaning pretty much the direct opposite, still trying to get her fingers into the metal teeth.

"Here," Letha says, chickenwinging her arms out and breathing in for the coming effort. "Cinn and Ginn aren't even supposed to come out this far."

"Me either," Jade mutters, and draws her lips back from her teeth when Letha jams her fingers down along her calf. That she can at all tells Jade there's blood. But it bit shut from side to side instead of front and back, meaning her shin bone isn't involved, just her muscle.

"Do it," she hisses, looking behind them.

A head-height pinpoint of light is bobbing through the trees, taking an indirect line towards them.

"One, two," Letha says, and on three she gives all her muscles and weight and effort to the bear trap, and, impossibly, it creaks open. Jade guides her foot up, up, and . . . her boot.

"You—have—to—" Letha strains out, her shoulders starting to tremble.

"Already doing it," Jade says, and reaches under to undo the knot her laces are in, slither her foot up and out, just making it past the teeth when the trap springs shut with a hard *clack*.

"Where are we going?" Letha asks, handing Jade's boot over.

"The long way around to Proofrock," Jade says, lacing up,

standing with Letha's help, giving her right leg what weight she can.

It's not broken, she's pretty sure, but she's not running anymore. *Or* hiking the long way around the lake.

"Shit," she says, trying to take another step.

"Here," Letha says, ducking under to be Jade's too-tall crutch, and Jade lets her for a hopping step or two. Until she stops them.

"What?" Letha asks.

"Do you know how to recock it?" Jade asks about the sprung trap.

Letha looks behind them, must not see the headlamp. She is sensing this danger, though. It's palpable. Anything can happen, and's probably about to.

"Why?" she asks.

"Why do you think?"

Letha considers, considers, then gently lets Jade stand on her own. Together—but mostly Letha—they wrench the steel jaws open again, this time far enough to click the trigger in place.

"Worst mousetrap ever," Letha says, stepping away, the trap practically humming with tension.

"*Best*," Jade says, then lowers in her unbalanced way to grab the trap's chain, drag it over from where it was, moving slow so it doesn't spring, chomp into her thigh this time.

"Why move it?" Letha asks.

"Maybe he knows where it used to be, right?" Jade says.

Letha looks at the tree it was at and then at the one it's at now, like clocking for difference, then shrugs whatever, steps under Jade's arm again. When Jade sneaks a look back, the headlamp is closer now. Though she's seeing it now as the mining light on Harry Warden's helmet.

"Go, go," she says to Letha, and they hop-crutch ahead, moving so much slower now. Jade knows that if she were even ten percent as wholesome as a final girl, she'd push Letha ahead, tell her to save herself, that her survival is what's important here, that she shouldn't endanger herself for someone whose timer's about up.

But the thing is, Jade's discovering, she doesn't want to die. Not really. Not out here in the dark, with whatever new and terrible construction tool Theo Mondragon's swinging.

Speaking of . . .

Jade peers behind Letha, across the lake. Not to the barge that makes a daily crossing, but to the idea of it.

Right?

Except tomorrow's a holiday, and the lake's closed to all powered watercraft. Only paddles and oars. Because everyone not checked into Pleasant Valley is going to be watching the movie from innertubes and canoes and dressed-up rowboats tomorrow night. Unless of course word of this massacre in Terra Nova makes it across the water. Then the staties will break Hardy's injunction, and the media won't be far behind.

Jade hitches along with Letha, looking behind them again—no light, which is fifty times worse—and reaches into her pocket, comes out with her phone. With her *dunked* phone. Her phone with the case still leaking lake water.

Jade holds it out to the side and drops it, says to Letha, "Breadcrumbs."

Letha nods about the solidness of that idea, pats her pajama bottom pockets for the phone she doesn't have.

"Oh," Jade says then, when they stumble back out into the moonlight of . . . of the meadow Mr. Holmes was showing them. Sheep's Head, something like that?

"Too exposed," Letha says, looking around like a prairie dog with a hawk complex, and Jade agrees, is letting Letha turn them around to hug the treeline, but then . . . there's that light again. Even closer.

At their new rate of speed, he's going to catch them inside two minutes, maybe less.

"No, no," Jade says, turning them back the other way, to cross the meadow. Which no way can they do.

"Is that my dad?" Letha says, then comes up onto her toes, waving one arm. "Dad, Daddy!"

Jade winces and Letha feels it, comes around, her eyes questioning.

"It is him," Jade says.

Letha studies Jade's face about this, then looks up to the light drawing closer, making more of a straight line now that it can echo-locate. Maybe Theo Mondragon can even see them now, for all Jade knows. One wounded duck with a shaved head, one improbably-alive daughter.

"You don't mean . . . ?" Letha says. "He would never—he couldn't—"

"He is," Jade says. "And he has been. Sorry. I saw."

"But Tiara."

"I don't know why yet," Jade says.

"Mr. Pangborne, Mr. Baker," Letha says. "Ladybird, Mrs. Todd, Mr. Singleton—"

"Deacon Samuels," Jade adds. "Those two Dutch kids."

"*Two?*"

"The other one . . . she's still out there somewhere." Jade tilts her head lakeward.

"And that—in the propeller?"

Clate Rodgers.

Jade blinks, looks behind them again, to the light bobbing in.

"Wave again," Jade says. "You'll see."

Letha stares into Jade's face again, harder, deeper, then turns to call her dad in but this time with hesitation, and not as loud: "Dad! Daddy!"

The light keeps on coming, keeps on, and then—

Snap!

Yes.

The bear trap.

Letha turns to Jade and pushes her hard enough Jade spills into the tall grass. "You *used* me!" she nearly screams, getting what just happened. "You used me to hurt my dad!"

"To keep him from hurting *us.*"

Out in the trees, her dad is bellowing.

Letha steps forward but Jade grabs her by the knee.

"If it is him, and it is," she says, "then we approach, we're dead. If it's not, and we stay here, then . . . my leg is a lot wimpier than his, right? He can't be hurt bad?"

"No, I—"

"Five minutes," Jade says, not letting go.

Theo Mondragon is free in two, standing again.

The chainsaw he's carrying rips awake and Letha steps back involuntarily.

"What was that guy's name in the stairwell?" she asks, even though she knows. Just, Letha needs to be seeing the two halves of Ross Pangborne up and down the stairs right now, and what might have made him like that.

"It can't be," Letha says, but she's talking to herself now.

"Do you want to stay and find out?" Jade asks, Theo Mondragon slinging the chainsaw back and forth before him like Leatherface's last dance. He's cutting the brush and limbs out of his way, and kind of lurching now from the bear trap's bite.

"Shit," Letha says, looking around for what to do, where to go, how to live.

"This is gonna suck the big one," Jade says, standing with Letha's help, then pointing with her lips to where she means.

Letha looks across, doesn't get it at first, then does.

"No," she says.

"Only way," Jade says.

"We can—" Letha tries.

"Not enough time," Jade says back, not letting her finish because whatever she's going to say isn't taking her hurt leg into account.

"You're sure he won't look there first?" Letha asks.

"Would you?" Jade asks.

When Letha has no answer, the two of them lunge ahead to the pile of rotting elk. That's what it is now. Not a killing field anymore, but a mound of corpses, which Jade guesses must be some stage of cleanup: pack them tight enough that a front-end loader can scoop them up in as few runs as possible, since heavy machinery leaves deep ruts in the national forest.

"How are we going to—?" Letha asks, then they both see the answer: there's a sort of tunnel in, held open with fresh-cut lodgepole pine. Which explains why the chainsaw was handy. But why would Theo Mondragon have been boring a temporary tunnel into all this rotting meat and bone, all this horn and hoof?

There's no time to figure it out. He's almost to the trees now, his chainsaw already ripping the night in two, its pungent exhaust seeping in ahead of him.

Jade pushes Letha in first, not because she's suddenly valiant or anything, but to be sure Letha doesn't chicken out, start running.

But would that really be so bad? She *could* stay ahead of her dad, scary limp and all.

This is already happening like this, though. For better or worse.

Jade still has her open hand to the small of Letha's back when Letha's muscles contract in a way Jade's are already starting to: the smell in this tunnel, this literal *hell* hole. It's almost sweet, but it's oily on the roof of Jade's mouth, too. Thick and oily and there's not a clean breath anywhere. Worse, they can't see what they're touching, can only hear it squishing, feel it between their fingers, and on their lips, against their eyes.

It's warm, too.

Because . . . Jade tries to remember, isn't sure she can: does decay kick off some sort of methane gas, maybe? She becomes extremely aware of the lighter already in her hand, that she was about to spark into light for them.

Shit. Shit shit shit.

They're only about ten, twelve feet in, too. And hunched over, the only thing keeping the pile up is two X's of cut tree trunks.

Is this his evil lair, what? At least Jason had the decency to have candles. At least Freddy's kind of fit a theme. Jade doesn't have time to wonder anymore, as Theo Mondragon's headlamp is washing across the elk, the chainsaw idling. Jade lunges across, clapping her right hand tight over Letha's mouth, pressing her back into the wall of flesh and skin.

Letha's tears drip down over Jade's skin, but, instead of fighting free like she could, Letha covers her mouth as well, both her hands over Jade's one.

The light peers in but the stubby tunnel's not a straight line, is more like a comma curving to the right. Theo Mondragon makes a retching sound, and now Jade understands why he *really* had that gas mask. This is even gross to him.

"Hold on, hold on," Jade whispers to Letha, and Letha nods, and when the light flashes over her perfect face for a tenth of a second, what Jade sees to either side of her is the reason Theo Mondragon was prospecting into these elk: Cody's pressed into the meat and bone to Letha's left, and Mismatched Gloves is impaled on sweeping antlers to her right, one of the tips coming out through his mouth, the velvet horn dark black with gore, now.

And then Theo Mondragon's gone, calling his daughter's name elsewhere.

Jade lets Letha's mouth go and Letha sucks air in.

"Now we can—" Letha says, pushing off either Mismatched Gloves or Cody to escape this fetid pit, but Jade blocks her in, whispers, "What slashers do is make you *think* they've left."

Letha stiffens, is maybe going to make a break for it, but then she falls back, sobbing.

It's the proper response, really. And why Jade isn't best friend material, even if she'd ever had one? It's because she's not thinking about consoling Letha right now. What she's running through her head is that paper she wrote for Mr. Holmes, about how final girls curl up into a chrysalis before emerging as their true killer self. And what is this elk pile but a custom-made transformation chamber, right?

Everything's working out. It doesn't smell good, it's dangerous as hell and twice as hot, but it's also just what Letha needs in order to become her truest self.

"We need a high school annual," Jade says. "Henderson Hawks, 198—when did your dad graduate?"

"You're trying to distract me," Letha says.

"No—"

"Keep going, please."

"He must have passed through here for a year, a semester," Jade says. "And—and I don't know. Something happened while he was here. Maybe he took a history class, maybe one of those four kids who bought it at Camp Blood back when were related to him, maybe he was there when Hardy's daughter—"

"I wasn't looking for you," Letha says.

"Say what?" Jade says, trying to see through the darkness.

"I told you I was looking for you earlier, in the Pangbornes' house," Letha says, sobbing now, but quietly, thank you. "I—the sheriff *did* call, but, but—"

"Shh, shh," Jade says, reaching across for Letha's mouth, finding her shaking shoulder instead. Letha's hands immediately clamp onto Jade's own.

"I'm sorry, I'm sorry," Letha's saying.

"You were looking for your dad?" Jade asks, trying to give her a way out—trying to be *sort* of a friend, anyway.

"I was going to burn it all down."

Jade tries to process this, finally says, "With that candle?"

She feels Letha nodding.

"Why?"

"We shouldn't be here," Letha says, shuddering now, holding the back of Jade's fingers to her mouth, speaking warmth right onto them.

"In Proofrock?"

"This side of the lake," Letha whispers, the hush of her words rushing up Jade's arm to the base of her jaw, the center of her chest.

"But—"

"*People*, I mean," Letha goes on. "This side of the lake isn't for *people*."

"Why do—*why*?" Jade asks.

"I've seen her," Letha says, barely able to get it out before pulling Jade closer all at once.

"No, no," Jade says, letting herself be drawn in. "This isn't the Golden Age, that's—it was your dad in a wig. I saw him too, from the water. That's how these things—"

"On the *water*," Letha says.

Jade's skin prickles.

"Paddleboard," she says.

"He doesn't know how," Letha says back.

"Where's your mom?" Jade asks, her lips right against Letha's neck, she's pretty sure.

Letha stills, then pushes Jade's hand away from her lips.

"You think *she* can paddleboard?" she asks, and like that, the possibility crystalizes for Jade: Letha's real mom, the left-behind ex–Mrs. Mondragon, the left-for-*dead* Mrs. Mondragon, follows her philandering husband and spirited-away daughter out to this mountain retreat, and she—she starts taking her revenge throat by throat, maybe even boiling a rabbit in the process.

It fits. No wig necessary.

"*Could* it be her?" Jade asks.

"She's . . . I went to her funeral," Letha's barely able to get out, make real.

Like slashers can't rise from the grave.

"Next you'll think it's me," Letha says, but Jade can still see her in her bedroom, unsure how to hold the machete.

The machete she . . . left behind? Not "dropped on purpose."

Jade forces her eyes shut, won't allow that to be true.

"And it's not him," Letha says, her voice more sure now.

"I'm just saying—" Jade starts. The reason she doesn't finish is that Theo Mondragon *is* close.

"Lee! Lee!" he's calling, his throat ragged.

"That's him," Letha says, in little-girl wonder.

"It's not your dad," Jade tells her. "Not anymore."

The silence that follows is Letha trying to process this, Jade knows: is Jade saying that the killer's impersonating her dad, or that her dad is no longer who he used to be?

"But that's what he calls me," Letha says, sitting up, Jade sloughing off.

"*Lee!*" Theo Mondragon says again, closer still.

"I've got to—" Letha says, surging forward, and Jade doesn't need eyes to see what happens half a second later: instead of darting easily through the drippy wet tunnel of gore, Letha conks almost immediately into the two lodgepole pines crossed beside them, holding the elk up.

It's enough to dislodge them.

"*No!*" Jade says, trying to stand now herself, but it's too late. The ceiling of meat is already coming down onto them. A full-grown elk is six, eight hundred pounds, and . . . how many did Mr. Holmes count? Nineteen of them? However many are directly above Jade and Letha come down like judgment, hardly any sound, and in the small breathing space Jade has directly under her face—air thick with rot—there's at least Letha's fingers to her cheeks.

Except those fingers aren't moving. And they're too thick anyway, are either Cody or Mismatched Gloves—probably Cody, then, since Mismatched Gloves would have gloves *on*, wouldn't he?

Jade breathes the decay all the way in, forces it back out in all the scream she can manage.

It's not enough.

SLASHER 101

How about we just consider this the very end of
my extra credit career if that works for you,
Mr. Holmes. And before I start, first let me say
that I know you're honor bound to not believe me,
to believe Manx and Tiffany K and also Gretta who
was only there at the end, but me standing on top
of the toilet in the last stall wasn't me reaching
up through the ceiling to find something to tie my
neck to. What about the black robe and Ghostface
mask I was wearing? If I have to divulge a secret
it's that I was standing on that toilet in the
Scream stall to pre honor the coming holiday,
Mr. Holmes. Not Spring Break and not tax day two
weeks after that, though that would make the
perfect slasher, "The Tax Man Cometh" -- ka-ching,
my idea, thank you -- but the SLASHER one that's
here this week: Friday the 13th. And yes I was
reaching into the ceiling, but it was only for my
emergency cigarettes, from the stress of the day
and the week and the year, which is a habit I think
you of all people can understand.

Anyway since you'll be watching it with the rest
of us this summer 1 more time, let me add an extra
credit to the kitty here for my tragic absence in
the nurse's office yesterday, which is feeding a
shark to the cat, yes, when really it would be the
other way around.

I'm talking about Jaws from 1975 here, sir.

It's a monster movie, but it's got the beating
heart of a slasher. You can tell from memory of
having seen it every year probably since 1975 and
probably even having been on the Indianapolis
with Quint that it has these characteristics
of the slasher, which I'll list now. Just like

with Michael Myers or Jason Voorhees, there's a
signature THEME, those 2 piano keys going back and
forth. Just like those 2 but also Freddy Krueger,
Jaws also has a SIGNATURE WEAPON, which is in the
title, that being Jaws and teeth. Jaws also has
kids partying it up with beer and a bonfire for the
BLOOD SACRIFICE, and it also has the COPS who are
useless at least until the very end and it also has
a BIG PARTY like Scream, which is July the 4th, and
a REVEAL that results in that line about a bigger
boat, and it even has a RED HERRING, that being
that license plate eating tiger shark.

Very importantly, Jaws also has some excellent
SLASHERCAM action, which feels exactly like a
giallo OR a slasher, just it's underwater this
time. Jaws also has GORE and SET PIECE KILLINGS
and a killer who doesn't use his words and a THIRD
REEL BODYDUMP. It's just one head kind of in the
middle I guess, but it still counts. And if NUDITY
floats your boat into slasher land, then Jaws opens
with some of that. And, did somebody say SEQUELS,
that being the "killer" coming back over and over
even though it's killed each time? Check. Is there
STALKING? Yes. Is there SLICING and DICING? Yes,
yes. Is there one of the best JUMPSCARES in all of
horror except for The Exorcist III? Yes definitely.
Is there a Crazy Ralph who knows what the real
horror is? Yes, in the body of Quint, who knows
sharks from fighting with them, but also Hooper,
who has shark scars himself.

But where is the REVENGE you promised, Jade? you
might be asking.

Let me tell you, and I have to go to the
history books and also a 3rd page for this, sir,
sorry, just give me extra points if you need to, I
understand. But I'm talking about that story Quint
tells below decks about his experience when the
Indianapolis sank in the ocean and was swarmed by

sharks which ate so many sailors and soldiers, the
thing he doesn't say about that is that his ship
then was delivering an atomic bomb called Little
Boy. So this is by some views already a guilty
ship, a punishable offense. But what do sharks
care about bombed cities or ruined centuries?
They don't, sir. But they do care about their
reputation, and their reputation went bad when
so many of them came in and ate the lower halves
of all these floating sailors and soldiers, which
started a different war, this 1 against shark
kind, BY humans. So that's what sharks can be
generally mad about and need justice for, their bad
reputation.

But also, why THIS shark. My idea which tracks
is that since in the world of Jaws we don't know
how long sharks live or if they even die, that
the great white attacking Amity Island could have
been AT the Indianapolis, and because we didn't
know radiation shielding the same back then, maybe
it even got some glowing green atomic rays in it,
making it big AND smart. Even smart enough to cross
over half the world and come to get revenge on a
sailor soldier who escaped its teeth in 1945, but
is now spreading word of sharks' lifeless doll
eyes, making everybody just shoot sharks on sight,
when really they just want to swim and eat fish and
stuff.

Which is why Jaws is a slasher, Mr. Holmes. In
addition to all the outer characteristics of a
slasher it has, it also has the internal and most
important trait of REVENGE, and it has 1 more too,
that being a FINAL GIRL, who is this time a guy,
Chief Brody, who starts out meek and afraid and
flinchy but gets brave and killy in the scary scary
open sea by the end.

This is how slashers work, sir.

See you in the water.

HELL NIGHT

There's something wriggling on the back of Jade's neck, multiple wet somethings, but her arms are too trapped to get at them. Maggots, she knows. She can't fault them, though. They're just the hungry kids muscling their way to the front of the cafeteria line, right? They want to be there waiting when the doors open, when the meat's the warmest it's going to be.

Jade chuckles and then finds she can't expand her chest out as much as it was before. Because of the weight. Because of her weakness. Because this is it.

She's not sure how long she was out, or even if she for sure *was* out. One moment there was bloody mucky darkness all around, and the next moment there was bloody mucky darkness pressing her down and down and down, the most full-body hug she's ever gritted her teeth through. Luckily her head cocked to the side right at the last instant, probably an instinct to save her teeth from getting crunched in, or else she'd have already smothered.

As it is, the air she's breathing is air she's *been* breathing, and has to be about eighty percent gore and rot, and some part sharp stabs of elk hair—sharp to her lips and eyes, anyway. The drowning feeling is completely real, but panicking doesn't make any difference. She can't move even a little. To keep from going even more batshit than she already is, she counts bodies from her and Letha's big nightmare run through the SS *Lazarus* of *Jason Takes Manhattan*, which wasn't the rush Jade had always imagined it to be.

There was . . . first there was Ladybird Samuels in the hallway, then Ross Pangborne in the stairwell, then Mars Baker up in the window, and Tiara pedaling out through open air, and Lewellyn Singleton in the shallows. Oh, and probably Macy Todd in the room on the other side of Letha's wall. She was really first. Except for Mismatched Gloves and Cody and Shooting Glasses. And now at the bitter end—for them anyway—Jade and Letha. Really, if Letha's lucky, then she was crushed instantly, or got the kindness of a shattered elk rib pushing up through an eye socket, into the big off-switch of her brain.

Faster has to be better.

As for Jade, she imagines her skull's going to turn up in years, when some kids not even born yet are building skeletons from this fun mess of bones, don't even realize they've found the last victim of the Lake Witch Slayings.

At least then she'll really be part of it, right?

Don't laugh, she warns herself. Any space her ribs give up, she doesn't get it back.

It won't be long now. It can't be.

Unless . . . are the state police already crawling over Terra Nova with dogs and cameras? Is the whole nation focused on Indian Lake again, now that not just one Founder's died, but a whole clutch of them?

If so, great, wonderful.

But the dogs and cameras can't be ranging out this far yet. They're probably still trying to talk Lemmy and Galatea out of the cabinets they've wedged themselves into on the yacht, that they're never really going to crawl all the way out of again, no matter how long they live. They're probably trying to raise Cinnamon and Ginger on their big-girl cellphones, except those twins are long-legged, are probably down the mountain already, and not stopping until they see Texas. They probably still think Letha is in the water, needs to be fished out. And what of Donna Pangborne, Lana Singleton, and, so far as the law and the media knows, Theo Mondragon?

Probably Donna and Lana were slashed open deeper down that hall, before Jade and Letha even woke—before Theo got to the room beside Letha's, maybe caught a pellet or two from Mars Baker's shotgun. And the kids could be piled down that same hallway, but . . . Jade doesn't think so. Even the Dutch kids sacrificed to start this whole cycle, they were probably nineteen, weren't they? How could they rent American cars if they weren't? And, *since* them there's been Deacon and Clate and the construction grunts and everybody on the yacht, none of whom were kids either.

Maybe Theo's like Jason?

The reason Jason never takes kids, Jade's always figured, is that he feels a dim kinship with them. Not just on a developmental level, but . . . his last good memories, they have to be *of* camp, don't they? Of eating hot dogs in the canteen, roasting marshmallows over the bonfire, shushed laughing from the bunks after lights out?

But, too, if kids are off-limits for Theo Mondragon, the slasher, and his daughter's the final girl, and she'll *always* be a kid to him, then . . . how's it supposed to work at the big movie on the water? Will he be pulling his punches, just knocking her to the side so he can open a few more necks, split a few more shoulders, leave a few more severed arms drifting down to Ezekiel's Cold Box?

If Jade had any wishes left, if she hadn't burned them all just to get a slasher to Indian Lake in the first place, she would want a few more hours of life, please. She'd wish to be there at the movie with the rest of Proofrock. To thrill in the carnage and narrate it all in her head, but . . . now that she's dying she can say it, at least to herself: the reason she needed a slasher to come to town, it was so he could cleave through her dad at some point in the rampage. Or, failing that, Jade could do that cleaving herself, and let Hardy assume the slasher did it. That being a trick he's already used himself, Tab Daniels being no friend to law enforcement, maybe Hardy'd let it slide, right?

But now Jade's just going to suffocate. Unless of course her sternum crushes in first, splinters through her lungs. She clenches her fist as much as she can at the stupidity of it all, grits her teeth until she tastes blood. Maybe her own, maybe the elks'.

And now she's crying, she's pretty sure. It's hard to tell, but she thinks maybe she is. Probably.

It's because she should have done more—she *could* have done more. If she'd just insisted instead of been all polite and asked, Jade could have prepared Letha for all this better. What she should have done, she knows now, is kidnapped Letha, tied her to a chair over in Camp Blood, and somehow wired a TV and VCR in, force-fed this nascent final girl all the slashers she needed to have on file, to not have ended up in this cave of rotting meat. This *collapsing* cave of rotting meat. Slasher movies are supposed to be these grand fairy tales where the princess is a bad-ass warrior, but Jade never showed Letha that, did she? She never showed her anything, really.

You'd have been the best of them all, Jade tells her all the same. Letha Mondragon could have swung her machete further into slasher immortality than any of the other final girls.

But, because Jade didn't think to kidnap her, now she's just down here with her, or with her corpse, anyway. Which is a kindness. Or, it's only fitting that Jade eke a little more life out, so she can soak in this rancid stew she deserves, wallow in her own failure.

"I'm sorry, I'm sorry, I'm sorry," she says as best she can, and then she thinks the unthinkable: that it would have been better for everyone if she'd just bled out in that canoe back on Friday the 13th. Or, no, the real dream, it's that her dad rolls his high school Grand Prix the weekend *before* he smiles his smile to Kimmy Daniels. Then Jade never screams her way into the world in the first place, making it easier on everyone. Sure, that means never getting sprayed with that thrillingly cold water from Hardy's airboat, that means never finding *A Bay of Blood* in the bargain bin, it means never visiting the Skank Station, never sitting through detention or history class, never running away to Camp Blood over and over, coming back to find she wasn't even missing, but it also means she doesn't ruin so many people's lives just by wishing a slasher to their pleasant little valley.

Jade's breathing fast and shallow now. This has to be the end. Her—her vision's even starting to glow at the edges. No more putting it off with slasher facts. No more slowing the moment down with heartfelt apologies. What confirms she's being pulled into another, even harsher reality is that the heavy dead body she's pressed alongside writhes into sinuous motion, since—of course— it's probably about to stand up, run away into the afterlife of elk, which is all grass and cold sunlight.

Except this elk, once the glow suffuses down onto it, isn't an elk at all, but Cody, because now him and Jade are just two more Indians at the bottom of the pile of massacred Indians. They're circling the drain of history together, while Letha and Shooting Glasses and Mismatched Gloves are over at some other drain, with harps and angel food cake. But so be it. At least Jade's not alone. Cody's eyes are open now, his head's shuddering like something hungry's pawing at him, and Jade, with her foggy thinking, decides that she must be Alice at the end of the first *Friday*, Ginny at the end of the next one, Nancy in the closing scene of *Nightmare*, when the rules of reality go slack so the dream can seep in—

And now her hand is glowing? Meaning she's reaching for Cody's face. Meaning she *can*.

There must be a reaper in whatever next stage of death this is, some dead-alive dude who sorts people into piles for processing. No, Jade says inside, not a reaper, a *Reeker*, like the movie.

"2005, Alex," she thinks she creaks. Her mouth is trying to move, anyway.

Unless it's the antropophagus from 1980, of course. In which case she's screwed, as she doesn't think she can run right now. She's not even sure she can raise her head. All she's sure of, or sort of hoping for, is that a glove of knife-fingers is about to burst up from the sand, wrap its blades around her face, draw her down into a forever *Nightmare*, which will be her own little back alley of heaven.

Jade starts to smile at the delicious horrible wrongness of it all, but then Cody rolls away and more light spills through, its impossible brightness blinding her so that when she looks up to who's doing this, it's an angel in a halo of blazing light, her hair wet with gore, face red and black with chunks, chest heaving, fingers curling open and shut like the talons they are.

Letha fucking Mondragon, reborn.

"You," Jade says with what feels like her last breath.

"Me," Letha says, and falls down into the pile alongside Jade, spent.

Their hands find each other in the rot and blood, their fingers intertwine like best friends, and Jade opens her mouth to the sky, breathes all this fresh crispness in.

They're alive, and they shouldn't be. They made it through the night somehow. This is the other side, Jade lets herself think for a hopeful moment—this is the sun rising over Woodsboro, Gale Weathers narrating the terrible events of the night.

Except: "*Where is he?*" she says, trying to push up, but her coveralls are full-body blood-glued down, so she has to peel up piece by piece, limb by limb.

Letha looks around casually, as if being polite, and they survey this serene meadow, Indian Lake glittering out past it, going forever.

It's not noon on the Fourth, it's *late* afternoon on the Fourth already, shading into dusk. Jade was out for . . . twelve hours? Seriously? Is that what breathing maggot air can do to you?

Shouldn't I have to, you know, pee? she thinks, but doesn't check. All the same, hours-old urine would be an improvement.

Letha stops scanning, as if re-hearing Jade's words. Or, only just now actually listening to them.

"My dad, you mean?" she asks, the insult there in her voice.

Jade nods once, nearly falls forward from it.

"It's not him," Letha says again.

"If he's not here, that just means he couldn't find us," Jade says, throwing her chin across the water. "He's already over there, getting ready for tonight. Snorkel, waterproof chainsaw, speargun, belt sander—"

"*Stop!*" Letha says, high-stepping out of the muck. "Do you know how long it took to dig you out?"

Jade stands, her whole body stiff and bruised, her balance not quite catching up with her yet, blood rushing here and there in the least comfortable ways, but with a lot of stinging urgency.

Both of them are head-to-feet gore.

Jade pats her pocket for her last cigarette, tries to light it but it's been in the lake, it's been soaked in blood, it's been crushed. She flicks it into the elk and it pretty much just crumbles mid-air, becomes an offering of tobacco above all these dead.

"Why isn't the sheriff here yet, you think?" Letha asks. "I kept expecting him to show up."

"Why would he call it in?" Jade says back.

Letha hears exactly what Jade's saying, but still says it anyway: "My dad, you mean."

"Your dad."

"Who would never do a thing like this."

"Who *did*, then?"

Letha just sits there, and after a few seconds of it, Jade notices she's crying. No sound, just tears.

"The twins," she says, about the massacre on the yacht. "And L-Lemmy. Gal."

Because of course the final girl doesn't think of herself first.

"If it matters, then . . . I think they're all right, probably," Jade says.

"Why do you think that?"

"Kids believe in the boogeyman. They know to hide."

"Thought you were going to say that my dad wouldn't do that."

"That too," Jade says, uselessly.

"So, what now?" Letha asks.

"Want to go to a horror movie with me?" Jade asks back.

Letha just looks up to her about this, like checking if this is even a serious question.

"Hardy'll be there," Jade adds.

"I know where the keys are," Letha says, tossing her chin to the yacht. "We can—"

"Going back on that boat is a death sentence. He—*whoever* it is, he's probably there waiting. He knows we need a phone. So they're probably all already overboard."

Letha looks down to what she's wearing: her ruined camisole and pajama bottoms. No shoes. Aside from covering her in the most minimal way, the only real purpose her sleep clothes are serving anymore is to keep the gore and blood close to her, which might be good if she were going up against Van Damme in an alien suit, but Theo Mondragon doesn't have heat vision, just slasher goggles.

Still, instead of already having sneaked over to the yacht for a clothes-change, here she is, right?

"Thanks for digging me out," Jade tells her. "You didn't have to, I know. I'm not worth it."

"Please shut up."

"You could have split, really."

"Jade, you—it's not your fault, what your father . . . and why you're . . . you."

"Yeah, I know, wow, it's terrible, isn't it?"

"I didn't mean it like that. You're you, and that's great."

"We should get going," Jade says, high-stepping out of this moment.

She swings her hurt leg ahead of her and brushes past Letha.

"And we've all got daddy issues, right?" she can't help but mumble, wincing the instant it crosses her lips.

"My dad isn't the one—"

"Then why didn't he dig you out?" Jade asks, playing with her lighter now, wishing so hard for a smoke.

"He didn't know where we were," Letha says, stepping out now as well, her voice rising a bit, in defense.

"If he felt that collapse, or heard it, or smelled it, whatever," Jade says, finally getting a strong flame going to occupy her eyes, give her somewhere else to look, "then . . . then either he thinks we're dead, which is score one for the good guys, or he went for help."

"Instead of digging us out?"

"How long did it take you?"

Letha narrows her eyes across the lake, considering this.

"He'd have had to go all the way around," she says, liking this.

"And his leg's like mine now," Jade adds with a shrug.

"He used to play football," Letha says. "He says he played one game with his kneecap all the way behind his knee."

"There you have it," Jade says, moving her lighter back and forth, daring the flame to flicker out. "But"—and she does look up for this—"why isn't anybody here yet?"

Letha flicks her eyes away.

"Whatever you believe or want to believe or won't believe," Jade tells her. "We have to get across the lake. We can't stay here. Here's done."

"Terra Nova."

"Terra Nova's done, yeah."

Letha steps past Jade for the boat garages.

Jade shrugs to herself, and, being sure Letha's clear enough, tosses her lit lighter into the dead elk, trusting the pent-up methane to catch that lick of flame, whoosh up into a bulbous explosion, one Jade can walk away from in slow dramatic motion.

Instead her lighter just adheres to a low wall of meat and hair, is upright enough that it's still flickering a weak flame.

"Thanks," Jade says to it, and turns on her heel, following Letha through the trees, Letha's long legs eating up the ground, Jade's limp still there so Letha has to stop, wait for Jade to catch up, then offer her a shoulder.

"You don't have to," Jade says, latching on.

"I'm not leaving you," Letha says. "I know you think this is some big horror movie we're in, and that you're going to get to choose your death, but—this is real life. A tragedy, but it's real, and it doesn't have to follow any rules."

Jade doesn't argue, tells herself to let the unfolding events prove her case.

Now that she's moving, though—

"I have to pee," she says, stopping them.

Letha extracts herself, steps away, turns politely around but that's not quite enough for Jade. She limps to a tree, pushes off it to the next, and the next, struggles twenty or thirty feet between her and Letha before feeling through the gore for the snaps and gummed-up zipper of her blood-matted coveralls.

When she's shouldering back into them is when she hears the groan. She radars in on it, the rest of the world falling away.

A low, long shape maybe fifteen feet back in the trees.

Theo Mondragon.

Clamped around his leg—same one, different one?—is *another* bear trap. One he didn't have the strength to push apart, apparently. Is he passed out from blood loss, from fatigue, from grief, what? Where's his kneecap *now*?

"Doesn't matter," Jade says, actually out loud, just, very quiet. "You'll get out just in time, won't you?"

Unless it's not *him*, Letha says in Jade's head.

But still, right? Jade knows for sure and certain that he put nails in Shooting Glasses and Cody and Mismatched Gloves. No way is she announcing him to Letha, so she can use her final girl determination to wrench the jaws of that bear trap open. This is a Let-Nature-Take-Its-Course situation if there ever was one.

"You okay?" Letha asks, meeting Jade halfway to crutch her along again, some part of Theo evidently cueing in that Jade's close, so he should groan again, louder, longer.

"Are you?" Jade says back, then has to stop when Letha does.

"Hear that?" she asks.

"Mountain alligator," Jade tells her, doing her eyebrows to show how much she doesn't mean this. "I scared it, I think." But challenging Letha to call her on it, too.

Letha considers this, listens harder, and when the groan doesn't come again, they move forward, Letha going from garage to garage to garage along the shore, coming out of each shaking her head no: all the boats they never even use are trashed. Not the engines, but the hulls. The boats are taking on water, foundering, the only thing holding them up their mooring lines or the straps looped under them.

"He *wants* us to have to walk it," Jade says.

"You can't," Letha says back.

"You could swim it," Jade says.

Letha nods, already knew that.

"The yacht," she says finally. *Again.*

"No motors on the water for the Fourth," Jade recites.

"I think this would be an exception."

"Except I'm not going on that boat again."

"Yacht."

"Whatever."

"Where's that . . . the *Umiak*, right?"

"Hunh," Letha says, looking around for it just the same.

"He already sunk it, didn't he?" Jade says.

"There," Letha says, and she's right. The *Umiak* is drifting out between Terra Nova and Camp Blood. Not sitting quite level anymore, either. It's the *Orca* now, after the shark's been chewing on it.

Letha shakes her head in frustration.

"They'll have hot dogs and stuff over there," Jade says, about Proofrock.

"I don't want to go through that . . . that old camp, cool?" Letha says.

Jade nods, doesn't explain that they'll just be looking down on Camp Blood from the bluff.

"We're gonna miss the movie if we don't—" she says instead, but Letha's silence and stillness stop her.

Jade follows what Letha's staring at.

It's . . . a head bobbing in the tall grass? An *ostrich*?

"You," Letha says to the ostrich head, pulling Jade ahead with it. "Pedals only," she narrates, "no motor."

Jade tries to force this into a statement that makes sense. But then all at once it does: the swan boat, the one Deacon Samuels was playing on in that memorial slideshow. They have to wade out to it, then Letha has to push and pull to get it unmired, but it's whole. The only boat over here that is.

Jade looks around to Letha to confirm that they're doing this, but Letha's gone. Jade spins around, about to panic, which is when Letha bursts up from the water, still trying to wash her face.

Jade follows suit, lowering herself under the surface in what she hopes is a more menacing fashion, swishing left to right, coming up to breathe, then doing it again, and again, until she feels halfway clean. Clean enough for a massacre.

Letha's already up in the boat's fiberglass couple's seat. She holds her hand down, hauls Jade's wet heavy self up as easy as anything, the swan boat tilting and rocking, but there's no hull for water to slosh over, really, no bottom to have to bail out. Just a footspace for water to wash across, run down. Jade clomps her heavy boots down into that slurry, watches the lake run red around her feet, then clear.

"You should—" Letha says, about Jade's boots. "If we end up having to swim, I mean."

Jade looks down at her combat boots, the ones she pulled on for battle each morning of the war called "high school." But Letha's right. She should have kicked them off last night, really. That's why Letha was able to swim so much faster than her. Well, that's one reason.

She unlaces them, works them off, sets them gently down into the lake. It takes them as it takes everything it's offered.

"The—" Letha says then, pulling at the nonexistent zipper over her chest, which is her way of saying maybe Jade should leave her coveralls behind as well?

Jade shakes her head no. Letha might look more killer with each article of clothing she loses, but Jade needs these, at the very least. She gathers her hand over the collars, pulling them together like fighting to keep them on.

"I feel like we're going to get noticed in this," she says about the swan boat.

"Good," Letha says, and starts churning them through the water.

Jade tries to figure out how to place her feet on the spinning pedals, pitch in.

There's a steering wheel of sorts—a joystick with a big white fiberglass egg for a handle, that must be connected to a rudder under the sweeping-back tail.

"Not exactly how I envisioned my return," Jade mumbles.

"Black swan fit you better?" Letha says, not quite with a smile—this isn't a time for that—but it shows she's waking up a little anyway.

"Ever done this before?" Jade asks. "Pedaled across?"

"We'll make it," Letha says, and pedals harder, surging them forward for a few feet. "Isn't this where . . . you know," she asks, sort of.

Jade rotates her left wrist up so her scar's right there.

"It didn't want me," she says. "The lake, I mean."

"Why not?"

"There's this preacher Ezekiel down there, purifying the water," Jade says. "It makes this a Christian burial ground, and, you know. I'm Indian."

"You and your dad."

To try to head this off, stop Letha's accusations before they can rev up, Jade says, "I'm sorry about your—your stepmom," Jade says. "She didn't deserve that. None of them did."

"I should have burned the whole place down months ago," Letha says. "We never should have come here."

"I'm glad you did," Jade can't help but say. "I mean, tragedy aside and all."

Letha's hand comes off the steering egg, finds the top of Jade's for a quick sisterly squeeze. Jade looks across the dark water to Camp Blood, lurking on Indian Lake's shore like an infection, like a bad memory.

Theo Mondragon's about to be walking through it, isn't he? And maybe pulling all its ghosts in behind him.

"Along with my axe," Jade adds to that visual.

Letha comes back with, "Say what?"

Jade shakes her head no, nothing. It's just what she thinks would look coolest, dragging behind a slasher who's limping across the narrow whiteness of Glen Dam: the heavy long-handled two-bit axe she buried over there, once upon a runaway night. But, axe or no, if he's going to make it, he needs to get to hopping to make an appearance before the movie's over, right?

Even in this ridiculous swan boat, they're getting there a half-hour ahead of him. At least half an hour. Which doesn't mean they're exactly skipping across the lake. First, they're bucking the breeze. In town, it never seems to matter. But try to row against it—or pedal—and it stands you right up. Even Letha.

"Gonna be dark," Jade says.

"I'm trying," Letha says back.

Jade tries to help with the pedaling but seems to slow things down more than actually contribute to their forward motion.

"Look," Letha says.

It's the inflatable movie screen.

Chrissie is running across the dunes, leaving her clothes behind her.

"Hey!" Letha screams, standing to wave with both arms, the swan tilting back and forth.

"They crank the sound all the way up," Jade tells her, holding on.

Behind the screen, by decree, Proofrock is inky dark. And there's no phone screens glowing on: nobody wants to douse them when their boat tumps, or when they find themselves in the middle of a splash fight.

"Y'all do this every year?" Letha asks, out of breath.

"Halloween for boats," Jade says. "I mean—everybody dresses their boat up like a parade? Hardy even looks the other way about beer."

"He really cares for you, you know?"

"I remember going in third grade. One of the high schoolers was dressed up as Jigsaw, and I—"

"He from *Bay of Blood*?"

Jade pretends that didn't just happen, rolls on: "I couldn't stop watching him."

"Or her."

"Jigsaw's a him. When you're in that mask, you're a him."

"Until two, yeah," Letha says. "And what about four?"

Jade looks over in wonder and Letha shrugs, the boat drifting a bit under them.

"The fuck's your problem?" Jade says, straight from the movie.

"*You're* my problem," Letha quotes right back, quirking her mouth just perfect.

"I thought you didn't—"

"That . . . the night of Banner's party?" Letha says, pedaling again, having to haul hard on the egg to try to control their drift.

"The bonfire," Jade says as if from a dream. "The Dutch boy in the lake."

"That's what we were watching in Banner's garage," Letha says. "But we didn't get to finish, and my—my therapist said it's unhealthy to leave a narrative incomplete. That it'll haunt me if I don't finish it, especially taking into account the . . . the trauma of that night."

"Y'all were watching the first one, then?"

"I told my dad I needed to finish it in my room. He sent all seven." Letha shrugs as if embarrassed.

"You dog," Jade says, impressed.

"It's nothing like . . . like back there, though," Letha says. "Who do you think did that to those elk?"

"Supposedly a bear."

Letha looks over like waiting for Jade to say what she thinks: it was Theo Mondragon, either trying to do the killer version of masturbating—animals, not people—or he was out there giving his shiny killing implements a run, seeing if he really had the nerve to go blade-on-skin. He'd have had to drug them first, a little ketamine in the salt lick, but . . .

Jade shrugs, and neither of them say anything for a while. Letha's got a sheen of sweat on her face now.

"Rest," Jade tells her, and Letha shakes her head no but does anyway.

The silence is amazing. They must be just farther than the speakers can reach, even across the water.

"I can't believe you know Jigsaw," Jade says, still catching on that. "*Saw*'s . . . *Saw*'s like *Hatchet*. What you *graduate* to, not where you start."

"I've never seen this one, if that helps," Letha says, nodding with her head to the inflated screen.

"You're from Boston, right?" Jade asks. "That's pretty much where this one happens, I think."

"And you've seen every mountain man movie?" Letha asks right back.

"Point," Jade says, and Letha starts in pedaling again.

"I can't believe we're talking about what we've seen and what we haven't," she says. "I can't believe we're talking at all, after . . ."

She bats her eyes about the yacht.

"I'm never eating elk again," Jade says, a laugh slipping out her lips.

Letha smiles too, has to cover it with her hand as if embarrassed, shaking her head fast that no, no, she'll never eat it again either.

"Or maggots either," Jade can't help but add.

"Stop!" Letha pleads.

Now it's Jade who's having to blink the feelings away.

"Everybody bumps their boats into each other for this part," she says, chucking her chin ahead of them, to the movie. It's all the wannabe trophy hunters crowding the boating lanes of Brody's harbor to catch the killer shark, get that reward money. Invariably some seventh-grader drops an M-80 into the water, in honor of the dynamite one of those fishermen have. Even the adults bring buckets of chum: red Jell-O run through the blender.

"Why that movie, though?" Letha asks, pedaling slower either from fatigue or inattention. In that lull, a bottle rocket arcs up into the velvety sky, its sparks drifting behind it. Jade feels the muted *pop* in her chest.

"Because of that," she says. "I mean, *Jaws* happens on the Fourth."

"Wouldn't a monster-bear movie fit better up here, though?"

"*Prophecy*, 1979, yeah," Jade tells her. "But we've got bears. Bears are a fact of life. Sharks aren't. Sharks are the fantasy. It's fun to scream about them."

"Fun?"

"Fun," Jade says, grinning in the dark, and doesn't even fall into some involved lecture about where *Jaws* can fit on the slasher evolutionary chart.

Letha holds the top of Jade's hand again, and keeps holding it, and Jade doesn't pull away, just rides, and watches the movie. It's not *quite* on mute anymore for them, but on "distant burble." She pictures Hardy up on the pier, trying to zero in on who that is on shore with the roman candle. "I thought I was going to die back there," she says all at once, surprising herself. "I guess I thought I already was dead, sort of."

"I wouldn't let that happen," Letha tells her, and she's so earnest that Jade almost has to chuckle, just as counterweight.

"How'd *you* get out?" she asks instead.

When Letha doesn't answer at first, Jade looks over just casually, catches her blinking a touch faster than she has been—like Jade just was. Except, Jade was trying not to let her emotions get the better of her, wasn't she? And . . . Jade's dialing back, back—back to Melanie's bench a week ago, yeah. When she clocked this exact tell from Letha.

"What?" Letha's asking.

"How'd you get out of the pile of elk?" Jade hears herself asking, a coldness washing up her, gripping her heart, her face, her hand slithering back into her lap. She can't remember how many of the who's-doing-it breed of slashers have been eureka'd just this way: a dumb, inconsequential question that exposes some simple gap in logic.

"I wasn't as deep in as you?" Letha is saying from what seems like far away.

"Because you're faster," Jade hears herself saying back, just to finish what she knows Letha is going to say. "You were almost all the way out when it fell down."

"Lucky," Letha says.

Jade looks behind them into the darkness, as if she should be able to see Theo Mondragon slouching along the shore, dragging that shiny axe behind him. Or, she can't lie to herself: she's studying the shore for even just a distant *glint* of that axe, please. Because that would mean that she's just light-headed from lack of calories, lack of real sleep, a concussion—that she's thinking wrong. That she's *not* sitting right by the one somehow behind it all.

Did Letha see her dad in that bear trap too, and walk away? Is this all a ruse? Did it really take her all day to dig Jade out, or did she need that time to bash holes in a few hulls? Was the swan boat really there by accident? Is the machete tucked behind the seat?

"What's wrong?" Letha asks.

"Somebody *threw* your stepmother," Jade blurts out, clasping hard to that certainty. Because no way was that Letha. And how to have choreographed that shotgun blast through the wall? Why cut it so close just to convince the horror chick, whom she could have just killed easy as anything?

Unless she can't. Unless that horror chick's about to get framed.

Unless that horror chick's been the patsy all along.

Speaking of, shouldn't Letha have been reduced to a crying ball of fear by now, not relaxed enough to be idly talking about horror movies?

"My dad would never do that to her," Letha says, still talking about Tiara's big slow-motion fall. "Not to anybody."

"Did you . . . *like* them?" Jade asks. "The *Saw*s?"

"I watched like this," Letha says, doing her fingers over her eyes, still playing the horror wimp.

Jade breathes in deep once, twice, and on three she says it: "Is that Michael Myers?" When Letha leans forward to follow where she's pointing—past the swan's regally arched neck, to Hardy policing fireworks from the pier—Jade slips quietly over the edge, under the water, no splash at all for once in her life, she's pretty sure.

Her gamble is that by the time Letha realizes she's gone, she'll spend thirty seconds or a minute standing in the boat, calling, before she dives in for a look around. But Indian Lake is big, and dark, and quiet, and it's been swallowing bodies since forever.

Jade kicks to the side, reaches with her right hand and pulls ahead like gathering water into her hip bag, and then she does it again, and again, her lungs burning. When she finally comes up, she's alone. Freezing, but alone, just a prickly-scalped seal bobbing in the water, her eyes barely above the surface.

She takes her apology to Letha Mondragon back.

Sure, she might have dreamed of and begged for a slasher to stalk into town one fine day, but that doesn't mean she wants to pedal into the big crowd along*side* that slasher.

Except—it can't be Letha, can it?

You're being paranoid, Jade tells herself, tracing slow figure eights with her hands. Paranoid and stupid. This is why nobody hangs out with you. This is why everybody hates you.

There's only about a quarter mile to go to Proofrock, now. To *Jaws*.

After looking all around, certain no ostrich-size swans are about to glide up on her, Jade starts pulling for that glowing screen, trying not to broadcast her location with white water, praying she can get there before hypothermia sets in.

Halfway there, the dialogue of the movie is coming through clear. Quint's just tacking that third barrel to the shark, and assuring Brody and Hooper that no fish can dive with *three*. When Jade looks behind her this time, she has to admit that it's to see if she's dragging a yellow barrel, as idiotic as that would be. But she is a monster, as far as this town is concerned.

What she sees instead of a yellow barrel is the dull silver prow of a sudden and completely soundless boat, bearing down on her. Not sucking air in this time—no time—Jade slips under, instantly clamping her hands to her head to keep her hair from tangling in the propeller, but then just having bare scalp to hold.

It's just a little trolling motor burring past, though. Jade watches it churn past inches from her face, a turbid cyclone of bubbles ensconcing the whirling blades. It's like a free-range garbage disposal, gone feral in the lake—it's the last thing Jason sees, in *The*

New Blood. Jade rotates in the water, tracking it until the darkness swallows it away, and . . . and, and standing in the shadows of Banner Tompkins's party a week and a half ago, she was *right*, wasn't she? This—a trolling motor, a light little boat—is exactly what Theo Mondragon's been using to cross the lake under cover of night. With it, and especially if he's got the sides blacked out, he might as well be walking on water.

She comes up a second after the aluminum hull's gone and gasps air in, her vision swimming from lack of oxygen, and from certainty, from relief.

It *is* him. Jade was—she was wrong about Letha, she was reading the moment wrong. But it doesn't matter, now.

"Right on time," she says to Theo Mondragon's wake, and then watches as he does the impossible: stands up in the prow of the little boat like George Washington crossing the Delaware—the poster's on Mr. Holmes's wall, has been since forever, even after Jade used her pencil eraser to give him Little Orphan Annie eyes. In the poster, what George Washington has running down along his leg, ready for battle, is a long curving saber.

What Theo Mondragon has is the machete, the one Jade never bothered to tell Letha is the same model Quint uses to save the *Orca*. And, not only is Theo Mondragon standing up in the boat, his hand no longer to the steering control of the trolling motor, but the boat, unlike Washington's . . . it's *sinking*?

Because he took one of the boats with the crashed-in hulls, Jade can see now. If he was sure to keep his weight all the way in the back, then the nose of that boat would ride out of the water, the big hole up front in the open air. Theo Mondragon must have gambled the boat would wheelie up like that, anyway. And, like every stock purchase he's taken a chance on, every merger, every takeover, every board meeting, his gamble is paying out.

Right as the boat swamps, he steps forward like he's going to continue with that forward momentum, walk across the water, start the blood harvest now, meaning . . . Jade doesn't even know what that would mean.

Luckily, instead of her whole world collapsing from *a human standing on the surface of the lake*, he drops into the water instead of balancing on top of it, is just a head like Jade now, pulling for shore. But, forty yards closer than her, his jaw probably not shivering yet.

Jade tries to fix on the shape of his head, track what part of the crowd he's going to drift into first, but then has to whip her head around again, sure that great white swan's about to pedal her under. By the time she spins back around to the crowd, locates a head bobbing in the water, there's . . . two more beside it?

"*No!*" Jade says, trying to climb out of the water.

What she saw for an instant, she's ninety percent sure, is the glint of glasses on that face barely holding itself above water. Yellow glasses.

Shooting Glasses.

He had been deeper underwater than Theo Mondragon's golden nails could reach, hadn't he? Because it's steeper on that side of the lake. It drops off faster.

He's alive.

And . . . and those two smaller heads it looks like he's carrying, that must be Cinnamon and Ginger, the twins? Mars Baker's daughters. Shooting Glasses has been swimming them across the lake for the last who knows how many hours, because . . . *he's* not the final girl, is he? Not because boy final girls are illegal or break the machine, but because . . . because if Theo Mondragon's the one with the machete, then that means that Letha can be what *she* was meant to be. What Jade meant for her to be.

Except Letha's own words are echoing: this is the real world, not a movie, and the real world doesn't have to follow any special rules. It just does what it does. You can't pick your genre, no. Has that been what Jade's been doing all along? Trying to shape an unwieldy string of dead people into a movie, just so she can have a minor role? So she can feel some sense of control?

If so, all her slasher homework has just been to delude herself, not to live through this night. Or, if she does live, then she lives knowing that there never was any slasher cycle, that slashers aren't real, are just pretend, and what kind of life would that be?

Jade closes her eyes, shakes her head no, balls her fists by her face and sinks under, doesn't know if she's crying or not. Hanging under the surface like that the world's so quiet that . . . what is that she's hearing?

A choir? Ezekiel's still down there in Drown Town, holding his last mass. And—and if *that* can be real, if Jade's really and actually hearing music, then . . . then anything can be true, can't it?

She reaches up, climbs the water handful by handful, finally surfaces a *third* time, her lungs hungry, her vision blurred, her nose running, skin number than numb.

She bobs, bobs, tries to jump up to see higher, not sure if her teeth are chattering from cold or from excitement.

He's almost to the back of the crowd, Shooting Glasses. And, maybe twenty yards to the left of him, *unaware* of his escape, so is Theo Mondragon. And Letha must be already in the crowd, her unsteerable swan just another ridiculous float in a night of ridiculous floats. On-screen, Quint is screaming, the giant pissed-off shark chomping him in bite by bite, leg by leg, shutting him up once and for all.

"*Somebody!*" Jade screams, clapping her hand on the water, but she wasn't lying: the movie really is cranked. And this is everybody's favorite scene, anyway. In honor, the Proofrockers are singing farewell to Spanish ladies, their arms hooked into other arms over gunwales, across bows—was this what Jade was hearing underwater? And, zero surprise here, isn't this where she's always been? Way on the outside, everyone deaf to her cries? Deaf *when* she cried?

She screams in fury, just to be heard, and when no official flashlight stabs a dusty beam of light out into the darkness to guide her in, she leans sideways, does her best approximation of a freestyle stroke until she pulls close enough to hear distinct words from the speakers.

And—oh shit.

This cannot be happening, can it?

Every year there's a sort of last-minute theme, circulated in the halls of both schools, scribbled on bathroom walls, left in code on the bulletin board at the drugstore: this year's costume. It's a game the whole town plays.

The year she saw the high schooler in the Jigsaw getup, the reason he stood out was that everyone was wearing nun costumes.

This year, some of those long black habits have been recycled, but mixed with hag masks, with zombie make-up, with long stringy J-horror wigs.

The theme this year is "Lake Witch." Stacey Graves. Because of course.

Right as Jade drifts in behind the last line of floats, one of those Lake Witches even comes flying across the screen, which is another tradition: dressing up, pole-vaulting off shore, into the stretch of water left free specifically for this year's jumper to splash down into.

Because jocks and the black t-shirt crowd don't exactly trade phone numbers and social calendars, Jade didn't track who this year's Henderson High *Graduation Day* pole vaulter was going to be, but whoever it is—Lee Scanlon, maybe?—he's silhouetted in front of the bright-bright screen now, his robe ragged and back-swept, never going to catch him, and it's like Stacey Graves has come back.

Good for her.

Just, this time, this cycle, the slasher's more mundane, more human. More *real*. Sorry, Stacey, Jade says in her heart—she's already seen this year's killer, and he's more from the Ghostface era than the Golden Age.

That doesn't mean his blade is any less sharp, though.

Jade latches onto the first hull she can and uses it to pull ahead. It's the librarian float: the boat's papier-mâché'd into a giant open book, but the gluey paper is mushy under Jade's hand already.

Connie the Librarian looks over, crosses her index finger over her lips to shush Jade.

What Jade wants to yell back is to clear the beaches, that the theater's on fire, that there's a werewolf in the subway, but she doesn't have enough breath, and Connie's just playing the role that goes with her float, anyway. Shushing people on tonight of all nights would be hopeless. Like every Fourth, there's elementary kids with shark fins tied to their backs, snorkels wrapped around their faces, there's junior highers wading among the boats, sneaking up on ready-to-shriek friends, there's sophomores making out in the water, seniors going further under cover of gunwales and blankets, and then there's dads keeping one hand in the water, to guard the beer they've got on a stringer, and those dads' wives drifting in innertubes, already on the day's second bottle of wine.

Somewhere in there is a hero in yellow glasses, Jade knows. He's trying to save two little girls whose father is dead, whose whole lives have turned into a screaming nightmare, who are probably chattering their teeth with hypothermia right now, since no way do they have enough body fat. Jade's not a good person, she knows she's not and never can be, it's too late for her, but that doesn't mean she can't try to find them, help them onto a boat, onto the pier, into one of Hardy's crunchy silver blankets.

Shooting Glasses, Shooting Glasses . . .

She steps up onto a raft built to be a living room, complete with couch and standing lamp, the man on the couch in comical boxers, a swimsuit under them—it's Lonnie, from the gas station—looking over to her in a drunken way, then lifting his beer to her as if to tell her, Look, I'm not in just an innertube anymore. Jade gives him a nod and holds on to the lamp, casing the crowd. Three or four boats over is a bass boat made into a bassinet, which must be someone's baby announcement, and there's Hardy's airboat tied to the pier like a guard dog, and—seriously?

Her father and Rexall are in a wooden paddleboat draped in what looks like ratty old elk hides that are taking on water. But who cares about their stupid boat. It's their idiot selves Jade is wincing from: her dad's got his face painted like Johnny Depp from *The Lone Ranger*—half-black, half-white, all "Indian"—and is drunk enough already to be shirtless in the open air. The better to see his gut, the skin stretched tight as a drum, his ribs traced in yellow for some reason. Maybe he saw it in a vision, was told by an eagle that if he painted his ribs yellow like that then he could fit not just two or three more beers into his body, but a whole twelve-pack.

Score.

Rexall's worse, and . . . maybe it's because he's white? The headdress he's in says he's the chief of their two-person tribe, though, and if beer guts are a status symbol, a sign of prosperity, of having enough buffalo to eat, then . . . he doesn't even need the turkey-feather headdress, really.

Jade's not sure how the eyepatch he's wearing is supposed to be part of his Halloween getup, but the monkey-doll clamped onto his shoulder probably isn't culture-specific either—what did she expect, really?

From him: nothing.

From her dad, who actually *is* Indian?

Jade makes herself pull her eyes away from the insult they are, fixes for a moment on the cheerleaders in their matching bikinis, all of them sitting front to back on some giant shark built over a canoe, it looks like—real original, girls, nobody's ever thought of that one for this movie. And talking canoes: like every year, Principal Manx is just past them in his clear plastic canoe, sitting alone, looking like he's just floating there, like if you believe hard enough that you're in a boat, then you can float.

And—

"Shooting Glasses!" Jade yells, her hands cupped around her mouth.

Which is when she realizes that she doesn't know his name. That, to him, those are probably safety glasses. Maybe he's never even fired a real gun, only knows nailguns. And more intimately than he ever hoped.

He doesn't turn around to her plea, is just trying to push either Cinnamon or Ginger up onto the pier, but there's no ladder on this side, Jade knows, and when that wood's wet, it's slicker than slick. But he finally does it, finally gets one of the girls up there enough that she can latch on, clamber up, and the other twin's pushing too, and . . . shit, that's not one of the *twins* turning around on the pier to help the other one up. It's Galatea Pangborne. Meaning the other twin . . . ? Jade sneaks a look across the lake, as if her mind's eye can bore into the bowels of the yacht, pick one dead twin from that carnage. Or one hiding twin left behind by her and Letha.

Jade comes right back to the pier as if to apologize, ask for a do-over, she'll just swim across right now, make everything right. But she's never been in time for anything, has she? Is this the "Indian Time" her dad's always using to explain his lateness? Growing up, she thought "Indian Time" meant "just one more beer," as in, Tab Daniels was going to be however late it took to cash another can, but maybe it covers leaving a terrified little girl on the wrong side of the lake, too.

Not that this is necessarily the right side.

Jade pushes up as high as she can in the water to get Shooting Glasses's attention, but he's . . . he's already got others' attention, doesn't he? Three, four flashlights are holding on him, helping him help these kids, who probably fell off their own floats. It should be a good thing, a happy thing, except—except he's Jada Pinkett Smith at the front of the theater in *Scream 2* now, isn't he?

Just, hopefully, without the slow, over-dramatic dying.

Either Cinnamon or Ginger is almost up onto the pier, though.

Which is when Jade's Spidey-sense gets her head turning, her eyes zeroing in on . . . on . . . Theo Mondragon.

He's bobbing in the water, using the baby announcement boat to see higher, and what he's seeing is who everybody's spotlighting for him: Shooting Glasses. Who's supposed to be dead.

"No," Jade says, but yes: in one of his bobs, or one of the water's dips, the tip of Theo Mondragon's Quint machete pokes up, is practically that long drill from *The Slumber Party Massacre* poster. And, on tonight of all nights, no one will take it seriously, everyone will think it's a prop-weapon. There's probably one that looks the same on every third boat, shit.

"*There he is!*" Jade calls out, slapping the surface of the lake with her hand, which is when the first scream comes. She looks over like she has to, and cheerleaders are bailing off the back of the shark, falling one after the other like a choreographed dance number.

But *why*?

Jade clambers up onto Lonnie's living room float again, using his floor lamp to steady herself, the lamp's chain evidently caught in her grip enough to pull the lightbulb on. Meaning there must be a battery on this raft somewhere—of course Lonnie would have a battery.

It lights her up, draws Theo's glare to her.

"*You*," he says, Jade somehow hearing it.

"Go to hell!" Jade screams back, and then tilts the lamp forward. It douses in the water, Lonnie lunging after it.

Jade steps back into the lake too, never mind the cold. She's roiling with heat, now, has no choice but to keep Theo Mondragon occupied long enough for Shooting Glasses to climb to safety, long enough for the final girl to gather her wits, find herself, and—

The cheerleaders, screaming again?

Jade whips her head around.

It's . . . Jocelyn Cates? Proofrock's beauty queen and onetime Olympic swimmer—the final girl hopeful of her day, surely. Had there been a slasher in Proofrock twenty years ago. She's standing up from her pink-frilled boat, and Jade's blood, she's pretty sure, actually drops a degree or two—*all* the degrees.

Jocelyn Cates is screaming because her husband beside her, whatever his name is, has black spreading over his chest. From his face, his mouth. Where his mouth used to be.

His lower jaw has been ripped off. All the flashlights within shining distance hold on him long enough that everyone can be sure. Long enough to track his slow slump forward.

Like that it's panic at the disco.

The bass-boat bassinet fires up its outboard in response, breaking whatever promise this mom-and-dad-to-be had to make to Hardy. It stands up in the water and tries to spin around but there's no room. Instead of executing a neat flipturn, the propeller wraps in the float beside it, the Henderson High float the teachers always do—the same "classroom" as every year—and all the teachers in the bolted-down chairs of their "desks" grab on to those desks, their hidden beers and glasses of wine exploding up before their faces, and, and—

Among them, Jade sees the last person she ever thought she'd get to see again. All other sound falls away.

Mr. Holmes.

He's there in a wheelchair, his right leg in a trash-bagged cast in front of him, a cigarette in his hand, hidden down by his spokes. And the float he's on is being chewed into by an illegal propeller that's screaming higher and madder, faster and faster.

"*Sir!*" Jade shrieks, and doesn't even think, just runs to him, climbing up and across Lonnie's living room, falling almost immediately back into the water, conking her chin on the hard side of some boat, its mushy paper clinging to her face so she has to duck below the surface, swim *under*.

She comes up into absolute madness.

On-screen, the *Orca* is sinking, and right beside her, a much smaller *Orca* is too. The papier-mâché shark is floating free, getting batted around, and—no. No no no.

The lower part of Jocelyn Cates's husband's face is snagged on a half-gone six-pack, is floating with it, right by Jade's face.

What could even *do* that? An M-80 in the *throat*?

There's no time, though.

Jade jerks away, trying to find Mr. Holmes. The bass-boat bassinet's outboard is coughing down now, maybe has too much of the teachers' float wrapped into its propeller. Jade can hear it, not see it. She looks around for anything to climb on, something to latch onto, and—the pier.

Either Cinnamon or Ginger has Galatea up on her hip. They're waiting for Shooting Glasses, who's having to find his own way up, and with, Jade can see now, a line of nails angling down across his back. Theo Mondragon *did* get him. Just, not enough.

Or: not yet.

Jade shakes her head no, can see this happening but do nothing about it: Theo Mondragon is gliding to the pier in—in Manx's invisible canoe. Which he *is* using like a paddleboard, Letha. He even has an actual paddle.

Give him a robe, a wig, and he's Stacey Graves.

And he must be soundless, too, or else his paddle dipping in is hidden by all the splashing around him, by *Jaws* still playing so loud through the speakers, by all the screaming. Shooting Glasses doesn't hear him until it's too late, anyway.

Theo Mondragon pulls him back hard, all at once, hard enough that the nails in Shooting Glasses's back stab into Theo Mondragon's chest and stomach, sending both of them spilling over the side, the invisible canoe continuing on invisibly, maybe, who knows.

Jade looks up onto the pier for where either Cinnamon or Ginger is looking, as they might have a better line on what's going on right under them, and—and it's Tiffany Koenig standing there now.

She's got her phone aimed down, is recording whatever's going on, and probably this whole disaster.

Jade waves as big as she can to Tiff, but her arm's just one of a hundred, and when she rises up high enough again to see the base of the pier, the foundering librarian float is in her way now.

"No!" Jade says, clawing at the soggy paper, her hand painfully connecting with the aluminum boat hidden underneath.

When she pulls it back to coddle it for a moment, stop the stinging, she makes herself try to remember if Theo Mondragon had his machete or not when he pulled Shooting Glasses down.

No, he didn't! He had *both* hands on that tall paddle, didn't he?

"Please please please," she says, and a heavy hand plants on her shoulder, its owner just trying to pull past, get away from whatever this is. It dunks Jade before she can breathe, and she comes up sputtering.

To her immediate right, bleary and blurry but clearing up,

too many Proofrockers are on Lonnie's raft, and it's sinking, the upright-again lamp flickering yellow somehow.

And the screaming, god. Jade can hardly hear herself think. Every mouth is open, and every second face is Stacey Graves—this night isn't a night, it's a series of heart attacks waiting to happen.

Jade finally fixes on her father, standing unmolested in his boat, his left hand to the toy saber strapped to his belt—aisle 3, Family Dollar—his right clutching the neck of his beer bottle. In the water at his feet is Alison Chambers, floating faceup, her chest leaking out into the lake. From that bass boat's illegal motor? But . . . how does that motor explain Jocelyn Cates's husband's jaw being ripped off, especially when that jaw being ripped off came before that outboard even fired up?

There's Judd Tambor standing in the water, holding a child up above the fray, the image of that wavering in Jade's head with the image of him at graduation, holding a kid above his head just the same, everybody clapping for her.

They're not clapping now, even though she was right about everything.

She backs up, feeling the water behind her first, and her fingertips find warmth.

Jade turns and the warmth is the inside of Misty Christy's chest. Misty Christy's daughter, the one Jade saved from the bus, is treading water while trying to hold her mom's head up, but it doesn't matter if Misty Christy's airways are clear anymore or not.

Jade pulls Misty Christy across to her.

"Go!" she tells the daughter, "find the sheriff, I'll keep her safe!"

The girl is about to cry, this is too much, but after a moment more of treading water, she turns, is a minnow cutting for shore, for the sheriff, for someone to save her mom.

Jade lets Misty Christy drift away, and has to swish her hand in the water to clear the blood. Dan Dan the mailman rises up under her hand, his bald head a nervous periscope, the pole vaulter's pole slips past like a rigid snake, and then some float is jouncing Jade forward. She looks back to who hit her. It's Dorothy, of Dot's. She's holding on to the innertube she has made up like a coffee cup, like every year. Holding on and thrashing. She latches onto Jade, pulls herself up with Jade's shoulder, which is when Jade sees Dorothy's face.

The right eye is gone, and a good chunk of the skull, too.

Jade flinches back, gulps bloody water in and swallows it before she can tell herself not to.

Because it's too crazy up here on the surface, she lowers everything but her eyes under, pulls from this boat to that boat, coasting through either blood or Jell-O. Her main hope now is to drift unobserved to the edge of this, and then float quietly out into deeper, more hidden waters. Except—her feet are tangling in something? She jerks, pulls, finally has to just duck under, see.

It's spokes. Of a wheelchair.

Mr. Holmes.

In this comparative calmness, she studies the water around her but can't even see past her hands. All the blood, all the silt, all the bubbles. When she comes up she's instantly swamped by she's not sure what—somebody cannonballing in? getting *thrown* in?—and when she clears her eyes, there's Mr. Holmes right in front of her, trying to float on his back, but the lake is going in and out of his mouth, and his cast is heavy, trying to pull him down.

His head's been opened at his hairline, about, probably from the prow of the bass boat, is spilling dates and history out into the water. His twitching left hand finds her right, and Jade pulls him to her, looking around for what she can protect him from.

He looks over to her, spits the water from his mouth and smiles, says, "Jenn—*Jennifer.*"

"Jade," Jade says back to him, her eyes hot and crying now.

"I—I—" he sputters.

His left hand finds the back of her head. He runs his fingers across her stubble and she pushes back against this touch, shaking her head no but holding his hand all the same.

A spasm passes across him: his head injury. His brain, failing.

Jade pulls him closer, tries to hold him higher.

"Just, just—" she says. "We can, I'll get you—"

It was a lie when she said it to Misty Christy's daughter, though, and it's a lie now.

The corners of Mr. Holmes's eyes crinkle like he appreciates the effort.

"Will she or won't she what?" he manages to get out, and the massacre they're in becomes just mute backdrop for the moment, a movie going on in the next theater over.

Will she or won't she? Jade repeats, inside, feeling through it.

Where is this from? She knows, she does, she—

No.

She closes her eyes.

It's what she told Hardy and Letha and Mr. Holmes her mom was asking herself, sitting in the car at that gas station in Idaho Falls, wasn't it? It's what she wrote in her letter to Letha.

And—and her deal with Holmes, to get her diploma. She has to pass her orals. She has to answer this one question for him truthfully, the same as he confessed to her about having started the fire in 1965.

His fingers tighten in her hand.

Jade opens her eyes, still shaking her head no.

"Will she—" she starts, breathing so deep now to finally be saying it, after all these years, "will she or won't she . . . be a grandma before she's thirty. The doctor was—was to see if he'd gotten me preg-preg—or not."

And Jade only *thought* she was crying before. Her whole face is leaking now, though, and it's from—it's from deeper than she's ever felt.

She's finally telling someone. She's finally saying it. It's not just inside her, now, it's out in the world, it's real, it really happened. She wasn't down in Idaho Falls to get baby aspirin pumped from her stomach, baby aspirin was just the first thing her mom saw on the impulse rack by her register, Keyser Söze–style. No, they were down there to see if—if she had something else inside her.

Mr. Holmes closes his eyes like this hurts him more than his head injury, more than his leg, more than anything.

"I'm—I should have—" he says, and uses his left hand to pull her face to his neck now, and, this close, Jade can feel the tremor passing through his body, the . . . *Twitch of the Death Nerve*, yes. Also known as *A Bay of Blood*.

Thank you, Mario Bava.

Jade pulls Mr. Holmes closer, as close as she can, but she can't stop it. He's dying. Right now this actual instant while he's in her arms, he's dying.

"Somebody should, somebody should . . ." he says, and Jade mumbles the end into his neck, her lips right against his rough skin: "Somebody will, sir."

When she looks up to him his eyes are glassy, and he's gone, is—say it, she tells herself: he's history.

Jade lets him float away, back into the frothing blood, the screams, the mayhem, all the volume dialing back up for her now. Where she's looking is to her father, still standing on his boat in the middle of all this madness, untouched, his black-and-white warpaint not even running.

For the moment.

"You're getting all the wrong people!" Jade screams to Theo Mondragon, wherever he is, whoever he's carving through now.

Jade's not moving stealthily anymore. She doesn't have to. All around her it's craziness, it's blood in the air and screams cutting through it, multiplying. And Letha was right, these coveralls are heavy, but Jade's fingers are too numb to get a grip on the wet zipper, so she just pulls ahead, pulls ahead.

On the way to her dad's boat she collects a shattered piece of a wooden pole—a rib from the cheerleader's shark, probably. Her dad's not a vampire, but the thing about stakes to the heart is that they work on non-vampires just the same. And this is one bloodsucker that needs to die. And in carnage like this, nobody will question one more body facedown in the mix. That's a lesson she's learned from the sheriff.

"This is for you," Jade tells her eleven-year-old self, a completely weird thing to say, but she's got to say something.

She comes up behind her dad's boat, glides up into it as stealthy as any slasher. Everything's already rocking, so a little more rocking—her climbing aboard—doesn't draw his attention. Before she can talk herself out of it, she steps cleanly ahead, takes his neck from the back in the crook of her arm, and presses the sharp leading point of the pole into his back, his chest swelling away from this pain but she has him by the neck, so he can't get away from this.

Of all the lines Jade's tried to have ready for this moment, all she manages to come up with is, "I wasn't for you, Dad."

"J-Jennifer?" he says back, realizing that it's her, that this isn't the end he thought it was, and for a bad flash—his tone is so *surprised*—Jade lets herself believe that he was drunk enough that night that he doesn't even remember what he did. How else does he get across the last six years in such good spirits?

It doesn't mean it didn't happen, though.

It doesn't matter, it doesn't matter, Jade's telling herself. Whether he remembers what he did or not doesn't mean it didn't happen.

When her dad tries to twist, see her face, she tightens her arm on his throat, shoves the splintered point of the pole maybe a quarter inch in, blood spurting warm onto the web of her hand.

She's in the shower again, which is where it happened. The water heater's failing, so they're doubling up. He's washing her, his bottle of vodka up by the shampoo, he's washing her and he's— he's—

"*What if Janet Leigh was* waiting *for Norman?*" Jade says through her sudden tears, or tries to say, but her throat is clenching, her whole body is trembling, is cringing away from this skin-to-skin contact with him, and—and she wants to spasm her head back and forth faster and faster like *Jacob's Ladder*, to shake free of this *Lost Highway* memory, she wants to remember things her own way, please, she wants to blur that whole year away, smear it into just a bland sixth-grade nothing, and she *still* isn't stabbing this sharp pole into her dad's back like she needs to.

"I'm really going to," she makes herself say, like hearing it out loud might make it true.

But . . . she can't?

She looks down to her hand like to clock where the betrayal is, but it's not there. It's in her head. Her head is what's betraying her. Her heart.

She can't do it. She's not a killer.

"Jennifer?" her dad says, a sort of confident chuckle to his voice that makes her want to hurl.

"No," a voice says from just past him, "it's *Jade*," and then Tab Daniels's head conks over to the side fast and hard. He falls away, slumps ahead into the water, out of Jade's arm, blood from his face coating the water.

Letha. It's Letha.

She's holding a board with a nail in it, but to her it's a bat. The nail, and the force behind it, tore Jade's dad's temple away from his skull. Some of him—cheek muscle, nose tissue, a whole eyebrow maybe—is still on the sharp end of that nail, even.

"He's never going to hurt you again," Letha says, breathing hard, which is when the world turns white and fast and stinging. Letha disappears into it and Jade falls onto her knees, shielding her face, her newly exposed scalp.

There's a sound too, an everywhere sound, a deep dangerous *whirring*, like a weed whacker the size of a car, which means—

Hardy's airboat.

He's got it revved high, all his lights shining through the mist and droplets his great blades are spitting across the water.

Until that fan cycles down, anyway.

Monstrous shadows surge through the light, and all Jade can see is Hardy teetering there now from whatever just happened, one hand still to his high captain's chair, his stomach open to the night air, his hand already clamped to that line of pain. But his hand's not big enough for this. At first a little blood seeps through his fingers, and then the rest, slick and bulging, glistening gray.

Jade's breathing hard now.

She looks back around to Letha, still standing exactly where she was, the nail-board down by her leg, and . . . *she* didn't do this to Hardy, she was right here, doing what Jade couldn't. And—and Theo Mondragon, Jade can see his hulking shape on the pier, one hand trying to keep his seeping nail-tears shut, the other shielding his eyes from the projector light, Brody huge on-screen behind him, lining up on that oxygen tank one last time.

"I don't—this doesn't—" Jade says to Letha, reaching forward not so much to pull Letha in as to just hold on to her, but . . . a small hand is reaching up from behind Letha, is taking her chin, and is wrenching it to the side, Letha's own hands coming up fast to try to hold her face together but even her final girl strength isn't enough.

Her jaw is tearing away, her head trying to go with it, her eyes blown wide because this can't really be happening, and finally her reflexes and muscles are able to clamp her hands onto whoever's doing this terrible thing to her, so her whole body can ride this tearing-away motion.

Still, her jaw is definitely creaking away from her face, opening her screaming mouth unnaturally wide, and crooked—a dark chasm Jade's seen a hundred times through the tracking lines of a VHS tape, but up close and personal like this, it's so much more intense. The top and bottom rows of teeth, they're—they're supposed to be parallel to each other, pretty much, but Letha's lower teeth are angling fast away, and there's the distinct sound of the hinge of her jaw cracking, the skin there tearing. There's not any blood yet, this moment is being sliced too thin for the blood to be coming yet, but if the skin is parting like this, if the bones are shattering into the muscle, if the ligaments and tendons are popping like rubber bands—

And then this instant catches up with itself and Letha is being flung away, her body ragdolling across the remains of Lonnie's living room, thunking into the side of the jauntily floating but thoroughly abandoned bass boat, and . . . then sinking, with no ceremony.

The final girl is dead.

Jade looks into the space Letha just was, to whoever just did this impossible thing.

It's a little girl with long black hair, a little girl with pale dead skin, a little girl with a dress both rotting away and rolled in stabby elk hair, a little girl with forever-cracked lips and shattered fingernails, thin black veins spidering away from her black-black eyes.

Stacey Graves, the Lake Witch.

She opens her mouth to hiss but her *own* jaw dislocates on one side, falls out of joint, stretching the dry skin on that side of her mouth down. She screeches, draws one hand up to stop this pain, and cocks her head over to some angle she must know, jams her jaw back up into place.

"*You*," Jade says, falling back, catching herself on a gunwale, and it all comes home for her in that instant: a little girl, afraid of what she is, gallops across Indian Lake on all fours, away from the boys who played this trick on her, away from the town that never fed her, away from the father who never wanted her. All she's looking for her is her mother, stashed in a crevice over there, one deeper than the buzzards can find, because Letch Graves doesn't need any more attention from the sheriff.

But Stacey Graves is no buzzard, and she has weeks to find her mother, and finally does, right at the water's rising edge.

Stacey Graves wriggles into the shallow cave with her, drapes her mother's arms around herself, and goes to sleep until the hated water seeps in with them, bringing its faint music with it. Because it's the water coming up over her, not her trying to get under it, and because she's wedged so tightly in her mother's embrace, Stacey Graves is able to go under at last and be with her mother, which is all she's ever wanted.

But then a sharp black hook finds her, ends her sleep.

She comes up, frees herself, and, looking for her mother again, kills anyone she finds hunting on that side of the lake, making those woods so sacred they become national forest almost on their own. But she does manage to find her mother again, dragged out along with Stacey, just floating at the surface of the lake now.

Stacey leads her to a better cave, a higher-up cave, one the singing water will never find, and then blocks the entrance up behind them, and this works for decades, until the forest becomes a furnace, dripping enough sparks and hissing pitch down that her mother's dry skin sizzles, flickers, catches flame.

Stacey Graves pats those little fires out, waits for the larger one to die back, and then she climbs up, goes for the first culprits she can find. They're at the edge of the lake, are in a series of little houses that aren't the town she hates, but will do.

Afterwards she retires to her cave, sleeps the sleep of the dead with her mother again, hopefully this time forever, but then someone drops in *with* her. She hisses at him, scratches at him, and then thick grey water starts to spurt down into her cave. But it's not water at all. It's melted rock.

Stacey Graves fights through before it can dry, rises that night, and takes the first lives she chances upon: elk, foraging close to shore under cover of darkness. But she's not done yet. There are voices out on the water. Laughing, happiness.

Not on her watch.

She rushes out there to that green canoe, silences them both, and, looking for another cave to ride out eternity in, she hides from the sun—it makes her skin hiss, her eyes smolder, her lips and nailbeds steam—in the only cave she can find: the elk she slaughtered, which embed their stabby hair into her rotting nightgown. But it's nice in there, it's dark and pressing like a hug, like her mother's there with her, and for weeks and months, it's enough, until a saw made of screaming metal tears into her rotting cave, splashing light in.

Stacey Graves retracts from it, squirming deeper into the decay, and then she pushes hard enough that she falls out into the open air again, after which she races to the loudest, most obnoxious sound she can, the one that must be responsible for disturbing her: the yacht. After tearing up and down those tight halls, slashing across those slick decks, crashing through door after door, she hides from the sun again for the day, and then—then this, the party on the water, disturbing her sleep, invading her lake. *Her* lake.

How Jade knows she's right about all this, it's not that the dates or the logic line up, it's that this little dead girl is standing *behind* where Letha was—*on* the water.

It *hasn't* been Theo Mondragon impossibly being here and then there at the same time. It's been a little dead girl flitting across the surface from person to person, a little girl not slowed down by having to wade or swim—she couldn't if she wanted to, because this Christian burial ground won't take her Indian self, won't *let* her step through.

Right when Stacey Graves starts to surge forward, for Jade, a bellow stops them both.

It's Theo Mondragon.

He's standing in Hardy's airboat, is looking at the bass boat Letha just died against. He's looking at the water his only daughter just sank down into.

And then he's looking at Stacey Graves.

He's got the machete back, now, must have had it slid into his belt at the small of his back.

"*You!*" he says to Stacey Graves, and she angles her head over, maybe surprised to be called out instead of retreated from.

But, does she even understand words anymore, or does she only understand death?

She seems to get it when Theo Mondragon points his machete at her, anyway.

Stacey Graves darts forward and Theo Mondragon cocks the machete back to cut her in half, but at the last moment she swerves, slides under his swing, stands up behind him.

Before he can orient, set his feet in the rocking airboat, she's reached around, has him by the jaw the same as she had Letha. She flings him hard to the side, not even bothering to tear his face in half, just cracking him into the side of the pier, probably fifteen feet away.

Theo Mondragon's legs and shoulders try to keep going, and do, folding around the unmoving side of the pier, and something cracks inside him. His back, surely, because people don't fold sideways, do they?

He sloughs off, down, and it seems for a moment that the empty green canoe is going to catch him, but it only catches his machete.

Stacey Graves, after watching that slow drip into the waiting water, maybe even appreciating it, turns, inspects the red surface of these waters, her eyes settling again on Jade.

"No," Jade whispers to her, like that can work. But it's not a completely voluntary thing, either. Is just a prayer, really.

It's answered by the night splitting in two from . . . gunfire?

Four fast shots, grouped tight in Stacey Graves's back, flinging her small body ahead, sending her skidding across the surface of Indian Lake, which looks so wrong.

It's Hardy, Jade sees. He's dying, is still trying to save her, because he's not going to let Jade die in these waters like his daughter did.

It's what dads do. It's what they're supposed to do.

After those four shots, though, Hardy slumps forward into the water, and Stacey Graves is already there on top of the water he just disappeared under. Just like when Hardy was eleven at Camp Blood, she's tearing at the surface, trying to get to him, but again she can't. Jade uses this distraction to push back, to hide, to *live*, and once under she kicks back and back, so that when she rises amid all the floating dead, she's just one head of many. Right beside her, faceup, is Mr. Holmes. And Misty Christy. Gliding past on a paddleboard is Lucky, the school bus driver, using a long blue paddle to pull himself ahead, ahead. He locks eyes with Jade for a second or two, pleading with her to be still, to be quiet, to let him sneak away, through all this, but then he thunks into the green canoe, over here already somehow, and loses his balances, has to step over the side, slip into the water.

On the way down his chin connects with the paddleboard and that leaves his tongue jumping on that gritty surface. When he comes up gasping for air, chin bloody, eyes panicked, Stacey Graves is standing right there, the holes in her chest and shoulder not even bleeding, just black at the edges of those craters.

She hauls Lucky up to her level by what hair he has and, moving slowly, deliberately like an experiment, she pushes her other hand into his chest, rotates it left and right to ease the insertion. Instead of pulling Lucky's heart back out, she holds it, it looks like, holds it in her small hand until he sags, becomes even deader weight.

When she drops Lucky's body back into the water along with his heart, she's already staring at Jade, treading bloody water, Jade's friends and enemies all dead around her, and—but it can't be, she's not a final girl . . . she hasn't been a virgin for six years now, almost seven. But she's the only one left who can do this, isn't she? The only one who can stand against the slasher?

Is *she* the final girl?

Jade shakes her head no, but Stacey Graves lived before movies, lived before John Carpenter and Wes Craven, before Jason and Ghostface, so she doesn't even know what Jade's saying no *to*.

I'm not ready, Jade wants to tell her. *I don't—I can't—I've never—*

It doesn't matter.

Stacey Graves lunges ahead to take Jade by the hair the same as she just took Lucky, but Jade has no hair for Stacey Graves to grab on to. Her little fingers scrabble on Jade's stubbly scalp and Jade slips under, away from them. She drops into a quieter world. Up above it, Stacey Graves is clawing at the surface of the water, clawing and, it looks like, screeching, the same as she was about Hardy. At least until her jaw cranks out of place and she has to stand, line it back up again.

Jade uses that to drift away, under some boat melting paper down.

She comes up as quietly as she can right alongside that boat—it's the librarians'. She can tell because Connie is hanging over the edge, her face in the water like she's looking for something she just dropped.

Jade breathes deep and slow, not sure when she's going to have to go under again, but she's fighting blind panic, too. It *can't* be her! It's supposed to be *Letha*! Letha could have done this.

Jade, she's—she's just the horror chick, the *fan*.

But then she hears a commotion, looks up. It's Lee Scanlon, trying to wade-run through the shallows, escape up Main Street.

Stacey Graves surges ahead, her bare feet on the surface making little sucking sounds, part of her dress ripping away behind her, clinging to the shape it caught on: the machete. It's stuck point-down into the high side of the green canoe, just as Quint left it—no, no, as Theo Mondragon dropped it.

This is no time to lose the line between movies and the real world, Jade tells herself.

With Lee's first, maybe last, scream, Jade reaches up from the water, grabs on to the handle of that machete, works it free—not as easy as it looks—sheathes herself back into the water.

You can do this, you can do this, she's telling herself. You can take down Stacey Graves. You have to. She killed Mr. Holmes. She killed Theo Mondragon. She killed Letha, the actual final girl.

Making no waves, Jade dog-paddles to the side, just away from where Stacey Graves knows she's supposed to be. The first body she comes to, she grabs on for purchase, to pull ahead, and it's Jocelyn Cates, playing possum, making hot eyes to Jade about *just keep moving, I'm not really here, don't say anything*.

Jade can't help it, she flinches away, surprised to have someone she thought dead making eyes at her, and only realizes the mistake after she's made it: Stacey Graves keys on that flurry of motion, is already coming over, *is* that hag from *Curtains*, moving so soft and perfect across the top of the water.

In the movie, though, it's slow motion, it's beautiful, it's serene.

In real life, in Indian Lake, it's all of about two terrible seconds.

Jade tries to duck under again, but this time Stacey Graves has her by the shoulder, her sharp little fingers pincering in through the skin, latching onto tendon and bone.

She hauls Jade up, and now her rancid scent—rot, decay, elk—assaults Jade's nose, her mouth, her lungs.

She lifts Jade higher, higher, maybe not sure where her feet are going to be, and Jade's shoulder is screaming, her neck too even though it's higher up, and her first instinct, it's that little-kid response: reach up, grab Stacey Graves's wrist, take some of that weight that way, just like Letha tried to do.

But that didn't work out so well for her, did it?

Instead, Jade takes the handle of the machete in both hands, knows this is a one-shot-only thing, and slices from right to left with everything she's been holding inside for the last six years, with every ounce of anger and rejection, all the unfairness and resentment, and she hears herself screaming exactly like a final girl when she does it, and it's not even on purpose, it's just coming, it's pure rage, it's having so much inside that it's got to come out, she's Constance in *Just Before Dawn*, she's finally turning around to fight, is insisting on her own life, is refusing to die, isn't going to take even one more moment of abuse, and, and—

The machete is factory sharp, and her grip is solid, and Stacey Graves's side is stretched tight from having to hold Jade up and up—she's short, never got past eight years tall.

Jade's scream dies away, her scream spent, her rage falling from her eyes so she can see again, and . . . the leading edge of the machete is maybe an inch into Stacey Graves's ribs, has done no more damage than Hardy's bullets. Way less, really.

Stacey Graves looks down to it, drops Jade to lower a hand, extract this irritation, and Jade slips under the water for what she knows is her last time. Now there's no one left to distract Stacey Graves. Now she's just going to squat down on the surface like the kid she is, wait for the living girl to come up for the air she needs, isn't she? And, even if Jade had all the machetes, they wouldn't matter, would they?

But . . . but why did that *hook* work on Stacey Graves all those years ago, and not the machete now? Is it that Jade's not the real final girl? But how could that keep a machete from acting like a machete? It doesn't make sense, it doesn't—

Steel, Jade tells herself. Of fucking course.

That's what the machete is made from, right? Because it needs to be sharp. And because this is the twenty-first century. But, didn't Christine Gillette say that that iron hook cost two dollars at the hardware store? Key word, there: *iron*.

Iron works on whatever Stacey Graves is. Steel machetes don't.

Like Jade has any *iron* ones four feet underwater.

This is it, she tells herself, and the way she knows it really is is that she's not running through a list of apologies and regrets, isn't talking to anybody right now. But—but at least she can deny Stacey Graves the pleasure of eviscerating her, can't she? At least I can die with my jaw attached, Jade tells herself, and blows all her air out, butterflies her arms out to go lower, lower, into the deep dark.

After thirty seconds of it, her body bucks, her mouth opens, draws in a deep breath of cold water, and she can't help it anymore, she's fighting up, she's clawing for the surface—

She gasps up, and almost before she can breathe in, she's puking water, her body still bucking, her hands out, fingers reaching for anything, please.

What they find is Stacey Graves's ankle.

Jade looks up along the rotted gown, and Stacey Graves is looking back down to her.

She works her jaw back into place again and steps neatly forward, out of Jade's grasp, squatting down to look Jade right in the face, her scent a sharp oily assault.

In the movie version of this, Jade knows, she'd have found

Mr. Bill's old dredging hook buried down on the floor of the lake, and this is when she'd sling it up and around, bury its sharp point in Stacey Graves's temple.

Letha was right, though: this is real life.

Stacey Graves cocks her head to the side, her eyes no longer on Jade's face, but on . . . her scalp?

She's never seen a bald girl, has she?

Jade closes her eyes, can't stop this inspection from happening: Stacey Graves's nose snuffling against her scalp, trying to get a read on this strange girl-person. Not exactly trying to get away anymore, that's useless, Jade retracts all the same, slips just barely under the surface, looks back up through it, and what she feels like is Hardy at eleven years old, hiding under the water while Stacey Graves stands right above him, unable to get down *to* him, because this water, to her, is cursed, is cursed with Ezekiel's unholy choir, which allows no intruders as corrupt as a little monster of a girl.

Then Jade finds a calm place inside her.

There's a thought bubbling up into her head, with the last of her oxygen. No, an image: Stacey Graves, thrown by the boys, screaming with joy, hanging above the water. But then *bouncing* on the hard-to-her surface. But—but if that elk hunter Mr. Bill hooked her under the water all those years ago, if the cover she was hiding in got submerged in the rising lake, then that means she *can* be under it, just . . . she can't get there herself. But it can rise over her. She can't be dropped in, can't be thrown in, but . . .

Jade waits until she feels Stacey Graves's nose right above her forehead, and then she shoves her right hand, her non-suicide hand up through the surface of the water as fast as she can, her fingers forcing their way between the blackened stumps of Stacey Graves's teeth, because—because the only weakness Stacey Graves has, aside from maybe iron dredging hooks, is her messed-up jaw.

Jade yanks down on it with everything she has, feels bone

creaking against bone somewhere in Stacey Graves's small skull, and she falls back with it as hard as she can, forcing all her air out again, no preparation, and—yes, yes yes yes—Stacey Graves's face plunges down *through* the surface, followed by her whole little body.

Her sharp broken teeth bite into and it feels like *through* Jade's fingers, but she keeps pulling, keeps dragging, Stacey Graves no longer mad but scared, shrieking under the water, clawing up, up, for where she belongs.

Jade pulls her deeper, deeper yet, until they reach a still point and Jade can hug Stacey to her, hug her tight with arms and legs, caging her, her small body bucking and writhing at first, but then, gratefully and by slow degrees, stilling, stilling enough that . . . is that music Jade's hearing through the water, or the end of the movie?

She lets go and Stacey Graves just hangs there, motionless in the silt.

At least until a large pale hand comes up through the muddy water, wraps around her thin ankle, and pulls her away all at once, down into the real and permanent darkness of Ezekiel's Cold Box.

Jade panics, her last lungful of air long since used up, and now she's the one bucking, now *she's* the one unable to climb up to the surface, but . . . but it was worth it, wasn't it? To die killing the slasher? To have got to actually and really *be* the final girl, right here at the very-very end?

Jade full-body convulses, her traitorous mouth opening to suck water in, the lake suffusing her chest, with its icy-everywhere-at-once fingers, and, and this is what death is like, some part of her realizes, and it's not soft or easy at all, it's a panic you're both trapped in and distant from, and it's—

Another hand coalesces a foot in front of Jade, which is . . . which is *up*, from above, not from below? Before Jade can process it anymore it has her by the front of her coveralls, is ripping her to the surface.

It's Letha Mondragon.

She's not slow-motioning it through the science hallway of Henderson High, though, her shampoo-commercial hair billowing behind her. No, now she's gasping, blood sheeting down over her face from a gouge across what used to be her eyebrow, and that eye's not moving with her other one anymore, but that's nothing—her *jaw*. It's been wrenched out of place, cracked away at the hinges, so her chin's hanging low and crooked. The only reason it's still even close to in place, isn't torn away and tossed aside to sink, is . . . it's her moisturizer regimen, isn't it?

Her skin was elastic enough to hold on.

And if she can make it through that kind of violence, then taking a header into a boat isn't going to end her.

Some girls just don't know how to die.

Jade wants to reach for Letha, to hold on to her, to be *held* by her, but there's a coldness surging up through her chest, there's a new burning she knows is air, wonderful air, and then she's puking lake water onto Letha. And Letha just lets her, lets her, doesn't drop her or anything. At least not until she has to, the last of her strength spent on Jade.

Jade reaches for her, for real now, to try to save her back, but she doesn't have to: Banner Tompkins is standing with her in his arms, is the one doing the saving here, his surge of water pushing Jade away.

"*She—she did it!*" Banner calls out, turning around so everyone left can see the hero, Letha Mondragon.

The final girl.

"*She did it!*" Banner repeats, louder, standing higher now with Letha, holding her like a trophy, like a hero, and Letha's a good-enough person to shake her head no about this, try to give slasher credit where slasher credit's due, but the effort to try to rise from Banner's arms to direct attention back to Jade is finally too much. Letha passes out into Banner's heaving chest, her long hair trailing down into the water, which somehow makes the whole scene more dramatic, more perfect.

Jade wouldn't just be the bad guy for messing with it, she'd be the worst guy.

Worse than Proofrock already thinks she is, anyway.

She lowers herself into the cold water so as to disappear and frog swims to the side, having to navigate all the half-sunken floats, all the cold dead arms hanging down, all the blood swirling around her outstretched fingers.

Underwater, it's not really crying.

But it is cold, now.

Jade surfaces with a gasp, the night air not doing much to warm her, and stabs a hand out for something to help her stay up.

The town canoe.

Jade clambers up, over, in, shoulder screaming, fingers throbbing, her hurt leg dead and heavy.

Collapsed down between the seats, her face to the green fiberglass, she laughs and sobs and hates everything, but she loves it all too, wouldn't trade it for anything.

Finally she rolls over and there's nothing but stars overhead. She drifts like that, just checked out, spent, imagining she's on a raft of the dead, imagining there's credits rolling somewhere in her foreground, imagining—

Her hand finds the machete under the bench.

She lifts it, inspects it like the wondrous thing it is, and, trying to be cool like Quint, slams it down into the side of the canoe. It falls over so she tries again, standing to swing, and just gets the edge to chisel in enough so the machete can stay there like it's supposed to.

Sideways in the canoe now, Jade hooks her legs over one side, hangs her head back over the other side, and for the thousandth time she's Alice at the end of *Friday the 13th*, Alice in the long sigh after all the screaming, Alice reclining back into that dream which would wedge the door of sleep open for Freddy, for this whole Golden Age.

Just for a moment, before Jason bursts up from the water, hugs her from behind, everything's pretty all right, isn't it? Pretty perfect, really. The horror's been dealt with, this long night is over, and there aren't even any hard questions to be answering yet.

It's the best tease in the long and storied history of teases.

It makes Jade breathe in, to get ready for the next part, her hand finding the handle of the machete on pure instinct.

"One last scare," she recites.

On cue, a great splash rises behind her, and, because she's ready, because she fucking *knows* this genre, Jade is already coming up to her knees and spinning, already swinging, already screaming for all she's worth.

But, again, her machete doesn't cut all the way through. Because evidently machetes don't really do that.

What they *are* good at, it would seem, is going a few inches in and stopping.

Except—except this isn't Stacey Graves?

It's Jade's dad, it's Tab Daniels, somehow floated out here too, just trying to survive, one eye and part of his head gone, the rest of him latching on to whatever he can, grabbing on to Jade to pull her back into the past with him. Because of *course* Letha's nail-plus-board didn't really kill him, now that Jade's having to think it through. Letha's too pure to kill unprovoked like that. The world won't let her deliver a blow that deep, that permanent.

Leave that for the Jades of the world.

The machete isn't even halfway through his neck, but that's far enough.

His blood—his *life*—slips out for real this time, coats the blade, and the one eye he has left is locked on Jade's, and she says it to him at last, what she always meant to, the only thing she ever had: "I *trusted* you, Dad."

When she pulls the machete back, he slips under, Indian Lake slurping him down, Drown Town calling his name, and Jade, the guilty party now, the Indian with her ear to the train tracks, feels her senses prickling, looks over to the side.

She's not as far from the pier as she thought, is she?

And, who she felt watching her, it's—it's Tiffany Koenig.

She's still recording all this on her phone.

"No," Jade says to her, trying to explain but not nearly loud enough, "you don't understand, he—he—"

She gives up.

Why even try?

Instead she covers her face with her hands and *screams* into her palms, screams and kicks, and when she looks up the next time, she's drifted farther out, and there's red and blue lights in Proofrock now, there's helicopters beating in over the trees.

So it begins.

Jade watches, her heart reaching across the water but her bloody hands staying right here. She uses one of them to pat her chest pocket for a cigarette she knows isn't going to be there, and then she works the lid off the little cooler, uses it like a paddle, two groaning pulls on the right side, two on the left, and going gradual like that, gradual and silent, she drags herself across the dark water.

She's crying again, because this is it. This is her last time to run away. No way can she go back now, not with what Tiff's got recorded on her phone. With Jade's luck, all the stories of this night's massacre are going to coalesce around her until she didn't just kill her dad, but everyone else too—all this blood in the water was her calculated revenge against the town that never accepted her, that treated her like it had treated Stacey Graves, once upon a time. They can even dig in her old history teacher's student files for her papers. They'll be all the proof needed, and more.

Theo and Letha weren't framing Jade, Jade's been doing that all on her own, all these years.

No, there's no going back. This is it. It has to be. Mr. Holmes is dead, Sheriff Hardy's dead, and she's officially a killer now.

Even if Proofrock would have her, there's nothing for her there.

She ships her oar—the cooler lid—runs her fingers up to the name-patch on her coveralls, works the two earrings loose. One's the comedy face, one's the tragedy face, right? Add them together and you've got a slasher, pretty much. That would have been her last paper for Mr. Holmes, she thinks. How the slasher is a bloody coin flipping through the air, showing a smile for a flash, then a frown, and then another smile.

Jade would have that coin never land.

She makes one last fist around the two earrings, the back of her fingers seeping from Stacey Graves's teeth, and then she holds her hand out over the water, lets the earrings go, closing her eyes for that small *plunk*, and so she can see them in her head, swirling and sinking, one laughing, one crying.

Before her on shore is a string of dark cabins against a chalky bluff. Camp Blood. If she had a best friend with her, or any friend at all, she'd point ahead with her lips, say how she was conceived there one bonfire night, she's pretty sure. And now—now they'll find her starved and frozen in one of those dark cabins, won't they? The horror chick turned into a leathery mummy, scavenged on by turtles and raccoons and crows, her knees still hugged to her chest, her heart finally buried in the only soil that would have it.

But she had a moment, didn't she? She screamed until that's all there was in the world and then she stuck her hand as deep into the killer's mouth as she could. Maybe for as long as that lasted she sort of *was* a final girl? Just a little?

Close enough.

Jade drops her name-patch over the side, lets "JD" sink as well, and then she peels out of her coveralls and shirts and pants, why not, pushes them over the side, holding herself against the cold at first but then remembering, taking the cooler lid up, dipping it over the side again and again. She doesn't want to die out here, in this green canoe, but up there.

"Momma, I'm coming home," she says between pulls, her teeth chattering, shoulders twitching, hands numb, and the mom she's talking to carries a hunting knife at her belt, the mom she's talking to would kill a whole *camp* of counselors if anybody so much as looked at her daughter wrong.

Jade pulls harder at the water.

She can't wait.

THE FINAL CHAPTER

What brings Jade out from her chosen cabin isn't dawn glowing behind Terra Nova, but she thinks that's what it's going to be.

It's the fire she guesses she probably started. The fire from the lighter she left flickering in that pile of elk. It finally singed some hair enough to rough a little flame up, and that flame caught some more hide, found the grass, felt across to the trees, and . . . and now Caribou-Targhee National Forest is burning. For the first time in fifty years. Every Idahoan's worst fear is climbing tree after tree, the crowns bursting sparks and embers into each other like an endless stand of matchsticks.

Jade shakes her head in apology, in regret, and kind of smiles a bit on accident, even.

This too, slasher gods?

"*The Burning*," she says, obviously. "1981, Alex."

It's the main slasher to have made of fire something formative, but, for an actual *forest* fire, not a misdirected prank, you have to dial all the way back to *The Prey*, Jade guesses. *The Prey* opens with a fire that burns across an innocent family, leaving one of them disfigured enough to Cropsy back up years later, when partying teens show up for a camping trip. But *The Prey* was only in theaters for a week at most in 1983. Or was it '84? Never mind that it was actually *shot* in 1978, meaning that, unlike all the other slashers of the Golden Age, *The Prey* wasn't really riding *Halloween's* coattails, was probably surfing the same cultural wave that spit *Halloween* up onto America's screens in the first place, that wave being the sweet spot where the grindhouse of the seventies and the giallo of the sixties overlapped with someone with Herschell Gordon Lewis dollar signs in their eyes—Sean Cunningham in early 1979, pretty much, taking out an ad in *Variety* to fund a little horror movie set on Friday the 13th that he wanted to make.

Call it what you want, Jade tells herself. The truth is, the same as you can't be cruel to animals in the production of your slasher— that poor innocent snake in *Friday the 13th*—you also can't light some random woods on fire just to make your movie cooler. What else she tells herself is that she kind of always knew it was going to come to this, didn't she? Her citing slasher trivia to herself over here in Camp Blood.

Who else would even listen?

She was always trying to be Randy from *Scream*—the Cassandra *Scream 2* would nod to, who would become a literal Cassandra-on-videotape in *Scream 3*—but she knows that, if anything, she's Crazy Ralph.

Definitely not the Girl Who Saved Proofrock. Or, as much of it as she could, anyway.

Hugging herself from the chill—it's always coldest just before dawn—she looks away from the flames consuming Terra Nova and the national forest and probably all of Idaho behind it, considers Proofrock watching this same tragedy unfold across the water.

As if ten or fifteen people floating in pieces in the water isn't enough, now there's a fire to try to deal with.

"Sorry," Jade says, wishing Mr. Holmes were around to shake his head at this prank to end all pranks. In trying to turn her back to it so as to maybe soak up at least the idea of some of that wonderful warmth, she finds herself facing the chalky white bluff behind Camp Blood, the one Hardy said it used to be a big joke to climb, so you could moon everyone at once.

Sounds like fun.

Jade grins a guilty grin—this is no time for smiling—and rocks back on her heels, imagines the cliff of water to the left of that bluff, that she used to dream of someday releasing down-valley, just for kicks and grins, and because she kind of wanted to see Drown Town, not just make dioramas of it for art class.

Now, after the fire feels around this side of the lake, ravages through Camp Blood on its way to taking Proofrock down, now the next generation's dioramas are going to be of Pleasant Valley, before it burned to cinders.

It's a foregone conclusion: that's the way the wind's blowing, and the skies are clear, no clouds building to release nature's fire extinguisher down.

Jade can try to climb the cliff when the flames get close, but . . . does she really want to? Better to just sit in her cabin hugging her knees and rocking. Maybe imagine that the flickering on the windows is from a bonfire burning into the night. Maybe the ghosts of the kids killed here will feel that heat, even, and raise their voices in some campfire song, the rhyme-y one about the dam bursting, and—

Jade stops rocking back and forth on shore.

She looks to the chalky bluff again.

Hardy didn't just tell her about that mooning stunt, did he?

He also made that big deal about . . . how long ago was this? Sophomore year, was that when Jade had to do her interview project a second time? Shit.

But: yeah. That story about that *other* old sheriff, the one who saved Pleasant Valley from the last fire by shooting out the windows of the dam's control booth and raising the level of the lake, dousing the flames.

Jade looks up the bluff again.

Could she?

If the wind's blowing the fire towards the lake, and the lake's rising, then . . . it *should* work, shouldn't it?

Hardy's not around to drive up to the dam and shoot the windows of the control booth out, though. And everybody in Proofrock's probably still got shriek-faces on about their dead friends and family, and everybody else is packing their cars and trucks, because this is the big one, this is the end of Pleasant Valley, the end of what Henderson and Golding started so long ago.

But it doesn't have to be.

Jade lowers her hands, trying to shake blood back into her fingertips, and for the fiftieth time she wishes hard for her coveralls. It was a good and necessary gesture last night, but dealing with that gesture in the morning is seriously sucking.

But this tracks, too, doesn't it? All of her armor's been stripped away, is part of the lake already, but there's still one fight to fight. Jade hates Proofrock through and through, doesn't have enough fingers or toes or math to even count all the ways she hates it, but that doesn't mean she can watch it burn, either.

She limps back to cabin 6, the one that was supposed to have been her own private *Mausoleum*, her high-altitude *Mortuary*, her American *Burial Ground*, and pries the loose floorboard up, stands with the shiny-new double-bit axe she stole once upon a childhood, to deal with anyone who ever followed her out here to her safe place.

Instead of dragging it behind like would look cool, she carries it low in front of her hips, runs for the bluff.

The lower ten feet are dotted with old rusted rebar hammered into the rock for a climbing patch. Jade tests that rebar, gives it her weight, her shoulder screaming for mercy, her fingers just screaming, and earns her climbing patch in her underwear, in a twenty-mile-per-hour wind.

From here on up, though, it's all fingertips and toes, it's all crumbling rock and untrustworthy roots, the axe hooked over her right shoulder from the front, its lower tip gouging into her back each time she has to reach farther than she can reach.

Letha Mondragon would make short work of a task like this, Jade knows, but Letha Mondragon is receiving medical attention in a tent right now, the reporters already carving her hero's journey in stone.

It makes Jade jam her bloodied fingertips deeper into the crevices. It makes her scrape her knees harder against the face of the rock.

Finally she births over the top of the bluff, lies there on her back panting, the axe clutched tight to her chest.

It's not over yet.

She rolls over, comes up to a knee, then three points, and then, because she doesn't trust herself to stand all at once without wavering back off into the open space behind her, she's running ahead as best she can, still holding the axe with both hands.

Ten, twelve minutes later, there's the dam like a big toy dropped down from orbit, its top lip of concrete probably twenty feet tall. Meaning: that's how high Jade can bring the water up, if she can just convince Jensen Banks, the dam keeper, to crank his controls that much.

Will he remember her from all the presentations he gave to the elementary classes? Presentations Jade groaned and squirmed through, not caring about the volume, the rate, any of that stupid stuff.

It matters now, though.

She runs harder, the smoke engulfing her for feet at a time, leaving her bent over and coughing from the absolute bottom of her lungs—it's like inhaling a whole pack of cigarettes at once, and then, before you've got your breath, inhaling *another* pack.

The Girl with the Black Lungs pushes on.

The Girl with the Stubbly Head doesn't stop.

Finally Jade crashes out onto the flat spine of the dam, her momentum plus the unwieldy axe nearly overbalancing her over the dry side, the long drop side.

She reins it in by swinging the axe back behind her, just holding on to the handle with one hand.

It works, but barely.

Jade makes herself *walk* the fifty yards to the control booth, her steps stiff and mechanical again, because Jensen's probably watching her through the peephole of his door—watching this girl in her underwear make her way to his booth, left foot dragging.

She taps on the door with the side of the axe, and, when there's no tap back, no anything, she knocks harder, with more insistence.

Still nothing.

Why didn't she check for Jensen's truck on the way in? But . . . but of course: he'd have seen the emergency lights down in Proofrock, wouldn't he have? He'd have seen and puttered down to see how he could help. Either that or he got a heads-up from the Forest Service about the fire headed his way, so he set the controls on the dam version of autopilot, abandoned his post.

Either way, Jade hauls the axe back behind her, swings it ahead with everything she's got, fully intent on Jack Torrance'ing the door to splinters.

The axe hardly makes a dent.

The door's metal, and thick, solid metal at that.

Jade swings at the doorknob now, misses, but connects on the second try.

The door handle clatters off, falls into the lake.

The door's just as fast, just as solid.

"*Shit shit shit!*" Jade says all around, to all the nature she's *also* trying to save.

Hating having to do this, she sucks in, tightropes around to the other side of the control booth. The three sides that don't have a door *do* have windows, but the one opposite the door is the only one you can actually do anything with, or to, as it's the only one you can really stand by.

Halfway there, Jade's bare foot jerks up all on its own from a sharp fleck of gravel or a rusty nail head or *it doesn't matter* and she throws her arms out like to keep from falling, her hands completely forgetting about the axe.

It falls, falls, one of its two bits catching on the concrete lip between Jade's feet instead of gouging into either of them like it should have, and that sends it cartwheeling out and back in what feels to Jade like the slowest motion ever—slow enough that even a nonathletic horror chick can plop down to her ass, her legs hanging out over the water so the top of her right foot can just cradle that axe head, guide it back up to her waiting hands.

The fall from here wouldn't kill her, but there not being anywhere to beach for a quarter mile would.

Slowly, carefully, the top of her right foot cracked open like an egg, she stands again, this time paranoid about keeping a grip on the axe, trying with each step to will her back adhesive, prehensile, whatever it takes.

It works—*just.*

She steps around the corner onto the comparatively wide spine of the dam, knocks on the glass with the axe.

Jensen's not home.

"I'm sorry," she says to the idea of him, and tries to wait this next breath of campfire smoke out to swing, but the smoke's like from a train in a tunnel, now. Just coming and coming, thicker and thicker.

It doesn't do anything to help Jade's balance.

Whenever Doc Wilson gave her a physical in elementary, before she stopped going in for them—for reasons—the portion of the test she always failed was when he'd tell her to stand on one foot and close her eyes.

Each time, she'd waver, almost fall.

Like now. She might as well have her eyes closed.

She taps on the glass with the axe, not swinging it, just expecting the big window to shatter because it knows this is an axe, she guesses.

Stupid.

She hauls back again, isn't sure about proper form or anything, but what she does have is a whole childhood of anger to swing, six years of the other kids' parents sneering at her, of teachers sending her to the principal for being sick—all of it. And then having to go home to Tab Daniels and his dirty dishes.

Jade opens her mouth in a scream she didn't know she had and swings forward with all of her weight, and, and—

The axe bounces off, bounces hard enough that it comes straight back for her face. She dodges it, watches it twirl past, then spin down the dry side of the dam, maybe never even hitting, it's so far down there.

"What?" Jade says.

But of course: since this is glass that got shot out once, and because the woods on the Proofrock side fill with hunters, these windows are all reinforced, aren't they?

Of course they are.

Still, all her effort did leave a chip deadcenter, at least. Like when gravel catches a windshield wrong.

Through the smoke chugging all around her, Jade guides her hand to that powdery crater in the glass, pushes on it with her index finger, and, as if that were the release button, the whole window collapses in.

Jade nods thank you thank you to the slasher gods and follows that glass in, clambering over the desk that's there, her knees and the heels of her hands gathering crumbles and shards, her eyes roving for dials and switches, levers and wheels.

They're all there, and more.

And there's no manual.

"Shit," Jade hisses.

There's no slasher movie that can help her with this, either. Maybe there's some submarine film or lighthouse movie that might could, but probably not. Dam control booths aren't that damn interesting—the joke whispered before all of Jensen Banks's talks at assembly.

All she can do, she supposes, because she has to do something, because something's better than nothing, is . . . is push the biggest, most central lever from its three-quarters *down* point to "all the way up?"

When the two wheels on the back wall are mostly turned over to the right, it feels like, she hauls them back to the left until they stop, imagining the dam is a giant water spigot. And it sort of is, isn't it?

To prove she's doing it right here, a whole bank of lights start flashing alarm, and a robot voice comes from overhead, not asking if she likes scary movies—the question she's forever waiting for— but telling Jensen to attend to the levels of "1" and "2," as failure to do so will result in a reduction in flow that could lead to dangerous back pressure if left unchecked.

"Exactly," Jade says, nodding about her handiwork.

She hovers her fingers over this big industrial dashboard like seeing what else she can do. When there's nothing left to push, nothing left to turn, she opens the door from the inside, having to force it with her shoulder.

It spills her out into open air with too much momentum but she was expecting that, knew to have a good hold on the inner doorknob.

Now if only the control booth would blow up with a big mushroom cloud as she walks away from it, down the dam.

How long will the lake take to rise, though?

Will it be fast enough? What brick by the bank will the waters reach over in Proofrock?

It'll be soon enough, Jade decides. And: it'll be *all* the bricks.

When the control booth doesn't explode—it's not packed with demolition supplies, and there are no sparks in there anyway—Jade keeps walking all the same, her hands fists, eyes fixed on Camp Blood's white bluff through the smoke, and she only stops when . . .

Holy fucking shit.

Galloping ahead of this fire is a grizzly. Not the trash bear that killed Deacon Samuels, part of her mind registers, because that cub she saw down in Proofrock earlier, it's trying like hell to keep up. With its momma.

"Run," Jade says to it again, and then realizes where they're running: right to her, right along the top of the dam.

She turns, is running hard herself now, her one chance in a thousand to plant her bare foot on the round knob inside that door she left cocked open.

It catches her right in the arch painfully, the door swinging out with her weight, trying to send her down and down into open space, but now her midsection's catching the flat roof of the control booth.

She starts to scrape back and down, the door coming back to hit her hanging legs, but . . . she scrabbles, she grabs, she pulls, she makes it up onto the gravel roof and whips her feet up fast, before any sharp teeth can snag them.

When she turns to peer through the gusting smoke, though— this momma bear and her cub aren't even halfway to the control booth.

"*Don't fall, don't fall,*" Jade whispers to them, not wanting to give her safe place away either—nine feet isn't much to a bear at least that tall—but . . . why have they stopped?

Jade looks behind them, down the line of the dam, and—they weren't running from the fire, they were running from what's *running* from the fire: the trash bear, a big ragged boar, his fur scorched and smoking, his face scarred from claws and teeth, or maybe fights with dumpsters, it doesn't matter.

What does is that, just like with hamsters, Jade knows— everybody in Proofrock knows—Papa Bears eat Baby Bear every chance they get. They're easy pickings, and tasty besides.

Jade stands, shaking her head no, no, please.

At the end of the dam, the air swirls clear enough for her to make out this trash bear standing, carving the air with his massive claws, his roar filling every iota of space, and then—then what Jade's always known to be a lie, what she would never believe, what all the nature shows have been lying to her about, what starts her heart like the chainsaw it is: the Momma bear tucks her cub up under herself, steps forward over it, and roars even *louder* than this trash bear, her lips quavering from it, her rage-saliva misting out before her, and Jade doesn't speak bear, but she gets this all the same.

This mother's saying that if this bad man wants her baby, then he's gonna have to come through her to get it, and Jade has to look up to the sky to keep her eyes from spilling, and for a moment the smoke parts enough for a grainy line of sunlight to filter through, find the palm of her hand when she reaches up to try to hold this feeling for as long as she can.

ACKNOWLEDGMENTS

First I'd like to thank a certain video rental clerk from Wimberley, Texas, in about 1985, 1986. Without you slipping a crew of eighth graders five or six Freddy and Michael and Jason movies every Friday after school, so long as we had them back first thing Saturday morning, then . . . I can't even imagine a life so bleak, so unslashery. Next I'd like to thank one of those eighth graders' dads, who would always wait until we were two or three tapes in to come drag his Freddy fingers on the metal door of the garage we were in. We'd fall off the saggy couch we were piled onto, we'd blast out the side door, and we'd run like I've never run since, tears slipping back from my eyes, my mouth actually hurting because my smile was so wide, nothing but darkness yawning open in front of me.

I ran into that darkness, and am still running.

Next I want to thank you, reader, for running with me.

If we go fast enough, if we close our eyes tight enough, if we ball our fists tight enough and lean forward far enough, then we can still remember what it's like to not just be terrified, but to be so terrified that we start grinning, and finally laughing, and then whether we get away or not doesn't matter anymore, because whatever's after us can never touch our smile.

Next I want to thank some writers who are involved with *My Heart Is a Chainsaw*, though they don't know it. The first is, once again, Stephen King. His story "The Raft" is shot all through *Chainsaw*. I may hold the record for having read that story the most times. And Emil Ferris's *My Favorite Thing Is Monsters*—holy something, Batman: How could I have even pretended to write *Chainsaw* without her book to guide me? And, talking comic books, I maybe smuggled a certain scene from the original *Secret Wars* (#4) into this novel. Mostly because that issue, more than any other book ever, changed my life. And William Vollman's *13 Stories, 13 Epitaphs* is part of this as well, in kind of the same way J. R. Angelella's novel *Zombie* is, the same way S. Elliot Brandis's *Young Slasher* is, the same way Zachary Auburn's *A Field Guide to the Aliens of Star Trek: The Next Generation* is, which is to say: me, stealing stuff. And Jeffrey Eugenides's *The Virgin Suicides* is here as well. I was so enchanted with its first-person plural delivery that all I wanted to do was hotwire it into the slasher. So, in 2013, over about three weeks, I did. I was fresh off my second slasher, *The Last Final Girl*, so I figured this would be easy. Wrong. *Chainsaw* back then was "Lake Access Only." And, while Indian Lake and Proofrock were there, Jade wasn't.

I should probably say up front here too that "Jade" is the name of someone not around anymore, someone who meant a lot to someone who means a lot to me, and Letha was a girl I knew in high school, when I was seventeen and living with a different horror crew in a trailer house in a junkyard in Midland, Texas, when we were all trying to be either George Lynch or Jon Bon Jovi. Letha's cool last name . . . it seems everybody back then had better names than me. I was a Jones moving among Stoneciphers and Outlaws, Ledbetters and Mondragons. But I was Jade, too, having to stand up bigger than I was in all the high schools I kept ending up in, all over Texas and

Colorado. Jade wasn't narrating this 2013 version of *My Heart Is a Chainsaw* yet, though. That duty fell to a boy in an iron mask, a boy I'm pretty sure was me ripping off the narrator of *The Tin Drum* and dressing him up like Quiet Riot's *Metal Health* album art. As you do. The whole story back then hinged on what the backside of certain turtle shells looked like, which is another way of saying that the novel Was Not Working. So I shelved it for when I could maybe be a better writer. Four years later, fresh off *Mongrels*, I thought I was that better writer. Wrong again, dude. I redid "Lake Access Only" from the ground up, no more first-person plural, no more turtles, and managed to find Jade and Letha in there, Hardy and Camp Blood, but the novel still wasn't working. So I wrote some different ones instead. One of them was *The Only Good Indians*—another slasher.

Chainsaw's heart started to beat again, like Jason's always does.

I started a new file, wrote it from the ground up *again*, and, even though I still wasn't a good enough writer—are you ever?—I had learned that, with good enough first readers, I could fake it. So, thank you from the bottom of my slasher heart to Matthew Pridham, Krista Davis, Michael Somes, Cara Albert, Paul Tremblay, Kelly Lonesome, Adam Cesare, Matt Serafini, Jesse Lawrence—I think Jesse's read most of these recent versions, even. But so has Mackenzie Kiera, so has my agent, BJ Robbins. Both of them pushed me and pushed me to make it better, when I kept thinking it was done, it was ready. I should know by now that I'm gonna be wrong, though. Luckily, I have people to remind me of that. And thanks too to Billy J. Stratton, for always being up for some in-depth Jason Voorhees discussion, thanks to Theo for letting me smuggle his name into this book (this is me asking for permission, Ted), thanks to Joe Ferrer for always hitting me with slashers when I need slashers, thanks to Rob Weiner for always having another title, another horror movie that, if not for him remembering it, might have been consigned to the heap. Thanks to Sandy Smith for helping me with a thorny possessive apostrophe and a lot else besides, thanks to Jessica Guess for believing in slashers—it means everything—thanks to Jason Heller for helping me with a certain t-shirt in here, thanks to Walter Chaw for always talking about horror in a meaningful, heartfelt, nothing's-out-of-bounds way, thanks to Dan McKeithan for some nursing home details that used to be a big part of *Chainsaw*, thanks to Vince Liaguno for a last-moment catch, and thanks to my sister Katie, for help with a plant thing late in the game.

Anyway, I guess I'm in here pretending like a lightbulb just went off randomly in my head, and standing in that glowing cone was Jade. Wrong. What happened was I'd written that first, broken version of a slasher set around Indian Lake, but swirling it all around this kid in the iron mask wasn't working. I thought the story was hopeless, was all shine, no substance. But then—and I can't find this article, don't want to search for it either—I stumbled onto a read about a young Native girl in Arizona who had killed herself after being molested by her (Native) father. I distinctly remember reading that article over and over, trying to make it make sense. It wouldn't, though. But whoever had written it had done their research, pulled in the statistics, and . . . this girl was alone, yes, but she also wasn't. The numbers for this happening among Indian communities was higher than it was anywhere else.

I won't lie that I crumpled that article up, dropped it in the trash, and opened up a new file to do this novel right. But I did now have someone to write *against*: that father who was never a dad. And all I had to do then was let Jade stand up from the shallows by the pier, look around for who was first on her list, here. The only real guide I had for that was Mona Simpson's story "Lawns," which David Kirby selected as the one story his grad class would read over and over for a semester. So, thank you, David Kirby and Mona Simpson. And also, for damming up Indian Lake, Tony Earley—the dam in his "The Prophet from Jupiter" story is the first and only literary dam, for me, and, if I'm being honest, I think that story's where I found

Hardy. Well, there and *The Howling*. There's also a poem in that old anthology *Vital Signs* that's important to Indian Lake—well, to Jade being Jade—but it'll be more important later, so maybe I'll remember to say something about it then. And thanks as well to an English teacher I had my senior year at Robert E. Lee High School in Midland, Texas, a teacher whose name I don't remember, since I only went to one day of my senior year. But that one day I went, you had a broken leg from a motorcycle accident, and you also had a . . . I don't know, a kind of glitter or humor to your eyes that reminded me of Dr. Johnny Fever from *WKRP in Cincinnati*, and I knew that if I stayed in your class, you would recognize me, the real me, you'd see past the ripped jeans, the rattlesnake earring, the skunk stripe in my hair. And so I quit, I left, I ran away. But I went back and let Jade stay, and that means a lot to me. It means everything, sir. You were there for her, I mean, when no one else was. Thank you for that.

And, of course, thank you forevermuch to Carol J. Clover, for mapping out the final girl for all of us. And thank you to Kevin Williamson for giving her the perfect story to run through. And thanks to Ryan Van Cleave, for knocking on my apartment door over winter break in January 1997 in Tallahassee, Florida, and making me go see this movie he said I had to see. I didn't want to go, I wanted to write instead, but you insisted, man, so I did. That movie was *Scream*. I was there on my own the next six nights in a row, soaking it in. I could feel the folds in my brain shifting, writhing, grinning. All the homework I'd been doing my whole life, it was suddenly worth it.

And—Wes Craven. I don't take many selfies, at least not on purpose, but one I did take, and still have, is of me in a Ghostface mask in 2015 in Salt Lake City, Utah, the day Wes Craven died. There's a reason *My Heart Is a Chainsaw* is set when it is, I mean.

Thank you, Mr. Craven.

You changed my world in 1984, and you changed it again in 1996. I wouldn't be the same without you.

And, *Chainsaw*, it wouldn't be the same without my champion of an editor, Joe Monti. Him and the whole Saga and Simon & Schuster team: Lisa Litwack, for the amazing cover, and all the hard work to get *to* that cover; Sherry Wasserman and Dave Cole, for saving my life in copyediting; Jaime Putorti, for designing this amazing interior; Kaitlyn Snowden, production manager, for keeping all the wheels turning; Madison Penico, for keeping versions straight, for keeping the manuscript sensible, for keeping all my paperwork in order, which I could never do alone; Caroline Pallotta, Allison Green, and Iris Chen, in managing editorial; and Jennifer Bergstrom, publisher, Jennifer Long, associate publisher, and Sally Marvin, VP of publicity and marketing—there couldn't be a better team. And thanks to Lauren Jackson, the most amazing marketing and publicity magician, statistician, and make-it-happen-inator I've ever worked with. But, Joe Monti: it would have been so easy for him to make me resculpt this novel such that Jade being Blackfeet would be instrumental instead of incidental. But Joe never even considered that, I don't think. Instead he did what good editors do: he crawled inside the story, looked around at what it was trying to do, and offered up a list of ways it could do that better. He got *Chainsaw* in order, I mean, the same as he'd done with *The Only Good Indians*, once upon a fairy tale. And the story, it just . . . it started locking in place. It was all I could do to write fast enough to keep up. You remember in *Cat's Cradle*, how all the water turns to ice-nine? That's what happened with *My Heart Is a Chainsaw*, after I touched Joe's notes to the manuscript.

Thanks, Joe Monti. You saved me again.

Here's to many more saves.

I just searched my inbox, too. My search was "Lake Access Only," *Chainsaw*'s old title. The first time it shows up is July 15, 2010. It's second in a stack of four titles I thought it might be fun to write into slashers some fine day.

This is that day.

Again, thank you, reader, for coming all the way out to Indian Lake with me, where the air's thin and the water red, and thank you to my two kids, Rane and Kinsey, for always watching slashers with me and talking slashers and dressing up as slashers. It's meant the world, y'all. I treasure it like nothing else. No dad's ever been so lucky as I am, getting to watch you grow up. And, thank you to my wife, Nancy. Back when I was writing *Demon Theory* in 1999—my first slasher—the video rental places in Lubbock, Texas, would always do 99-cent horror movies, and I'd come back with a stack of Jason and Michael and Freddy tapes night after night, but I would always be too scared to watch them on my own. This was the first house we lived in, remember? Your grandparents' old house. I have such a distinct memory of standing in their doorway and meeting them in 1991 and looking past them to the console television with Lawrence Welk playing. Eight years later, it was you and me there, Nan, and the television was in the same place, only, instead of Lawrence Welk, it was chainsaws and machetes, masks and screaming, and me in a chair soaking it all in until the small hours, and you, who had to get up at five in the morning to work the payment window at the power company, sleeping on the old couch in the glow of that television, sleeping there because you knew I wouldn't be safe with all this scary stuff alone.

Thank you, Nancy, for keeping me safe all those nights. I think the only time I haven't been wrong was when I said to you that maybe we could make a life together, and grow old holding each other's hand.

My heart is a chainsaw, yes, but you're the one who starts it.

Stephen Graham Jones
Boulder, Colorado, USA
November 27, 2020